The Champagne Slipper

The Champagne Slipper

Joann G. Layne

Authors Choice Press
New York Lincoln Shanghai

The Champagne Slipper

Copyright © 1998, 2005 by Joann G. Layne

All rights reserved. No part of this book may be used or reproduced by any means, graphic, electronic, or mechanical, including photocopying, recording, taping or by any information storage retrieval system without the written permission of the publisher except in the case of brief quotations embodied in critical articles and reviews.

Authors Choice Press
an imprint of iUniverse, Inc.

iUniverse books may be ordered through booksellers or by contacting:

iUniverse
2021 Pine Lake Road, Suite 100
Lincoln, NE 68512
www.iuniverse.com
1-800-Authors (1-800-288-4677)

Originally published by Vantage Press

ISBN-13: 978-0-595-36780-1
ISBN-10: 0-595-36780-1

Printed in the United States of America

To Bobby Bates,
who guided me from shipwreck
and helped me walk on water

Man's great guilt does not lie in the sins that he commits, for temptation is great and his strength limited.

Man's great guilt lies in the fact that he can turn away from evil at any moment, and yet he does not.

—Rabbi Martin Buber

Introduction

It was late into the seventies, and street life had been good. The rate of homosexuality and transexuality was at an all-time high. Although not accepted by society, they marched right into the mainstream of life and refused to be rejected. If prostitution was their source of occupation, it was paying off at fabulous prices. For example, the "drag queens" were making five hundred to a thousand dollars a night. Therefore, the doctors who injected them with hormones and put silicone implants and silicone injections into their bodies and faces were making cash dollars like they would never see again.

Insurance fraud was high, with the insurance companies neither aware nor able to do anything about it. Prescriptions were being written for all kinds of narcotic pills and sold to the highest bidder. Pharmacies were cutting medication capsules in half with sugar and making enormous profits. The sniffing of cocaine was at an all-time high. Condoms were sitting on the shelves rotting away with expiration dates long gone. The stock on latex was at an all-time low and medical personnel were not using gloves to handle bloody emergencies. Patients were insulted if you approached them with gloved hands. The medical profession still retained an attitude about washing hands between patients.

The police ran the real girls and queens off the street when it was time for elections. Most everyone had their stroll. No one interfered with another's territory. Killings were subtle, not open and brazen. Money was flowing, corruption quietly flowed, and the sex magazines and parlors were going big time.

The seventies had been prosperous for many people and professions. It would soon end, and the next decade would be full of tragic results stemming from the freedom of the past decade.

The Champagne Slipper

1

Cautiously, she emerged from the subway onto the streets of midtown Manhattan to begin her evening trek. Answering to the name of Ms. Honey Babe, she was a prostitute, whore, and lady of the night. Carefully, she surveyed her surroundings. She would look from back to front and side to side. This night, she looked strikingly beautiful, with her flaming red wig and milky white skin. She was confident that tonight would be as profitable as the other nights. Ms. Honey Babe definitely had sex for sale. It was what her present life was about.

The night air was chilly, but the thin short jacket protecting her from the cold was part of her street-walking outfit—a short, tight skirt with a sheer blouse exposing a brassiere. She glided her tall frame along the Avenue of the Americas towards Forty-fifth Street. There she turned west and continued strolling through the block, smiling at passing cars, taxis, and limousines. Catching a trick on New York streets was similar to fishing. You had to bait the line and hold still for a few minutes. If no bite, then you moved to another spot. Ms. Honey Babe laughed. She called it baiting and waiting.

Her route tonight would be the same as it had been for the past six months. The time was usually seven-thirty when she hit the streets. Honey Babe checked to see if she were being followed. There were the small-time punks who might try to rob her. She was relieved to see it clear.

It was theater time. As she passed the fur-clad ladies, their dazzling jewelry caught her eye. The men were handsome, clean, and interesting. She smiled at them. Some stared, some smiled, some were embarrassed, some distressed by her wardrobe, and some expressed pity for the street wench daring to exhibit herself in front of them. The women in the crowd displayed an air of superiority, confident that their husbands would never have anything to do with that kind of woman. Honey Babe enjoyed the outside show. She spoke loudly as she began moving her body.

"Hope your show inside is as good as the one I can give you outside."

Catching their attention, she opened her jacket wide and gave a wiggle. Sensing she was no threat, they relaxed, laughed, and gave her big applause. Then she continued her jaunt up Seventh Avenue. *Damn*, she thought, *it's starting to get cold in this fucking city. It's going to get more difficult selling this sex. Whores will outnumber tricks.*

Undaunted by the dim prospects, she continued walking and paused outside the Metropolitan Cafe, where the lights were extra bright. In case anybody was looking for a whore, she could be seen from one end of the street to the other. During her fifteen-minute walk, she whispered and smiled at all passing males. Remaining fruitless in her endeavors, she turned east on Forty-Ninth and walked across Sixth Avenue and continued onward to Fifth.

The lighted display windows of Saks attracted her attention. For a moment, she forgot her mission. She pressed close to the cold windows and could almost touch the fine fabrics and perfect tailoring. *One day I'll have all of that,* she promised herself, *and I'll be rich and a real proper woman.* She moved from the window. No time for dreaming. She had to make money. Her stroll continued west on Fifty-third street and back to Seventh Avenue. Reaching Seventh and Central Park South, she stood beside the elegant and mysterious New York Athletic Club building. She remembered that one night she had five tricks from this area.

However, she knew that business would not be good on this corner. Two girls across the street were waiting for the same merchandise. It was the policy to stay out of another girl's territory, but nowadays, there was no honor among whores or thieves. She turned the corner at Central Park South and walked east to Sixth Avenue. After lingering and surveying the area for ten minutes, she decided to move on. There were no tricks, therefore no money. She headed down Sixth Avenue slowly, passing the Hilton Hotel. Doubling back, she moved closer toward the entrance of the hotel.

"Get away from here," the outside doorman warned.

"Fuck you," she answered and moved back onto the sidewalk toward Forty-fifth Street. Honey Babe had made one whole cycle without scoring one trick. Checking her time, she was glad it was only eight-thirty. She wanted to be off the streets by three in the morning. This was her stroll every evening for six months, and it was a good run. She always walked the odd-numbered side streets. It was her good-luck strolls. Never busted, never molested, never robbed, and always made three to five hundred a night. By two o'clock, Honey Babe had rounded her stroll ten times. Business had flourished. She had picked up six tricks. Four were blow jobs and two hand jobs. Her money had been skillfully tucked into the zippered back pocket of the skirt.

Now she had three hundred and seventy-five dollars. One hundred and twenty-five dollars was needed to complete her goal. This would be the hardest and longest wait. She lingered slowly in the darkened doorway of the Time Life building. If she waited long enough, someone would come. Then she saw him. He was short, hatless, and pudgy. There was a slight limp in his stride. She braced herself for the cold as she opened her coat exposing herself. He glanced and continued walking. Her eyes quickly patrolled the area for a cop. Few of them walked. They rode in cars and vans and were known as the anti-crime unit. They brought in twenty or thirty girls at one. She quickly drew her attention back to the man who was getting away. She hurried after him.

"Hey, baby," she moaned.
"Leave me alone," he blurted out, not even looking at her direction.
"Won't take long." She informed him as she fell into stride.
"Tell me what you'll do," he demanded, still moving.
"I can suck it good, baby."
"How much?"
"One hundred."
"Too much."
"Seventy-five." She snapped.
He laughed and kept walking.
"For that much I'll go home and pay my wife. Ten dollars, that's it."
"I got something your wife ain't got."
He slowed his pace.
"What's that?"
She pulled him towards the darkened doorway, grabbed his hand, and thrust it between her legs. Either he'd go for it, or she would get a fist in her face.
"Feel that? How do you like that?"
His cold and groping hands met with something totally unexpected. The message was sent.
"Do you like that? Ever had that before?"
She scrutinized his face, ready to make a quick move if he appeared repulsed. He groped blindly and fondled what was between her legs. His experienced hands let Honey Babe know he had sipped from the champagne slipper. He had become victim. His voice quivered when he spoke.
"Oh, my, I never dreamed . . . you look so real . . . oh, my, you're perfect."

Quickly his hands went into his pocket, fumbled together five twenties and thrust them into Honey Babe's hands.

"Get it hard, baby. Get it hard," he moaned as he fell down on his knees in front of the raised skirt. He held his own penis in one hand while the other was manipulating Honey Babe's large penis into his mouth. Honey Babe, transvestite, was the prize of the night for this trick. Honey Babe was not concerned about her own penis getting hard. That was impossible, but she knew that in less than a minute, the act would be over. A few choice words from her hurried up the process.

"Suck it like a good little boy. You're such a freak!"

Those were the magic words. She could feel him quivering as he frantically jerked himself off with Honey Babe's penis in his mouth. She kept a sharp glance in search of the police or other punk criminals that lurked Sixth Avenue looking to prey upon hookers and johns. Honey Babe hoped that his come did not drip onto her new boots.

"Come on, baby, let it go," she begged softly.

He held it fast in his mouth.

"Shit, let go of my dick." Now she was angry. Reluctantly, he loosened his grip.

"Get yourself together," she warned him.

He was off his knees. His composure had returned, and once more, he was the astute gentleman.

"Where can I find you again?"

"Right here every night. Gotta go. Thanks, baby."

"What's your name?" he inquired as he moved away.

"Honey Babe. They call me Ms. Honey Babe."

Quickly she moved up Sixth Avenue in search of a cab. Cabs were selective this time of night. The red wig and white skin would be in her favor. They would pick up a white girl, but the black girls were left waving their arms in vain. When the traffic lights changed, she spotted an approaching cab. The cold air nipped again at her as she frantically waved her arm. The cab stopped.

"Where you going?" the cabby questioned her through a half-opened window. "I know it ain't uptown."

"Darling, I'm just going to Seventy-ninth and Third." She used her most captivating southern accent.

"Get in."

She was glad to be in the safe and warm environment. Another night, and she had made it safely through the streets. There was a time it was not so dangerous, but now the streets were bad. This kind of life was bad. But it was almost over for her. In a few months she would be making a most important decision to change her life.

"Did you have a good night?" The cab driver looked at her through the mirror.

"Yes, I had a real good night," she sneered back at him.

Honey Babe, prostitute, whore, and transvestite, settled back and thought about how it was going to be after the operation that would make her a woman. A real woman with a real pussy.

2

"I got pain, dammit! Pain, pain, and more pain," she cursed loudly, unaware and uncaring of the attention attracted as she continued towards Dr. Peter Edgewater's office. As she bumped her way through the crowded sidewalk, people stared in astonishment at the tall black figure draped in flowing designer clothes. The makeup transformed her face into a painted mask. The eyes were heavily lined with three colors. The lips, large and pouting, were painted a glossy red. The cheeks of her face, pumped round with silicone, appeared to dive-bomb into her chin. A wicked stubble of beard was breaking through the skin around her chin and mouth. The hair-weave onto the short, nappy stubs was ridiculously long, thick, and flowing.

"I can't fall out here in the street. I got to make it inside the office,"she moaned quietly as she took the last painful strides to the door.

She banged on the door. It would not open. Desperately, she hit the door with her foot.

"Dammit, dammit, let me in!"

The last assault on the door brought results. It opened. Michelle Wilson, ex-transvestite, postoperative transsexual, dramatically stumbled into the office of Dr. Peter Edgewater. Slowly and carefully, she slipped to the floor, avoiding any injury to herself. She glanced quickly at the other waiting patients. Most of them ignored her. The others displayed their disgust of her antics. She continued her show.

"Oh, God, help me. Help me! I can't pee!"

Her cries pierced the waiting room, the treatment room, the bathroom, and the office where Jolena Taylor, nurse, secretary, and receptionist was arranging the files for the day's visits.

Taylor, annoyed and curious, moved toward the cut-out opening which separated her from the patients. She viewed Michelle lying prostrate on the faded blue carpet.

"Well, good afternoon, Michelle." Her voice was clear with experienced cynicism. "You finally pulled out the catheter. You just could not wait. I knew this would happen. I knew it! I knew it!" Jolena threw her hands up in disgust. She seemed almost pleased with her prediction.

"I couldn't pee with it in, so what's the fuckin' difference. I pulled it out. Oh, Ms. Taylor, help me. Look, look at my stomach. It's all hard and puffed up," she cried.

The other patients, silent, waited and watched.

Michelle, aware that she had center stage, had now pulled up her dress, revealing a bloated belly. Also available for general observation was the revealing results of the surgery performed on her less than a week ago.

"It looks real. Just like a woman's thing," some anonymous voice murmured. Patients pressed closely for a better look at what they might decide to do in the future. Michelle proudly spread her legs for all to see. It appeared that she had forgotten about her pain.

Jolena appeared in the waiting room and stood over Michelle.

"Close your legs and get up. I'll have the doctor see you first."

She made no attempt to help Michelle. Problems and exhibitions like this were commonplace in the office. Michelle glared at Jolena.

"He ain't here yet?"

"No, he ain't here yet!" Jolena mocked. It was one of many ways she had to deal with some of the mentalities encountered in the office.

"I need help now. I can't pee. I might die."

"Just get up, Michelle, and I'll put you in the treatment room."

"Oh, God, help me, help me," she continued to moan, curling into a fetal position, her face twisting with pain, her long, masculine arms reaching upward.

Jolena continued indifferently.

"I'll be in the back. When you decide to get up, come in." She turned to leave.

Suddenly a loud masculine voice shook the room.

"Get up you big, dumb, ugly she-he."

Michelle surveyed the room, searching for the owner of the insult hurled at her. For a moment, the pain was forgotten. She spied a large figure sitting in the corner laughing at her.

"Fuck you, you dick-hanging drag queen, faggot, homosexual, and pervert," Michelle hissed back. Tension mounted. Many of the other patients began to move closer together. Jolena Taylor spun around and returned to center ring.

"Damn you, Michelle, get up! I've told you I don't want problems in here." Her eyes darted toward the corner. "And you! You know better than to say anything. One day it could be you."

Michelle joined in.

"Yes, and then see—"

"Shut up! All of you. Shut up!" Jolena Taylor ordered. She boldly eyed the masculine drag queens.

The room became quiet. No one moved except Michelle, who promptly got up and proudly proceeded to the treatment room. Jolena followed.

"Stay on this table until the doctor comes. He will examine you and do whatever is necessary."

"When will he be here? I hurt." Michelle spoke softly.

"I know he's on his way. Be patient. If he doesn't get here in the next thirty minutes, I'll take care of it." Jolena touched her softly on the cheek.

"Why don't you just take care of it now? You know I trust you. We all trust you."

"I have to wait, Michelle. You understand how it goes. I'm just the nurse."

Jolena left the room and returned to the files. Another patient, with a more dramatically made-up face, appeared at the window.

"I'm sorry, Ms. Taylor. I didn't mean to upset you, but she should have just gotten up when you told her."

Jolena smiled at the apologizing patient.

"I understand. It's no problem."

"You're a good person, Ms. Taylor. You're kind, even though you are tough on us, all the time trying to make us big-ass freaks act like real women. With all the silicone and surgery, we are still men. How come all this new pussy they be getting, they still act like a man and look like one, too." The patient, seemingly satisfied, returned to her chair. All was quiet.

Jolena Taylor, a registered nurse, was in charge of what she privately termed the "zoo." That word would cross her lips each morning as she readied herself for the office. She had started this job five years ago. Then, it had been new and challenging. Now, it was always the same routine and the same type of patients. Some mornings she shuddered at the prospect of going to work. Jolena had managed to maintain her professionalism amongst them, but now it seemed as if her energy had run out.

She was now forty years old, and the thought of working twenty more years administering to a bunch of transsexuals, transvestites, and homosexuals was beginning to be a constant nightmare. She missed real nursing, the recovery rooms, intensive care, and operating rooms. Five years ago, when she worked in the operating room, it had been hard and honest work. It was then that he had enticed her to work for him.

"Come work for me, Jolena. I can use a good nurse," Dr. Peter Edgewater asked while she assisted him during a surgical procedure.

The surgeon she had worked with had retired, and the budget crunch at the hospital had eliminated any hope of overtime, and she needed the extra cash.

"You had mentioned something about cash?" she inquired carefully.

"Yep, no problem. Come tomorrow night at eight. You can help me with a minor surgical case. All local anesthetic." He reassured her.

"I'll be there."

When she arrived at the office, he immediately directed her to his treatment room.

"The patient is in the dressing room. After she has changed, put her on the table. Instruments are in the sterilizer. It's minor surgery. You make yourself familiar. You know what to do." He disappeared into his private office.

Jolena surveyed the surroundings. It was not a large office. There were two treatment rooms, a small room for the receptionist, and a large waiting room, and his own private office, where he continually retreated. In the treatment room, she removed the instruments and carefully placed them onto a sterile field atop the small table. She was proud of her ability to cope within an environment that did not have all the necessary equipment and space. A strange and husky voice addressed her.

"Hi, I'm Marlene. I'm the patient." She was tall with graying hair. The face was painted discreetly; however the lines and furrows of aging peeked through. The eyes, bright and clear, glowed with confidence.

"I'm Ms. Taylor. Here, allow me to help you onto the table." She instructed the patient to lie down, covered her with a sheet, and went to inform the doctor that all was ready. While they both waited, Jolena surveyed her surgical setup to assure that everything was in readiness. She thought about how much he would pay her for this small amount of work. Maybe twenty-dollars, twenty-five? *I should have settled that in the beginning*, she thought. *Oh, well, too late now. If it's not enough, I won't come back.*

"Hello, Marlene, my dear. Are you all ready?" Dr. Peter Edgewater, tall, blond, and quite handsome, spoke softly to his patient.

"Oh, yes, doctor, and I am very relaxed. I am so glad you have a nurse to help you. You need help. You are much too busy these days to do everything alone."

"Yes, Jolena is very experienced."

To provide proper assistance to the surgeon, she positioned herself across the table from him. When he lowered the sheet and raised the patient's gown, Jolena stared in disbelief at Marlene's exposed nakedness. There was a penis and scrotum! This patient was a man! How did she ever mistake—*well, of course,* she thought, *the patient is a cross-dresser.* It was a common occurrence. Her experience had been mainly in the operating room when they came in for the final sex change. She had never really seen one outside the operating room. Therefore, she was not familiar with their mode of dressing or life before or after surgery. She watched as the doctor's gloved hands roughly scrubbed the genitals with the antiseptic solution. Jolena watched and was amazed that the patient did not make any complaints about his roughness.

"Marlene, dear, I am going to inject you below with a local anesthetic. The same medication a dentist would use." His voice was soft and reassuring.

Jolena stared in disbelief when he began injecting the local anesthetic into and around the scrotum. *My God,* she thought, *is he going to do what I think? Maybe I should ask? What about consent? Oh, shit! What did I get myself into?* She remained quiet. He was the doctor.

Finishing with the injections, he held out his hand in the usual manner which indicated that he was ready for the scalpel. Quickly, she responded. He made a medium-sized horizontal incision, and the blood flowed. She slapped a clamp onto his open hand and expertly sponged the bleeding area. Staring intently, she watched his fingers manipulate the sack until a small glistening white and pink testicle was squeezed out through the small incision. He cut it away from the clinging membrane. Bright red blood began to gather at the severed spot. Quickly, he clamped. Jolena handed him the catgut suture to tie off the bleeder. A husky moan escaped from the patient.

"That is the only pain you will feel, dear."

"Why does it hurt in the bottom of my stomach?" The patient's voice was calm.

"It hurts there because of the nerve structure."

Jolena listened to the informative conversation. Suddenly, as the doctor fingered the small glistening ball, it slipped away from the gloved hands and landed onto the floor with a wet plop. Jolena apologized for not being able to stop the incident. He murmured that it was not important. She felt sick and concluded that she would not return to this place. She raised her eyes to see if his face showed any signs of remorse, regret, or distress. He continued without expression. Quickly, he tied off another bleeder, and Jolena dutifully assisted him.

When he asked for the scalpel again, it took her by surprise, for she had forgotten there was another testicle to be removed. Strength ebbed into her from unknown reserves. She could never desert a doctor in the midst of surgery. Remaining to the end was without question. It would be unprofessional to express her opinions during the surgery or in front of the patient. Immediately, she became the astute surgical nurse assisting him without hesitation as he removed the second glistening slippery ball. This time she did not allow it to fall, but carefully retrieved it from the doctor's gloves, preserving it in a gauze. She had regained her composure.

After the surgery, she took the patient to the dressing room and left her with directions to rest before getting dressed. Later, she asked Dr. Edgewater what to do with the specimens.

"Throw them in the garbage. They are of no use, are they?" He smiled and returned to his office.

Marlene appeared in the door, dressed and ready to go. Jolena stared at her, trying hard to conceal her disbelief.

"Here is a little something for you." She handed Jolena a twenty-dollar bill.

"No, no. I can't take that." Jolena pushed the money back toward her. She had been taught that it was unprofessional.

"I insist you take it, and I don't want to hear any arguments." She shoved the money into the nurse's uniform pocket and disappeared into the doctor's office.

Jolena had always maintained her professionalism by not accepting gifts or money from patients. However, she made no further resistance. She certainly could use the money. The patient had made it easy. While cleaning the room, she retrieved the dropped specimen from the floor and threw it into the garbage. *Strange,* she thought, *it no longer bothers me.* She did her usual good job of putting the room in order. Jolena could see that he needed someone to organize and keep the small treatment room clean. She frowned at the disarrayed and dirty instruments. She would be glad to get out of there.

"Jolena, dear, this is for you." Dr. Edgewater's voice startled her. She turned to face him, and he handed her a fifty-dollar bill. She flushed.

"Thank you, doctor, thank you." *Don't say too much, just take it and be glad,* she thought.

"I'll need help tomorrow evening. Can you please help me?" He smiled, that ever-gentle smile, that only he owned.

"Tomorrow? . . . tomorrow? Let me think . . . well . . . yes, yes, of course. I can make it. Oh, doctor, please, tell me why Marlene did not wait and have the complete surgery like we used to do at the hospital?"

"Well, she is considering the sex change, but in the meantime, removing the testicles eliminates most of the testosterone. Now she will have less hair growth on her body. Also, the female hormones that I prescribe for her will work better."

Jolena nodded in agreement.

"I was never involved with them at this level. Only in the operating room, and then, they were asleep. Strange how much I didn't know."

He laughed.

"I'll bring you a book, and you can read more about it. It's not a popular subject with the doctors in the hospital. The less you say about it, the better for both of us."

She understood all he said and all he didn't take the time to explain.

"No problem with me, Dr. Edgewater." Jolena understood well that she was not to talk about this office. She didn't even want to think about it. If there was something wrong with the way he did his procedure, who was she to question. She had been prepared to tell him that she would not return, but he had been kind and needed help. It had been the first time her ethics in nursing and money had been tested. She was aware that money was a persuasive factor. Her monetary rewards in nursing were small. She would help him out until he found a replacement. She pressed the seventy dollars carefully into her pocket. It would take her two days to earn that and then it would be taxed. She was pleased. Her pay and this extra money would make a difference. When she left that evening, Jolena Taylor had no idea that she would remain for five years at that job and that job alone.

"Jolena!"

His voice snapped her out of the past. She had not noticed that all conversation had ceased in the waiting room. Jolena perked herself up.

"Daydreaming? Surely, not you!" He smiled that charming smile. She noticed he looked exceptionally handsome this day. A brisk aroma of after-shave filled the room. "Who do we have in the treatment room?"

She followed him to his private office.

"Sorry, I was in deep thought. Well, your favorite patient, Michelle, is here. She pulled out the catheter."

"Oh, damn her! What a mess to deal with after all day in surgery. Why didn't you put it back in and send her on her way?"

"I've done that before. And if it doesn't work out right, who do you blame? Me. And who will you blame if any complications set in? Me. No, my dear doctor, you replace the catheter. You're the doctor." She was firm.

Often, through the years, he had relinquished duties to her that were not in her nursing description. She had performed those duties diligently and often with better technique than he would have employed, but if a complication occurred, no matter how insignificant, he would indicate that it was her fault. That taught her to wait and allow him to do his own administering. She would always be there to assist him. They were doctor and nurse, and their professional relationship worked. He trusted her and she protected him.

Together they had set up the office and schedules so that there was no need to hire additional personnel. This kept everything very private. No one could pry into charts and other documents. Jolena was able to handle the difficult personalities and eliminate the troublemakers and gossips. Jolena was the catalyst that had made the office successful.

He smiled at her.

"You are a good student."

"And you are a good teacher."

Dutifully, she took his hand and led him to the treatment room. Michelle's voice came alive when she saw him.

"Doctor, oh, doctor, I can't pee. What happened? Why can't I pee?"

"Because you took the damn catheter out. Why in the hell do you do this? This is the second time." He spoke harshly. Jolena was surprised. She had never seen or heard him so irritable.

"I'm going to replace this catheter, and I do not want it out until I remove it. And if it comes out, don't come back to this office!"

He grabbed the catheter setup, quickly put on the gloves, and slowly began inserting the catheter into the meatus leading toward the bladder. The urine began flowing into the large basin. He then took a syringe and inflated the miniature balloon that was on the tip of the catheter enabling it to stay in place. The moans had now turned to sighs of relief. He shook his head in disgust, yanking off the gloves.

"Clean her up. Reattach and tape that catheter into place, Jolena." He left the room.

"He sure ain't in a good mood, Ms. Taylor."

"No, he's tired. Lots of surgery today."

Jolena put on gloves and applied an antiseptic solution, cleaning the newly formed female genitalia between the legs.

"Now, you have pulled out that catheter twice, but don't you dare touch or pull out that vaginal packing, Michelle, or you will be in a world of trouble. You understand that, don't you?"

"Yes, Ms. Taylor. You explained it to me many times before. Nobody but you. Even that new girl who works with him in the operating room didn't tell me nothing. Even when she came around after the surgery, she never told me nothing. I think he's kind of sweet on her. Everybody at the hospital said so. She is young and pretty."

"She was in the operating room during your surgery?" Jolena inquired. She had never heard him mention that he had an assistant or girl working with him in the hospital.

"Oh, yeah. She was always there with him, even when he made his visits."

"Okay, Michelle, you can get up and go. Don't stop to visit or say anything outside. Just go straight out that door. Be good, and call if you have any problems."

"I'm glad you're here. You're nice to me."

Jolena nodded in approval. Quickly, she called in the first patient. "Coco! Come in."

The tall transvestite glided through the door and into the treatment room. He looked as he was: a man dressed in drag.

"I want body, body, and more body."

"Strip from the waist down. The doctor will be in soon."

Jolena left the treatment room and hurried to the files. She pulled the last five postoperative reports. Leafing through each one, she stopped at the operative sheets that listed who had performed each operation and the assistants. The same name appeared: Belinda Koski. Slowly, she closed the files. He had never mentioned having a permanent assistant in the operating room. Was he having an affair with this one? It was certainly his personal business. He had just gotten rid of the last girlfriend less than two months ago. She had never known him to pick anyone from the hospital. How long has this been going on? Was this the reason for his recent rash of lateness and careless attitudes toward the patients? Well, if this was a new affair, she'd hear about it sooner or later.

"Doctor," she announced on the intercom, "there is one in the room waiting."

"Michelle's gone?" he asked, on his way to the treatment room.

"Yep, and I took care of everything. She'll be okay. You want me to help you in there?"

"No, I can manage." He disappeared into the room.

At first, the sounds were low moans, then the screams began to seep from the patient to the outer office. Jolena, oblivious to all of this, continued her work. However, the painted and poised patients, hearing the disturbance, became restless and uneasily shifted in their seats. Screams pierced the silence. They glanced at each other, shaking their heads in disbelief. No one left. There was no other place to go. No other doctor wanted them in their office. They were tall, out of shape, illiterate, loud, disheveled, overdressed, underdressed, bewigged, bewildered blacks, whites, and Hispanic men who desired to look and feel like women. They were the outcasts, the scum and the slime. They were the transvestites of New York who desired to become the women of the future.

Jolena knew he would be out soon, sweating, swearing, and complaining. The door opened.

"Dammit! It is always the new ones who make the most noise. Finish up for me, Jolena." Sweating profusely and wiping his glasses, he retreated to his office.

She went to the treatment room. It was in disarray. Jolena carefully discarded all the needles and syringes. The patient, half-nude, was laying on her stomach. Jolena threw a sheet over the red and swollen buttocks that had just received the injections.

"Thank you, nurse." The patient was crying softly. "I didn't know it would hurt so much. He sure ain't nice."

"He's okay. It's just a bad day for him. Lots of surgery and other things." Jolena defended the doctor. That was her professional duty. Never talk about the doctor. "Here, dry your eyes." She handed her tissues.

Her attitude, in the beginning, toward these patients had been matter-of-fact. However, after years of listening and observing, she had become more sympathetic. She realized one basic fact. They were human. Perhaps misguided or misdirected, but they still had the ability to think, dream, laugh, cry, eat, drink, and hurt. She listened to their ideas and dreams of a better future. She could feel their hurt when they had been rejected or met with an injustice. The same things had happened in her life. She found it was necessary to maintain firmness in her guidance but with a gentle touch.

"Now, listen carefully," she spoke softly but with authority, "I am going to massage your buttocks where the doctor put the treatments. Then I will clean the area and apply the dressings. Do not take them off until tomorrow morning. After that, massage every day just like I did, and always scrub your skin every day with a brush or a rough washcloth. Now repeat what I've just told you."

Coco repeated the instructions. Jolena firmly massaged the reddened buttocks where Dr. Peter Edgewater had injected a large amount of silicone. This substance would eventually gel and cause the buttocks to appear larger and more attractive for those men who wanted to be female; men who wanted to dress as women; men who wanted female names; men who wanted to have breasts like women but retain their penes; men who wanted to paint their face and nails like women, and men who wanted to eventually cut off their male organs and possess vaginas. Jolena finally put on the bandages. It saddened her to look at the result of his injections. The work was sloppy and indifferent and it showed the doctor's total lack of concern.

"Coco, I'll give you an appointment in two weeks."

"He said I could come back in a few days."

Jolena knew the rule was two weeks.

"How much did you spend today?"

"Oh, I spent a thousand dollars," she answered proudly.

That's what you think, Jolena thought.

"You wait two weeks, Coco. Listen to me."

"Okay, Ms. Taylor. The girls say you know."

Jolena sighed deeply. Would they ever learn?

Coco walked slowly into the waiting room. All eyes riveted to her. Silence was deep. She stumbled to where her companions waited with open arms. Her ordeal was over, and she had survived. The other patients became cheerleaders, throwing supportive therapy to their brave comrade. Soothing words filled the room.

"Good girl." "Hang in there." "All for beauty." "No pain, no fame." "You made it, baby." "Hang tough." Their praises and voices had risen to a loud crescendo.

"Okay, ladies, not too loud." Jolena commanded. The voices quieted. It never ceased to amaze Jolena how much control she had over a roomful of men. She had surmised that it had to do with their sexual identity problems. They were also like children. All you had to do was to maintain discipline. And because she was honest, kind, and willing to listen to their problems and fantasies, they did not object to her discipline.

Jolena never shunned or ridiculed. If she had to give criticism, it was done in private. Any complications, treatments, or complaints suffered by one patient was never discussed in front of or with another patient. Privacy was protected. The patients were also aware that Jolena did the best body sculpturing with the silicone. The doctor only started the new patients, because the beginning treatments were easy and the patients uncomplaining. The remainder of the treatments, often painful and time-consuming, were left to Jolena.

"The second time is better, Coco," her friends whispered. "Taylor will do the work, and your body will begin to shape. She's the one, not him."

As the patients dwindled down to the last seven, Jolena knew the time to work her artistry was near. The seven that waited were to have silicone injections. In the beginning, Jolena had been reluctant to do the treatments. She knew little about the product and the results it produced. After watching them go through such painful procedure, it was apparent to her that out of desperation and desire to obtain a woman's shape, they cared little about dangers or future side effects.

Dr. Edgewater's offer of extra money persuaded her to assist with the injections. He would do the first treatment and Jolena would finish the entire shaping of the body. It was time-consuming and could take as long as one or two years to make a shape similar and oftentimes better than a genetic woman's body. It took endurance and extreme patience from both parties. The total cost could be astronomical. The beginning fee was one-thousand dollars, and all work after was five hundred dollars for each treatment, and he reassured everyone that his nurse, trained by him, would complete the shaping of their body in a manner that they could be proud to exhibit.

Jolena made her announcement.

"Ladies, please hand me the money for your treatments."

Everyone lined up, and each gave their five-hundred dollars for the second treatment. Jolena placed the money in an envelope.

"Have a seat, and I'll be with you shortly."

Calmly they waited.

Suddenly, the silence was shattered by a banging on the outside door. Jolena buzzed the door open. She stared at the patient. Anger consumed her. *Be calm,* she thought. *Don't let this one bitch get you angry. That's what she wants to happen.*

Lita Lopez swept into the office. Lita, twenty years old, was already a street legend in New York. It was rumored she was the youngest transvestite to have a sex-change surgery. She was considered a real woman by her peers. The other patients' eyes widened with amazement; eyes narrowed with hatred; eyes squinted for a closer look; eyes rolled in disgust; and eyes stared in admiration. The aroma of her personality smothered the office.

The makeup of her flawless tan skin was always perfect. Her hair, as a result of overindulgence in hormones, was long, black, and silky; her face, free of hair growth, was painted to perfection. The common Adam's apple and muscular composition of man was absent. The shape displayed beneath the tight clothes was her most intriguing attribute. The large, pumped breasts bounced freely under the blouse. She boasted of having had her "Adam's rib" removed, which helped create a smaller waistline. However, she boasted more about the many thousands of dollars in silicone that she had injected into her hips, thereby creating a perfect hourglass shape.

Besides her obnoxious personality, the only flaws existing in Lita's body were her flat buttocks and her thin, unshapely legs. Lita was not happy about these defects and heavily padded her buttocks and enlarged her legs by wearing several pair of pantyhose and pads. This created an illusion that she had a perfect shape for all others to envy. It worked, but Jolena knew the truth.

Lita leaned into the window opening. Jolena looked at her, but Lita spoke past her.

"I want to see the doctor."

"Have a seat, Lita, and I'll tell him you are here," Jolena said softly and turned away from her.

"I don't want a seat. I want the doctor. Now!" She spoke loudly as she glared at Jolena.

Jolena took a deep breath, turned and stared directly into Lita's face.

The tone of her voice was not soft this time.

"Don't even try it with me today. I asked you to take a seat, and I will tell him you are here."

Lita continued to stand. The feud between them existed because Jolena refused to inject more silicone into Lita's body. Jolena had complained to the doctor.

"She's greedy and obnoxious and wants to tell you how to do everything. There is something about her I don't like and I don't trust. You take care of her. She likes you."

Dr. Edgewater had reluctantly complied. Lita spent a lot of money, and he did not want to lose her cash business.

Jolena called out to Lita.

"Come here, Lita, because I have something to whisper to you."

Lita, curious, smirked and leaned toward the opening to hear what Jolena could possibly have to say to her. Everyone in the waiting room watched with fascination. There was silence. They strained to hear.

Jolena whispered with articulation, "I am the bitch here, Lita. You are a man in drag with a sex change even you would like to get rid of. If you want to act like a bitch, I'll start by giving you a few lessons, like telling all the girls about what is really under that dress. Now, be a nice lady and sit down!"

Lita, careful not to display defeat, turned and sat in the nearest chair. Jolena smiled. The other patients, having observed the entire scene, were pleased. They knew Jolena could handle Lita. It was a quiet victory for them.

Jolena knocked on the doctor's door and entered.

"Lita Lopez is here and wants some work done. You know what I mean."

"My God! I'm already late for an appointment. Why does she always do this? Always the last minute." He angrily pounded his fist on the desk. He knew this job would take at least forty-five minutes, but he also knew that Lita would be spending a thousand dollars in cash.

"Jolena, I'll start the treatments, and can you finish—"

"No! I told you before. I can't stand her. So the quicker you finish her, the quicker I can start on the others." She shoved the envelope with the other patients' money into his hand. It made the task in front of him easier.

"Put her in the room."

Jolena returned to the window and requested that Lita come to the treatment room. Triumphantly she strolled past the other patients. Jolena informed the doctor that Lita was ready.

The remaining patients knew that the waiting would be prolonged. They stirred restlessly. Some cursed, some murmured, some sighed, and everyone resented that they had to be pushed aside by some "queen diva."

Thomas Blake sat silent and forgotten through the whole dreaded scenario. Even Jolena had overlooked his presence. He was dressed in blue jeans, a heavy T-shirt, midthigh jacket, and comfortable walking shoes. He was as ordinary as his outfit. The medium-length blond hair had been pulled back from his face in a ponytail. The cap he wore covered most of his forehead. He wore horn-rimmed glasses and did not join in conversation or attempt to make friends in a crowd that could not fit in his future plans. He hated their vicious gossip. Their tongues would wag if they knew he was the painted and wigged Ms. Honey Babe, street walker of various Manhattan avenues. However, it was impossible for them to detect that this clean-faced, blue-eyed, blond boy was the same person. Slowly, he started toward the exit. Someone called out to him.

"Hey, baby, ain't you gonna wait?"

"No, I got another appointment. I'll try again next week."

Thomas exited with a sigh of relief. The sky hung low with gray clouds, and the air was still and cold. He shivered and tightly hunched his shoulders. The crispness of the air felt refreshing and welcome after that office scene. *I'll be back,* he thought. *But it will be a time when all those street drag queens won't be there.* He had observed that it wouldn't be easy getting close to Jolena Taylor. He'd have to keep trying, because Jolena Taylor was the only person he could trust to help him.

The ringing phone disturbed the peace that now prevailed in the office. Jolena answered.

"Has Peter left that office yet?" The voice was young, abrupt, and demanding.

"No. Dr. Edgewater is here. May I take a message? He is busy with a patient."

"This is Belinda, his assistant. Just tell him I will meet him at the restaurant. Gotta go."

The connection was quickly broken. Jolena at once recalled the name on the operative sheets. She opened the door. Dr. Edgewater, sweating, was bent over, pumping the thick liquid substance into Lita's buttocks.

"Doctor, your assistant, Belinda, called and said she would meet you at the restaurant."

"Oh, yes, thank you."

Jolena closed the door. Now at least he knew that she knew he had an assistant. Her mind was full of questions. Was this the Belinda that the patient had mentioned and whose name she saw on the hospital records? Was he getting involved in another affair? How much was this going to cost him? An assistant? She remembered that he had hinted needing help. What would happen to her extra money if he brought in some outsider? Everything had gone so well all these years. Why start changing things?

When the doctor finished with Lita, he approached her.

"Jolena, I wanted to talk with you about my new assistant."

He continued quickly, as though he was trying to justify the long delay in telling Jolena that things were going to change.

"She is a big help to me at the hospital, and I am thinking that maybe she could help us out here."

Jolena was quick and to the point.

"Personally, I don't think we need a third person. But that's up to you. It's your office."

She had made it apparent that she resented the idea. He did not bother with any further explanations.

"I'm in a hurry now. I'll talk with you tomorrow. Good night, my dear." He was gone.

Lita was dressed and moaning with pain.

"Oh, God, did he leave a prescription for me?"

Without uttering a word, Jolena handed her the prescription.

"I apologize, Ms. Taylor."

"Accepted." She never looked up at her.

"Why don't you like me? I know you don't."

"You're greedy, and I don't trust you. Let's leave it at that. Good night, Lita."

Lita lowered her head and left. The pain had taken its toll.

"You sure got her pegged, Ms. Taylor," one of the girls called out triumphantly.

"Let's not talk about it," Jolena replied.

There was no victory in the war with Lita.

3

When Peter entered the restaurant and saw her, all else was forgotten. Being in love with Belinda awakened his whole body. He wanted her with him at all times. With her, he was able to forget the little problems he had encountered. She smiled deliciously at him. He knew that she was in love with him. Peter had no doubts about her feelings. He reached over and kissed her.

"You're late again, Peter," she complained acidly.

"My darling, do forgive me. It's the office again. Always so many patients." He sighed heavily as he took a menu. "It gets to be a bit too much at times."

"I told you I would come in and help. If I can assist you in the OR, I can certainly help you in the office."

"Well, I have Jolena helping me. She does an excellent job."

"She's only a nurse. After all, I am a 'physician assistant' and more experienced."

Peter didn't respond. He thought about what she said, but he also knew the truth. He had forged her papers so she could come into the hospital and work with him. How quickly she had forgotten that she was a fraud. She really believed that she was a real physician assistant. He smiled. She was young and naive.

"We'll talk about it later. Let's order a drink and some food. Allow me to feast on that lovely face of yours."

She reached over, took his hand, and smiled seductively.

"I love you, Peter."

He knew that being a doctor was impressive, but he also believed she loved him. He could feel the love coming from her.

"And I am in love with you. I can't stand to be away from you. I think about you all the time."

When the waiter approached, he ordered a double martini. It helped Peter not to think about the difference in their ages. After all, he was now forty-five years old, and this beautiful girl was only twenty-two. What would he do with her in ten years? Would she still love him? He thought about her in bed and how she made him feel. Nothing mattered now except the two of them being together.

"I think we should make different living arrangements," he said with authority.

"Like what?"

"Like you moving in with me. Then, later, I might just marry you." He smiled as he watched her face break into a big grin. She was happy.

"Oh, great! That way we will always be together. I can work with you in the hospital and office."

"There's much to consider as far as the office is concerned. I've had Jolena there for five years. She runs the place effectively and profitably."

Belinda lowered her eyes and became silent.

"What's the matter, pet?"

"You talk as if I can't handle that office. As if I am not as capable as that nurse."

"No, no, my darling. Let's forget about that. Let us enjoy our dinner."

Belinda would not forget. She carried on a conversation, smiled the beautiful smile, was as seductive as a public setting would allow, but she did not forget. Whoever this Jolena was, Belinda did not intend to work with her. She had never seen her but had understood through the doctor's conversation that Jolena was black. She had planned never to work with black people unless she had no other choice. Surely she should have a choice in Peter's office. It might take a few weeks or months to get rid of her, but she would accomplish that task very easily. Peter would do anything for her. She would make very sure of that.

Dr. Peter Edgewater hated the drive up the Bruckner Expressway and eventually into Co-Corp. complex where Belinda lived with her parents. He had wanted her to sleep at his apartment tonight, but she began to complain of stomach cramps and wanted to go home.

"I was hoping we could go to my place. You could spend the night, and in the morning we could go to work together," he explained as he drove up the long stretch of the expressway.

"Oh, Peter," she complained. "I am having such bad cramps. It's time for my period, and I have pain all the time. Also, I have to talk to my parents and let them know I'm moving into the city, but I don't want them to think I am living with you. They wouldn't like that. They want me to be married."

He could sense that she was looking to hear some kind of positive response.

"Well, who knows? Marriage might come very soon." He stole a glance and could see that she was pleased with the statement. He had thought of marriage with her but had not quite worked out the plans. The car was nearing the multibuilding complex. "I'll be glad not to make this long ride again."

"And I'll be equally glad. I hate it up here. It's getting worse. All kinds of people are moving in."

"Don't worry, precious; after tomorrow, you will be free of this."

He turned the car into a large oval driveway of the multiplex buildings. When he leaned over to kiss her, she wrapped her arms around him, responding passionately.

"It's not too late," he begged. "We can turn around and go back downtown."

"Peter, for goodness sake, can't you wait until tomorrow?"

"It's the way you make me feel. Whenever you touch me, I am ready." He stared longingly into her young face. "But you're right. I'll see you at work tomorrow." They kissed again.

Belinda got out and hurried toward her building. She turned and watched Peter drive away. After entering the building, she went to a different floor from the one on which she lived. She rang the bell.

"Elaine, it's me, Belinda. Quick, open up. I've got something to tell you."

A sleepy Elaine slowly opened the door.

"Oh, Belinda, it's late. What's the matter?"

Belinda, ignoring her apparent tiredness, pushed by her.

"Dr. Peter Edgewater has finally asked me to move in with him."

"For real?" The announcement alerted her.

"Yes, and tomorrow I will be moving in with him."

"What about your parents, and what about that boyfriend? What story are you going to tell them?"

"Oh, I can handle all of that. I won't tell my parents that I am living with him. I'll just say that I am living with a girlfriend. And Ricky, well, I'll just tell him it's over. I'm tired of him. I have a doctor who has money, and I am not going to lose him for any reason." She was emphatic.

"Will you still be working in the OR with him?"

"Yes, and also in the office. I am now his right hand."

"Wow, you will be with him all the time. Since he will have you around him that much, why should he marry you?" Elaine sounded sarcastic.

"He will. He will. And after the marriage, my dear Elaine, I will not be working anywhere. I am going to be a doctor's wife."

"Lucky you! Out of here, and soon to be a doctor's wife."

"Yes, and I am never coming back."

The two women said their good-nights, and Belinda made her way to her parents' apartment. She thought about Ricky and began to long for him. They had been going together for almost two years. She liked the way he made love to her. It wasn't sloppy and indifferent, like Peter's lovemaking. She picked up the phone and dialed. Ricky's voice answered, and she responded.

"It's me."

"Baby, my God, when am I going to see you? Goddamm, I miss you."

"I told you I was busy working. I am moving up in the world."

"I'm not concerned with that. I only want to see you."

"You know what to do. Come here now. I'll be waiting by the door."

She hung up the phone. After checking to make sure that her parents were asleep, Belinda went to the door and waited for the sound of the elevator. When she heard the elevator door open, she opened the apartment door; her heart pounded as Ricky emerged and took her into his arms. It felt good, comforting, and safe. She never wanted him to let her go, but then she remembered her ambition and wrestled herself free.

"Let's go into my room. Be quiet so my parents don't hear us."

Once inside the bedroom, they frantically undressed and became consumed with each other. There were quiet moans and confessions of love. But Belinda remembered her ambition.

"I'll be moving to the city tomorrow."

"My God. When will I see you?"

"I'll call you. Don't worry; I'll keep in touch."

He took her in his arms again, and again he made love to her. Belinda responded openly and with all the emotion she possessed. She knew that it would be a long time before she saw him, or ever again. She shuddered at both thoughts. But then, again she remembered her ambition.

4

Thomas Blake returned to his small East Side apartment. He was elated. He had finally found the Jolena he'd heard so much about. Thomas prayed that when he went back at his own planned time, she would help him. He flipped the radio on, and the sound of classical music filled the room. He sighed with relief. Patience and planning had been important. He wanted everything to be almost perfect. It would be important to have a flawless body, a classic, sculptured face, and a vagina that not only looked like a vagina but functioned. It would cost much money for him to acquire what he desired. And Thomas Blake desired not only to become a female, but a rich and famous female with no past that could be traced.

Money spent in the right places would take care of everything. Thomas was a firm believer that money opened doors, windows, hearts, minds, bodies, and souls. Now he began removing his clothes and studied the male form in the mirror. Quickly, he covered himself. He hated that image. Thomas lay on his magazine-cluttered bed to take a short rest before preparing for his nightly stroll. He hated that part of his life, but it served his purpose in life. He remembered that earlier his uncle had been an unpleasant part of his life. Thomas blamed him for everything. He hated to think about the past, but sometimes he had to, sometimes he had to remember....

The house had been big. The biggest house he'd ever seen. Brent was his real name, and he was twelve years old. Both parents had been killed in a car accident, and he was brought to live with his aunt and uncle. He couldn't understand death snatching his parents from him. He became very quiet and withdrawn, but his uncle was always there to comfort him, even more than his aunt. Her social activities caused her to neglect her husband and Brent.

But the uncle was not at all neglectful of Brent. He took him almost everywhere he went. Even to the office and to lunch with all his lawyer friends. Brent was enjoying a good, rich life and the attention. But when the uncle began to fondle him, Brent became frightened.

He did not understand this kind of relationship, neither did he understand the kind of feelings that were being aroused in him. He could not discuss it with his aunt. Besides, he was enjoying all the trips, clothes, and shoes, and most anything he asked for, the uncle, without reservation, would buy for him. He had no place to go, and there were no other relatives. So he continued to be quiet and silently submitted to his uncle's advances.

He hated him and wished he would die, but that wish did not come true. His uncle was in politics, and Brent seemed to sense that those kind of people never die. So through the next four years, he learned about sex perverts who claimed to be for white supremacy and against homosexuality. His uncle reminded him that leaders of the world had all indulged in these kinds of sexual acts without acting like "faggots" and that most of them were intelligent, strong, and honest men. He had named Homer, Socrates, and a few others Brent knew who were not alive to defend their sexuality.

Brent had grown into a handsome young boy. He was tall and thin in stature. His blond hair was straight and thick, his nose angular, eyes widely set, jaw line well defined, and his cheekbones chiseled to perfection. His looks were Aryan, with his blond hair and striking blue eyes. Often he stared in the mirror at himself. He never felt like other boys and knew that something about him was different. Sometimes he would wrap a towel around his head and was aware that he looked beautiful. One day, he wandered into his aunt's bedroom and began experimenting with her makeup. His uncle caught him.

"Well, look, what have we here? A girl?"

Brent was frightened.

"No, no, Uncle, I was just pretending." He began removing the makeup.

"You look beautiful," his uncle whispered. "It's amazing! A person would never know the difference if you didn't have that little pecker hanging down there."

Brent tried to move past his uncle and out of the room. His uncle grabbed him.

"Maybe I should treat you more like a girl. You want to be a girl, don't you?"

Embarrassed and frightened, Brent started to cry.

"Stop that! You're too old to cry. Go to your room before your aunt returns. I'll be there."

Brent ran to his room. He was frightened. His uncle entered, carrying a small, flimsy nightgown. He threw it to Brent.

"Here, put this one. Let's see how you look."

Reluctantly Brent put on the gown. He and his uncle gazed into the mirror.

"My God, you are just like a girl. Do you like how you look?" Brent was mesmerized with the reflection. "Yes," he whispered.

He continued to stare at himself. If he had long hair, it would have been complete. A strange feeling was aroused within Brent. One day he would fix all of these wrong things about him.

His uncle began to run his hand around Brent's buttocks and small penis. Brent tried to move away, but his uncle held on to him and began whispering.

"Oh, you sweet little girl. You beautiful bitch. I'm going to make love to you. I've waited so long." Brent began to try to break free. "Be still. It won't hurt. It'll just take a minute. Don't try to get away from me!"

He pushed Brent down on the bed. Quickly, he dropped his pants and raised the young boy's legs high. Before Brent could comprehend what was happening, his uncle had his penis inserted into the young boy's anus. Brent moaned with pain, then slowly, it disappeared and a pleasure consumed him that he had never before experienced. He watched as his uncle's face grimaced as he ejaculated.

"Did you like it? Did you like it?" the uncle demanded.

Brent didn't know how to answer. He said nothing. He only turned his head away. He didn't want to look at him.

The uncle kissed him on the cheek and warned him.

"Don't you tell anyone about this. Not even your aunt. If you do, you will end up like one of those jiggaboos we dump out there in the woods."

Brent, shaken back to the real world, felt the pain around his wet and soggy rectum. Later, in the bathroom, he gazed in the mirror. His uncle was right. He should have been a girl. But that was impossible.

The following year, Brent ran away from the well-kept lawns and comfortable home of his uncle and his continual sexual abuse. Chicago was the closest city and his first stop. After hanging around in the bus depot and sleeping along Lakeshore Drive, he finally got an offer from a passing gentleman. Brent needed the money, so he went home with the stranger. His name was Joseph, and he told Brent he could stay as long as he desired.

After listening to Brent describe his past life with the uncle, Joseph did not make any sexual advances toward him. Instead, he saw Brent as someone he could teach and guide. During the next six months, he taught Brent correct body hygiene, how to dress and eat, and the proper wines to order. He taught him how to answer the telephone, write checks, answer questions correctly, count money, when to say yes or no, and when to keep quiet. Brent was an excellent student. Joseph molded him into a handsome gentleman who knew how to service older, wealthy gentlemen who paid well for the privilege of his company.

It had been two years since he left Cicero. He had learned to save his money. Very rarely did he spend any large amount of money. Dutifully, he had put his money away in a safe deposit box.

Frequently when Brent was in the company of the men he serviced, he heard rude remarks about women and worse about transvestites. Brent remained silent. He had never forgotten about his desire. Whenever a transvestite who looked exceptionally good was pointed out, Brent would be fascinated. He wanted to know so much about how they made themselves look like a woman. He'd never mention such a subject to even Joseph, who had expressed his opinion on transvestites as being real sick in the head. At every opportunity, he would search through the fashion magazines, admiring the tall, lean models. He wanted to look like the women he saw in the magazines. This was his secret desire—to be a beautiful woman. He had no one in whom he could trust or confide. Brent did not want to spend the rest of his life fucking men in the ass or getting fucked.

He started developing a plan. The first part of that plan was to continue saving his money. Without money he was nothing. The second part was to get out from under Joseph and make a life for himself. He carefully guarded his most deep desires and trusted no one. When Joseph inquired about what he did with his money, Brent mentioned that he sent money home to help care for a retarded brother. It was accepted.

Brent had adapted well into his living situation, especially since he now had the plan set into motion. However, an incident occurred that caused him to make a quick change in his plans. A newly elected congressman was being honored at a large political party. The congressman wanted a white, blond, blue-eyed young man to be his companion after the party. Brent was to service this gentleman for a fee of one thousand dollars. Brent hated having to be with politicians, but they paid well and usually drank too much and fell asleep quickly before the sexual act could even begin.

That evening, Brent arrived early at the ballroom. He was handsomely dressed, and many of the women turned their heads to catch an extra glance. He, in turn, admired the woman in their beautiful beaded and silk gowns. Whenever he saw them, a longing filled him—not a sexual thing, but a desire to be like them.

He had found himself a good corner and was enjoying his champagne as he awaited the arrival of the "man of the hour." As he began to sip on his second glass, all attention turned to the fanfare at the door. The congressman had arrived. Brent moved closer to get a look at the politician he would service tonight. He laughed to himself—a real government job. He took one short glance at the man and quickly moved out of sight. He felt sick. He made his way to the bathroom and rinsed his face with cold water. The congressman was his uncle! *The fuckin' bastard,* he thought. *How quickly he had moved up the ladder.*

He hated him. No way was he going to be exposed and trapped by him. Quickly, he left the bathroom and made his way out of the ballroom without being noticed. Joseph would have to find someone else to work him. It would not be Brent. He returned to the apartment and packed whatever clothes he could manage to squeeze in the two suitcases.

He knew he had panicked. Sit down and get your plans and thoughts together. There was no place to go at this hour in the morning. He needed his money, therefore, he'd have to wait until the bank opened at nine o'clock. He hoped that Joseph did not come home this particular evening. Joseph had been good to him. He did not want to feel guilty, but he knew it was time to leave Chicago. He pulled out a bottle of champagne, opened it, and sat on the terrace overlooking the tremendous lake.

"Here's to you, Chicago. You did me well. This will be the last time I see you. And to you, dear uncle, may you die before you fuck all the young white boys of America."

As he sat through the night into the morning, going over his short life, he realized that he had stayed in Chicago too long and it was time to make a change. He thought about Joseph. How he would miss him. He was a good person and had helped him.

"You taught me well, and I owe you. Maybe one day we will meet again," he whispered.

The sun was coming up over the lake. It was time now. He left the keys behind and closed the door. The doorman quickly got him a cab. Brent directed the cab to Michigan and State.

"Please wait. I am going to the airport. I tip well."

The driver nodded in agreement. The business at the bank took less than fifteen minutes. He had scooped his fifteen thousand out of the box and was soon on his way to O'Hare Airport. There was a plane every hour to New York. At the restaurant, he ordered breakfast. During his meal, his attention was diverted by the television news announcement that a well-known congressman had been accused of propositioning a young man to have sex with him. The young man in question had been an undercover cop who had been assigned to a case involving rich men soliciting young boys. Brent sat, astonished, as he watched the television showing his uncle being led handcuffed by a policeman. Brent laughed, and then laughed louder when he saw that the policeman was black.

5

When Dr. Peter Edgewater opened the door to his apartment, located on the nineteenth floor of a luxury apartment building, the painting caught his eye. It was an original Van Gogh. He sighed in extreme delight, as always, to know that he owned such a treasure. As a young man, he had adored art and had shown great promise of being an artist, but a dominating mother had insisted he become a doctor. It was useless to go against her, so he accepted a medical school scholarship and finally specialized in plastic surgery. That was the closest specialty to being an artist.

But he discovered it was also long and tedious work and not at all rewarding if you were not in with the "right group" of plastic surgeons and if you did not have privileges at a prestigious hospital. Later, he was trapped into marriage with a social climber, who discovered he was not as ambitious as she wanted him to be and who he discovered did not have the money or clout she had professed having. Disappointed in each other, they divorced but not before he was forced to give her a five-thousand-dollar settlement. The only sadness he could display over the divorce was the loss of money he had to borrow to pay her.

He racked it up as a lesson for all his future dealings with women or wives. He vowed never to make that mistake again. All women he met from then on would pay a price. If they could not promote him or help in his quest for whatever he wanted, they were of no use to him. Peter Edgewater used all of his attributes to move himself into a financial setup.

Step by step, he had worked his way to his own office. The majority of his patients were by no means the socialites he had desired, but they had their own society. They were the transvestites of the streets of New York. But they came with cash in their hands, requesting any type of surgery that would make them look more feminine. Their greatest demand was the silicone injections. Edgewater had the only silicone business in the city or, at least, the most well known.

When a resident, he had learned from a famous plastic surgeon the technique of injecting the silicone. The wife of that surgeon had been extremely attractive to Peter and, after many weeks of secret meetings of lovemaking, revealed to him knowledge that enabled him to purchase the silicone that he began to use in his own practice with a great deal of success.

The subculture that he treated was wild for silicone. He had become their savior. It was strictly a cash business. He was able to hide away, along with all of that money, other small treasures he had acquired, mostly from admiring women and patients. Some had been his lovers and some had not. He hardly remembered or cared to remember.

Peter poured himself a drink and settled down into a chair that enabled him to look out over the city and its lights. He thought about Belinda, and a smile came over his face. A glance around his large bachelor apartment reassured him that she would be happy living with him. He could handle her. Already he had trained her to do as he requested. There were few negative responses from her. She was the youngest woman he had ever had, and he indulged himself to every delight with her.

He was aware that Belinda was impressed with his being a doctor, and that was his good fortune. He trusted her but would have to be careful not to allow her to become too knowledgeable. Especially about his money. It was time now for him to have somebody, and she was what he wanted. Belinda was the right ticket. He would marry her but not right away. There were many of her habits he would have to tolerate or change. If he was happy, then everything would be perfect.

Together they would work hard, and within five years they should be able to seek an easier way of life. Whether this would be acceptable to Belinda was the last thought on Peter's mind. He knew what was best for her. After all, hadn't he made her a "physician assistant?" It had cost a lot of money to have the papers processed, but he did not have to worry about her working for anyone else. However, Belinda did not realize that she was and would be *his* physician assistant and *only his*. The license that she thought she had didn't exist. Telling her the truth would only shatter her little world, deflate her ego, and make her think ill of him.

Peter had envisioned plans for the future, and those plans were to get rid of the transvestite patients. They were, however, a rich source of unreported cash. Peter was beginning to view them more and more as monstrous, dirty, and obnoxious. He wanted the high class and rich society women. If he intended to belong to that social crowd, then he would have to clean up his office image. It would be necessary to redecorate, buy new equipment and furniture. Of course, a new face in the office, preferably a white face, would be impressive. Surely he would never relate this to Jolena. It would only hurt or offend. He felt a small tinge of guilt even harboring such thoughts. However, with the passionate thoughts of Belinda flooding his mind, he unwittingly began plotting a way to lessen Jolena's position.

Jolena was important, but not enough that it should interfere with his life and money. At one time, he thought that without her, he could never manage his office. Why not train Belinda, just as he had Jolena? It was important that she be trained to function alone and take over Jolena's job of doing the silicone injections.

Performing the injections was difficult and dangerous work. Jolena, however, had acquired a knack for that job. And he was paying her cash money for her services. Of course, Jolena could become upset and quit. But isn't this what he wanted? She would have no problem getting another job. His only concern was for Belinda and himself. He could never pay her as much as he gave Jolena, but whatever she got would be sufficient. That way he would be able to save more cash. Now would be the right time to start disposing of Jolena.

He was amazed that he had never thought about this before. Was it his love for Belinda that had finally opened his eyes to a better way? Peter always felt that if he began to feel right about an idea then it should be put into effect. How could he have held Jolena in such high professional esteem? Sure, he had been impressed when he saw her functioning so efficiently with Dr. Bernie Charles. Later, he had been fortunate to get her to work for him, but now, was she really necessary? He was smarter now and knew what was necessary to make his professional career function. It was also apparent to him that she knew too much about his office, his surgery, his false insurance records, his bank accounts, and his personal business.

He contemplated how he had never really been fond of nurses. From the time of his internship in the hospitals, he disliked nurses. They seemed to stand there to watch you stumble through procedures on patients. Some never uttered a word; some ignored your mistakes; some verbally criticized you; some pushed you aside before you made a mistake; some hissed at you; some openly laughed at you; and some reported you to the chief of the service. He had vowed he'd never have a nurse around him, but Jolena had been an exception.

She had been kind, helpful, loyal, honest, and a friend. So he had to admit that the problem wasn't with Jolena or the nurse in Jolena; it was the money, and one other matter that was beginning to bother his rather inflated ego. The patients who came for the infamous silicone injections requested that she, the nurse, work on them because they liked her method. Her method! He had been silently appalled. He could never understand how she had managed to become so creative, much less establish a "method."

Naturally, he didn't want to think about the fact that she was black. No, Peter was not prejudiced. Color was the last thing he thought about, but it did begin to creep into existence. Beautiful Belinda had mentioned it several times. So was he jealous of the nurse or of the black nurse? Black or whatever, he narrowed it down to the fact that she had no special talents. Rather, she had carefully scrutinized his technique. On second thought and after a second drink, he had to admit that his technique did not work and he had no creativity. All he ever did was pump one big syringeful of silicone and send them on their way.

He had expected that she would follow his method. Left to her own devices and without his advice or assistance, the nurse had become a supernurse, and in his own office. However, after viewing the results of her work, he had to admit, inwardly, that the bodies were shaped and flawless. That took time and patience. He possessed neither. Belinda would be his answer. Eventually, she would replace Jolena. He smiled again as he admired the painting and the new plan he had formulated tonight. Now he raised his glass in a toast to himself.

"To a job well done, Dr. Peter Edgewater, despite all the obstacles in your way." He gulped a big drink.

His thoughts now turned to his skill as a surgeon. He was especially proud of his operative procedures. According to "the book," some procedures were impossible to do or impossible to do in such a short time. Peter had found ways to shorten procedures. His longest operation might be two hours. There were complications, but those were to be expected, and Peter handled them well. He cared little about his patients' complaints. After all, to him, they were just a bunch of "freaks" looking for the impossible dream.

They voiced complaints but never did anything about it. Where could they go to put in a serious complaint against him? The changes they wanted done on their bodies was against nature. How could they ever dream of being beautiful women or handsome men? Nobody really cared about their feelings, thoughts, or dreams, much less their complaints. Therefore, he felt free to do the various procedures and operations upon them that he knew were against all medical ethics. He fulfilled their wishes for a more pointed chin, a narrow nose, implants in the cheeks, implants in the hips, implants in the breasts, and silicone injections everywhere and anywhere he could or would put it.

Peter looked in the mirror. He was pleased with himself. He liked the way he looked. Being middle-aged was not as bad as he had heard.

But then, every man did not have a Belinda—dear, sweet, dumb little Belinda. He could feel himself getting an erection just thinking about her. She sucked his dick so good! So young, and yet, so experienced. How did she ever get so experienced? Well, that was not important now.

What was important was that he teach her how to do the injections of silicone. He needed someone she could learn from. And suddenly the answer was there. Belinda would pump Lita's body. Jolena refused to touch her, and now, Belinda would be perfect. He knew that Lita didn't care who pumped her body with the dreaded substance. She always brought cash and never less than a thousand dollars. *Brilliant idea,* he thought. And that deserved another drink.

Later, in bed, Peter tossed and turned. He was lonely. He needed Belinda. Perhaps he would just call her and hear her voice. No, that would be silly. He did not want her to think that he was a silly old man. *Tomorrow night she will be here,* he thought. And that helped him to sleep.

6

Lita Lopez was in pain when she left the doctor's office. The verbal incident with Jolena annoyed her. Lita found it difficult to deal with Jolena. She had tried to buy her, con her, convince her to continue pumping the silicone into her body, but Jolena refused. She hated to be injected by the doctor. He was not as creative with bodies as Jolena, and he always gave her a rush job. Lita knew damn well he never gave her what she paid for. One day she'd find a way to get even.

As she made her way down Eighty-sixth Street, a short, round, and ruddy-faced priest passed and slowly nodded. Lita, transsexual, thief, prostitute, turned quickly and stared after him. A strange chill swept through her. It had nothing to do with the cold outside. There must be a church near, she thought. As she turned the corner and approached Park Avenue, she saw the tall, formidable sanctuary. Since Lita had no appointments or nowhere to be at any given time, her curiosity caused her to enter.

It had been many years since she had been in a church, but the immediate odors of muskiness and burning candlewick permeated her brain. Without respectfully genuflecting, she sat down. Here, she would rest, and maybe the pain would ease. It was peaceful and quiet. The clinking of coins into the church box broke the silence. Lita looked around and saw a well-dressed gentleman walk past her toward the alter and kneel.

He looks ripe, she thought. When he finished praying and approached where she knelt, Lita made her move.

"You want some religious fun?" she whispered.

He hesitated, then moved into the pew with her.

"What did you say?"

"I want to know if you want some religious fun?" She smiled.

"What do you mean?"

"I mean that I can give you a quick blow job right here. It's dark, and nobody will notice. We are the only ones." She gestured.

"This is not right. This is . . ." He began to move away. She reached out and touched him between the legs. It was hard. Experience taught her he was ready. She quickly unzipped his pants.

"Give me fifty," she demanded.

"I don't have that much."

"Come on, yes, you do. It's gonna be worth it. When have you ever had a blow job in a church? Just keep your eye on the blessed sacrament. Watch how it lights up when you come."

He quickly groped two twenties and a ten, which he shoved towards her. Lita quickly went to work. It was only a matter of two minutes, and she was finished. He was devastated.

"That was so good. When can I see you again? What is your name?"

She got up and looked down at him. The name seemed to bellow throughout the church.

"Jose." She hesitated, then continued. "Lita Jose Lopez." She strolled out of the church. Lita was laughing.

The children's eyes, wide with excitement and curiosity, watched the newborn baby slip down from between the mother's legs. It was not a special phenomenon to them, nor was it the first time they had seen babies come out of their mother. Consuela Lopez had just delivered her sixth child. She quickly made a sign of the cross.

"Please let it be a boy. Please God," she muttered.

Her prayers were answered. This would be the last baby. No more babies. After five girls, a boy would make her husband happy. She wrapped the baby in a blanket and smiled. At last, at last, a boy.

"Rosa, go find your father and tell him he has a son!"

She was the oldest child and knew where her father spent all of his time and money. Later that night, the child returned, but the father was not with her.

"He said to tell you that it was good he has a son and he will be home later."

Consuela, disappointed as always, went about her various household chores. Now she was tired and wanted to rest. She had to call on her little girls to help her with the new baby.

The father celebrated the birth of his son by getting drunk and having sex with any one of the local women in the cantina who would have him. Drunken and wasted, he stumbled home, demanding sex from his wife, who had less than twenty-four hours earlier delivered his son. As he attempted to beat her into submission, Consuela plunged a knife deep into his belly. She cried only for the sake of her children, for it would be a long, harsh prison term, and the children would be placed in various homes and orphanages.

Jose, the last born, was shifted from home to relatives, to more various and distant relatives and orphanage to orphanage. At the age of eight, he was taken to a small church and parish. It was considered an honor to be selected to live in the parish. There he would be the altar boy and administer all chores necessary to keep the church functioning without their having to pay salaries. Father Emmanuel had taken little Jose, who had never known love or affection, and changed his life forever.

Father Emmanuel was fond of little boys. Since there were no relatives or parents to be concerned about Jose, he would be the perfect child for the priest. Not much time passed before Jose, who thought of the priest like a father, discovered that late at night Father Emmanuel dressed up like a woman. He quickly explained to Jose that it was a game they both would enjoy. Jose was delighted.

"Remember, Jose," Father Emmanuel had warned, "if you want to stay here, you can never tell anybody about our game, or God will strike both of us dead!"

Those words horrified Jose. He didn't want anything to happen to Father Emmanuel.

"I will never tell."

Jose was sincere and loyal. He did not want to leave the parish. It was clean, with lots of good food and no need to share with anyone. Jose was also fearful of being struck dead.

"Now, late at night when I become your mother, you have to call me mommy. Then I am going to show you how a little boy must treat his mommy."

Jose listened carefully. He never had a real mommy. What he could not understand through explanation he would through feelings. Father Emmanuel was an expert in arousing the feelings of a virgin boy.

In the evenings after the church was locked, Father Emmanuel and Jose would return to their own private quarters in the rectory. There, the priest would dress as a woman. Jose would laugh with glee.

"Hi, mommy," Jose chirped.

"Hello, my son. My sweet little baby." Father Emmanuel spoke in a high falsetto voice. His wig and makeup gave him all the appearance of a middle-aged woman. His manner of dress was similar to what any female parishioner would wear. The nylon stockings that flattered his hairless legs were held in place by fancy garters. He pranced about in the highest heels Jose had ever seen. He pulled his dress up to show Jose the pretty lace panties covering his male anatomy.

"Mommy has something for her little baby tonight."

Jose was delighted. Almost every night since the priest had revealed his secret to Jose, he had given him a small toy or candy.

"What? What?"

"Come over to the sofa, and I'll show you."

Emmanuel slowly unbuttoned the top of his dress. Jose watched with fascination as breasts plopped out.

"Oh, mommy, what are they?" Jose was mystified. He had never seen breasts and never on a man.

"They are breasts, and they are for you. They have milk in them, and mommy wants you to help get the milk out. You want to do that, don't you? Just like a baby?"

Jose, astonished and mystified, nodded with approval.

"Climb up here and put your mouth on them and suck real hard. Don't bite mommy. Be gentle."

Jose climbed into Emmanuel's lap and maneuvered a breast into his small mouth. The priest enclosed Jose in his arms and softly moaned while Jose sucked from one breast to the other. Often he complained that he was not able to taste the milk. Father Emmanuel told him he was doing a good job and to continue. Eventually Jose fell asleep. He was not aware of the wetness between Father Emmanuel's legs or that the job of making "mommy" happy would be extended to other duties.

Father Emmanuel had not fathomed that such a prize could be awarded him. He would carefully lead the small boy through the stages of accepting all he offered. However, Jose made the task easier by asking for the nightly treat of getting the milk out of "mommy's" breast. Father Emmanuel found it easier to go a step further.

"I know you would like to make both mommy and daddy happy, and that will make us give you anything you want."

Jose nodded in agreement. At this point, he was becoming confused about what more he could demand. He had been showered with all kinds of toys and food. Whatever the new game, he was willing. Up to this point, everything had been fun and new. Most of all, he had pleased Father Emmanuel. This would be Jose's first introduction to a devastating sexual pleasure. How could it be distasteful if he had never been introduced to any type of sexual act? Whatever request was presented to him by this mommy and daddy figure in the church was correct and it was all right.

Father Emmanuel took off his clothes except the brassiere, garter belt, and stockings that he constantly wore under his habit. His penis was small and firm. His directions were simple enough for the child to follow.

"Take my little rod in your hands and rub it." Jose grabbed the penis and began to rub.

"Oh, ouch! No, no, you must do it softly." Jose loosened his grip and began rubbing it as directed. "That's better. Yes, that's nice." Father Emmanuel sat down in the old sofa taking Jose with him.

"Now climb up in my lap and keep rubbing my rod, and you can begin to suck on mommy's tits." The old priest was in his most glorious moment. God was surely good to him. A young innocent boy to be made to his perfection. He suddenly wished that the boy would never grow up.

"That feels so good." He spoke softly and stroked his head. "You are a good little baby, and you are making both your mommy and daddy very happy. That is a wonderful thing for you to do."

The feel of the small warm hands rubbing his penis and the sound and feel of Jose's young hot mouth on his breast aroused such excitement in the priest that it took all in his power to hold back the ejaculation. He didn't want it to end. It was too good to end. Finally, he pulled away.

Jose, astonished, cried.

"Why did you do that? I like it. I want to do more. More!"

The youngster grabbed the penis and began sucking it feverishly. Father Emmanuel was shocked. He had not planned this. Not yet. He moaned and mumbled, lost in his ecstasy.

"Oh, Jose, what a sweet little baby. Daddy loves you for doing this. Be careful, do not bite me. Up and down, up and down." He took the small head in his hands and carefully guided it as Jose sucked on the penis. Suddenly, he could no longer hold back. When the white, sticky, thick substance jumped into Jose's mouth, he jumped away, leaving Father Emmanuel to finish ejaculating on himself.

"What was that?" Jose was wiping his mouth. His face grimaced in disgust.

"Oh, you naughty boy. You must never jump away like that. You must keep it in your mouth till I am finished. I'm so sorry. I forgot to tell you." He was careful not to show his anger.

"I didn't like that. It didn't taste good." Jose started crying.

Emmanuel gently took him in his arms and held him.

"It's okay, baby. It's something new. You'll get used to it as soon as you understand. Now you just suck mommy's tits and go to sleep."

Soon Jose was sleeping. Father Emmanuel had experienced a great satisfaction. Soon Jose would need no directions. Everything would fall into place.

Within two years, Father Emmanuel, priest, homosexual, and pederast, had managed to secure a full sex life with Jose. The priest now had everything. He had a good and loving parish, a good and loving boy, and, as far as he was concerned, a good and loving God.

Jose had accepted his way of life merely because he had no other. He was not interested in playing with other children. His schooling was limited to a half-day three times a week. He attended to his numerous duties around the church, such as dusting the seats, cleaning the floors, collecting the coins from the various boxes, and when no one was watching, he'd steal into the blessed sacrament and drink a little wine. Later, he would sit in the darkened church and breathe in the aroma of the candles. Jose was ten years old and had not been introduced to television, movies, magazines, or children games. He had already decided to be a priest and stay in the church with Father Emmanuel forever. He had no idea that forever could be as long as it could be short.

Father Emmanuel, overweight and sixty-five, was not in the best of health. The overindulgence of the mommy-and-daddy act had taken a toll on him. However, Jose, young and strong, had developed increased sexual desires. The priest attempted to keep pace with Jose's increasing demands but found himself more tired. Jose began to feel abandoned.

"Why don't you want to play more mommy and daddy with me? You fall asleep and never wake up till the morning, and I am waiting to play, and you say you are too tired?"

"You are a young boy, full of energy, and I am an old man who does not have so much energy. So we have to take it a little slow," the priest explained quietly.

"You're not going to make me stop, are you?" I don't want to stop. Never!"

"No, no, but just one or two nights each week. You have to start thinking about your future. In a few years, you must decide what you are going to be or do."

"I want to be a priest!" Jose bellowed.

"I thought about that also. I think that is wonderful."

"But I want to be something else before I am a priest."

"Oh, and what is that?" the old priest smiled. He was pleased with his pupil.

Jose tossed his head proudly.

"I want to be a woman!"

"A what?" The priest was shocked.

"A woman! A mommy! You know. Like you are at night."

"But that's just a game we play."

"I like it. I like that game. It's a good game."

42

Father Emmanuel looked at the small face. He had noticed how smooth and clear his skin was. The eyes were big and brown, the nose small, the lips full and sensuous. Jose would grow up to be a handsome man. He had to start correcting the damage he had done to the thoughts of this child.

"It's not possible for you to be a woman or a mommy."

"But I want to try it. So why can't you buy me a dress and let me put it on at night like you do?"

Father Emmanuel was angry. His voice was harsh.

"Jose, I told you no! Stop thinking about it."

"I want to try it! I want to dress up like you and look pretty. You told me you'd give me anything I want." Jose looked at him and smiled. "Just one night. Please." He knew how to persuade the old man.

Emmanuel did not want to lose the trust or love of the young boy. That might cause him problems.

"Okay, I'll get you the dress, and you can wear it for just one night. No more. You cannot be a girl all the time!"

Jose jumped with glee. He hugged the priest and began stroking him between the legs. He was now well adapted in the art of sexual stimulation.

"Do you want me to put my pecker in your pussy now, mommy?" Jose could feel his own penis getting hard, and he wanted relief.

"Don't talk like that. Haven't you had enough. Learn to control your desires."

Jose was stronger than the priest. He gently pushed him to the sofa and quickly mounted him. There were no complaints.

Three nights later, as they prepared for bed, Father Emmanuel gave Jose a box. Despite all the other gifts, he knew this was special. The dress was pink and white with many ribbons and bows. Jose danced with excitement. He put it on immediately.

"How do I look?" he pranced around the bedroom.

Father laughed.

"You look like a girl. A beautiful young girl. Very beautiful! Amazing!"

"You see! I know what I want. And I want to wear it all the time," he demanded as he stared into the long mirror.

"No, no, Jose, we will get in trouble. You don't want to get mommy and daddy in trouble, because they will take you away and take our church, and God will not be able to protect us."

Jose was disappointed but understood about being safe. It had been safe in the church.

"Are you ready to play daddy?" Jose looked seductively into the priest's eyes.

"I am ready." He was aroused even though he was tired. He couldn't disappoint this little boy he had trained so well.

"Since I have my dress on, I want to be the mommy tonight. Can't you do it to me like I did to you?"

The priest was hesitant. He had always directed Jose to do things to his body. Now Jose was desiring that these things be done to him.

"Come to bed, and take off your little dress."

"I don't want to take it off. I'll put it up, and you do me like I do you."

Slowly the priest began working on Jose's body. He was young and strong. His penis had grown bigger and hard. Father Emmanuel sucked it with all the passion he possessed.

"Suck it more! Suck it more!" Jose was wild with excitement.

Emmanuel stopped.

"Calm down. I am going to make you feel like a woman. Pull your pretty dress way up and raise your legs as far as you can."

Jose quickly followed directions. His penis was hard. Emmanuel was excited. He wanted to consume it all. This was the ultimate act for him. With Jose in position, he kissed the boy's anus, and after lubricating his penis, he slowly began to insert it.

"Be brave now because this will hurt at first, but then it will make you feel good, just like you make me."

"Quick, put it in. Do me like I do you!" Jose demanded.

Emmanuel had never dared to violate Jose rectally. But now, the young boy was ready and demanding it. That made it right. It had all worked out the way it should. The priest took his small, hard penis and slowly worked it into the boy. There were shouts of pain that quickly turned into sighs of delight, moans of pleasure.

"Don't stop, daddy. Don't stop," Jose screamed. He knew he would never take off that dress.

Whatever the visions were that passed before Father Emmanuel's eyes as he ejaculated into Jose, they were filled with fires of hell and damnation. Whatever he saw, he never lived to tell about it, because at the last drop of pleasure he experienced, he also experienced his last breath of life.

Jose was disappointed because the priest had suddenly stopped and rolled over.

"Don't go to sleep now, daddy. I want more." But the priest did not answer. Jose knew that he must be sleeping, and since he could not rouse him, he covered the naked body and curled up next to him and fell asleep in his pink dress. The next morning, he was still unable to rouse the priest. The body had become cold and stiff. Jose sensed death. He had seen dead people. But not his priest! He never thought a priest could die.

Crying and hysterical, he ran to the police station. Everyone looked astonished to see the small altar boy in such a fancy dress. They followed him to the living quarters of the church. What they saw was shocking. There lay their priest with large pendulous breasts, and panties and garter belt, naked and dead. Jose stood crying and mumbling about something had happened to his daddy and mommy.

It was impossible to explain anything to Jose. The funeral was quiet and quick. It was rumored that the priest had done wrong things to the boy. Jose would not reveal anything about his life in the rectory. His only comment was that he was beginning to be a girl. The officials sadly shook their heads. He was sent off to a state boys' school. Five years later, Jose slipped away from the compound. He had learned that his keys to survival were sex and money. He managed to work his way across the border into the United States. There, he had been told, he could become a real girl.

7

When Brent left Chicago to live in New York, he changed his name to Thomas Blake. It was not a complicated process to change a name. You simply changed it.

Thomas's life was not without purpose. Each day and evening had a mission. During the day, he would wander through the various museums and art galleries and attend auctions. He found the experience educational and invigorating. Thomas had dreams of owning expensive art. He had dreams of owning many expensive items out of his reach at this time in his life.

However, his plan was to educate himself. Thomas, handsome and tall, was constantly approached by men during his jaunts through the galleries. He would smile and politely turn down the numerous offers and invitations to apartments and social parties. He avoided these gatherings. A social life, friends, or any close human relationships were strictly avoided. All of that would come at the proper time.

Thomas had a plan and direction for his life, and if he followed the format, one day he would be exactly what he wanted to be and have exactly what he wanted. Therefore, in the evening, Thomas had a different and interesting life. These were the hours he dressed in drag and became Ms. Honey Babe, street-walking whore from Salina, Mississippi. He himself laughed and wondered if there was such a place as Salina. Between the hours of ten at night and three in the morning, he dressed in a most exotic outfit, painted his face, put on an alluring red wig, and would begin his stroll of the avenues and streets of midtown Manhattan.

He avoided making friends with other prostitutes. His business was tricks and money. The money was necessary to solve his problems and secure his future. The dressing in drag was the best part of his life now, and it was his best act. It served as a pilot for the future when he would make a permanent change. He had studied and acquired a sweet, purring Southern accent. Walking the streets as a hooker at night was like going in front of a camera. Every night was a dress rehearsal. What better practice than this for when he finally begins his complete transformation?

He had carefully planned his future, and nobody could stop him. That is the one reason he remained aloof and alone. He hated hustling the streets. It was low class and dangerous, but it allowed him to remain anonymous. He could have worked for a madam, but he'd have to split his money and everyone would know him, never forget him, and that would follow him the rest of his life. That was not part of the plan. As he climbed the ladder, he wanted no one to be able to pull him down. The less attention he drew to himself, the better. The only person he needed was Jolena. He had no intentions of ever meeting the doctor or being treated by him. It was Jolena who held the answers and the help he needed. He had to trust in one person, and it would be her.

Today his mission was to go to the office early with the hope that he could get to see her alone. When he entered the office, it was empty of patients. He was elated. However, Jolena looked at him in a rather annoyed manner.

"Can I help you?" Jolena knew he was not one of the regular patients, and he was much too early for office hours.

"My name is Thomas Blake. I have an appointment for today, but I am early, and there is a reason, if you will let me explain."

Jolena was listening and checking her appointment book. She did not find his name.

"You should have called if—"

"I know," he interrupted, "but I wanted to be here when it was empty because I want to talk to you about something very private."

Jolena was curious. It was probably another "queen proposition." She looked at him and was taken aback by the blue eyes and beautiful face. *My God,* she thought, *he should have been a girl.*

"Come around and tell me about this very private matter."

Quickly he made his way into her office. He removed his jacket and sat down, looking at her with a very serious expression.

"I want to be something one day. Rather, I want to be somebody; not just another queen or queer walking the streets or dressing in drag."

Jolena had heard these statements many times. Not as intense as she was hearing now, but the words still struck familiar cords.

"Apparently you have a plan?" she inquired.

"Yes, I do. But in order to implement this plan, I need your help. You are the only one who can help me. You are the only one I can trust. Only you, Ms. Taylor."

Jolena felt puzzled and hesitant. To be put into this position of trust was a big responsibility.

"What can I possibly do to help you?"

"First, you must never tell anyone about anything concerning me, or that you ever knew me."

"But what about the doctor? We will have to talk to him—"

"No, no, I don't even want him to know anything."

Jolena leaned forward with interest.

"What do you want done that we cannot involve him in the process?"

"I know about your work. I hear it said that you do the best, flawless work on bodies. Look at my chest." He jumped up and opened his shirt. His chest was flat.

"I want you to do my breast. Small ones. Something like an A cup and perfect in shape. I know you can do that." Excited, he continued. "Let me show you the rest of my body. I need my hips and buttocks rounded out just enough to look feminine."

He had lowered his pants. She was astonished at the smoothness of his skin. There was almost no masculine hair.

"Yes, that can be done."

"But I want only you to do it for me. And in private. I don't want the doctor or anyone else to touch me. I don't want to come here to this office. You come to my apartment. That way, no one would know anything. I will give five thousand dollars if you just do my body work. Please, please help me."

She heard what he said about the amount of money, but it was the pleading in his voice and eyes that touched her. She would have to give this consideration, a lot of thought. The money was appealing and she needed the money. She also remembered that Peter hinted that his assistant might be coming to work in the office. Where would she be pushed to?

"Thomas, I would have to think about this. Give me till Monday or Tuesday. I do understand your need for privacy. Give me your phone number, and I will call you. In the meantime, stay away from this office, so if we do launch this project, no one can ever remember you."

"If you help me, I will be grateful to you the rest of my life. And one day, I will make it big. I will forever be in your debt. You will be the only one who ever knew this part of my life. I am formulating a new identity. I will need to find the name of a doctor in Canada who does the sex change surgery. That way, I can go across as a tourist and come back without showing identification. I'll go over as a boy and come back as a boy, but as soon as I get into this country, I will get rid of Thomas and Ms. Honey Babe."

"Who is Ms. Honey Babe?"

"That is my drag name, my street name. You would never recognize me. If those street drag queens can't recognize me out of drag, no one can."

She was amazed. He had formulated his plan. In fact, she was so fascinated by the whole idea that she had already decided to help him. It was not for the money as much as it was the desire to see him succeed against the odds. To be actually born again into a different gender.

"What is your final goal, Thomas?"

"You have to believe this, because I believe it. I am going to be one of the top models in the world."

She would have to try hard to believe that story because of the many times she had heard a "girl" exclaiming that she wanted to be a model, but she had never known one who qualified or ever succeeded being much of anything. They did succeed well as peep-show models.

She studied him closely and thought there was potential. He did not have masculine features. His hands were not large, and his arms were not long, like the arms of a man. He would need a slight nose job. Nothing major. There was no Adam's apple, and his neck was not muscular. In fact, he had a perfect swan neck. His jawline and cheekbones were sculpted flawlessly. He fit the model profile.

"You'll need your nose narrowed. It's a good nose, but it has a slight masculine touch. You can get that done by any plastic surgeon, and you don't have to even tell your correct name."

"I plan to do it in Canada."

"Good. You know, Thomas, I think I will help you. When do you want to start?"

"Oh, God, thank you, thank you. You are going to be so proud of me. Just you wait." Quickly he scribbled down his phone number and address. "Call me as soon as you can start."

"Okay. Now you'd better go before someone comes in early. Also, I'll bring the hormones and give them to you. Remember, trust no one. Never tell, and let me warn you, never trust a woman! When you get out in that "real" world, never trust any woman, no matter how good a friend she might be to you. They will turn on you. They will be jealous and envious, and they will tell." He would always remember the warning.

"You won't be sorry. I am going to make you proud." He was jubilant as he left the office.

Jolena had been impressed, both by the fact that the young man had a plan and that he had the money to carry it out. He claimed to have visited the office one time, observed, and left. She didn't remember him, and probably no one else had paid attention to him. Jolena smiled, shook her head, and continued her work. Yes, she thought, someone would be in for a big surprise one day. Maybe the whole world if he indeed become famous and nobody ever knew. As the eventual transformation would come about, not even Jolena would remember him looking as he did this day.

8

Jolena was glad to get home that evening. When she opened the door to her small Harlem apartment, she was immediately greeted by her large calico cat. "Hello, Ms. Meow." She spoke softly. "Did you miss me? No, I don't have anything for you."

The cat scampered around the room, displaying pleasure that Jolena was home. She finally settled down but kept a steady eye on her mistress.

If life was ever boring for Jolena, it was now. She had few friends and little time to socialize. She had vowed many times to take time to go out and meet with old friends or make some new ones. Time, however, seemed to move without warning, and Jolena seemed to be standing still. Jolena was forty, and that was closer to fifty than the twenty she had once enjoyed. She shook her head in amazement. What had she done with her life in all those years? What were her accomplishments outside of being a registered nurse and now in charge of an office that catered to a group of mixed-up and misguided transsexuals and homosexuals?

Perhaps it was time to go back to the hospital and work. Just leave the office to Edgewater and the new girlfriend, whoever she was. Financially, she couldn't afford to leave. She had nothing saved. Things were changing in nursing. Everybody was getting degrees, and more and more, they were requiring that nurses have additional educational skills. Jolena would have to make some kind of move soon, or she would be left out in the cold, out of this very profession. She fixed herself a strong drink of vodka and stared down onto the Harlem night scene from her window.

She thought back to the time when money flowed and life was fun. Night life was good in Harlem. On the weekends, music could be heard coming from many clubs. Sex, love, and money was at an all-time high. Harlem number's bankers and controllers were impressed with light-skinned, tall, and long-haired, educated women. Jolena had fit the qualifications, and she was the beauty they carried on their arms to the fights, the casinos, and the hideaways in the Bahamas. The men treated her with respect and gifts because she was a beautiful, educated, and professional person. Within their criminal environment, it gave them a sense of respectability.

It was while she enjoyed this lifestyle that she met Ricco. It had been one of those nights in her life that she decided to go out and listen to some music at Sleepy's, where her favorite jazz players performed. It was summer, and she was tanned and beautiful and in a white dress. The bar was not crowded that night. When she walked in, her eyes met Ricco's, and she felt a surge go through her. Their eyes locked for a few seconds, and she knew the meaning. She had quickly looked away.

Ricco, black, rich, and the biggest Harlem number's banker, had felt it also. It was a feeling he had not felt for a long time. His life was set, straight and solid. He was married and a father. Turn away, he had told himself, but instead, he went right to her.

"I'm Ricco. I've seen you here before."

"I'm Jolena." She paused, looking at him with intensity. "I'm glad I came out. Is this our destiny?"

"Yes, baby, this is our destiny." He didn't attempt to deny or fight it. He smiled that smile she would never forget. That was the beginning of a happiness Jolena would always remember—and never forget all that it cost her.

The blaring fire truck that raced down the avenue below her snapped Jolena back to reality. She took another drink of vodka. She didn't want to remember. That was seven years ago, and she never wanted to remember the tragedy. Lifestyles had taken a different turn. There were no more rich boyfriends. The Harlem world of criminal activity began to change. The gentlemen bankers and controllers were slowly forced out or taken over by young drug dealers. Nothing—person, place, or title—was important to them. Only territory and money. Young girls were always accessible and free, and cocaine was GOD.

Jolena surveyed herself in the mirror. The slim figure was still there, and a few gray hairs were showing. But at forty years of age, that was to be expected. However, Jolena's black silk hair was still her crowning glory. The laugh lines had deepened, but she was still pleased with her looks and, most of all, her survival. Now the battle to keep her job was in front of her. She leaned over and stroked Ms. Meow, who was rubbing against her leg.

"If only I had some money," she whispered. "If only I had managed things differently."

She remembered that it was a waste of time having regrets about yesteryears. It was today and tomorrow that was important. After finishing her last drink of vodka, she took a shower and went to bed.

Jolena lay very still in bed, waiting for sleep. Sleep was important. Tomorrow was important. To persevere was important. Money was important. And so, Thomas Blake had become important, because he offered her an amount of money that she could use to fall back on just in case things did not work out at the office. She would call him tomorrow. Now, time was important to Jolena, and that was fleeting.

Ms. Meow jumped up and curled alongside her. The purring lulled Jolena to sleep.

9

It was showtime. Arnold Brown emerged from his Bronx apartment building. He was the drag queen of the neighborhood. However, this evening, the weather had turned cold and there was no audience. When he came out, it was a big disappointment to him. He always made it a point to pose in front of the building and give his neighbors an eyeful of drag. He considered it a privilege for them to be able to cast their eyes on his transformation. This night, he was dressed in red, and the sight of himself caused him to sing the tune about the lady in red. He posed, pursed his brightly painted lips, and riveted his eyes back and forth, hoping that anyone, just anyone, would be so fortunate to see him in all his splendor. No one appeared.

Disappointed, he walked down the street to catch a cab. Already his feet were hurting in the high-heeled red sandals. The toes hung over the open front of the shoes, periodically scraping the ground, serving notice that he had to pick up his feet in a more ladylike fashion. The red dress that reached just below his knees fitted tight around his obese hips and ass. Underneath, his penis and balls hung freely through a split made in the panty hose. After all, Arnold, known as Lottie Lee when in drag, did not have time to stop and stoop to make pee. He merely found a tree, doorway, mailbox, phone booth, or whatever could afford a minimal amount of privacy and pulled up his dress and let it flow.

Arnold was almost six feet and weighed two hundred pounds of solid, black flesh. Anybody, even a blind man, could tell that he was a man dressed in women's clothes. A drag queen. Arnold couldn't care what anyone, blind or not, thought about how he appeared when he dressed. He thought that when he dressed in drag, he was lovely and every man wanted him. He would walk slowly, turning and smiling at all men, black, white, and yellow. Some men were embarrassed, some laughed loudly, some snarled angrily, some shook their heads in disbelief, some stopped and took a good look. His smile sent a message: "Hi, come and have some fun with me."

His makeup was done to perfection. It covered his beard, which would not appear till at least the next morning. His structure was exciting. His face was large, with small, penetrating black eyes. His lips were large and sensuous. But it was his nose that was the most beautiful part of his face. It was perfectly shaped within its triangle. His nostrils were enviously narrow. His chin came to a perfect point, and his neck was long.

His height and largeness gave him the appearance of a Watusi in drag. His silicone-pumped breasts bounced heavily, and although his stomach had begun to take on a few folds, his shape was attractive. His buttocks were a legend by themselves. They were round and large, provocative of devious sexual fantasies. The upper half of the body was supported by two large, muscular thighs and hefty legs, further supported by large feet. Arnold was truly built.

His best asset was his personality, in or out of drag. He was a charmer, and he was clean. He bathed every day. He always smelled good. Arnold lived for the evenings that he cross-dressed. He enjoyed walking the streets and turning tricks with old and young white men, who were fascinated by the apparition. If they were embarrassed to ask if he was a man, he quickly solved the problem by lifting up his dress and displaying the large piece of dangling meat. That charmed them. He would then speak in his most falsetto voice. That charmed them. Gently he would touch them. That charmed them. He whispered and moaned desired words. That charmed them. Money then became the main topic. That charmed Arnold, who always stated his price in dollars.

He never dealt in francs, marks, Canadian dollars, yen, or xu. To receive a real fast blow job or hand job, he charged fifty dollars. And that was only for two minutes if the victim lasted that long. To take Arnold home cost more, and despite his large and monstrous looks, many tricks did take him to their elegant East or West Side apartments and penthouses.

Arnold never went with more than one man at a time. He didn't like "parties," for the men tended to get out of control; when their conscience finally woke them to the realization that they had enjoyed sex and had an orgasm with a black man, they wanted to blame him and would proceed to get violent. Many times, Arnold would have to lose his falsetto voice and charm when a macho type man would attempt to attack him. Then Arnold became a real man as his viciousness matched his blackness. He would then display his favorite weapon, a stiletto that rested between his fat breasts. It was his only and favorite weapon. Like the sea, Arnold was experienced.

Tonight, he felt that he was looking rather tasty as he stood at Central Park South and Columbus Circle. The evening was getting more chilly, and he was wishing for a quick trick. But he also toyed with another idea. He could forget about money tonight and find some "free trade" sitting on a park bench. He thought longingly of a fine, young, muscular boy whom he could take home for a day or two. After that, he'd throw him out. Suddenly his decision was made when he saw a man wobbling toward him. *My, my,* thought Arnold, *come into my parlor.* This was going to be easy pickings. Arnold walked towards the man.

"Hi, sweetie, want some fun?"

The man raised his head. He was obviously drunk.

"Yeah, baby. Goddam, you are big and black. That's what I like."

Arnold was amused. He had already spied the expensive watch. He knew that it and a wallet filled with credit cards or cash would net him a nice profit for the night. One good sting, and he could call it a night. He moved close to the man, rubbing his arms and shoulders. He spoke in his charming voice.

"Here, sweetie, put your hand on my pussy. You'll like my pussy."

As soon as Arnold caught hold of the man's arm, he had the watch off and dropped between his tits. Quickly, as he maneuvered the victim's hand up his dress, he reached around and nimbly lifted the bulge he had felt in the back pocket. Arnold's hands were quick and nimble. He was no amateur, for he had been picking pockets and watches since the age of thirteen. What made him so good was that he'd take the wallet, empty it, and put it back without the victim's awareness. The bulge felt big and rewarding. *Put the fuckin' wallet back and tip,* he told himself, *before the drunk realizes that he's been robbed.* Arnold knew there was nothing more sobering than finding out you've been robbed.

"Wait one minute, sweetie, I'll be right back."

"Where you going? I'm ready for fun." The man stood there, looking silly.

"I'm just going back behind this wall to pee."

"I want to pee with you." The drunk laughed.

"Sweetie, I'll be right back, " he reassured him.

Arnold eyed the street for the police. He had to move quickly. Forget about putting the wallet back. His inner sense was telling him to go now.

Suddenly, the man yelled!

"Where's my watch, my watch, where's my watch? Hey! Hey! You took my watch!"

What the man saw next was a large black figure jumping the thick stoned wall. Arnold was fleeing.

"Help! Help! I've been robbed."

The shock of having been robbed triggered the adrenalin to his brain. Suddenly, the victim was alert and yelling. Arnold continued to run the best he could in the high heels. He was now somewhere in the middle of Central Park. *That stupid bastard,* he whispered angrily, *why in the hell does he have to make all that fucking noise?* He can always get another watch and more money. I didn't hurt the dumb fuck. I don't kill people. Arnold could hear the low moan of the sirens heading toward the area of the distressed victim. Oh, shit, I got to move faster. He ran deeper into the park. Out of breath and his feet hurting, Arnold could not think of a way to get out of this situation.

The sirens sounded closer. He hid behind some bushes. The plainclothes police had entered the park and were shining a flood light. Arnold stood quiet. But he knew they were going to find him. Quietly, he dug into the ground and placed the watch, wallet, and his stiletto into a pit and covered it with dirt. It was a choice of keeping the goods or discarding them; being caught without them or not caught at all. Either way he would lose. He would go to jail. Without the evidence, it would be his word against the victim's. He could make bail and be free. If the victim was from out of town there was a ninety-nine percent chance he'd never show for the hearing.

Arnold moved quietly from the bushes and made his way back to the area where he had robbed the man. *All my hard work gone to hell,* he thought. He hoped he could come back and find the spot where he had hidden the loot. Well, he hummed sadly, Arnold is going to jail. When he reached the stone wall, the police were waiting. They smiled.

"Well, Lottie Lee. We knew it was you."

"Oh, officer, how are you?" Arnold's voice was sweet and condescending. Suddenly, he changed into a deep man's voice.

"Knew it was me? Knew it was me doing what? Doing what? I ain't done nothing. I'm just looking for a little trade." Arnold grinned wide with innocence.

"C'mon, Lottie, we got to take you in."

The man ran up to the trio.

"That's her. That's the black bitch who took my watch and money!"

"I ain't got your watch or money. Are you sick, white man?"

"It's you! It's you! How could anybody forget something as big, black, and ugly as you!"

The police listened to the accusations.

"Fuck you! You were the one who told me you like them big and black."

"Officer, I never said that! She robbed me! Give me my watch and wallet."

"I ain't got nothing of yours, motherfucker. Dumb, motherfucker. Here, search me."

Arnold pulled up the skirt, and the large black penis and balls presented themselves. The police laughed.

The man gasped.

"Oh, my God, it's . . . it's . . . a man? Oh, shit, I didn't even know."

The police, acting in a serious mode, shone their flashlight over Arnold's body and searched for the stolen goods.

"See, I ain't got nothing," he lashed out at his victim. "And don't act like you didn't know I was a man. You have to be a dumb fuck not to have known that!"

The officer spoke.

"You are lucky, sir, that it was Lottie Lee. Lottie only robs you. He never beats or kills."

"Well, thank you, officer, I consider that a compliment, but I didn't rob—"

"Okay, enough! C'mon, Lottie. We got to take you downtown. You know how it goes."

Arnold took one big deep breath. It was over for him for tonight. Now he'd spend the night and all of tomorrow in jail. They handcuffed him and put him in the back of the old automobile in which they patrolled. He smiled. *Lord,* he thought, *there has to be an easier way,* and he did not mean getting a job. That was out of the question. Well, at least he didn't have to ride the wagon with all the other street whores.

10

Shit, she thought, *that fuck is hard again.* Lita Lopez, queen, transsexual, had been awakened from her deep sleep. She ran to the bathroom to urinate. Sometimes that would reduce the swollen penis stump. She returned to bed and waited. It began to subside. This was one of her many problems she did not want to think about. Lita, legend amongst all the street drag queens, had made many mistakes in life, but the one mistake she would regret most would be her so-called sex-change operation. Slowly, she reached over and picked up the hundred-dollar bill that contained her precious white cocaine powder. She sniffed greedily and relaxed. There was plenty of cocaine to last her throughout the day, and that made her comfortable.

It was the horror after that surgery that she would never forget. There was pain she would always remember. There was the "vagina" she fantasized was in place. There was the rejection she would endure, and there were the nights she would cry alone and remember that time in California eight years ago. . .

Jose had slipped across the Mexican border into California. He had learned the trade of selling his body. Now, he was a complete cross-dresser and felt himself every bit a woman. He even had a boyfriend, with whom he was living. They were young and "in love," but Jose, who now called himself Josie and preferred to be referred to as "she" and "her," was not happy. Josie wanted to be a complete woman. Even though her lover was satisfied with the anal and oral sex, this was not the way Josie wanted her sex life to remain.

She hated her penis, even though she could see her boyfriend's excitement whenever she emerged from the bathroom with her small hormone-induced breasts, long black hair, made-up face, and, above all, the large penis swinging between his legs. However wild and consuming the lovemaking became, Josie wanted to have a vagina. Josie wanted to make real love, not this faggot love, as she described it. The constant complaints of not being complete was expressed to Olga, one of the street girls Josie hustled with and who finally admitted she knew a good doctor who would do the sex-change surgery without question.

"He can make me a real pussy?" Josie inquired.

"Sure, he does it all the time. And it doesn't take long, and he's cheap."

"What's cheap?"

"Two thousand dollars."

"I can get that together. I have half of that now." Josie knew that in one more week the rest of the money would be secured.

"How long before I can come back to work?"

"Oh, maybe a day or two."

"That soon?" Josie was impressed.

Josie scrutinized Olga closely. Olga had had the surgery and looked like a woman. She never heard Olga complain about her vagina, and she was using it every night. Josie envied her, and envy was a bitter pill that Josie had not yet learned to swallow. A vagina was important at any cost. She had to have that surgery.

"Please set up an appointment for me to see him."

"Girl, you don't need an appointment. He ain't talking to you on the phone. Just go to this address with the money and be sure to tell him that Olga sent you." She scribbled an address and shoved it to Josie.

Josie was ecstatic. It was unbelievable. No examination or explanations. *Well*, she thought, *that's the way it should be.* She took the card and tucked it safely away. It would be a new beginning for her. She could then get proper identification and a real job. Josie had already decided she wanted to work with makeup. Maybe in a department store. She was good at doing makeup. It would be a relief not to deal with the streets and freak men. Just to feel and look like a woman down there would be the most glorious happening for her. Then if she ever had to prove that she was a woman, it would be very simple to pull up the dress and say, "There is my pussy." Josie's dream was going to come true. She could have almost cried.

One week later, Josie went to the address on the card. The building was rather shabby, but she surmised that this had to be the doctor's office, and from here she would be transported to the hospital. The hallway and stairwell reminded her of places she had slept and worked in when she had first left Mexico. The surroundings were dirty and dilapidated. A baby cried from somewhere. Televisions and music blared. In the dimly lit hallway, she found the apartment. Josie knocked and was answered by a tall white man with a large nose, puffy face, and bespectacled, squinty eyes glaring at her. Behind him stood a fat beastly woman whose appearance resembled a man.

"Olga sent me. Are you Dr. Smith?" Josie Lopez, streetwise streetwalker, thief, liar, and transvestite, humbled herself before this man. This man who would change her life. This man who would take away the one thing she hated. This man who would cut away the past. This man who would make Jose, a.k.a. Josie, into a true woman.

"Come in. I'm the doctor." His answer was quick. He observed the small boy in front of him. This would be an easy and fast job. He hated the big fat one. Too much bleeding. Josie eased into the apartment.

"Did you bring the money with you?"

"Oh, yes, I have it. Can you please tell me how long this will take and when I will be getting out of the hospital?"

"It will take about an hour, and the hospital won't be necessary. We do everything here. You can go home when I am finished."

Josie surveyed the room. It didn't appear to be much of a doctor's office and didn't look like an operating room. But what did she know about a doctor's office or an operating room? She had never been in either. They led her to another room.

"This is the room where we will do the surgery. You see I have all the equipment here."

"Yes, yes, I see." Josie looked around. She had no idea if it was right, wrong, nice, or nasty.

He turned and pulled the woman forward.

"This is Laura. You give her the money. She will be helping me. Now, what was your name again?"

"Josie. But after my surgery I want to be called 'Lita.'"

The doctor was amused.

"Lita? Well, any name is good. Laura here had the surgery, so she can reassure you that all is going to be well. Tell her, Laura."

Lita handed the money to Laura who counted while she talked.

"Oh, yeah. It was good for me. Made me into a real woman."

Josie was unaware that Laura never had a sex-change operation, simply because she was born a woman. The husky-voiced woman continued to explain.

"You'll be so happy when it's all over. You'll have a little discomfort, but in the end, it pays off. It'll look just like mine. Let me show you."

She lifted her dress, and there were no panties. Laura slowly parted the pubic hairs to display the amazing results of her "operation." The doctor smiled. Josie knew she had come to the right place.

"Okay, girls, let's go to work. Laura, get the patient ready."

Josie was instructed to undress. There was no place to hang her clothes.

"Where shall I put my clothes?" Josie asked Laura as she disrobed.

"Oh, just pile them on this chair. I'll take care of them." Laura threw a soiled green gown around Josie and instructed her to climb up on the table. Josie's heart beat fast. *At last,* she thought, *my problems are going to be over.*

Laura took Josie's arm and announced that she was going to inject her with medicine that would relax her. Josie was glad.

"Will I go to sleep?"

"In a way. You won't feel any pain. You will be so spaced out." Laura laughed.

"What about when I wake up. Will I be in pain?"

"Well, a little, but that will go away. We'll give you medicine. Okay. No more questions. You are going to sleep now."

Laura jabbed the needle into Josie's vein and administered the medication.

"God, that hurt," Josie mumbled. Slowly she began to feel that she was without a head or that it was detached and left her body on the table. She was not in any further control of herself.

Dr. Smith looked casually at Laura.

"Is he out?"

"Excuse me, doctor; you mean is *she* out?" Laura laughed and continued. "Yeah, she is out, and you would be also if you had that cocktail of Valium and methadone."

"It works well on the small ones," he murmured.

Laura raised Josie's legs into a lithotomy position and tied them onto the worn stirrups. The genitals were exposed. There was no concern for aseptic technique. No one washed or scrubbed their hands. No one washed down the operative area. They put on gloves to keep their own hands clean. Quickly, he injected a large amount of local anesthetic into the scrotum sack. Taking a scalpel, he slit the sack open. Bright red blood flowed and spilled onto the floor, which had been covered with newspapers. The contents of the scrotum bag, which consisted of two pink gristlelike balls plunked onto the floor. Laura kicked them aside. She was busy trying to stop the bleeding.

"Shit, you need to clamp something here."

He moved her aside, took a small clamp, and after dabbing the area with paper towels, he expertly clamped the small bleeding vessel.

"You want to tie it?"

"Later."

He continued to cut away the remaining skin from the scrotum. He trimmed it close to the perineum floor. After applying three more clamps, he announced he was ready to tie. She handed him a roll of black heavy suture from the table, which was in complete bloody disarray.

"Well, he didn't want balls, and now he doesn't have balls," He remarked as he began to suture together the now empty scrotum sack. "By the way, when is the next patient?"

"In about two hours."

"I've got to move faster on this one. I lose money spending so much time on such surgery."

"You already do three or four a day. Shit, what do you want! You are a greedy fuck."

Laura talked to Dr. Smith in that manner because as his assistant she knew all about his sex-change surgery ploy. The price was twenty-five hundred dollars. That was cheap enough to make every drag queen who dreamed of having a pussy come running. He took two thousand, and Laura got five hundred. The operation was simple enough for him. All he had to do was cut out the balls, scrotum, and cut off the penis. There were complications, but by the time they occurred, the "office" had been vacated and they had moved on to another section of the sprawling city.

Dr. Smith had been a first-year resident in surgery when he was let go by the hospital after making a fatal decision on his own. Unable to adjust being kicked out of the medical profession, he became addicted to cocaine and emerged in the company of people with devious methods of survival. Surrounding himself with the company of homosexuals and transsexuals, he chose to form close and sexual relationships with the "girls." His money enabled him to have a constant supply of cocaine, affording him a constant high from the moment he sniffed cocaine until he put himself to sleep with Valium. Dr. Smith needed money for his habit, and he had found the perfect victims.

Often he got annoyed with Laura's show of disrespect toward him.

"You shouldn't talk to the doctor like that."

She ignored his statement then warned him.

"You'd better hurry or he'll be screaming. Remember what happened the other day. That one woke up on you."

He remembered the screams. The sound was unbearable. Men screaming like women. After injecting more local anesthetic into the shaft of the penis, he took the scalpel and made a slit down the undershaft of the penis. Minimal amounts of blood flowed. He proceeded to clamp off one major vessel and then asked for a sharp blade. Laura, fumbling, finally handed him a large, sharp blade.

"You gonna cut it now?"

"Of course. What do you think I'm gonna do, stand here and hold this useless dick for the rest of my life?"

"You said to remind you to put a catheter in and then cut around it. Remember what happened before?"

"That's a lot of unnecessary work. I'll cut now and suture. I'll put the catheter in last."

And so he cut the penis down close to the base of its shaft. Josie was beginning to moan and move about on the table.

"Give him another shot of methadon."

Laura administered more medication. The methadon had been bought from a druggist who was willing to sell at a high price. It was a synthetic heroin and the best pain medicine.

Quickly, he sutured up the bleeding wound. He inserted an unsterile catheter. He was satisfied with the flow of urine. Dr. Smith wiped the area clean with some water Laura had retrieved from the faucet. After covering the area with unsterile dressings, he gave Laura instructions.

"Give him some Narcan, and get him up."

"You could at least refer to him as 'her.' You converted him to her. The name is now Lita. Lita. Lita." She glared at the doctor.

"Stop the fucking lecture, and make sure she, Ms. Lita, gets a cab and rides out of here. Don't forget to give her instructions."

He left the room. Laura began shaking Jose and calling her by the name she had requested when she became a woman.

"Lita, Lita, wake up. You're a complete woman now."

Lita Lopez opened her eyes. At first, she did not remember who or where she was until she kept hearing her new name. Then she knew that it was over and she was a real woman. The pain was intense, but she realized that pain was often the price to pay for desired effects. Lita was happy in the midst of all her pain.

However, Lita's happiness would be short-lived. Her choice of a doctor had been a tragic mistake. Dr. Smith had not been skilled enough to construct a vagina in the area between the penis and rectum. Had he attempted such a maneuver in the setting in which he worked, Lita Lopez would have gone into shock and never survived. She had desired a sex change, and Dr. Smith had given her his best version. He had removed her testicles, and scrotum and cut her penis down to a small stump. The operation was over.

Laura helped her to a taxi, and the medicine had enabled her to arrive home with a minimum amount of pain. She had forgotten to give her the written instructions, but even Laura knew they were of no value.

Later that night when her boyfriend arrived, she was awake and in severe pain.

"How did the operation go?" He had not been happy about her having such a drastic procedure.

"Well, I guess okay, but it hurts real bad."

"What did the doctor tell you to do? Do you have any medicine? When do you have to go back? When can—"

"He didn't tell me anything. I don't know anything. It just hurts," she was crying.

"You want me to look down there?" He was curious.

"Look for what?"

"I ain't gonna touch anything. I just want to look. I've never seen a brand new pussy before."

Despite all the pain, she was proud to show him. She tried to pull her legs up.

"Oh, God! Look how swollen my legs are. And my stomach."

"Yeah, you look pregnant."

The boyfriend removed the large piece of dressing. His eyes searched for the vagina.

"I don't see anything that looks like a pussy. I don't see a hole."

"Get a mirror and let me look. Oh, God, I'm in pain," she moaned.

He brought her a mirror and watched while she searched. Her face grimaced in pain and bewilderment.

"I can't see it. But I feel like I have to pee, but it won't come out."

"Maybe it's supposed to come out of that tube hanging out where your dick used to be."

"Do you think I should take it out? Maybe that's why it's not working."

"You better go to the bathroom."

He helped her out of the bed. In the bathroom, she sat and sat. The pain was as if a small fire had been lit in the operative area. She pushed to try to make pee, but nothing came out except the catheter.

"How long you gonna sit there?"

"I got to wait. It feels like it's going to come out."

"Now you're sitting on the toilet like a real woman." He remarked.

Despite her pain, that statement made her feel real. She managed to smile.

"Yes, I am. But I think I'm going to stand up like before because it'll feel better. Maybe that's the reason it won't come out." Lita stood. She stood for almost fifteen minutes.

The urine would not come out because the urethra was already closing up due to stenosis. The catheter had been of no use because it was not the correct one and it had been inserted too late. Dr. Smith and Laura both knew that. In desperation and ignorance, Lita had pulled it out. Her stomach had become much larger and hard. The pain was more intense. She climbed back into bed.

"I can't stand anymore," she moaned and moaned.

He was standing with the mirror in his hand.

"Here take this, and look at what's down there. It just doesn't look like a pussy is there. Maybe it grows out later."

She took the mirror and spread her legs again. Removing the remainder of the bandages, she stared down at the mutilated genitalia. She forgot the intense pain as her fingers groped frantically trying to locate the vagina.

"I can't feel it, and I can't see it. What do you think happened? You better call the doctor." Lita was crying.

"Give me the number," the boyfriend said.

"I don't have it. Olga made all the arrangements."

He dialed Olga's number.

"There's no answer."

"Keep trying. Something ain't right. Go out to the street, and see if she's on the stroll. You got to get the doctor. Something ain't right. My stomach and legs are swelling up!"

He stared in horror at how, little by little, Lita was changing. She looked pale and sweaty. He was afraid to leave her alone. He dialed Olga again.

"There still ain't no answer."

"Leave it ring."

He sat the phone down, allowing it to remain ringing the dialed number. At moments, he would pick it up, but no one answered.

"I think something is wrong with this whole thing."

"What is wrong?"

"I don't think he was a real doctor, or he would have given you a number to call in case of an emergency."

"I'm tired. I feel sick. Look, look at my stomach."

He stared horrified. Her stomach had swollen so much, the belly button was pushed out in a distorted shape.

"I think you better go to the doctor."

"No more doctors." She was firm.

"I mean to a hospital."

"No! I'm going to sleep. Maybe when I wake up, everything will be okay. Maybe it will be there."

"What will be there?"

"The pussy! The vagina I paid to have put in there!"

"Lita," he yelled, "if it ain't there now, how's it gonna get there?"

"Maybe I have to go back. Maybe he couldn't do it all in one operation."

"I think he did something wrong. Didn't he tell you anything?"

"No. Nothing."

"But he took the money?"

"Of course. That was first. Then he told me I would wake up a woman. I feel bad. I keep seeing things in front of my eyes."

"Like what things?" He was pacing the floor like a caged animal. He had never been in this kind of situation.

"Spots and colors. I feel sleepy. I'm going now. Cover me up. I'm cold."

He went to the phone and listened at the receiver. The number for Olga was still ringing. He hung up the phone. Now he began to put the whole scenario together.

"Lita, I think the doctor did a wrong job on you. I think you better go to the police or to a hospital. I also think that Olga knew that he was a quack."

Lita did not respond. She was either sleeping or near unconsciousness.

"Wake up! I think you better go to a hospital."

He went over to shake her, but she only mumbled incoherently. Her skin felt cold and clammy. He shook her head and was yelling.

"Lita, wake up, wake up. You got to go to the hospital."

She was not alert. Mumbling, she fell back into a stupor. He ran to the phone.

"Operator, get me the police. I need an ambulance. Lita is dying!"

Dr. Smith's surgical castration of any transvestite seeking the sex-change operation was always the same. Collect the money, cut off the scrotum sack and its contents, lobe off the penis at its base, and insert a catheter, and the surgery was over. The patient was bandaged and sent home with written instructions and a phone number to call in case of an emergency. The instructions were simple: No bath or shower for five days; cut catheter and pull out after ten days; remove dressings before first shower. End of instructions.

The main complications following his version of the operation was stenosis of the urethra, a condition that closes the opening of the urethra due to formation of scar tissue. This complication causes the bladder to become swollen with urine because there is no exit for the urine. It eventually distends until it bursts open, which would cause an immediate peritonitis, septicemia, and death. Infection was the other culprit.

His technique was not even clean. Just plain dirty. He was handling an area that was highly susceptible to infection.

By the time Lita Lopez was brought to the emergency room in the city hospital, she was in shock. An intravenous was started and oxygen administered. When the doctors were told what sort of operation had been performed, they were puzzled. Upon examination, they shook their heads in disbelief. No doctor, however, inept, would perform this type of surgery on a human being. How could this be allowed? After listening to Lita's friend explain the circumstances, they began to understand her desperate situation. She, or he, had been at the mercy of an enterprising quack.

Lita Lopez was taken to the operating room, where a revision of the butchery was performed. The opening to the stump of the penis was slightly revised so it would heal without the incidence of scar tissue. The catheterization relieved the pressure on the bladder, thereby eliminating the danger of a rupture. A few days later, the doctor explained to her what had been done by Dr. Smith and what revisions they had made to save her life. The doctors further explained that she did not have a vagina and to attempt such an operation would be disastrous. The penis was reduced to a small stump, making it impossible for her to ever use it as a sex organ.

Lita was inconsolable. She considered herself useless, a freak. Her dreams of being a real woman, of having a vagina, of being rid of the organ she hated were over. For days and weeks, she talked to no one. When her boyfriend came, she hid her head under the covers. She was of no use to him and begged him not to return. It was time to rearrange her life. Time to face up to what faced her. Finally, she had the courage to look down to what had been done to her body. She had no testicles or penis. Only a stump. From that stump she passed her water. Instead of sitting, she would have to stand and manipulate the stump so that the stream would go straight.

The other problem explained to her by the doctors was that whenever she felt a "hard" coming on, the stump would swell and become very hard. Often it would take a long time to reduce itself, unless of course she chose to masturbate. If she desired, Lita would only be able to accept anal sex. Therefore, she was back to where she began. What enjoyment would there ever be for her when it came to the sex act? Lita realized that she must make adjustments and new plans.

Of course, she would remain a prostitute—but what a prostitute! The best! She would prostitute her body to the highest bidder. Money would be her master. Money would be her god, her lover, her life, her food, her drink, her poison, and her death. What man could sincerely desire her? There would be no close friends, and no one would know her secret. Lita Lopez, the freak. The tricks wouldn't care. Most of them loved a freak. There would be plenty of men who would sip champagne from her slipper.

The time came for her to leave the hospital. There was nothing more that could be done. All sympathy for her had been used up. She had become an object for hospital gossip, ridicule, and jokes.

Lita's main concentration was upon Dr. Smith, who had so ruthlessly ruined her life. One day she will find him. That would be no problem. The only problem would be how she will kill him and not be a suspect. The answer to that was patience. She must have patience.

Eight months after Lita was discharged and forgotten, a patient, known only as Smith, had been brought to the emergency room. He had been brutally stabbed. He died as they were administering emergency care. When his clothes were removed, they counted at least twenty stab wounds. Worst of all, he had been castrated. It was determined that his death had been slow. . . .

Lita sniffed again from the one-hundred-dollar bill that held the cocaine. She liked sniffing her cocaine from large denomination bills. Made her feel rich. Now she was more alert, and her spirits were soaring. Today, she would go to Dr. Snyder's office. He would give her the silicone injections. If Edgewater thought he was the only act in town, then he should think again. Snyder would give her more than Edgewater. She laughed and got dressed.

11

"You dirty bastards!" Louis Frazier's voice resounded throughout the hospital ward. "Somebody come and untie me. Let me get up! I want up!"

The staff, familiar with Louis and his outbursts, unanimously agreed that moving him into a small private cubicle at the end of the corridor would ensure a quieter ward. But Louis yelled louder and longer.

"I want a doctor. I want to go home. Help me. Help me!" Incessantly, he hollered day and night.

Two months ago, Louis Frazier, his brain dazed from alcohol, had staggered out of a Lenox Avenue bar into the busy Saturday-night traffic. He remembered only the impact of the car. When later he awoke in the hospital, he found the intravenous fluids, Foley catheter, and nasal tubes extremely annoying. He was never alone. The constant attention from the doctors and nurses impressed him. He felt special for the first time in his life.

Young and pretty student nurses were assigned to bathe Louis. It amused him to see the amazed expressions on their faces when they gazed at his nakedness.

"How do you like the looks of that?" he would ask.

They dropped the covers, pretending not to hear. However, one morning, he heard a bewildering statement.

"How are you going to like it when you finally realize that you will never use it again."

When Louis was moved to the ward with other patients, he was subjected to the same inattention for which the hospital was renowned. So Louis created loud verbal noises to gain attention. Success was limited. He could look at his body, but he could not feel it. For long periods, he would try to catch it moving, but to no avail. "Move dammit!" he had demanded. It remained stationary. Intently he'd watch the tube with urine flowing from his penis. Why did he have it there? The fact that he had experienced no pain from the many needles that pierced into his flesh convinced him that something was missing in his body. Louis wanted some answers.

"I want a doctor, I want a doctor," he chanted until he fell asleep.

When he awoke, his outcry was halted only by the sound of feet shuffling toward the cubical. A short, squinty-eyed doctor arrived.

"Hey, doc, I'm sure glad to see you. I ain't seen a doctor all week. I want some action here. Like getting out of this bed and walking around." His voice was deep and commanding. "I want to get moving, and I want to go home, and I want this thing out of my dick!"

The doctor, unperturbed, spoke in broken English.

"Nobody tell you?"

"Nobody tell me what?" Louis mocked.

"You no walk."

Louis gawked at the dingy lab coat and the stethoscope dangling snakelike from his neck.

"I thought you scream 'cause you have pain, but you cannot have pain because you not feel anything. So, why you scream all day and most of the night? You disturb all people 'round here." He made a wide gesture with his arms.

"This place is a pain, so I do get pain," Louis hissed.

The doctor methodically took his ballpoint pen and glided it on Louis's body.

"You feel?"

"Feel what?"

"Feel pain?"

"Man, what are talking about? What kinda doctor are you?"

"I try to show you, Mr. Louis, you no feel pain. No more. You no move arms or legs. No more. You like vegetable from neck down. You similar to car without engine. No move."

Satisfied that he had made the situation clear, the doctor sent him a final glance and started to leave.

"Don't give me that Chinese laundry opinion of yours," Louis screamed. "You're a fuckin' liar, and I bet you don't even got a license!"

"You upset. Relax. One day we get you in chair, but it will be necessary to tie you in chair. That way, you no fall out. Chair will be good for you." He smiled at Louis.

"Fuck a chair. When will I walk? That's all I want to know? When can I use my arms and get this tube outta my dick?"

"You very stubborn man, Mr. Louis. You no try to listen. Just yell, yell all day. Ask questions, but don't listen to answers. Very pitiful. You no walk in life anymore; no use arms anymore; never be able to know when you want to make water. Very bad situation for rest of life. No more sex. Nothing. You lucky man to be alive. Now, give everybody a nice rest."

The doctor disappeared.

Louis Frazier was mute. *They got to be joking,* he thought. His eyes darted to the lower part of his body. It was there. His arms were there. But why couldn't he move now? Why couldn't he feel? This business about being a "vegetable" was not clear. He heard about people who were like that. What did it all mean? He was baffled. The doctor's words riveted to that section of the brain where the truth is stored. Tears flooded his eyes and rolled down the sides of his face. Wiping them was impossible. He began to understand.

The days were long for Louis Frazier, but the nights were unending. He would sleep continuously. After being fed, he would return to sleep. This peaceful sleep was punctuated by nightmares. He saw himself walking up the walls or on the ceiling. He fantasized that a part of his body was floating away or that he was wedged or tied to the bed. He began to doubt his sanity. He feared sleep. He feared being awake. The inability to remember words hampered him from singing a simple song. However, he remembered one little prayer his grandmother had taught him.

Now I lay me down to sleep,
I pray the Lord my soul He'll keep.
If I should die before I wake,
I pray the Lord my soul He'll take.

That's the answer, he thought. He would merely change the word "soul" to "body" and ask him to take this body and give him back the one he had before the accident. So in serious, muted, and respectful tones, he prayed. He was willing to wait until the next morning for the miracle. He wouldn't rush the Lord. That night Louis slept without incident. When morning arrived, it did so without any answer to his prayer. He wanted to cry, but the tears had run out. He wanted to yell, but his voice was hoarse. Silence and anger overwhelmed him.

"How are you doing, Louis?" an unfamiliar voice inquired.

"Who the hell are you?"

"Well, they call me 'Oldtimer.'"

A handsome gray-haired gentleman smiled down at Louis. The rough-dried hospital robe indicated he was a patient. A cane assisted one arm while the other dangled at his side.

"What kinda name is that?"

"It sorta means 'wisdom', especially around here and out on the avenue. You know how that goes."

"Yeah," Louis laughed.

"Yeah, man, I hear you yelling and carrying on all day. You in a bad way. I think you gonna need some help and advice."

"What kinda help and advice can you give, Mr. Wisdom?" Louis mocked.

The man adjusted his robe. Smiling, he displayed a handsome set of teeth. Louis was impressed.

"Is those teeth real?"

Oldtimer laughed and lied.

"These teeth are as real as me. I'm mighty proud of them. But let's get to helping you."

"Helping me? Look at you. You don't look so together. Your arm hanging down at your side like a limp dick, and you got a raggedly-ass cane holding up the other. How you gonna help somebody?"

"But I can walk, Louis. I can do a lot of things you can't and never will do. So why don't you let me give you some advice now and then?"

Oldtimer's words galvanized Louis's brain. Conditions were harsh. Food was shovelled into his mouth. A complete bath did not exist for him, and he had never sat in a chair as the doctor had promised.

"Maybe, just maybe, I'll let you give me a little advice, but that's not saying I'm gonna take it."

"I'm always hanging 'round. You just call when you need me."

The man hobbled away.

Louis lay alone, silent and inert. He was confused as to the day of the month. In the cubicle, he was aware of night and day because of the opaque window pane. Roaches scampered along the drab green walls and ceilings. Turning his head to the far right, he found himself viewing a picture of a nurse, complete in uniform, with a finger to her lips, indicating quiet. He smiled and greeted her loudly.

"Good morning, white-capped bitch!"

Louis envisioned himself sauntering up the avenue. . . . He passed the big hospital, the candy stores, the number holes, and the laundromats. The sweltering heat had been driving people from their apartments onto the sidewalks. They found solace in complaining about the weather. Louis drifted into the bar. It emanated the smell of beer and smoke.

"Hey, Maxie! Who's gonna win the ball game?" Louis lurched his body onto a bar stool. The jukebox blared. It was a festive atmosphere because a ball game was being played at the stadium.

"Man, it's gotta be our team. Charlie will be at bat and on the mound. How can we lose?" Maxie authorized.

"Right on!"

They slapped hands. Louis felt the sting. Then the music aroused him. He moved to the floor, oscillating his body to the sounds. He stopped, whirled on one leg, and, lifting the other, he gyrated his tall, lean body like a revolving top. Maxie and the other patrons explained. Bowing to accept the applause, Louis grinned.

"I'll take a rum and Coke."

The drink cooled his throat and soothed his brain. . . . He was enjoying the prestige until, suddenly, Louis realized this was not real. He closed his eyes tightly and prayed for sleep. Maybe, if he could go to sleep with the same memories, when he woke up everything would be okay. Louis would be okay.

12

Arnold had spent two miserable days in jail. He was tired and still dressed in the drag outfit in which he had been arrested. His makeup had faded, and now a shadow of a beard began to show. He reluctantly removed his beloved wig. His feet, still in high heels, were in constant pain and seemed to scream for help. He had no money for a taxi and was not looking forward to the subway. He stood against the wall outside the Tombs, looking rather forlorn and feeling real insulted at being released so abruptly, in plain daylight, onto the streets during the early morning rush hour. Arnold was a night creature, therefore, the brightness of the daylight actually stung his eyes. As he attempted to shield his eyes from the sun, he spied the tall, black corrections officer. Arnold knew he was getting off duty, and maybe this was a chance for a ride. He hoped he was going uptown or near the Bronx.

"Want to give a girl a ride? Promise not to rob you."

Clarence Brown turned and saw the horror standing a few feet from him. No way! He didn't want that piece of shit in his car.

"Sorry, baby, I'm in a hurry." He laughed and jumped into the car. Quickly he started the motor.

Arnold limped to the window and tapped.

"Listen, officer, I'm desperate. I got busted early, so I don't have a coin. I can't go in the subway looking like this. If I try to jump the turnstile, the police will arrest me again. Please. Just to the corner of 139th and the Concourse. I'll pay you, not now, but I'll pay you."

Clarence was familiar with Arnold's history. It was rumored that he had some honesty about him. He didn't do drugs, alcohol, or smoke. He only robbed, never killed, and wouldn't rob black men. Even Clarence hated the idea of the public having to look at Arnold in this condition.

"Okay, get in." Arnold joyfully jumped in the passenger seat.

During the ride, he remained silent because he knew that the officer was not pleased having him in his car. He didn't want to annoy him. However, it was difficult for Arnold not to be aroused by just being in the presence of the handsome black man. Arnold had a passion for corrections officers. He had sex with a few of them when he had been incarcerated. But he had never seen one as handsome as Clarence. He strained his eyeballs sneaking a periodical look at the officer. *Beyond my reach,* thought Arnold. But then his mind did a quick reverse. *Never say never.* He smiled.

"I guess you know that my name is Arnold."

"The whole system knows you. You're also known as Lottie."

"Oh, yes, that's me! And what is your name?"

"Clarence." He remained quiet during most of the ride.

The car was approaching the corner near Arnold's apartment.

"Is this your stop?"

"Yes, yes. Could you turn into the side street, and I'll get out? I don't want the neighbors to see too much of me looking like this." Clarence had to smile at Arnold's concern over the neighbors. "If the situation was different and I was a woman, I would invite you up to have a drink. But then who drinks this early? I am not a cook, and that's all I can offer." Arnold laughed, knowing that such an offer would be refused.

Clarence Brown had all the intentions of refusing anything that Arnold or any faggot offered, but he was curious about how a faggot lives two different disguises. Why not accept a drink? He was not afraid of faggots, and this would give him a chance to see if he lived as bad as he looked.

"I'll take that drink. I'm curious to see how a faggot and pickpocket lives." He hoped he had insulted him.

Arnold almost fell out of his seat.

"Oh, my, my, I'm most honored." Insulting names didn't bother Arnold.

Quickly, he was out of the car, with Clarence following him into the building. Arnold could not believe his good fortune. All he needed was a chance, an opportunity, an opening. He put the key in, opened the door, and switched on the light. Turning seductively, he spoke.

"Do enter my palazzo. My villa!"

Clarence entered and gasped. It was an enormous studio apartment. However, it had been furnished and fashioned after an Italian adventure. The walls were covered with expensive paintings. Clarence, not familiar with the art, was not aware that on those walls were Miros, a Judd, three Beardens, and a Katz. All other space had been covered with small and medium tapestries besides other miscellaneous paintings. Clarence looked further and spied two beautiful lamps. He had no idea that they were original Tiffany lamps.

"Is this stuff real or fake?"

"I do not steal fakes. I wouldn't risk my freedom on fakes. Of course, you don't understand that world."

Arnold proudly strolled around the studio, pointing out objects to Clarence.

"This is an original Warhol. You'd be surprised how I managed to get it. It's worth a fortune. As you can see, I have Tiffany lamps, Mexican and Latin American paintings, namely Rivera, Teledo, and Coronel. Some are prints, some are originals." He strolled to a far corner and posed as he pointed and elaborated.

"This is my Chinese antique corner. I have here small objects from the first through the nineteenth century, namely porcelain, jades, and bronzes. They are small but worth a fortune."

Arnold then turned and strolled to the magnificent four-poster bed that occupied the middle of the room.

"This is my only early American piece. I thought that I should sleep in an American antique. I love my country, and this bed is so American. No, I did not steal it. I'm good but not that good." He laughed, as did Clarence.

The ice was breaking. He could see that Clarence was impressed. This was pleasing and exciting to Arnold. His sexual hopes soared. Maybe there would be a small chance. Now, he must impress this man, but most of all, he wanted to have this man. Of course, experience had taught him that he must make his move slowly or he could end up with a big black fist in his precious face.

Arnold moved quickly to the cabinet where he kept his finest glasses.

"Let's not forget you came up for a drink. What do you drink, sir?" Arnold was trying to make Clarence feel every bit the man. He loved the play that was being enacted here. He wanted Clarence to request, to express, to demand, and to be in control.

Clarence, impressed by Arnold's apartment, settled down into a chair.

"I hope this is safe to sit on. Is it an antique also?"

"Oh, no!" Arnold laughed. "This is really a chair for my guests so they will not sit their black asses on my antiques. Of course, it would be different if you—" Arnold stopped and cut his eyes toward Clarence to see if he had caught on to what he was implying. Clarence was oblivious to Arnold's words.

"I would never dream you lived like this. How in the hell did you acquire all of these trappings?"

Arnold was quite candid.

"I bought most of them with the money, Rolexes, and credit cards I stole off of men. If I couldn't afford the entire price, then I laid it away and got it out when my criminal activity paid off. If the store owner was willing, I got it all for blow jobs or a reduced price. Sometimes I would be at a rich trick's apartment and when he fell asleep I walked out with whatever was most valuable. I know my art and antiques. Just because I'm a faggot, a thief, and black does not make me ignorant. I'm telling you the truth, Officer Clarence Brown, because you know my criminal history."

He noted that the officer's glass was empty.

"Would you like another drink?" Arnold, holding the bottle in a fanciful manner, stared the officer squarely in the face.

"Yes, yes, of course." Clarence was more relaxed. "Your brandy is the best."

"Oh, but of course, it's an antique in its own fashion."

Arnold's hopes soared. The officer had accepted another drink and did not appear in any hurry to leave.

"Please excuse me for at least five or ten minutes. I must go take a shower and clean the street and jail off my body."

Before he could hear a protest or approval, Arnold had disappeared into the bathroom. He showered quickly. He was concerned about how many brandies it would take to mellow out this big black man. Now, without the makeup, wig, and other feminine attire, Arnold was a handsome man. He had put on a pair of blue jeans and shirt. He rejoined his guest.

Clarence looked surprised to see him out of drag clothes and makeup.

"Damn, you look okay as a man. Why in the hell do you dress up in that drag shit?"

"I like to dress. I think I look good as a woman, and on the streets it gets me a lot of customers."

"I don't understand you faggots." His voice was harsh and he sounded a hard, soft laugh. "How can you think you look good as a woman, and why not just be yourself and get a job. All these ideas in your head are warped. Dressing up like a woman, cruising tricks, picking pockets and watches, you are a fuckin' menace to the world. They should lock all of you up and throw away the key. You're a fuckin' burden on the taxpayers."

Arnold could see that the brandy was making him angry. He decided it was better to say less and try to ease him out of the apartment before he got violent. He didn't want to be beaten by this big black man. He had known these scenes to happen. What he really wanted to happen was now out of the question.

"Well, I am tired, Officer Brown, and I think I will go to bed, even though it is daylight. Thank you for the ride home. I know there is no way I can repay you."

Clarence got up from the chair. He stared at Arnold in disgust and headed towards the door. He stopped and looked at a photograph on the wall.

"Who are these people?"

"Oh, that was me when I was ten. And there is my mother and my uncle. My dear uncle began fucking me at the age of seven. He was very helpful in my homosexual transition. You see, Officer, I was not born this way."

Arnold noticed the puzzlement in Clarence and continued.

"My mother died when I was ten, and my uncle kept up his 'treatments.' I was able to run away when I was sixteen. There's no more to say about it. It's over and done."

"Hey, I'm sorry. It's just that I see your kind every day. You are different than most. At least you're clean and intelligent, and I like the fact that you do not steal from your own color." Arnold, sensing compassion, was not frightened any longer. "Look, I'm getting ready to go, and I will not be passing your way again, so do me one favor, and I mean this is between you and me."

Arnold could not imagine what favor he could do for the officer.

Clarence took a deep breath, hesitated, then spoke.

"I can't get it from my wife, and I have never had it from a man. I want a blow job. Just once, and I am finished with it."

Arnold could not believe those magic words. He didn't hesitate, and before Clarence could think about changing his mind, he had already begun to push him over to the antique bed, where he would begin the most creative blow job he had ever performed in his life. Officer Brown offered no resistance. His large penis was hard and ready. Slowly, Arnold began licking it in a slow, rhythmic motion. Into his mouth and out of his mouth. Arnold enjoyed the hardness of the man.

It was perfect. Clarence Brown was responding and receiving a whole new sexual experience. He forgot who he was, where he was, and what he was. His eyes closed, his heart pounded, his dick throbbed, his body relaxed into a sexual pit, and when he exploded no regrets ever materialized. He wanted to say stop; he wanted to lash out at Arnold; he wanted to beg for it again; he wanted to forget what had happened and never come back. He left quickly without saying a word.

Arnold smiled. How perfect it had turned out for him. In fact, it had been more than what he had hoped for. Of course, he wanted more of him, but then, he'd have to wait. Wait for him to call. He would call. It might take a few weeks, but Clarence Brown would call. He had sipped from the champagne slipper. He would be back.

13

Within three weeks, Dr. Edgewater announced that Belinda, his new physician assistant, would be working in the office. Jolena, much to his surprise, accepted the news without questions. He was pleased and positive that everything would work out between them. But he knew also that before long neither woman would accept the other. Jolena was smart enough to know that he would not get rid of his beloved Belinda.

It was apparent to Jolena whenever the doctor entered the office. Greetings, sighs, and murmurs from the patients would rise to a crescendo. Jolena glanced through the opening and saw the doctor and the young, blond girl who accompanied him. He was jubilant as he entered Jolena's work area. She noted how the girl eyed the room with an air of superiority.

"Jolena, dear, I want you to meet my new physician assistant." He pulled Belinda forward.

"Belinda, meet Jolena. She is my right hand here in the office."

Then he addressed Jolena.

"And Belinda is my right hand in the operating room."

Jolena knew what to say.

"Hi, Belinda. I'm so glad to meet you. It is so good that we have extra help." She smiled and grasped the young girl's hand. Belinda was startled by the warm greeting. Jolena could sense dislike even in the handshake.

The doctor was elated that the introductions were over. He kept Belinda with him. She followed him throughout the office. The resentment Jolena had tried to harbor dissolved, but not the distrust. This was the new assistant he had announced would be working with him. Now she understood the reason for the changes he was displaying, short temper, neglect of the office, sloppy examinations, careless procedures, long and whispering phone conversations.

If this new employee was going to relieve her from having to deal with the results of his botched surgical procedures and listen to his false promises of how "everything will be okay"; "wait, my dear, give it time"; "wait two more weeks, my dear"; "come back in a month, my dear," and all his excuses he gave the unsuspecting patients, she was satisfied. Let the girlfriend have it. She herself would take care of the outer office and continue to make her extra money with the injections.

A month had passed without incident. Unmarked boundaries had been drawn, and each one stayed within those lines. Belinda, however, was taking on a greater air of importance and authority. She began to use this attitude with the patients. Many complained to Jolena. She advised them to speak to the doctor. It was important that she did not get involved in their petty complaints. It was difficult to trust any of them; therefore, she took no sides. Jolena stayed out of the presence of Belinda as much as possible. Any messages she had for the doctor she relayed through the intercom. She never attempted to assist him. If he needed her, he would call. One Friday evening, near closing, she counted five patients who would be receiving their "body treatment." Dr. Edgewater came to her desk.

"Jolena, dear, we are leaving now. How many bodies do we have?"

"Five."

"You collected?"

"Yes. It's all here. She handed him the envelope, which he slipped into his pocket. "I took mine out."

She noted that Belinda was standing in the background observing the transaction and conversation between them.

"I'll see you Monday. Have a nice weekend."

"Thank you, doctor. You both have a nice weekend."

She watched Belinda manage a stiff smile as she grabbed onto the doctor's arm.

She sat quietly until she was sure they had departed, then she went to the bathroom, shut the door, and splashed her face with cold water in an attempt to calm the rage that had come over her. She did not like or trust Belinda. Something was not right in this whole situation. Why did he bring her to work in the office? Why didn't he just marry her and keep her at home? Was this job coming to an end? When Peter Edgewater was in love, it was impossible to get any messages through to him. She was experienced enough to know that there were two types of people you can't help: a person in love and a drunk. Tonight she'd go and visit an old friend. He would advise her. Now, she had to concentrate on her work. She returned to her desk.

"Carla, come in. You'll be first today."

Carla, a tall masculine Spanish transvestite came into the treatment room.

"Who's the new girl working with the doctor?" Carla smiled slyly as she waited for a reaction from Jolena.

"Belinda is her name, and she's his physician assistant. She helps him in the operating room and treatment rooms."

Jolena appeared unconcerned. She never wanted the patients to know she was upset or worried about being replaced.

"Is she gonna do this body work?"

"No."

"Good! 'Cause I don't like her and don't want her working on me."

"Oh, stop being like that. She hasn't done anything to you. Pull off your clothes and get on the table."

Carla undressed and threw the clothes in the corner on the floor. The boy body was completely exposed. No silicone work had been done, and the shape of the body was that of a male. The hips were narrow and shapeless, the buttocks flat and shapeless. Carla had unsuccessfully used many hormones, hoping that a shape would develop. The body never developed a shape, but the effect on the penis had not been welcomed. Carla was unable to get an erection. This was not what she had expected, even though she had been told by Jolena that it could happen. Carla stopped the hormones. After all, she worked the streets as a prostitute and could not afford to have a limp penis. After all, what did tricks want? Yes, a hard dick.

"Carla, pick up your clothes and put them neatly on the chair. How many times—"

"Okay, okay, I'm sorry. I bet you two ain't gonna get along in this office."

"Why shouldn't we get along?"

"She's a bitch. I can see it. All the girls are talking. And let's not forget that she's white. You see, Ms. Taylor, you ain't white, and you ain't no bitch. Oh, yeah, you get on us and keep things in order and make us try to act like ladies even though we all ain't nothing but a lot of sick men. She just ain't to be trusted. You should see how uppity she is in that treatment room."

"Let's not talk about it. Everything will work out."

"Just watch your back. I don't trust either one of them."

"Stop talking, and do not move. I'm getting ready to work on you."

Slowly she placed the needles into the approved area of the body. She drew back the solution and slowly injected. She skillfully placed more needles. Carla was quiet.

"Now, let them set for a few minutes, and then we will begin."

Carla continued her summation.

"You ain't stupid. You know what's going on."

"It's not my business, and it's not yours." Jolena was annoyed at Carla's warnings. Already Carla and the others were sensing danger for her. Was she ignoring this warning or resentful that they had become so perceptive?

"I'm just trying to warn you. Watch your back. She'll get rid of you."

"Be quiet now so I can concentrate." She pulled up a stool and began injecting the silicone into the needles. She watched with admiration as the body slowly began to take shape.

"Your body is going to look great when it's finished. You might not need too many treatments."

Carla smiled. She was happy. Getting silicone injections was her dream.

"Oh, I want a lot more. I want it big. Bigger than Lita Lopez."

"Forget it. You'll look hideous."

"The big contest and dance is coming up, and I want to walk that ball for body!"

"You will look great."

"Are you coming to the ball? You ain't never been to one. You should come."

Jolena smiled and did not answer. No, she had never been to one of the "queen" balls. Maybe she would go this one time. After she had finished shaping the body with the silicone injections, she cleaned and taped the body.

"You can get dressed. Remember not to massage until tomorrow after you take off the dressings. Do not return here for two weeks."

After finishing, Jolena began to think about the conversation with Carla. For the first time she worried. She had an uneasy feeling from the day Belinda walked into the office. Resentment was on both sides. However, Belinda had the edge. She could influence the doctor against her. What chance did she have? She was replaceable. And Belinda would be the replacement. She remembered his suggesting that Belinda stay a few nights and observe Jolena's technique. It was hard to believe that he would do this to her. That he would systematically get rid of her. Now she'd have to take extra precautions. Sooner or later, Belinda would be looking over her shoulder, spying on her technique. *Well,* she thought, *I'll have to make it as unpleasant as possible.*

The office had emptied, but the ringing doorbell put a stop to her thoughts. *Who could that be at this time of the night?* she wondered as she went to open the door.

He stood there, tall and handsome. The blue eyes riveted through her. The face was strong and masculine. The smile was the best in the world. The brown hair slightly windswept.

Jolena was elated when she saw him.

"Oh, my God! Mark Nelson, my God where have you been? I was just—"

"And I was just thinking about you." He swooped into the office and immediately enveloped her into his arms. He held her tight, and it felt good for that quick moment.

"Is everything okay? Why are you here?" She looked up at him. She showed concern.

He didn't bother to answer her question.

"Did you miss me?"

"Of course I missed you."

"Jolena, you will always be my love."

"And you will always be my love. Now tell me everything that has happened to you." She broke away from his embrace.

"I've fallen in love."

"You traitor!" She laughed. "I was supposed to be your love. You were always supposed to love me."

She put her hand on her shapely hip and stared intently at him. He laughed, revealing his white and perfect teeth. Small insignificant wrinkles showed around his eyes.

"Jolena, this is the other kind of love you told me about. The kind you told me that has the passion and all of that other stuff."

She smiled and understood.

"Tell me about her."

"This girl! She is great! She is beautiful, educated, and she loves me. She actually loves me!" He spun around on his heels like a dancer. "For myself, Jolena! For me!"

"Then she knows!" Jolena's voice was serious.

"Yes, she knows. I explained to her that I was born a woman and gradually became a man. She accepts me. We are beautiful together. We have formed a love between us that I never knew could exist. It's tender, it's passionate, it's musical, it's everything I've ever dreamed about."

Mark had come to the office almost three years ago as a woman who wanted to become a man. Jolena and Mark, who was then known as Marsha, had struck up a close relationship. She was fond of him and wanted everything to work as well as possible in his life. He was extremely intelligent and kind, but she knew he was seeking more than the sex change had offered him.

She spoke slowly, looking directly in his face.

"Mark, can she live with the fact that you do not have a penis and you will probably never have one that will function?"

He hesitated and did a complete turn around on his heel. This was a habit he had acquired when questions became difficult to answer.

"Well, I have not told her all of that. That's why I am here. I want to know what is happening in the field of prosthesis. Maybe—"

"Mark, it's not successful. Not at all. I'll be truthful with you. I've seen one or two, and they have turned out to be disastrous. It's just not perfected. Even Edgewater does not talk about it. He tried one, and it turned out real bad. He's never going to admit that to you, so I'm telling you this in confidence. Wait a while. Since your girlfriend knows everything, can't you live your life together just like you are now?"

He slumped down into the chair. She could feel his disappointment. He stared at the floor. All the jubilation had disappeared.

"Forgive me I don't want you to feel bad or give up hope. Technology marches on. Forgive me."

He looked at her, and again his face beamed.

"You never have to ask my forgiveness. Tell you what; give me an appointment to see the doctor tomorrow. I'm only in the city for three days. And I'll love you forever!"

She laughed.

"What choice do I have? You just got the best appointment in the book. Three o'clock tomorrow." She knew it was useless to discourage him. Enough had been said. He would have to settle that with the doctor.

He got up, smiled, and hugged her.

"You'll always be my girl."

"And you'll always be my guy," she returned his embrace. Still joking and laughing, Mark left the office.

Jolena returned to the treatment room to tidy up before leaving. She was very careful, properly disposing of used needles and syringes. She had constantly cleaned up behind the doctor, who left dirty syringes and needles lying about. She knew that whenever he used the treatment room, he had the habit of automatically picking up whatever syringe was available, even if it had been used on another patient. The syringes for the silicone injections proved to be a constant friction between them. He preferred to use the large glass syringes because it was easier to push the heavy substance into the body. It was less expensive to use the same syringe rather than the disposable.

When Jolena would insist on sterilizing the syringes, he would get angry because the high temperature caused them to crack after sterilization. After having to buy new syringes, he instructed her not to sterilize, but wash and soak, them in special solution. It was useless to lecture him on clean or sterile technique. He was the doctor; he was knowledgeable of disease and techniques. This was his office, and he was in charge. Now, he was displaying less interest in technique and handling of patients. Jolena, however, had already discovered that she could use disposable plastic syringes. It took a little longer, but it afforded more safety for her and the patients.

Now, she had to worry about her future. She felt that she would soon be eliminated from the office. He had no use for her any longer in the treatment room. She had really become a secretary and receptionist. It would not be long before he eliminated her from the one job that netted him more cash than he dared to think about. Now, he suggested that he wanted Belinda to be taught her skills. It was upsetting to her that their professional relationship might end in this manner. Her loyalty, protectiveness, and honesty had meant nothing to him. Jolena was hurt. She felt tired and useless. Before leaving the office, she made a phone call. There was one person in whom she could confide.

"Hello, Bernie, it's Jolena. How do you feel, my love? Me? I'm fine, but I need to talk to you. I need a drink of that fine cognac. See you in about fifteen minutes."

Jolena left the office and walked up Park Avenue. The night was brisk. Spring would soon be here. It had surprised her that Bernie did not go to Florida this winter. She arrived at Ninety-fifth Street and entered the magnificent lobby of the building. The doorman, smiling, greeted her.

"Go right up, Ms. Taylor. He's expecting you."

Jolena rode the elevator to the top floor; it opened to the only apartment on that floor. She entered, calling out to him.

"Bernie, which room are you in?"

His apartment had ten rooms. She could not understand why he did not get a smaller place, since he was alone, but this was his way of life. It was a rich life that she was far removed from and would never possess. There were rooms filled with priceless art and sculpture. This was his world, his only world and all he had left.

"I'm glad you came, Jolena. I always look forward to your visits." They embraced. He held her extra long this time.

"I need to talk to you, Bernie. There's no one else I can tell these things who could understand or advise me."

Dr. Bernie Charles sat down and pointed out a chair close to him.

She took one of the fine crystal glasses and poured the brandy. Bernie knew she enjoyed the visits to his apartment. It was an environment in which she would never live. He enjoyed watching her stroll through his home, observing and studying the rare art works, books, and furniture that all belonged to his rich past. Bernie knew she appreciated and enjoyed his richness. He enjoyed her for that. There were no ulterior motives. No love affair, no sexual touching, no sexual conversation, just pure, sweet, and honest friendship and conversation. They both understood each other.

He had been the most respected and consulted plastic surgeon in the city. She had been one of his favorite scrub nurses. He was sixty-five years old when he was removed from his thirty-year position as chief of the plastic surgery department. Although the board of the large hospital respected his dedication and service, they wanted him out. Of course he could have remained as a member of the board, but that was not his desire. They wanted younger doctors with more incentive, doctors who did not demand so much and who could give more of their time, and cost the hospital less money.

He had sensed that his days of fame were over. Administration was not interested in his theories on infections and what it can do to a face lift, skin graft, flap, or whatever. Everything was time and money; money was the most important. Even to him, but he never allowed it to come before his patient's health. He had seen his other colleagues leave. All ousted by younger men with new and outlandish ideas. But before they could move in on him, he had resigned.

"Bernie! What are you thinking about? You were really lost there." Jolena asked as the brandy smoothed her nerves.

Her voice had snapped him back to the present.

"I was thinking back, Jolena. I always think back. Nothing much to think ahead about."

"Oh, stop! You have a lot of life in front of you. All you have to do is go out and mingle with your old friends. But if you are happy like this, then stay like this."

Another reason he liked her. She never tried to change him. He was sixty-five, his face, although it showed signs of aging, still showed the remnants of a once-handsome man. He had kept his body in fairly good shape by working out in his own exercise room.

"So tell me what the great surgeon is doing now." He spoke mockingly. Jolena knew he did not like Dr. Edgewater. Bernie never expressed that to anyone but Jolena. He seemed to receive therapy from the conversation.

"He's in love." Jolena waited for the reaction.

Bernie laughed and took a swallow of the drink she had poured for him.

"How old is she?"

"Hmm, maybe twenty-two or three."

"My God! Well, well, that's good. That's very good. Now we will see some real human emotions displayed," he mused.

"You sound happy for him but in which direction?"

"I am. I knew that one day it would happen to him."

"Why, Bernie, why do you dislike him? You never told me. I know you were never pleased with his carelessness, his haughty attitude, and his lack of consideration for patients, but there must be another reason. I've heard other rumors, but you know I would never say anything to you."

"It's a long story. I'm not in the mood to talk about it tonight. One evening I'll tell you. You know I will tell you. In fact you are the only one I will tell the whole story. I trust you."

He looked at her, and he liked her, as always. He wished that she had been the one he loved, but it was better this way. She was black and he white and Jewish. Society would have destroyed them. Still, he wondered how it would have been with her. If he could just hold and caress her for one night. Her voice broke the spell.

"A patient came in tonight. We operated on him two years ago. Woman to man. Now he wants to get a penis attachment."

"It won't work. Not even for a short while. He will never get an ejaculation, but he will surely get the biggest infection of his lifetime. That operation has not been perfected."

"He insisted on an appointment."

"You can bet that the 'genius' will try it."

"Yes, I guess so. His ego is really inflated now."

"He's got to show off for his new princess."

"I'm already barred from the treatment room when she is there. She is the assistant now."

"What is her title?"

"She is a Physician Assistant."

"I doubt that, but be glad you don't have to continue viewing the horrors he inflicts on those poor uninformed individuals."

"Well, Bernie, I think he is getting ready to eliminate my extra money."

"With silicone?"

"Yep."

"Get out of there, Jolena. It's not good. The silicone is bad news. Sometimes it works, but later on, it turns sour. I know you are good and you do excellent work, but he is going to get more and more greedy. Then you know what happens."

"Well, I have to stay until he takes the cash job from me."

"If that girl does that work, something will turn out wrong. She doesn't have the knowledge or talent. Remember, I taught you all the good and bad things about that product."

"I remember. If he tells her as much as he told me, she'll know nothing."

"It's dangerous, Jolena; it's dangerous." He finished his drink. She got up and poured another one for him. Jolena valued Bernie's opinion.

"I need the money, Bernie."

"Jolena, don't you have anything saved?"

"I have about two thousand dollars, thanks to you for guiding me in the right direction. Just a few more months, then I'm going back to work in the hospital."

"I've still got connections. If you want to scrub for a good plastic man, you know I can get you a job with a private doctor or even in any hospital."

"I know, Bernie." She finished the cognac. "I'm getting old. I don't want to be standing up all day in the operating room while the varicose veins grow larger in my legs and my hips spread and my face fades into old age. I'll be here next week, same time."

"Jolena, come Wednesday. You get off early. I want to talk with you."

She wondered why he had changed their schedule.

"Okay, Bernie." She leaned down and kissed him. There was sadness about him she had not seen before.

"Goodnight, my love, and think about what I told you, Jolena. Make plans. Make plans like I did. Be one step ahead."

He grabbed her hand, and she was aware of the softness of his hands. They were small, smooth hands that felt like the touch of velvet.

"I'll see you next week, Bernie." She embraced him. Again he clung to her. She felt sad, and it was hard not to cry. Why? There were no apparent emotion between them. Maybe it was his penetrating eyes and his touch. He appeared more lonely, or was she sad for his loneliness or her own?

Jolena stepped into the waiting elevator, and Dr. Bernard Charles was alone. He walked to the large picture window that focused upon Central Park. And he began to remember, and his thoughts reached back...

Dr. Bernard Charles was chief of the plastic surgery division in one of the most prestigious New York City hospitals. He ran the department with efficiency and to great profit. His own operating rooms were equipped with the latest monitors, anesthesia machines, and all kinds of necessary instruments. Bernie loved the days that surgery was performed. He was always there keeping watch over the residents and ready to step in and assist if there was a problem.

Three days a week, he operated on his own private patients. These patients paid a great fee for the privilege of having Dr. Charles operate on them. After all, he was the most capable surgeon doing the transsexual surgery. On the days he operated, there was much tension in the operating suites. Everyone knew that Dr. Bernie Charles would be operating today, and that would mean trouble if things were not as he desired.

In the scrub area, outside the operating suite, Dr. Charles and his two resident doctors were engaged in the art of scrubbing their hands. Only the sound of the water and the vigorous scrubbing of arms and hands were heard. When Dr. Charles dropped his brush and walked into the room, his assistants followed. Today there was a new doctor who would spend one year with Dr. Charles so he could learn his latest technique of transsexual surgery. He was Dr. Peter Edgewater.

Jolena was in the room before the doctors. She was situated behind two large sterile tables covered with sterile instruments. She had expertise with all instruments and plastic surgery procedures. Jolena looked at no one except Dr. Charles. He never had to ask for an instrument. He merely held out his hand and the instrument was placed there, his every move anticipated.

Once the patient was brought to the room, all talking ceased until the anesthesiologist put the patient to sleep. After the patient was prepped and positioned, the operation would begin. The gender-change surgery had become his specialty. He was proud of the progress and results he had obtained in this most controversial and difficult surgery. Silence was broken only when Dr. Charles began to talk.

"Doctors, it might seem strange to any of you who are new here that this room is silent, but I do not allow talking unless it concerns this case. And I do not allow talking concerning the patient. You must remember that with an anesthetized patient, we can never be sure what they hear. Also, I believe the anesthesiologist would agree, this is as close to death as a person can travel. We are walking on hallowed grounds. Our main concern is the patient. No matter who he or she might be, or how bizarre you might think the operation, we have taken on the task of performing corrective surgery, and we are obligated for all its problems. Also, from this moment on, we will all refer to the patient as she, her, female, woman, or Molly, which is this patient's name."

Dr. Charles had become increasingly aware that a transsexual patient had great difficulty in getting a proper operation in the United States. Physicians did not want to get involved with this type of patient, mostly due to their puritanical heritage and the sexual alteration. This was considered by some to be immoral. To remove normal genitalia could possibly subject a surgeon to almost immediate litigation. The surgery itself was expensive, extensive, and irreversible. There were almost no clues as to why certain people desired this operation. Psychiatrists who had no success in the nonoperative treatment of transvestites warned that they were impossible to treat, much less cure.

He spent three years researching and traveling to different clinics and hospitals in Europe and South America. His first visit and awareness of the surgery was in Mexico. He was impressed with the improvements made in surgical techniques but not with aseptic techniques. Later, he attended lectures in Chicago, Virginia, and Canada. He also spent four months at both gender identity clinics in Johns Hopkins Hospital and three additional months at the Gender Identity Program at Stanford University School of Medicine. After that, he began to make his plans to operate at his hospital. Now he was operating on his twenty-sixth patient.

"As you can see, doctors, the patient is in a hyperflexed lithotomy position. She has been prepped and draped to expose the genitalia and perineum."

Eyes were wide with curiosity as the gloved and gowned doctors stood in anticipation, waiting for the first cut to be made.

Doctor Charles continued his explanation.

"This patient is asleep. I don't have to ask the anesthesiologist, because he and I have worked together for years and we know each other's routine. That is important. Now the only thing desired by all transsexuals is a deep vagina. However, tissues would break down inside the newly made vagina and scarring can occur."

Everyone gathered behind Dr. Charles as he positioned himself on a stool between the patient's legs. Jolena moved closer with her Mayo stand containing the necessary instruments. Quickly, she slapped a scalpel into his outreached hand. He made a slow, long incision down the middle of the perineum.

"Also, the depth of the vagina would be limited by the length of the penis. As you can see, this penis is rather large and, fortunately, not circumcised, so we will have more skin to work with in making a deep vagina."

Jolena knew the young residents were having a hard time handling this part of the surgery. Dr. Charles clamped the end of the penis and held it up for all to see, then he moved it to the side and continued his incision and explanation.

"In twenty to twenty-five percent of cases, the penis is small and a graft would be necessary. This would be taken from the buttocks because that area is hairless."

"What are the complications in this surgery?" asked one of the residents.

"A good question. I'm glad you asked." Dr. Charles turned to see who had asked the question. It was Dr. Peter Edgewater.

"There can be shortness in the vagina, which would limit the sex act's rectrovaginal fistulas; vaginal stenosis; and bulbus urethrovaginal fistulas."

He explained to them that the rectum and vagina could erupt into each other, causing any semen from the sex act to leak through the rectum and any feces from the rectum to leak out through the vagina. The vaginal stenosis was a closure of the vagina, thereby making it impossible for anything to enter the newly acquired vagina. The other complication was a leakage of urine into the vagina.

"To obtain satisfactory surgical results, we must construct the female genitalia more than satisfactory in function and appearance. We want a capacious vagina. This is obtained by a split thickness skin graft, retrodisplacement of the urethra, a cosmetically acceptable and pain-free perineum, good donor sites for the skin graft, and careful, postoperative explanation to the patient about the care of the operative site."

By this time, Dr. Charles was deep into the perineum, cutting and clamping to prepare a vagina. It was a bloody operation, and one of the young residents left the room. Jolena smiled. She had never known a time when they all stayed.

"The vagina should be large enough to permit comfortable intercourse, because this is what we are making it for." He continued without even turning to see who had left the room.

"We do not want hair-bearing skin within the vagina, and its direction should be more superior than posterior. Now, a serious complication in gender conversion surgery is derived from mishandling the urethra. The meatus must be patulous, for stenosis is not long tolerated. The urinary stream must go in a direction that allows the patient to sit. The perineum must be as close to female as possible and be free from the discomforts of a tender penile stump and scar tissue."

At this time, Dr. Charles began to dissect the large penis. This was the longest part of the surgery. The penis would be stripped carefully until it was a small stump to be used only to urinate from. The total time of the operation would last as long as eight hours.

This surgery had been his creation, and he had become quite successful. He taught the technique to many young doctors from all over the world. He also taught Dr. Peter Edgewater.

"You are going to be a fine surgeon in this field. I hope you carry your compassion to your office and treat them as well as you do in the operating room," he told Edgewater privately. He also commented that after doctors started making large amounts of money, they sometimes fell down in their habits. Overblown egos and pockets had caused many of them to lose their sense of values.

He and Edgewater had become quite close. Many times they socialized together. It had been Dr. Charles's wife, Gloria, that seemed to cement the relationship. She had developed a liking for the young, handsome doctor. Bernie knew this, but he had trusted her discretion and good judgment. He later found out that she had neither when it came to Dr. Edgewater. By the time Edgewater left his training program, he and Gloria had become very much involved.

Dr. Charles had been openly humiliated by their affair. Neither Gloria nor Edgewater seem to care or realize the embarrassment heaped upon him. Then came the suffering that Gloria experienced when Edgewater dumped her, after using her as a stepping stone. Gloria had finally confessed to her husband her generosity to Edgewater. Besides large amounts of cash, she had even given him the ten-carat emerald Dr. Charles had bought her in South America. It had been a perfect stone, and he had been proud to present it to this wife. Now it was gone, her love from him was gone, and within two years, depressed and anorectic, Gloria committed suicide.

Bernie was devastated, destroyed. He resigned from the hospital and refused to see or talk with anyone except Jolena. Maybe it was because she was a "neutral" person. She understood and respected his habits and idiosyncrasies. She would listen to him, sit with him, and comfort him.

He became obsessed with Edgewater's career. When Edgewater emerged as the "new doctor in town," he urged Jolena to accept any job offer from him. He knew that Edgewater's greed would destroy him; Jolena would give him an account along the way. Edgewater had long forgotten Gloria and Bernie Charles. He never suspected that Jolena had remained fiercely loyal to Bernie, keeping him abreast of everything.

Bernie's desire for another cognac brought him out of the past. He poured a drink and walked back to the window. The bare limbs of the trees reminded him of naked women lifting their arms up to him for help. He took a large gulp of the cognac and smiled. It wouldn't be long. A young girl would finally destroy Edgewater.

14

"Take me to the Waldorf, please." Mark requested when he entered the cab outside the doctor's office.

"Yes, sir!" The cab driver was happy. It was a good fare downtown.

Mark looked around the city as the cab raced down Park Avenue. It was almost four years since he came to New York to see the doctor who would help alter his lifestyle. Then, he was twenty-three years old, had a degree in physical education, and was extremely unhappy that he could not live life as a man. He remembered the quizzical expression on Jolena's face when she called him in for the interview four years ago...

"Sit down, please, Marsha." Jolena was engrossed with the personal history report that Marsha had completed.

Marsha was frightened. What if they did not accept her? She had heard this was the office to get done what you wanted without a lot of legal hassles, especially the sex change operation. Marsha Hunter wanted to be a man. She had been raised on a Pennsylvania farm with a strict father and four brothers and no mother. After Marsha's birth, her mother had deserted the family. Marsha was raised in tomboy fashion. It was common and acceptable. Everyone said she would grow out of it. However, Marsha liked the way she was growing.

She believed that one day she would grow to be a man. She could ride a horse, run a tractor, and milk cows faster than her brothers. Education was pressed upon her by the father. Although her brothers quit school early, Marsha was compelled to finish. She did not mind going to school. There, she was able to see and be with Millie Downs. Millie had long blond curls, cow-milk complexion, and the largest blue eyes in the county. Marsha was stunned by her beauty. She did not want to be like her; she just wanted to be with her. Whenever the boys would pull on Millie's curls, Marsha would take over as the gallant knight and fight to keep all hands off Millie. They became best friends. At the age of fourteen, an incident occurred that caused that friendship to end.

Millie was a constant visitor to the farm where Marsha lived. She would travel each Saturday by bicycle and spend the day while Marsha attended to her various farm duties. Marsha was proud to show off in front of Millie. It made her feel proud, strong, and more manly as Millie watched her tackle the various farm chores.

"I bet you can't find me!" Millie yelled out as she went up into the hay loft in the barn.

"You go up there, and I can find you. I know every inch of that hay." Marsha laughed as she watched her pretty friend climb the ladder.

After a few minutes Marsha yelled out.

"You better be hidden good, because I am coming up there and I'll find you."

She could hear Millie giggle. Marsha swung her boyish frame quickly up the ladder and into the loft. She knew where Millie would hide. She pretended to search as she called out to her.

"Millie! You sure did hide out good." Slowly she made her way to where Millie had hidden down inside the hay.

"Boo!" Marsha yelled. Millie screamed and laughed.

Marsha laughingly fell down into the hay, and the two girls rolled around. Then Marsha found herself on top of Millie. They both became silent. Slowly Marsha reached her hand down into Millie's panties. She tenderly fondled Millie, pressing her body close. She gyrated slowly, rubbing her private parts against Millie. Both remained silent except for the heavy breathing. Marsha released her passion by urinating between the young girl's legs. It was then that they held each other and kissed. Without conversation, mystified, and embarrassed, Millie left and never came back.

Marsha was sad and confused. Deep in her heart, she felt that if she had been a male, Millie would have come back. She vowed on that day to leave that farm and become a man. After graduating from high school, she went to college and became a physical education teacher. At least in that field, she did not have to pretend femininity. She took on many masculine features and the trials and tribulations of dates with fellows who repeatedly tried to have sex with her. Sex with men did not interest her.

Gradually she appeared more masculine. Her wardrobe consisted of pantsuits, slacks, and jeans. Her handsome face was clear of all makeup. She had cultivated masculine ways of walking, standing, shaking hands, and talking. She lowered the tone of her voice and acquired a directness of manner and speech associated with men. These characteristics were carried to such an extreme that sometimes it was difficult to remember that she was Marsha.

Although the attitudes towards gays had not made a drastic change, this did not deter Marsha's plans to change her sex. She knew people considered her a lesbian, but she had no plans to live as a lesbian. She was now twenty-four years old, and she wanted a sex change. Although she had built her body into splendid muscular form, she hated to see her breasts and knew she had a vagina that was useless to her.

"Do you prefer for me to call you Mark or Marsha?" Jolena had asked.

"Please call me Marsha. I am gradually changing over in my dress habits. After my operation, you can call me Mark all the time."

"What about your job? Will this affect your job?"

"No, because as soon as I have my change, I shall move to another state. I'll make a clean break. With my education, I will have no trouble teaching."

"If the doctor approves you for the surgery, we can help you get the necessary document for your birth certificate change, and you can also change your educational records."

Jolena smiled at her. Marsha appreciated her kindness and found it easy to admire Jolena's manner and appearance. Her tan color and black hair were also appealing. She wondered if she was black or Hispanic. It didn't matter. To Marsha, she was beautiful. Jolena requested Marsha to roll up her shirt sleeve so she could look at the appearance of her arms.

"Well, Marsha, you have been pumping iron, or are you taking male hormones?"

"Both."

"What kind of hormones?"

"Some sort of androgen supplement. I get it from a druggist."

Marsha opened her shirt to display her chest muscles. The small breasts were almost lost in muscle bulge.

"Wow! That's great. It looks good." Jolena was impressed. Marsha felt proud.

"Miss Taylor, I hope the doctor can do this operation for me. I am so unhappy like this."

"I know, Marsha. Or, at least, I can imagine." Jolena smiled that charming smile. "I think he can help you. You go in and see him now. I'll speak to you later."

Jolena knew that Edgewater would take the case. She knew he had never done one like this, but he would appear experienced with the patient.

Marsha entered the treatment room and waited for Dr. Edgewater. When he entered, Marsha could see that the doctor was impressed.

"Marsha, glad to meet you." Dr. Edgewater extended his hand, and Marsha returned a masculine grip. "I read here that you are on hormones."

"Yes, but I have to get them on my own. It is difficult to find a doctor who is willing to talk with me about what I want."

"I understand, yes, I understand."

Dr. Edgewater quickly glanced over the chart. He looked again at the woman. He was impressed with the masculine details she had incorporated, such as the short haircut and the suit. She seemed a handsome man.

"Do you ever completely cross-dress, or do you keep it modest, as you are now? Will this surgery interfere with your job?"

"I dress like this most of the time, but I have dressed as a man. I really look better that way. I feel like a man. I wear a wedding band at work so no one will ask me out. The job is not important. I intend on moving."

The doctor scrutinized her face with its bony and prominent cheekbones and masculine jaw. Her hair was midnight black, and she had green eyes. The shape of her nose was perfect. Marsha could have been a very beautiful woman, but now she wanted to become a handsome man. *How sad,* thought Dr. Edgewater.

"I will have to do a total hysterectomy and a bilateral mastectomy."

"You have to interpret that for me."

"Sorry, of course. I would have to remove all of your female organs, uterus, and both breasts."

"All at the same time?"

"Yes, we might as well get it over."

Marsha sighed with relief.

"I will be happy to get rid of those things. I hate them. I should have never been born like this."

Dr. Edgewater continued.

"The total surgery will cost six thousand dollars, and I must have that before surgery. I will send you to our psychiatrist. You need only one visit, and he will approve the fact that you are a candidate for surgery. His fee is one hundred dollars. Jolena will make an appointment for you."

"One moment, doctor. I want to ask you about the most important feature. The penis. How does it grow on me, or how do you go about attaching one that is functional?"

Dr. Edgewater could feel his own uneasiness about that subject, but being a doctor, he had an answer for all questions.

"Well, that would have to come at a later time. Actually, it does grow, but it has to do with skin grafts and a lot of intricate surgery you just would not understand at this time." He had to admit to himself that he himself did not understand that type of surgery and had never taken on such a project.

"How long would I have to wait? That is very important to me. I would like to function as close to a complete man as possible."

Peter shifted uneasily in his chair. He was appalled that this woman could actually think about being a man. And a complete man. There was no way he could possibly think of attaching a penis onto her private parts.

"I am willing to pay whatever it might cost," Marsha added.

"Well, that would be at least a year or two down the road. But don't worry about it now. We'll take care of it then. Trust me."

And Peter Edgewater could be trusted to give it his deepest priority and the highest price he could charge. The thought of his fee for a penile attachment prompted him to read up on such surgery.

Dr. Edgewater shook Marsha's hand, and she left the room.

Marsha was disappointed with the quick consultation. There were other questions, but she would ask them later. Maybe the nurse would help. She appeared at Jolena's desk.

"Did you find out what you wanted to know?"

"No." The disappointment showed.

"Sit here and we'll talk. It's not busy today. Sometimes the doctor gets tired, but he has trained me to answer some of your questions. Do not feel that you have been neglected. He is going to do the surgery, but first I must make an appointment with the psychiatrist."

Marsha sat down and nodded in approval. She felt comfortable. Jolena had been kind and acceptable of her.

"Here is a packet of literature explaining the surgery. Afterwards, we will put you on hormone therapy. These will be injections. I'll teach you how to do your own injections. Never allow anyone to use your needle or medication."

Marsha was pleased, and her hopes soared. Jolena went into more detail.

"After taking the hormones, you will find more hair growth on your body. Also, your voice will take on a more husky tone. I know that will make you happy." She smiled. "Now, as soon as we get the letter from the psychiatrist, I will call, and we will set a date for surgery. The cost of the surgery is six thousand dollars. This will cover surgery and hospitalization. If you pay cash, then we do not have to go through a waiting period with the insurance company's inquiries, and your privacy is better protected."

"I'll pay cash so it can be over and done with." Marsha saw a way out of the life she was leading and wanted no interference.

"Call me later today, and I'll give you the appointment for the psychiatrist, and three days later, we can book your surgical date."

Marsha was pleased. She thanked Jolena and promised to call later that day. Jolena was pleased that Marsha left the office in such a jovial mood, but even Jolena knew there should be more than a one-day consultation with a psychiatrist or surgeon for the drastic surgery that Marsha desired. Surely Marsha should have undergone psychiatric, psychological, endocrinological, urological, gynecological, legal, and social evaluation. She was disappointed that the doctor had not incorporated these other areas into his final evaluation and decision on surgery. But Jolena also knew that if a patient had to wait for all the returns from all the proper referrals, it could take a year or two years before formal approval would be granted. Dr. Edgewater found a way to work around all that formality.

Within two weeks, Marsha had the operation. Within two more weeks, she was coming to the office for her postop visits. Now she dressed as a man and was referred to by her new name, Mark Nelson.

Even Jolena had to admit how handsome Mark had become. His manner of dress was always a suit, vest, and tie. He always carried his briefcase. He had grown a slight beard. It was extremely difficult for anyone to even think that this person had once been a complete woman. Jolena was especially proud of him. His body movements were masculine in motion. His stride was long and straight. He displayed more muscular control over his body. No feminine hand movements were displayed.

Mark himself was amazed at the change. He had never expected it to be so perfect. Now, he visited the office two or three times a week. He found himself thinking about Jolena more and more. She had become his fixation. Mark felt he had fallen in love with her, and Jolena was beginning to sense his feelings. She suspected that he was coming to the office to see her more than to be seen by the doctor. It had been three months since the surgery, and Jolena felt she had to speak to him about the situation.

"Mark, I do not think you have to come back for any more visits. I know that you are interested in a penile attachment but the doctor told you that would have to wait a couple of years. I think it's time for you to get on with that life you said you were going after." She looked at him directly. "You can't like me. I am not the one. You only feel that way because I've helped you and befriended you."

"Then you know how I feel?"

"Anybody can see from the way you look at me. Even one of the patients inquired whether you were my boyfriend."

Mark laughed and was relieved.

"I guess you are right. But you will always be my favorite girl. Well, I've got a job offer, and I'll be off to Maine in a few weeks. Now, does that you feel better?"

"I'm happy for you, and you will always be my favorite guy."

He embraced her, and she allowed him to hold her for a few minutes. Despite all she knew about him, she felt good in his arms. It made Jolena realize that she was lonely and would like to be loved and be in love. She allowed him to kiss her and then broke away. They both laughed.

It was the cab driver's husky voice that broke through his thoughts.

"This is it. The Waldorf."

Mark was glad to get to the hotel. He felt tired tonight. His first move would be to call Francine and tell her the good news. Francine, who he was going to marry, had never pushed him to have any additional surgery or "fixing." She was happy with him as he was. This was definitely Mark's quest.

As soon as he got to his room, Mark went to the bathroom and as he sat down on the toilet, he saw it again. It was blood and bright red in color.

"Oh, shit," he whispered, "I thought it had stopped."

Mark had been spotting on and off for almost six months. He refused to mention it to anyone, not even to Jolena. He was sure it was not serious. However, what part of his anatomy could this blood be coming from? The doctor had performed a complete hysterectomy. What started out as spotting had now become bright red bleeding. He found it necessary to wear several layers of tissue inside his underwear. Now he was wearing a pad. Maybe should have told Jolena or, at least, the doctor. No, that might delay his impending surgery.

Despite all that had been done on him surgically, the main thing he wanted had not yet been done. Would his life ever be complete? The doctor had filled him with great expectation. Jolena had not been too pleased with his seeking additional surgery, but he knew she had his best interest at heart. He did not want any more disappointments. Maybe he should call Jolena and tell her what was happening to him.

No, the bleeding would stop, just as it had before. He did not have time to think about that little problem. He put on the television. That would wipe away bad thoughts.

15

Arnold was well aware that Clarence had become obsessed with him. But then, wasn't that the way it always turned out with those big black corrections officers who vowed never to allow a faggot to touch them, much less suck their dick? However, Clarence had succumbed to the act more than a dozen times with Arnold. Each time, Clarence had vowed it would be the last. Now he was finding it more difficult to resist. He refused to even allow the idea of it being love. After all, he had a wife and two children. Every time Clarence thought about his children, who were boys, he shuddered. What if his boys grew up to be faggots? He didn't know which way to turn.

Arnold loved the intrigue! He was proud to have captured a correction officer. It had been fun, and he was enjoying every moment and every moment of Clarence's misery. However, Clarence began to interfere with Arnold's nightly stroll. He did not want Arnold out there, stealing from men and sucking dick. Of course, Arnold reassured him that he might rob a few men, but never sucked their dicks. He further reassured him that his penis was the only one he sucked with such love and tenderness. Strangely enough, Clarence believed him, but he still insisted that Arnold get a job.

A job! Arnold had never had a legitimate job in his life. His only job was thieving and luring men. What would he do with a real job? Every time Clarence got on his job campaign, Arnold pretended to listen, then responded with seriousness. He knew that a job would be impossible with his lifestyle. "Twiddle-de-dee," he whispered to himself, then stretched his large black body on his antique bed and dreamed of being Scarlet O'Hara. The ringing phone broke his daydreaming. "God, who disturbs me now," he whispered as he snatched the receiver.

"Hello, and why are you calling me, whoever you are?"

"Baby, it's me, Clarence. I'm calling you back. Get up now and go down to the hospital in Harlem. They are hiring. I know someone there, and they will hire you."

"Who? Me?" Arnold was shocked.

"Yes, bitch, you." Clarence yelled back. He had learned how to handle this drag queen.

"I ain't going. I ain't going. To do what? Scrub floors? Not me. I rather go out every night and suck dick." He knew that would upset Clarence.

"I made an appointment for you. Now you get up and go before I come there and kick your black ass all over the Concourse."

Arnold sat up. He knew Clarence meant business. Also, he liked Clarence to be authoritative with him. It made him feel like a woman.

"What name did you give them?"

"Arnold, Arnold Brown. What other fucking name should I give them?"

"Lottie Lee." Arnold's voice was firm.

"Lottie Lee! You dumb fuck. How are you going to work with that name?"

"Because I will be Lottie Lee. If you think that I am going to work looking like a man, you are dead wrong. If you want me to work, then I will work only as a woman. I will be a nurse's aide. I won't be no janitor. Now, since you are so damn resourceful, you call back and tell them that you are sending someone else and her name is Lottie Lee." Arnold was finished. There was silence on the other end. "Clarence, darling, are you there?"

"Okay, bitch. And you better go down there."

"Are you going to come and take me there?"

"Hell, no. In that costume! I told you I don't like that shit."

"You like that shit when I suck your dick."

"I'm hanging up!"

Arnold heard the click and knew that Clarence was mad. He thought again about the job. It might be interesting. Maybe he would give it a try. It might turn out to be fun. He might meet someone even more interesting than Clarence. Now Arnold felt energized. A new challenge. He got up and selected his daytime female clothes and makeup. Wouldn't the neighbors be surprised and impressed. Arnold Brown going out to work and in the daylight. Yes, he would be impressive.

Arnold had considered dressing in red to go for the job interview, but he thought it best to be more conservative. He chose a tank-type dress that reached almost to the middle of his hairy legs. His shape was that of a large woman. His makeup was quiet. His wig, decent in appearance, set sedately on his head. He hoped that the neighbors would get a peek at him. Then they would realize that Arnold knew how to dress in a proper manner, especially when he was going for a job interview.

There was never a doubt about his being hired, because all the arrangements had been taken care of in advance.

It was only the formality of the interview that raised many questions and eyebrows.

"What is your name?" asked the interviewer.

"Arnold Brown, but I demand to be called Lottie Lee."

"Lottie Lee? I don't understand?"

"Understand that I am a woman trapped in this horrible man's body, and I am truly Lottie Lee."

The interviewer, a woman, stared at him, puzzled.

"I don't quite understand the problem—"

"My main problem is a job. I need a job, and I am a good worker." Arnold stared directly at her face.

She avoided his eyes while she continued the interview.

"Are you experienced in taking care of sick people?"

"Of course. I take care of a lot of sick people."

"Do you have reference from any of the previous patients you took care of?"

"Of course. You just get in touch with Mr. Clarence Brown, no relation, and he will verify my previous experience. Now, when do I begin to work? And I want my checks made out to Arnold Brown."

"Okay, Mr. Brown—"

"No, sweetie, not Mr. Brown. Lottie, Lottie. Remember what I told you?"

"Oh, yes. Lottie, Lottie Lee."

After the interview and necessary signing of papers, Arnold was told that he would begin working the next day. He was quite annoyed. That hardly gave him time to get his busy life in order. When issued uniforms, he requested a dress type of uniform but was sadly informed that everyone wore pants and tops. Arnold made it a point that he should not be issued a male type of uniform. He got his wish. Arnold was also informed that he would be working in the medical ward, where he would be of great service, because with his large body build, he would be able to assist in getting patients in and out of bed.

Arnold did not take kindly to that and reminded them that he was a "woman trapped in a man's body." His statement was respected; Arnold knew that this was going to be a fun place to be in the daytime. Slowly, he began to feel pride seeping into his body. Now he was a legal person, with a job, getting a paycheck. He owed it all to dear

Clarence. He must remember to suck his dick extra super when he saw him again.

When he left the hospital and descended into the subway, he noticed that people took extra glances toward him. He was certain that they were admiring his daytime outfit. When he stood next to a gentleman on the train, Arnold's fingers itched to go into the man's pocket. *How easy it would be to take that wallet,* he thought. Of course the man was not rich, but who knows what is in a wallet. Arnold smiled and made his way to an empty seat. He looked at the gentleman and remembered his principles. The man was black.

16

Belinda knew for a fact that she was an expert at sucking dick. So did the various boys she had done in the quiet stairwells of the Co-Corp complex. In her senior year of high school, she had been a true free spirit and practiced fellatio on all the boys. However, she was not like the other girls who gave up their virginity. Not Belinda! She remained a virgin in spite of all the sex games she indulged in. Belinda was saving her virgin pussy for the right man, and he had to be a rich man who could remove her from her present living conditions.

Belinda hated being poor. Living in a high-rise in Co-Corp was what she considered even middle class. She wanted to live downtown close to the plush apartment buildings and have doorman service. She wanted to be rich, or at least, have a rich husband. After working summers in the various Bronx hospitals, she learned that the person in the hospital with money was the doctor. So her goal then was to capture a doctor. Now Belinda's aim was to be in the correct place at the correct time to meet the correct person.

After securing a job in the operating room at a small Bronx hospital, Belinda kept a keen eye out for an unmarried doctor who would cast a second glance. She had heard a lot about Dr. Peter Edgewater and had finally gotten the opportunity to circulate in the room in which he was operating. Belinda made sure her scrub dress was fitting a little tighter. On their first meeting, she was only able to make eye contact, but she could sense that he was interested. Later, she learned that he had made inquiries about her. Now she would have to be a little more aggressive.

She purposely lingered outside the operating room, where he could see her in all her glory, without the cap and mask. He looked in awe at the flowing blond hair, beautiful, white, flawless skin, and blue eyes set into a captivating face. He had to have her. Yes, Belinda, the little Co-Corp City, free dick-sucking whore had attracted Dr. Edgewater's attention. He invited her to lunch, she accepted. Later he invited her to dinner, she accepted. He then invited her to work with him as his assistant, she accepted. And when he invited her to bed, she accepted.

And it was there that she was the champion. She was the expert; she was the creator; she was in charge. Belinda took Peter Edgewater to bed and performed sex acts on him he had never experienced. However, when he discovered that she was a virgin and he would be the first to have her, he was as overwhelmed as he was impressed. He wanted her. He wanted to marry her. He wanted her to move into his apartment with him. She didn't care, just as long as she could leave the Bronx.

But Peter was more than generous. He made her his "physician assistant," a fairly new title at that time. And when he told her about the new title, she rewarded him with the most devastating act of fellatio she ever performed. She knew from then on that she was secure. Belinda had her doctor, and he was rich, and she was going to be his wife. Of course, it would not be easy at first. He talked of his plans for her to work in the office and assist him in surgery. She would go along with that for a while but not for long. Belinda wanted to relax and go shopping at Saks, Bloomingdale's and Bergdorf. After all, wasn't that what doctor's wives did while their husbands worked?

And then there was the young lover she had left behind in the Bronx. They had only engaged in oral sex, but now that she found the right man to give her virginity to, Belinda was disappointed in the small dick that Peter had put into her. It was then that she realized how much better one of those big hard dicks that she had sucked would fulfill the emptiness Peter had left her with. She thought about Ricky, who lived one floor above her parents' apartment. She had sucked his dick many times but never allowed him to fuck her. She had vowed to fuck him every night until she married Peter. Then she would have to arrange a different schedule, but that would be no problem.

Today was the first chance in weeks that she was able to get away from Peter. One free day was what Belinda needed. She had already alerted her girlfriend to get in touch with Ricky and tell him that she would be up in the Bronx. Peter was safely tied up in the operating room. That way, he could not make phone calls in an attempt to locate her.

Ricky was waiting for her in front of the apartment building. She went into his arms immediately. They kissed passionately from the lobby into the elevator. Once inside her bedroom, which her parents still maintained for her, they both stripped off their clothes. In a matter of minutes, he had inserted his hard penis into her vagina. She was ecstatic. Peter would never be able to fuck her this way.

"Why not tell the truth?"

"What truth? About what?"

"Why can't I find you. Where are you hiding? I know there is another man."

"Ricky, you got to understand. If you promise to understand, then I will tell you the truth."

"Okay, I'll understand. I can understand better if you tell me the truth."

"There is this doctor who is in love with me. Believe me! He's in love, not me! I love you! But it's all about money. Ricky, it's all about money! He has made me a physician assistant, with all the legal papers. Do you know what that means? I'm nothing but a high school graduate. I need this man, and I need his money and his influence."

Ricky lay back and listened to Belinda. It was always easier to listen to Belinda after sex. All the frustration and anger was out of him. He knew she was a common slut. A trashy white bitch who could suck your dick and make you love her. He loved her and thought they would be together, but he had forgotten about her ambitions. Belinda was a complicated person with problems that Ricky did not want to deal with. He knew that sooner or later he would not want her. Now he wondered if she had found a new source for her habit.

"You want that other thing I got for you?"

"Oh, God, yes!"

Ricky went to his jacket and pulled out the glasine bag containing the white powder.

"Does he give you this?"

"Don't be a fool! He knows nothing about this. He can hardly give me dick, let alone this."

Ricky prepared several rows of the cocaine for her to consume. Belinda wasted no time. She sniffed and sniffed. As Ricky questioned her, she answered all questions, talked, and sniffed more cocaine.

"His dick is small. I suck it almost every day. Sometimes twice a day. I thought once a week would be enough for him, but he has some kind of souped-up energy. I hate sucking his dick, but what can I do? When he fucks me, he comes almost before he gets it in my pussy, and he never puts his tongue down there like you do."

She reached for him, and he embraced her. Belinda lay back, twisting her body and moaning.

"Please suck my pussy. I need it. I need it. I need you to love me. Please, Ricky."

He put his head between her legs and made her feel the madness that accompanies the joy of a climax. After consuming and enjoying each other, they sniffed the cocaine and verbalized their cocaine fantasies.

"I am going to be rich, and it won't take all my life." Belinda assured him. "You must wait for me. Don't fall in love with anyone else. Wait for me. I'll be back."

Ricky knew that Belinda only came back for the sex. He knew that the visits would become less and less and he would lose her. She would find another man somewhere. Ricky had lots of women to pick from, and he was going to make sure he had one. He was not going to stand around holding his dick while he waited for Belinda to play her little games. He fed her some more cocaine and watched how greedily she sniffed.

"I have to pay for this shit, Belinda. Don't be so greedy."

"I have money. I'll give you money."

Ricky accepted it. He sure in hell couldn't afford to pay for her habit.

Later that afternoon, Belinda returned to the office.

"Good afternoon, Jolena." She was actually mellow as she spoke to the person she disliked.

Jolena looked at her in astonishment and returned the greeting.

"Is Peter in yet?"

"No, but he has called several times for you. He'll be here shortly."

Belinda went directly to Peter's office. She had to psych herself up to the routine again and prepare to tell the lies. She could certainly use that cocaine now. How foolish of her not to have brought some with her. It would have made the rest of the day easier to bear.

Jolena wondered why they were not together this day. *Well, little Belinda is taking off by herself,* she thought. *Wonder where she spent the day.* Jolena detected something not quite right. She smiled. Poor Peter. He really doesn't understand how life can be with a young girl. But he would learn.

17

Louis stared up into the large painted face. He was actually aware that Ms. Lottie Lee resembled a man dressed up like a woman. But a second thought reassured him that this would not happen in a hospital. Surely there were no drag queens allowed to work in hospitals. Louis was sure of only one thing; she was ugly! And he hated how the small, round, black suspicious eyes stared back at him. But he was fascinated by the nose. He had never seen anyone so ugly with such a perfect nose. He laughed and continued laughing. Louis continued to stare at her.

"So, what's funny? Have you got a problem with me?"

He noticed her even-spaced white teeth. Immediately, he ran his tongue across his own cavities.

"Oh, no. I ain't got no problem. I'm glad you're here. I sure can use some help."

"The nurses said you can't do anything for yourself. Can you or can't you? I gotta know, because I can't be wasting my time doing all the work if you can do it for yourself?"

He felt her resentment. The nerve of this ugly bitch, he simmered, talking to him like he was nothing. If he could move his hand, he'd smack her directly in the face.

"I can't do much today, so I would like you to help me out."

He spoke softly. He needed help and didn't want to chase her away.

Ignoring him, Lottie surveyed the small room.

"You are Louis Frazier?"

"Of course I am. Why?"

She placed both hands on her hips.

"Well, what do you mean by you 'can't do much today'? From what I hear, you can't do nothing today or tomorrow."

The thundering voice and its message sent shock waves through Louis's brain. He hated her.

"Bitch!" he yelled. "You gotta help me today because I can't move today. Maybe I'll move tomorrow or tonight, but can't you fuckin' understand that this body controls itself at certain times? I need to be cleaned. Now!"

His face was distorted with anger.

"My name is not 'bitch'." It is Ms. Lottie Lee, and I'll see you another time."

Lottie turned and left before she acted like the Arnold she was. *The nerve of this sick nonmovable fuck,* she thought. *My first day on the job, and this sick fuck is going to cause me to lose the job. Clarence, too, will be through with me.* So Ms. Lottie Lee, also known and loved as Arnold when he was in Clarence's arms, went to the nursing office and pleaded for another assignment for that day until she could gather her "emotions" after seeing poor Louis Frazier.

Alone in his small room, Louis Frazier cried. There was nothing else he could do. Oldtimer appeared at the door.

"Well, my man, you sure blew that," Oldtimer whispered, shaking his head regretfully.

"Man, leave me alone. I can't talk to you now."

Oldtimer retrieved some tissues from the bathrobe and wiped the tears flowing down Louis's face. He continued to lecture.

"You gots to think carefully, my man, 'cause the big ugly woman is your key. Yeah, she is your key to a lotta things. Like clean linen, a good bath, better food, and a lotta other extra things you didn't know existed in this place. But you talk all wrong to a woman."

"I know how to talk to them," Louis snorted.

"But you don't know the facts. Listen closely to Oldtimer's facts. Fact, the woman is ugly. Now what do all women, whether they is ugly or beautiful, want? Fact, to be told that they are beautiful. You gots to talk bullshit to them, my man. Fact, flattery, that excites them, makes them think you are what's at the end of the rainbow. You can't move them arms or legs, but, fact, you can talk. And, my man, you needs to talk fast, because you look in bad condition, and you smell real bad."

Oldtimer frowned and moved away from Louis.

"It's too late. She won't come back."

"She'll be back. So study your words for tomorrow."

When Louis awoke the next morning, he turned his head and his eyes met the nurse's picture. Just like him, he thought, it never changes. He'd try Oldtimer's way and concentrate on how to win over Ms. Lottie Lee.

Louis Frazier was awarded another opportunity.

"Good morning, Mr. Frazier."

It was her, and the voice sounded deep and stern.

"Good morning, Ms. Lee." He smiled. His eyes pleaded forgiveness. "I'm sure glad you're taking care of me today."

He lied, and yet, there was much truth in the statement.

"Well, I'm not glad to be taking care of you!" There was plenty of truth in that statement.

He reminded himself not to get upset. Surely, there must be some compassion in this ugly beast.

Lottie began bathing him. "I'm so happy to get a bath." Without a reply, she watched his face. "Damn, the water's cold."

She stopped and sneered.

"Cold or hot, you're lucky to get washed!"

"I'm sorry. I'm . . . I'm not blaming you. It's this damn place. I guess there ain't no hot water."

Silently, Lottie resumed bathing him. Carelessly, she splashed cold water on his body. He hated her. If he could move his hand from its anchored position, he'd slap her. There was a small area on his face she had not washed. This would annoy him all day.

"Ms. Lee."

"What?"

"There's a spot on my left cheek that you missed. Could you please—"

"I ain't got time now. Can't you see I'm busy? You ain't the only sick one I got to take care of." She gathered up her equipment and left.

"Ms. Lee, my face!" His voice was loud and demanding.

Her voice yelled back to him.

"I ain't got time, Mr. Frazier. I'll see you later."

That was the most familiar phrase used in the hospital. Later meant the next day, the next week, or not at all.

The malodor of his body, the feces, urine, and sweat permeated the small room. Louis smelled it. Oldtimer smelled it.

"Man, this place stinks so bad, even the cockroaches stay away."

"Get the fuck out! I'm tired of you and your suggestions."

"You gotta flatter her. Tell her you missed her."

"I could never miss her."

"Tell her you need her."

"I sure in hell don't need her. This body will move, sooner or later."

"Well, show me some movement, now."

"I ain't ready, and it ain't ready. Just leave me alone."

Oldtimer proudly left. Louis felt bitter frustration and disappointment.

Attendants came to feed and clean him. They performed their job with sloppy indifference. The realization of a better life in the hospital began to dawn on him. Was she the answer? If so, he had to secure her friendship and, above all, her affection. Oldtimer was right. He would make her his lover and provider. But he must not allow her to suspect his motivations, he was in no position to bear her wrath.

Now the plan was challenging and stimulating. His face flushed with excitement. His eyes darted down toward the catheter. He was urinating. It inched sluggishly down the catheter into a plastic bag. Louis knew he would have to get rid of that tube. How would he ever make love to Lottie Lee with that tube in the way?

18

There would never be enough silicone for Lita. No matter who pumped it. So again she visited Dr. Snyder's office. It was as she expected. Empty. He was not one for promoting business and had plans for retiring in the very near future. But only Lita knew that he would do silicone injections for the right amount of money, and Lita had the money. She never shared this doctor with any of the other street queens.

Despite her money, Dr. Snyder was not happy to see her come into his office. He knew that it would be a session of demands for more in this spot and more in that spot. He could hardly refuse her. She did bring the right amount of cash with her. That was the only thing that made her welcome.

"I need more body, and you gotta do some corrections on what you've already done," she complained.

Snyder knew damn well that all the imperfections she complained about did not come from his few sessions. Did she think he was so stupid that he did not know she visited Edgewater's office for the majority of her silicone?

Dr. Snyder did not get intimidated by Lita's complaints or demands.

"Stop complaining and get in the treatment room before I decide not to do you."

"And don't ask me how much I am spending," she retorted. "You know I always spend big money."

It made her feel proud and important to inform him that she had such large amounts to spend on her body. She went inside to the treatment room.

After she had stripped naked, he stared intently at the disgusting sight in front of him. He had to be kind.

"Now what could possibly be wrong with this body?"

"It's not even. I want it even."

He could clearly see the imperfections of the naked body, but did not want to be the one to say the truth.

"How much are you spending, Lita? And where do you want it put today?"

"Put in the usual thousand. And put some in my face and some more in my legs and ankles."

Dr. Snyder tried again not to show his distaste as he looked over the entire body. He could see that she had enough silicone for a lifetime. The uneven bulges of her buttocks and the discoloration of the skin was prominent. He knew she was not concerned. All she wanted was to be pumped! He sighed. A few more treatments from him wouldn't hurt or harm. If he didn't do it, she'd go somewhere else and spend the money. He might as well get it.

"Now, doc, don't forget my ankles."

"I think you've had enough there."

"I want more, please, just do it!"

He didn't argue. He'd just charge her extra.

"It will cost you another hundred if I do those ankles."

"I don't care. Just do them."

He could see the unshapely bulges and knew that the silicone had drifted. Well, he'd just stick in the needles and pretend he was injecting the silicone. Lita would never know.

"I will need some around my knees and in the middle of my legs. My ankles are getting bigger than my legs so I have to have them balanced."

She lay on the treatment table. He picked up a syringe and attached a large needle. Dr. Snyder used a large caliber needle in order to push the silicone into the body with ease and quickness. The silicone was thick and oily. Many transvestites had thought at one time that silicone was nothing but ordinary oil, that any oil would do; baby oil, cooking oil, cleaning oil, hair oil, face oil, and even motor oil. A few of them had attempted to inject each other with some kind of oil.

The disfigurations and complications were something they carried with them for life. There were large hard balls in the cheeks of the face. Eyes almost swollen shut due to large amounts of oil pumped into their face. Bodies that had turned black and rock hard from being pumped with the oil. Oil that had been pumped into the buttocks often drifted way down the thighs and onto the knees. Eventually, it made its way to the ankles and feet, where it caused painful swelling and inflammation. Later, sometimes a year or two, the entire thighs, knees, legs, and ankles would become inflamed, painful, and discolored.

Dr. Snyder repeatedly filled the syringe and injected the silicone into the upper portion of Lita's hips. They swelled and the skin turned red and shiny. He twisted and turned the needle in various directions.

He could hear the crunch of the silicone that had previously settled there. He pushed silicone until it seeped out of the previous needle holes.

"I'm finished now." He was tired of looking at the distortion in front of him.

"Don't forget my legs."

He wanted to slap her at that moment. He began to realize just how much he hated Lita. Well, this would be the last time for her. But he had said that before. It was useless to try and reason with her. He'd just have to listen to her mouth threats. So Dr. Snyder continued. He inserted a smaller beveled needle and injected the inner aspect of her lower legs. They swelled into a large bulge. He injected more. Now the legs were red and shiny. He taped her body and legs. Lita was pleased and happy.

"You can get up. And, Lita, don't come back for one month."

"Don't worry. I'm running short of money. I got to hit those streets." She reached into her bag and pulled out a pack of money.

"It's all there."

He didn't bother to count it. He just wanted her out.

Lita dressed quickly and left. He was relieved. For some reason, he did not feel comfortable with her. Something sinister seemed to accompany her presence. Next time, he would definitely refuse her. She seemed to have developed a habit. Her thinking was as distorted as her body. He grabbed his coat and left the office. The first horse race was at eight, and he wanted to play the double.

Lita was neither insulted nor were her feelings hurt by the briskness of that doctor or any doctor. She had been treated worse than dirt by most of them. Lita neither liked nor trusted those she had dealt with on a short- or long-term basis. When she returned to her apartment, her feet felt heavy. *It's the silicone,* she thought. *The fuckin' shit is moving down into my feet. The doctor knew that and wouldn't say anything.* But she did remember that he had warned her even as he continued to take her money and injected more.

Lita removed her shoes and lay on the bed. She needed to relax, because she had to make the stroll tonight. Her favorite hundred-dollar bill filled with cocaine lay on the night stand. Lita greedily indulged herself. The cocaine kept the depression away. It made everything okay. She lay quiet for nearly thirty minutes. Then she felt a tightness in her groin. She knew that the silicone had moved. It had drifted from the side of her hips to the place of least resistance.

She got up and observed her body in the mirror. The unevenness was more apparent. One hip jutted out further than the other. Her left buttock was bigger than her right and slightly higher. Most of the skin color of her buttocks had lost its white color and had taken on a brownish discoloration. The skin on the buttocks and thighs had developed erythematous skin nodules that took on an orange peel appearance. The inside of her thighs all the way down to the knees were enlarged from the silicone in such disproportion that when she walked, they constantly rubbed together, causing the skin to be red, and painfully irritated.

The lower legs, where too much silicone had been injected, were hard and very discolored. This was the reason she covered her body with two or three pair of pantyhose. The excess of the silicone had dropped down to her ankles, which were now swollen and discolored. At times she had sensations of pins and needles in her feet. Especially at night, they often felt cold and numb.

What Lita did not understand was that her body had been injected with more silicone than it was able to tolerate. Silicone is slow-moving. It will shift to the point of least resistance. There it becomes a well-formed bulge, stretching the skin out of shape and preventing the skin from receiving its blood supply. Gradually, that portion of the skin loses its natural color. Silicone finally attaches and mingles with the other fat globules, making it impossible to remove without creating horrible scars and indentations in the area from which the surgical removal had taken place.

She was not interested in these complications. Her concern was only in the way her body looked now. According to Lita's philosophy, today is tomorrow and tomorrow is today. Before going to the mirror to view the horror that stared back at her when she lowered her G-string, she walked over to the small night table and dipped her long fingernail into the cocaine and sniffed again. Closing her eyes in ecstasy, she enjoyed the full effects of the drug. She dipped again and again. It was only then that she could lower her panties. Then she stared bravely at the mutilated stump of her penis.

Only one person besides Dr. Edgewater ever saw the mutilation; that was Jolena, who for some reason, she trusted her never to tell, even though Jolena would threaten to tell. She smiled. She knew Jolena used that ploy to keep her in line when she came to the office and acted up.

Lita enjoyed being "queen of queens." The other transvestites were fascinated by Lita's being the first sex change in the city. They would seek her out to ask questions and get advice on the operation.

When questioned about the wisdom of having a sex change, her answer was standard: "Well, you see how lovely I am. I hope you will surely be as lovely."

When questioned about the functioning of her vagina, her answer was standard: "It works great! I can take up to thirteen inches." That statement was powerful and made her the envy of most queens seeking to have a sex change.

When questioned concerning regrets about having such an operation, her answer was standard: "How could I ever, ever go back to that life? I am a full woman. I'm lovely. Just look at me. I am a woman with a pussy. How could I ever be happy living part man and part woman?" Her answers had been cheered by most, jeered by some, and puzzling to the rest.

Another large sniff of the cocaine and Lita could not care about viewing her nakedness. Her pubic hair was unusually thick. She went into the shower and began pulling through the hair. Much of it dropped onto the shower floor. They were glued on to appear thick. After showering, she scrubbed and massaged her bruised body. Lita looked into the mirror and grimaced with disgust. Without the artificial pubic hairs, the small penile stump revealed itself.

She stared in hatred at what had been a penis. She dared not touch or stimulate it in fear it would swell and get erected. Then it would take almost an hour to reduce. But more cocaine would take care of that action. She took two more large sniffs. That would keep the stump of the penis from erecting. Although it was just a stump of the penis, it retained all of its functions. The erections for Lita were painful and mentally devastating. Next, she took a small envelope, opened it and selected from the various miniature hair pieces. She applied glue to the tips and slowly pressed them around her pubic area, thereby hiding the penile stump. She laughed, proud of her clever disguise.

She lay on her small bed in the cluttered studio. There were trunks in the far corner and a closet filled with gowns she could use at the balls. There were boxes filled with pictures and makeup. The studio stayed in constant disarray. She always promised herself to clean it up one day and throw away unnecessary things. But they were all Lita's security blanket. They all belonged to her, and she would never throw out her years of collections. But sometimes she was lonesome. Even Lita wished she had someone to love her. Someone to caress her, kiss her, and hold her. A man. If she could only find a man who would love Lita, the real Lita. With that thought, she took another sniff of the drug. No, she laughed, that wasn't going to happen for Lita. This was it!

She surveyed her surroundings again and took another sniff in honor of her studio. It was home for her. She liked living alone. Lita would not allow anyone to invade her sanctuary. She trusted no one; therefore, no one would know the secrets of Lita. And Lita had secrets! She took more of the white powder and laughed.

"Lita, the sex change, here's to you." And another sniff as she continued her speech. "Lita, boy, girl, man, or woman. What is she, folks? Lita, the silicone queen; Lita, the sex change in name only; Lita, the liar; Lita, the whore; Lita, the fool; Lita, the human; Lita, poor little Jose; poor little Lita, the mutilated!"

She took one more big sniff of cocaine and whispered.

"Oh, yes, let us not forget, Lita the murderess!"

19

A few days later, after a short course on taking care of the sick and becoming familiar with hospital policy, Lottie Lee was ready to take care of Louis in a more proper and professional manner. She swooped into his room, loaded down with bed linens and towels. She neither spoke nor looked at him.

Get out! Get out! He wanted to scream, but he remembered his resolution.

"Good morning, Ms. Lee. How are you today?" he chirped in a falsetto voice.

"You trying to be funny, using that kinda voice?"

"No, no, I'm just glad to see you."

"With the condition you're in, I guess, you should be glad to see anybody."

"No, I'm glad to see you. Not just anybody, Ms. Lee, 'cause I found out that you are the best nurses' aide on this floor." Falsity was easy.

Lottie knew it was a lie. This was her first job, but she'd accept the compliment.

"You're right about that. Can't nobody take care of sick people as good as me."

He remembered to apologize.

"I'm so sorry, Ms. Lee, for talking wrong to you the other day. I didn't mean it. I was just upset. Nobody helps me, and when you walked in, I thought you were just another ordinary worker. Please forgive me."

He waited and measured her response.

"I think it was my fault, Mr. Frazier. I thought about it later and realized I was wrong. After all, you're sick and need help. Now I'm gonna clean you up real good."

The covers were discarded. She was shocked at how thin and dry his skin appeared. Lottie was thankful she wasn't sick and lying in a hospital. Maybe her life was a doubly dangerous one, but at least she could function without depending on another human being. Tenderly, Lottie lathered and rinsed his body. Then applications of oils and lotions were massaged into his limbs.

Louis pretended to feel the massage and moaned in ecstasy.

"You can feel that?"

"Oh, of course, it feels good. I ain't had nobody do that since I came here."

"Those nurses say you can't feel nothing, and you can't move nothing below your neck."

"What can they know about what I can do or feel? They ain't in here like you."

"Maybe you can move and walk." Lottie's voice was filled with wonder.

"Sure, but we gotta wait until these legs and arms are ready. Now, don't tell them out there. This is just between you and me. You just help me out, and we are going to give them one big-ass surprise when we walk down that hall together."

Dubiously, she accepted his statement, and they laughed together. Now the first round between them was sealed. Lottie continued washing him. He was cleaned between his toes, between his fingers, behind his knees, around his neck, in his ears, around his scrotum, along his groins, along his back, between his buttocks, under his arms, around his eyes, and in his navel. Louis was elated. The repulsive odors had disappeared. The smell of clean linen, powder, and soap filled the air. Once Louis was cleaned, she began to perform her magic on the cubicle. She wiped the window and the sunlight filled the room.

"You are the most wonderful person I've ever met, Ms. Lee."

The words came easy. He had forgotten the ugliness he had seen the first day. Incredulous changes were made in Louis's lifestyle. He was provided with a better diet, clean bed linens, a firmer pillow for his head, and removal of the picture he disliked. The screaming, cursing, and crying had ceased. His nights were without incident. He awoke each morning to a new game: waiting. He waited for the dawn; he waited for the change of shift; he waited for lunch; he waited for the afternoon; he waited for dinner; he waited for the evening care; he waited for the night; he waited for her to leave; he waited for sleep, and he waited for her to return.

The job of caring for Louis Frazier gave Lottie Lee, also known as Arnold Brown, a sense of pride. At least that was how he felt, and he felt needed and even loved by this patient. He had told Clarence how much he liked his job and how he had been assigned to the special patient.

"He can't move anything but his head. I've never seen anything like that in my life." Arnold explained to Clarence one night after they made love.

"He's paralyzed. He'll never walk in life."

"Oh, yes, he will. He said he would."

"He can't walk or feel anything. I know about those kinds of accidents people have and get paralyzed." Clarence was annoyed.

"He told me that he could feel when I wash his body and massage him with lotion."

"You massage him?"

"Of course. His skin was in bad shape. That's part of my job. You wanted me to have a job, and that's my job!" Arnold glared at him.

"Oh, you are having a good time going to work all dressed up like a woman. You should be ashamed. If you ever see me on the street, please act like you don't know me."

"Not on the street, but it's okay here when I suck your dick, you big faggot."

"Don't call me a faggot. I'm a man."

"Sure you are. Married and with children. But you like this ass hole."

Clarence wanted to hit Arnold, but he knew that Arnold would fight him. He didn't want a neighborhood disturbance. After all, he was a corrections officer, and any scandal like that could cost him his job. He wished he could stay away from Arnold, but he had fallen into the trap. Too many times he had come back and sipped from the champagne slipper.

"I'm leaving. And I ain't coming back. At least you can be grateful that I helped you get a job and off those fuckin' streets."

Arnold sighed and strutted his naked body to the door.

"Here's the door. See you when you come back." He glared at Clarence. "And you will be back."

Clarence stormed out of the apartment. Arnold slammed his door and returned to his bed. He would get a few hours sleep and get ready for the streets. He laughed. Poor, dumb Clarence, did he think that Arnold had stopped making the stroll? Of course, he had cut down his hours on the street, but he still remained Ms. Lottie Lee in the very late evening. He would return home by three in the morning, get a few hours sleep, and then go to his job at the hospital.

The job was very important to him, and he liked that man, Louis, even though he couldn't move his body. Arnold would find something to do with him until he could move. After all, he had promised to move. Arnold enjoyed being Lottie Lee in the daytime. Louis made her feel like a woman. Why not! It's what he always wanted to feel like. No, he did not want one of those sex changes. Cut off his dick! Never! He wondered if it was going to be a problem when Louis discovered the truth about who or what he was. Arnold would enchant him so much that when he did find out, he would still want him.

A few hours later, Arnold changed over to Ms. Lottie Lee. He was in full drag and ready to make the stroll. He prayed to God to be able to avoid the police. Last night was a very close call. Poor Clarence would have a heart attack if he saw him being escorted to the jail in full drag and handcuffs. And what about poor Louis Frazier. Alone and waiting. His hopes dashed against the rocks. He would believe that she would ever return. Now Lottie Lee had an obligation to Louis! She must be very careful so she could take care of him. He would be waiting.

20

Belinda had been working two months in the office. Today she was in charge of the whole office because the doctor had insisted that Jolena take off on Wednesdays. Peter Edgewater knew that Belinda would be happy having Wednesdays without Jolena. Today, he had five patients to examine; they were all postop, and all had complications. He was exhausted with the complications and was quite sure that if they had not been "freaks," these complications would not occur. He was totally convinced his surgical procedures were perfect.

All the patients and their complaints had arrived. It took him less than an hour to examine them. In that short time, he had soothed them with promises. Promises that if they were patient, everything would be fine; promises that the implants would soften; promises that the newly constructed vagina would get larger; promises that sexual sensation would return; promises that the swollen nose would get smaller; promises that the ugly scars would disappear; and promises that the crooked chin implant would correct itself.

Just when the office had emptied, the doorbell rang, and before he could warn Belinda not to answer, Lita Lopez appeared. Dr. Edgewater was upset. *Shit,* he thought, *this bitch, what is she doing here on Wednesday?*

"Hey, doc! Well, I came at the right time. Office is empty. Now, you know what I want. And Ms. Jolena is not here." She strolled in and turned around to take a second look at Belinda.

"Well, who in the fuck is this? What a beauty. Is this the new girlfriend?"

"What do you want, Lita? I'm getting ready to close. I don't have time for a lot of conversation." He was annoyed.

"You only have one thing I want, and that's some silicone, and I'm glad that bitch, Jolena, is not here."

Belinda was fascinated by Lita and the conversation. She was more pleased to realize that Lita did not like Jolena.

"I have a thousand dollars." She pulled a pack of money out and slammed it down on the desk. "I know you ain't gonna refuse me."

He became less annoyed, smiled and shook his head in disbelief.

"How in the hell do you do it?"

"I suck dick. Men love it. They think I have the best head in New York. The fact that I am a transsexual makes my head job good, but they don't know the secret." She laughed.

Belinda laughed along with the doctor. Belinda knew instantly that she liked Lita. She was glad to have company in her camp against Jolena.

"Belinda, take her in the room and get her ready."

"I'll go get undressed. I'll be waiting." Lita announced.

Dr. Edgewater pulled Belinda aside.

"This will give you a chance to see how I do this work, and if Jolena quits, then you can take over. That way, we will keep the money in the family."

Belinda was ecstatic. Quickly, she went to the room where Lita was undressing. Lita had thrown her clothes onto the floor. Belinda looked at the pile of dirty underwear in disgust.

"So you are the new girlfriend?"

"Yes, but soon I'll be his wife. He will marry me, you know. I am also a physician assistant, and that is a higher position than Jolena."

In one stupid paragraph, she had given Lita all the information she needed. As she lay on the table in position for the doctor to inject her, she questioned Belinda.

"So you don't get along with Jolena either?"

"No, she tries to be in charge of everything and everybody, including the doctor."

"Yeah, you are right about that." Lita loved the direction the conversation was going. "And besides, you're not the only one who feels that way. A lot of the other patients feel the same way. He should get rid of her now that he has you helping him, and after all, you are a physician assistant." Lita hoped that would boost the dumb little bitch's ego.

"Well, I am learning how to pump bodies. In fact, he's going to teach me today, starting with you." She smiled hopefully at Lita.

"Well, they say Jolena makes the best bodies."

"She can't do any better than me. All I need is a couple of weeks, and I will have it down pat."

"Well, I'll be here every week, and you can certainly do my body. I don't allow Jolena to touch me." Now Lita was aware that Belinda knew nothing about the disagreement between her and Jolena.

Belinda never felt more fortunate. If she were able to work on Lita every week, she would become very experienced in a short time. Lita was equally happy. Now she had a little dummy who wanted to do the injections. *This little bitch is stupid and greedy,* thought Lita, *and I can use her to my advantage.* Lita didn't care who pumped her body. At this point, it did not matter. Her body was already messed up by Dr. Edgewater and Snyder, so what did it matter if dear little Belinda did some more damage to it.

When Edgewater entered the room, he quickly showed Belinda the setup. Then he proceeded to put the needles into Lita's buttocks. Belinda was shocked at the skin discoloration on the buttocks and hips. It was a stained brown against the rest of her whiteness. There were large bruises, unevenness, and lumps. As he injected the needles, the blood return was enormous. Most of the blood flow was almost black. Belinda wanted to ask him the reason but was beginning to realize that his mood was not too pleasant. After several minutes and the injection with the large-bore needles, he found areas where the blood flow was minimal. Satisfied, he beckoned Belinda to observe as he pumped in the contents of the silicone.

"Put in ten of these on each side and call me when you are done."

Quickly he left the room without any further instructions. Belinda struggled with the slippery substance. Most of the time, she could not get the syringe to stay on the needle, and the silicone ended up on the table or the floor. She was finding it tedious and slow work. Within twenty minutes, Edgewater returned to the room.

"My God, you have not even started the other side?"

He picked up a syringe and started finishing Lita's body. By now, Belinda was bewildered, tired, and frustrated. She put down the syringe and left the room in tears.

"Don't pay that any attention. She's young and inexperienced. I'm teaching her."

Yeah, thought Lita, *but she won't be a Jolena.*

"Oh, I understand, doc. I'm not in a hurry."

But I'm in a hurry, he thought angrily. He did not want to spend any more time than necessary with Lita. Money was the only important issue. Finally, he finished the other buttock. The redness and bruises, he ignored. He took a suture and quickly closed the large needle holes. However, the silicone still managed to leak. Then he took a large piece of cotton and pressed it over the large needle hole. After allowing her to stand, he wrap-taped her body with heavy-duty duct tape. Lita knew how painful all this would be to take off. She didn't care as long as she got pumped. She could handle the pain. It always seemed to be her reliable and constant companion. She got dressed.

"When can I come back?"

"Damn, Lita, you haven't left yet, and you're ready to come back? Haven't you had enough?"

"Well, I want to get finished. I'm making a lot of money now, and I want to spend it while I have it. How about next week?"

"Suit yourself."

"See you then."

She was gone, and he was glad. He knew well that she should never be injected again. Her body was in a mess, but he did not really care about that. *Jolena was right,* he thought. *There is something sinister about Lita.* But now he had a thousand tax-free dollars in his pocket, so he couldn't care less about warnings.

When he returned to his private office, Belinda was still crying.

"What's the matter, pet?" He took her in his arms.

"You hurt my feelings," she cried.

"Oh, sweetheart, I didn't mean to do that. Now dry your eyes, and let's go to dinner."

He reached into his pocket and pulled out two one-hundred dollar bills.

"Now here is your first extra money." Belinda was more than pleased.

"Oh, then I did all right. You checked my work out? Am I getting the hang of things? I know that Lita liked me." There were no tears now, just the beautiful, vivacious, and dumb Belinda.

"Just give it a little time, and you'll be doing excellent work."

"As good as Jolena?" She waited for a correct answer.

"Even better than her."

He lied to keep her pleased. Peter knew that Belinda would never do that work as well as Jolena. He had thought that maybe she would have the talent, but now he knew better. She had only one gift, and that was sucking his dick. He needed that now. He took her in his arms, and she knew what she had to do.

"Take off your clothes, Peter. I want your dick. I want to suck it."

Peter was weak. All he could do was to remember how good it was the last time, and he wanted it again and again. When her hot mouth clamped on his dick, then expertly moved to his balls and began the long strokes with her tongue, Peter was ready to come. All he could think about as he ejaculated was how soon he could get ready again. Belinda knew that a good blow job would cement her place in his office and in his life.

However, after her first introduction to pushing silicone, she was not sure if she really wanted to deal with that job. Maybe she'd better stop pushing the issue of getting rid of Jolena. But the bigot side of her determination to get rid of that black person was too overwhelming. She'd do it for a while, but as soon as she became his wife, that would be the end of this fuckin' office. As he came in her mouth, she thought about Ricky. She needed a good hard fuck and a taste of fresh young come, not the stale taste Peter left in her mouth.

21

Louis and Lottie had been kind to each other for almost three weeks. However, Louis felt the urgency to communicate with Lottie on a higher, romantic level, beyond words.

One morning, he leveled his eyes onto hers and began his words of love and gratitude.

"You know what you are to me?"

"Can't guess. What am I?" Lottie giggled. She knew his words would be flattering.

"You are my baby." The tone of his voice was soft.

"Oh, Louis, stop—"

"You're my sweet baby, my sweetheart, my soul, and my life." He was going strong with his words.

"Louis!" She was overwhelmed.

"I miss you when you're not here." He watched her smile. "You are the best thing that happened to me since my accident. In fact in my whole life. What would I do without you? I care for you so much."

"I care for you, too. I think about you all the time. I just want you to start walking real soon. And look here at these arms. You gotta start moving these arms."

She picked them up, but they flopped back onto the bed. Louis had no control.

"See that, those arms can't do nothing."

"Yeah, they can! I just ain't ready yet."

"Well, when are you gonna get ready? I been here with you over a month, and I ain't seen no movement. Maybe those doctors were right."

"Don't pay them any attention. I told you before that you and I are going down that hall and out that door."

She grinned. He knew she liked what he had told her.

"You and me, Louis?"

He heard romance in her voice. It was time.

"Yeah, who else? You're the only one that matters in my life. Who else do I wait for? Draw those curtains around the bed."

Lottie drew the curtains.

"Come to me, baby." Louis demanded. "Unbutton your dress; take my hand and put it on your breast."

Lottie was glad she had managed to grow some breast tissue from the hormones taken over the years. She took Louis's limp hand and maneuvered it to her breast.

"Can you feel them?" Lottie had to hold the limp hand to her breast. The hand made no attempt to fondle the breast as she had expected. She wondered again about how much truth Louis was telling her. Slowly she moved her hand down her stomach and between her legs.

"Can you feel that?"

She watched his face to see if he was able to visualize or feel what was between her legs even though she kept her organs tightly tucked up between her buttocks. However, she noted that Louis had closed his eyes. She allowed him to remain that way. Louis was remembering the time in his life when his hands had fondled and caressed; how his lips had touched on soft nipples.

Lottie moaned for him, and he answered the call.

"You like that, sweetheart?"

"Oh, yes, Louis, it feels so good." She now moved onto the bed in a kneeling position. She held his hand between her legs. Passionate sighing filled the cubicle. Lottie wiggled frantically while holding his hand in the place creating the most excitement. Her organ began to swell. "Oh, Louis, it feels good . . . I can feel myself. . ." Her words drifted. She was ecstatic.

"Good, good, baby, don't stop. It feels good to me. You feel good. I need it."

Louis was proud of himself. Nobody, not even Oldtimer, could tell Louis Frazier how to handle a woman when it came to sex.

"Lay on top of me," he demanded, "I want to kiss you and put my tongue in your mouth."

Quickly, Lottie placed the limp arm back in place and lay down on Louis. He was amazed at her swiftness. It was impossible for him to feel the many pounds of Lottie's weight because of being without feeling from his neck downward. She placed her lips on his, and their tongues locked together in wet darkness. They consumed each other's mouth until it was impossible to breathe.

"I love you, Ms. Lottie Lee," he whispered.

They were the words Lottie Lee, also known as Arnold Brown, drag queen, transvestite, thief, and man, had not heard in all of his life as he heard them now. Not even from Clarence and his possessive self. These words would have a lasting effect on Lottie Lee. She wanted to say them back to Louis but knew in her heart it was not time. However, another bond had been sealed.

After finishing his morning bath, she whispered to him.

"I'm so happy, Louis. I just can't wait until you show them out there that you can walk."

"Yeah, baby, I'll be glad, too."

Romance had seeped into Louis's life. However, with the happiness he was experiencing, there lurked an uneasiness. Something in his brain reminded him. How was he going to walk when he couldn't even move?

Oldtimer suspected something strange about Ms. Lottie Lee. After all, he had been in the world a long time and knew about women. But this woman was different. She seemed to be more man than woman. Oldtimer had come to the conclusion that Lottie Lee was a drag queen. He could see it, and he could feel it. She was too big and muscular. He swore he saw a beard peaking through the heavy makeup she wore everyday. Besides, her arms were long and her hands massive. Oldtimer felt that it was his duty to tell Louis. After all, poor Louis had no idea that a drag queen and faggot was taking care of him and administering all this loving care on him. But should he tell him, or should he just leave it alone?

However, Louis was his friend, and one did have to look after a friend. Would Louis be pleased or disappointed upon learning the truth about his caretaker? He was quite happy now, and Oldtimer did hate to upset him, but after all, he was man, and men should know when some faggot was sneaking around in a dress, pretending to be a woman and taking care of the sick. True, Louis was the cleanest he had seen him, and his whole attitude had changed. He was not cantankerous and had stopped the screaming at night. *No,* Oldtimer thought to himself, *leave it alone.* It was none of his business!

But then he thought about Ms. Lottie Lee strutting into the ward like she was something grand. He wondered what she had been doing to Louis in that small cubicle. He had heard moans and giggles. As Oldtimer gave it more thought, his dick began to swell underneath the pajamas. *Damn,* he smiled, *Louis is having a better time than me, and Louis couldn't move anything but his head. No way!* He'd tell him. Why should Louis be deceived? *Damn, Lottie Lee might even turn Louis into a faggot!* Oldtimer was devastated with the thought. Poor Louis had enough problems without becoming gay.

Quickly, he made his way to Louis's cubicle. In truth, he was rather distressed by the fact that Louis was getting all this attention.

He remembered when he himself was brought in with a stroke that no one cared or gave him the kind of attention Louis was receiving.

"My man! How are you doing today? You sure look comfortable, and it sure is smelling good in this little space."

Louis smiled with pride.

"Yeah, thanks to Lottie. Without her, I don't think I would have survived."

"Yeah, she sure has done a job on you. He smiled and couldn't help adding. "In more ways than one."

Louis smiled.

"She's my savior. You have no idea how good she makes me feel."

"Oh, I have an idea, and I can imagine what goes on in this small cubicle. I bet she is sucking on that dick."

"Man, how can she suck on my dick with this tube in there. If I didn't have that damn tube, she could suck on the dick."

"Can it get hard?"

"What do you mean, 'can it get hard?' Nothing wrong with my dick."

"Well, since you can't move any part of your body or feel anything, I can't figure out how it can get hard."

"Well, it does. So don't get that stupid notion in your head, and soon as I get this tube out, she promised to make good love to my dick," Louis bragged.

This was most distressing to Oldtimer. Just the thought of that sex act was enough to anger him into telling Louis what he thought of Ms. Lottie Lee.

"You know, friend, I think I should tell you something that I don't think you know."

"Don't bring me no bad news, man. I done had enough."

"It's not bad news. In a way, it's news you should know about before this thing goes any further."

"Before what thing goes any further?"

"This thing with Ms. Lottie Lee. I know you is sweet on her, but she is just getting your hopes up, and you are going to be real disappointed when she lets you know or when you discover the truth about her."

Suddenly, Louis knew! *This motherfucker is jealous over me. Imagine! Me! I can't even move, and he is jealous.*

"Man, whatever truth you are talking about, I don't want to hear it. That woman is good to me. She likes me, and she is taking good care of me. What the fuck do you know about Lottie Lee that is going to be so disappointing to me?"

"Man, Lottie is not all you think her to be."

"I don't care!"

"You would care if you knew what I knew."

Louis turned his head in an angry motion and responded.

"You tell it to her when she comes back to work. You tell her! I don't want to hear any bullshit from you. Get the fuck out of my room. You tell *her*! You know so much about her, you tell *her*! Get out! Get out!" Louis was screaming as loud as his voice would allow.

Oldtimer quickly limped away from Louis. He was somewhat scared by Louis's reaction, even though he knew that he couldn't physically harm him. However, if he was going to confront Lottie Lee, that would be a different story. What if she wasn't a drag queen, and what if she was a drag queen? Either way, Oldtimer knew that he might be in for a good old-fashioned ass-kicking. He would wait. The proper time would come. That fuck Louis could lay up there and get all the attention he wanted now, but one day soon, Oldtimer would put an end to all that.

Louis Frazier was angry. He'd like to kick Oldtimer's ass. What the fuck did he know about Lottie? When Lottie returned to work, he'd have to warn her about Oldtimer. He knew Lottie would take care of Oldtimer and his mouth.

22

It was troubling to Jolena that Dr. Edgewater was going to attempt an operation on Mark in the office. Her concern for Mark would make her ask if this was truly his intention. She knew he did not have the proper setup, and a sterile technique would be almost impossible to create in that treatment room.

A few days later, she approached Edgewater with the question. She felt awkward asking him anything nowadays. He hardly sat down and talked with her as they did even six months ago. They had laughed and talked during their almost five years together. But now, with Belinda in his heart, he had little time for any conversation. If any changes were coming about in the office, she only found out about them when they occurred.

Today was a rare occasion, because Belinda did not come into the office with him. Jolena hoped secretly that she had dropped off into space forever. Jolena was able to approach him.

"Dr. Edgewater, are you really going to do Mark here in the office?"

"Oh, yes. It's not complicated. It's only a skin graft."

"If you need any help, just let me know. I'll be glad to help you."

"Thank you, Jolena. I think that I can manage. I have Belinda helping me."

So she still existed, Jolena thought.

"Then you are going to eventually construct a penis for Mark?"

"Oh, yes. I have a new method. Of course, I've not tried it out, but I am positive it will work."

"What about complications?"

"Complications will only occur and do occur when these patients do not follow postoperative instructions. If there is a complication, it will not be from my surgery."

From that statement Jolena began to sense that there was a change coming over Peter. His very theory on complications, blaming them on the patients, had been cropping up too much. She could not begin to visualize what quick method he had for constructing a penis. Perhaps she had been out of the operating room too long and was not familiar with the new technology.

"Mark is so set on having this procedure. He believes in you. He will be so disappointed if this does not work out."

"I know your concern for him, Jolena. I will do my very best job."

His statement of reassurance and the charming smile he displayed put Jolena at ease. He was acting like his old self for that fleeting moment.

Jolena acknowledged that statement and attended to her own business in the office. However, she still felt an uneasiness about the entire procedure. If only she could talk to Mark and discourage him from going through with the operation. She did have to call and give him the date to come in for the surgery. Perhaps she could talk to him then. But he was so desperate to have it done. Would he even listen to her? Was it really her position to warn him of all the bad things that could happen? Wasn't that the doctor's position or even his brilliant assistant's?

What should she do?

Yes, she would speak to him when she gave him the appointment. She would ask him to reconsider. Did you talk to your fiance, Mark? Is this essential to your future happiness? Do you realize the dangers of a graft, and if he is going to do a thigh flap and skin graft, there is a possibility of it not taking well? All of these questions, and more, clouded Jolena. Maybe she should just mind her business and be the secretary as she has now been relegated?

"Jolena," Dr. Edgewater's voice broke through her thoughts of doubt. "You can give Mark an appointment for a Wednesday two weeks from tomorrow."

"Yes, I'll get in touch with him."

She had to tell him when she made the call or just be quiet about the whole situation. What was her position in this matter? On the next visit to Bernie, she would get that answer. Bernie would also bring her up-to-date on the latest techniques concerning penile construction. He had mentioned once that it had not been perfected. Jolena knew that Bernie would be very interested in this latest rapid method that Peter had developed.

Dr. Peter Edgewater, M.D., F.A.C.S. settled back in his comfortable office chair. He was pleased with himself. Every little plan he had constructed was working. He had brought Belinda in, and Jolena had wisely stepped aside. He had suggested she take off Wednesdays, and she had complied. Peter felt she was upset at not being able to make the extra money doing the silicone, but she had made no protest. He thought that strange, but maybe she was tired of dealing with the freaks. Now that he had set Belinda in motion doing the injections, all would work out well. He was glad that Jolena had not been a problem.

His conscience did twinge a little when he thought about the money he had eliminated her from earning. However, if she was displeased, she could always quit. That would be easier for him than having to fire her. Soon as he got Belinda conditioned to the office and his routine, he would not need Jolena. He had to make sure that Belinda could cope with all the problems as Jolena had coped. But surely she would. She was young and anxious. She would follow his orders.

Peter did have a feeling that Jolena knew his plans. She had worked with him too long and knew him well. Jolena was no dummy. She had to know the deal. She knew when he was in love. She had seen him go through many mini love affairs. However, this one was different; he could not and would not give up Belinda. His thoughts of her aroused him sexually each time. He was amazed at how she had him ready sexually each night and morning. Peter could not diagnose this as love or lust. But whatever it was, it pleased him, and he did not intend to lose her.

He wondered what she was doing right now. He knew she needed time off to visit her parents. Maybe he should call and see if he she got there. As he reached for the phone, he thought better about making that move. He did not want her to think that he was checking on her movements. She would surely be returning. Where could she go? What better deal could she get? He planned to give her everything he could. Of course, he could not do that immediately. He'd have to wait and see how she worked out.

He had to make sure that she was in love with him or was too 'crippled' to leave him or too insecure. Yes, he'd have to keep her insecure. If he built up too much confidence in her, then she would become independent and be a problem. No, she must rely on him.

He thought about marriage and children. That would be a good move. He had no children, but then, he had never been too sad about not having children. When he looked at all the homosexuals and transsexuals that flooded his office, he wondered if it was safe to have children. What would they grow up to be? There seem to be a plague of homosexuality and transsexuality. That was another thing bothering Peter. He wanted very much to change his office patients. He would have to slowly weed them out.

"Dr. Edgewater," Jolena's voice came over the intercom. "I have Mark on the line. I told him the date for the surgery. However, he wants to talk to you about something."

"Okay, put him on."

Peter picked up his telephone and settled back comfortably in his chair.

"Mark, I'm glad you agree with the date. So what is on your mind? Jolena said you had something to ask me?"

As Mark related to Dr. Edgewater his recent bleeding problem, Dr. Edgewater could feel that familiar but unexplained cold sensation going up his back as it did whenever he heard news which did not please him.

"How long have you been bleeding?" He tried not to sound concerned.

"About four months."

"Is the blood dark or bright red."

"Bright red. It has always been bright red."

"Is there a lot or just spotting?"

"Spotting at first, but now it's a little more."

"Maybe you injured yourself. It sounds like you might have torn the floor of the perineum. The opening there is very small. You come in two days before surgery, and I will put some packing in there, and I'm sure it will stop. Nothing to be concerned about. We can still proceed with the surgery. That area has nothing to do with the procedure we are doing. This is the first stage, and I am merely going to attach a skin graft to the thigh, and you will go home with that for a few weeks. Then when you return, we should be able to complete the attachment of a penis."

"That sounds good to me. I'll see you next week."

Dr. Edgewater hung up the phone. *Damn,* he thought, *what the fuck is going on with that body? Why in the fuck is he or she bleeding? I did a complete hysterectomy almost four years ago. Maybe I should just cancel this procedure. No,* he thought again, *that's five thousand cash he is bringing, and I can use that money.* The chill had left him, and he did not want to think about Mark anymore or the reason he had gotten that sudden chill when he heard the word blood. He immediately turned his thoughts to more pleasant ones, such as Belinda and marriage.

Jolena had listened in on the conversation. When she called Mark to give him the appointment, he had mentioned the bleeding to her. She had suggested that he tell the doctor. Jolena could not believe that he was going to proceed with the surgery and not do some sort of test on Mark to find the cause of the bleeding. This was a complication that even aroused Jolena's curiosity. She would be seeing Bernie soon, and he'd tell her what was happening. Maybe she should warn Mark, but she was unsure about getting involved. Bernie would be able to give her an answer to that problem also.

23

After Jolena's third visit, Honey Babe, or Thomas, had developed almost the perfect body. The breasts had been injected with enough silicone to enable them to become a respectable small size. The buttocks were injected to perfection, and the hips, after injections had been smoothed down to meet perfectly with the thighs. Jolena was pleased with her creation. She only hoped that it was not in vain. She hoped that Thomas would stay off the streets. His dream of becoming one of the top runway models or magazine models was rather farfetched for Jolena to comprehend. However, he was still committed to that dream. After the last visit, he announced to Jolena that the time had come for him to make his trip.

"Are you sure this is what you want to do?" she inquired again.

"Yes! Without the life that I dream will one day be mine, this life I live is over. I will never stay in this kind of situation. I will kill myself. There is no other way for me."

Jolena stared at him and realized he was serious. She scrutinized his face. It was perfect without makeup. Yes, Thomas would make a beautiful woman. What a joke this would be on the world. She was glad he had covered his tracks. He had not left out any details.

"Will you be coming back to this apartment when you return?"

"No. Never. I will be coming back to New York a woman, and I will go to the one place girls stay when they are from out of town and struggling to be an actress or model."

"And where is that?"

"The Barbizon Hotel. For women of course." Thomas laughed, and Jolena noted the feminine laughter that had moved into his voice.

"Good luck, Thom—What am I going to call you? What will be your new name?"

"I haven't decided, but I will call you, at your home, and you will know that it is me. Only you. I trust you."

"I never knew you. It's wiped from my brain."

Thomas embraced Jolena as she was about to leave.

"Thank you for helping me. I will always be indebted to you."

"You owe me nothing except to make a success of yourself. And that you owe to yourself. Always be good to yourself."

After Jolena parted, Thomas Blake, a.k.a. Honey Babe, began making plans to go to Canada. The doctor had been contacted, and all appointments made. Thomas would be hospitalized exactly a week. After that, it would be necessary to remain and be seen during the postop period. Now he would make his clean break with New York. Management had been notified that he would be vacating his apartment at the end of the month. The few things he had collected, especially the street clothes he wore at night, would be discarded. Everything he carried in the small suitcase to Canada would be all he owned. Thomas Blake would never leave Canada, at least not with that name or the body he went in with. The name would disappear forever, and so would the rest of the boy. When he returned to the United States, there would be a whole new physical and paper identity.

Money had already bought him a birth certificate, born in New York City, female with only a last name. When he returned from Canada, he would secure a social security number, and from there, he would start his life all over. He looked in the mirror. Did he believe he was woman? Yes! Did he believe he could become famous? Yes! Did he believe he was beautiful? Yes! Did he believe all of this would work? Yes! Did he believe he would be rich? Yes! There were no more questions for Thomas Blake to ask himself. The male components of him would soon be a thing of the past. Thomas Blake never existed.

24

After Jolena left Thomas's apartment, she decided to walk to Madison Avenue and catch a bus uptown. Today, her reflection in the passing windows became apparent and uneasy. It was going to be a difficult day to deal with herself. She was always good at solving everybody's problems and never appeared to have any of her own. She had always displayed a lighter side of life. Never complaining or talking about herself, her hopes, ambitions, fears, or the past, Jolena was excellent company for someone who wanted to talk. She had a gift for listening. One man she had dated remarked that when he was with her, he felt as if she had just been born or had dropped out of the sky from nowhere. But Jolena knew there had been a past to her life.

Today, that past was trying to break through her armored thoughts, and she refused to submit. Yes, today would be difficult and the night worse. Then she saw the Chinese restaurant. She entered and took a seat at the bar. Chinese bars were good to sit at, because no one really bothered you. As long as you showed your money and were quiet, no one talked to you, and Jolena did not want to talk. She ordered a drink. Today, it would be a martini. Chinese bartenders made good martinis, and she had discovered that the ingredients in martinis made you forget.

After drinking one martini, she began to feel better. When the situation called for alcohol, Jolena did not hesitate. It was better than popping a lot of strange pills and begging doctors for prescriptions. And alcohol was cheaper and legal. During the second drink, she remembered that she had to call Bernie. Before she finished the drink, Jolena made the call. As usual, he was there. Jolena laughed. Where else was he going? He has no life. Lost up in that grand apartment or, as she described it, the mini-mansion in the sky.

"Bernie, it's Jolena. I know it's early, but I'm off today and I'll be passing by your building. Would you like me to visit?" She spoke as always to Bernie, direct and honest.

He was delighted that she called and told her to come anytime. He also informed her that he would have a small lunch prepared for them. Jolena was glad. She would need a small lunch after two martinis. She finished her last drink and walked toward Fifth Avenue.

With the crisp air and walk to his apartment, the effect of the martinis would be reduced to a respectable level. Therefore, she would be able to answer all questions about Edgewater. Bernie lived for the next episode. But lately, there had been no exciting events. So Bernie would have to live with past stories about Edgewater and enjoy her company.

The doorman directed her to go up without announcement. Bernie seemed unusually happy to see her.

"Well, Jolena, this is the first time I have seen you in the daytime. To what do I owe this visit?"

"I was in the neighborhood and thought about you. I always think about you, Bernie. You are a dear friend to me. Don't you know that?" She laughed and pulled off her lightweight jacket.

She had on slacks that complimented her shapely body. Bernie noticed. He always noticed. Ever since Jolena had come to work with him at the hospital, he marveled at the quiet beauty she possessed. This awareness was beginning to come alive in Bernie, and the more she came to sit and talk with him, the more he harbored thoughts of holding her in his arms and even going to bed with her. However, to approach her in this manner was somewhat beyond his ability. He did not want to insult her with such a suggestion or make her think that he just wanted to lay with her because she visited him so frequently.

Jolena was still a mystery to him, despite all he knew about her. Bernie always felt that there was something more he never knew or that she would ever tell him. But he knew that life was ebbing away from him, and he wanted desperately to get some companionship out of it before it was all over.

But who could he trust? He could have his choice of young, beautiful white girls, prostitutes, or otherwise. Even astute Jewish widows would be glad to be with him. In bed or out of bed. His money was that important to them. But Bernie didn't want them slobbering over him, whispering lies, or scheming up plots so he would marry them. No, not Bernie Charles. He was old enough and wise enough to know what and who he wanted, and it was Jolena.

But what would he do with her? Especially in bed? He was unsure of being able to satisfy her. Outside of bed, what would he do with her? Yes, he would proudly walk down the street with her on his arm. Yes, he would take her to every grand restaurant and resort. Yes, he would spend his money on her. Yes, he would give her money. Yes, he would marry her. Yes, he would take her away from that damn office! Yes, Yes, Yes. But what about Jolena? He was too fearful to ask.

She interrupted his bizarre thoughts.

"Bernie, I'm glad I didn't disturb you. I must confess that I really needed to come here today. I just wanted to be around someone, and who else better than you?"

He was flattered.

"I guess we are in the same boat today. I felt the same way."

She felt that he still missed or thought much about his wife. Instinctively, Jolena embraced him. He was pleased to feel the warmth of her body and held her unusually long. Jolena noticed. For the first time she noticed and felt Bernie. She moved away.

"Well, what are we drinking today? And you did mention lunch?" she asked as she walked though the large room, looking at the various paintings and sculptures. Jolena could see the richness and value throughout the room. She wished she had more knowledge about art and artists.

"Bernie, I love this art, even though I don't understand any of it. It's just beautiful to me. You should educate me."

Bernie followed.

"I would be glad to tell you many things about art and teach you. Anytime you are ready. However, today, my dear Jolena, we shall drink champagne. The very best. Dom Perignon."

"I like the best." Jolena smiled.

"And you deserve the best. We shall have a small portion of the finest crab-meat salad. Just enough to make us want more."

The elderly oriental man servant, who had been with Bernie for thirty years, served the champagne and food. Jolena hardly saw him, because she usually came at night. He bowed politely and served them.

"These glasses, my dear Jolena, are Baccarat. Very fine glasses for very fine champagne." He wanted to impress her.

She was impressed and loved it.

"Yes, Bernie, I love it." She paused, then lifted her glass to him. "This is to you for being my dear, dear friend all these years. I love you for that."

He noticed the glistening in her eyes.

"Jolena, tell me about yourself. You know, all the years I've known you, I really never knew you. You've had a life; you've had love; you've had adventure. What happened in your life? You had a life before you worked for me. What happened? You never talk about the earlier years."

Jolena laughed a silly laugh.

"There was never earlier years. I had just been born when I met you in the operating room. I told you about all those bad affairs I had."

"Jolena, come now. What about the time before all of that?"

"Bernie, I won't talk about that. I did not come here to talk about that. We can talk about Edgewater. We always talk about him."

"I don't want to hear about Edgewater. I want to hear about Jolena." He paused. "But if Jolena doesn't want to talk about Jolena, it's okay. Let's go eat."

She was relieved. They dined on the fine food and drank the fine wine. Bernie related to her the history of champagne and the art of preparing fine foods. She was fascinated and amused. Jolena enjoyed this visit with Bernie more than other visits. Jolena felt mellow. The wine had taken away the wicked effects of the martinis. She expressed her feelings to Bernie.

"Too bad, Bernie, you are white."

He laughed.

"Too bad, Bernie, you are Jewish."

He laughed.

"Too bad, Bernie, you are rich."

He laughed.

"Too bad, Bernie, you are a doctor."

He laughed.

"Too bad, Bernie, because if you were none of those, I would go to bed with you."

Bernie did not laugh. He peered closely at Jolena.

"Pretend I am none of those, and come to my bedroom, Jolena."

He stood up and took her hand. Slowly, he led her through a section of the apartment she had never seen. The bedroom was plush and luxurious. The bed was a large four-poster with a canopy. The rest of the furniture was dark mahogany, very rich and very rare. The walls were covered with a rich damask. The lighting was low, and a rich aroma of musk permeated the room. Jolena was mesmerized.

"Bernie, I think it was the champagne that overtook me. I really did not mean to say all those things to you. Forgive me. I should go."

"Don't leave me, Jolena. Stay with me today and tonight. Don't leave me. We need to be together. Please, Jolena. I've been thinking about this—"

"No, Bernie, I'm just not some nurse you can go to bed with, and because I am black, you just can't use me."

"Jolena, stop that! You should know how I feel about you. I trust you and respect you. I want more in our relationship."

Jolena stopped. She looked around at all of the elegance. When Bernie was younger, she always thought of him as being sexy. She did like him, but did she like him this way? She noticed the champagne was by the bedside. Had he planned this? Jolena smiled and shook her head.

"Bernie, I cannot believe you. This is really different. I must admit I like the intrigue."

He was pleased. He had offered her the best in atmosphere. Maybe. Maybe. He poured her a glass of the champagne. When he turned to offer her the glass, she held her hand up. She then turned as if she were leaving the room. Abruptly, she turned toward him. Already, she had unbuttoned her blouse. He could see her beautiful honey-colored flesh. Slowly Jolena began to disrobe. Piece by piece. He studied her body. She was in excellent form. He had seen many women's bodies during his lifetime, but Jolena's body was smooth and curved. He was surprised that her breasts were large and firm. He wanted to bury his head in them. She took the champagne from Bernie. She drank.

"Take off your clothes, Bernie. You want me in your bed. Then you will get your wish."

Bernie never heeded the warning. He disrobed, took a drink of the champagne, and lay in his own bed, awaiting the beautiful black woman to come to him. His eyes feasted upon the tall, honey-colored, beautiful, sophisticated middle-aged woman. Jolena had thrown all caution to the wind. Bernie became to her someone she had not seen in many years. Someone she would never see again. Someone she had loved and lost a long time ago.

This day became another day, another place, and another person. Jolena made love to Bernie as he had never experienced. She was gentle, passionate, and consuming. Bernie returned all the passion she had aroused within him. It did not take long for either of them to satisfy their sexual needs. Afterwards, Bernie took Jolena in his arms and held her close. She was silent.

"I care for you more than you can ever understand. Please don't think that this is just for one time. I love to have you with me. I don't want to crowd you."

He kissed her on the face and the neck and held her again. The martinis and champagne were gone from Jolena's brain. She remembered where she was and with whom she had made love. Never in her life had she desired or made love to a white man. Why did she do this today? But then, who else in her life? Nobody. Bernie was different.

He had always been kind and respectful. She was surprised that he had such a keen sexual knowledge. There were no complaints.

"Bernie, you're not crowding me. I have enjoyed this day. Maybe I wanted to do this as much as you."

"Jolena, why are you such a lone person? I never hear you talk about friends or family. Even at holiday time. Where is your family? And boyfriends?"

"I have none. I have nobody." Her voice was cold and distant.

As he held her closer, he could feel her body shaking. She was crying.

"Why do you cry, Jolena? I've never known you to cry."

"Please don't ask me questions, Bernie. Just hold me tight. I only cry for a few seconds, and then it's okay. See, look at me. No tears. I'm fine." She laughed as he stared into her composed face. The tears were gone, and Jolena was smiling.

"Stay with me tonight," he begged.

"I would really stay, but I have an old ragged cat at home waiting for me. I'm loyal, you know that, even to a cat."

He liked that. Although he didn't want her to leave, he knew she was a responsible person. But Bernie knew there was something about her life she had not told him. From the first day she came to work for him Bernie felt there was something Jolena never talked about but never forgot. Maybe one day she would tell him.

Jolena was still dazed. She never imagined what happened between her and Bernie could ever happen. Surely, it had been the wine. But then, she had to remember that Bernie had not been intoxicated before, during, or after the whole affair. How could this have happened? They had actually had sex together. They had always been close friends. He had never made any advances toward her. They had laughed together, confided in each other, and she had even cried and held him when his wife had committed suicide, but never anything intimate.

What had happened to Bernie? How long had he been harboring these feelings for her? What should she do? Jolena knew that she would not be in and out of Bernie's bed like some whore, and he knew that. She could not quite remember his words to her, but they hinted at more than just sex. Could she possibly tolerate him all the time? He was not the man she hoped would come along one day and fulfill all her romantic fantasies. Maybe it was time to stop dreaming or fantasizing.

But the problem with Bernie was that he was white. This was the first time in her life that she had made love with a white man. It had not been difficult that afternoon because she had had a few drinks.

The atmosphere was perfect. It was rich and clean. Although Bernie was not handsome, he was gentle and experienced. He made love to her. They enjoyed each other. In fact, she could sense that he did not want her to leave so soon. Later, at home, she undressed and inspected herself closely in the mirror. Jolena was forty-one years old. Her body was still intact, but like all middle-aged women she had seen coming to the office, she too would begin to sag and look dumpy.

She needed to exercise, but there was no time for that and, certainly, no money to go to expensive health clubs. She would begin to watch carefully what she ate. Already she was plucking her gray hairs. And the laugh lines were deeper, and it wasn't from laughter. Jolena could begin to imagine how she might look in ten years and did not want to think about twenty years. She'd probably still be working in a hospital, walking up and down long corridors or standing for hours in the operating room. She could imagine her ankles getting fat and varicose veins pushing their ugliness through her legs. As a nurse working long hours, it would be more difficult to keep her shape and good looks. Life would probably not get easier. Already it had given Jolena her share of sorrow. She did not want to think about that now.

Quickly, she showered and washed her hair. It was still early in the evening, but Jolena decided to go to bed early. Ms. Meow jumped up to her favorite place. Jolena stroked her gently. Her confessions to Ms. Meow were safe and never revealed.

"Well, Ms. Meow, today was very interesting. I received my final cash payment from Thomas, who has gone away to disappear from his old life and come back in another form, and I made love to an old friend who is much older than me. And you know, Ms. Meow, a lot of that has taken my mind away from problems at the office. I am no longer annoyed with Edgewater and his girlfriend. I am only going to be concerned with myself. I don't want to be old and poor. I don't want to work forever. I want more out of life. A better life for you and me, Ms. Meow. What happened today might lead to that better life. I'm going to listen very seriously to what Bernie has to say."

As Jolena began to drift off to sleep, she thought again about Bernie. What did he have in mind? What was Bernie after? Why had he invited her to his bed? Where was all of this going to lead? She turned and curled her body into its most comfortable position and entered into sleep. Ms. Meow changed position and moved closer to her mistress. She nudged her body close to Jolena, purred softly, and joined in the sleep.

25

Lita Lopez was lonesome. She wanted love. Real love from a real man. These feelings descended on her one night as she prepared for her nightly stroll. Steadily, she sniffed her precious cocaine and sipped cheap brandy from a paper cup. Looking in the mirror, after the ingestion of cocaine and brandy, she concluded that she looked especially lovely tonight. Yes, why not let tonight be a night of finding a man. A real man who would love and want her for just being Lita. She would not lie to him. She would be truthful from the very beginning and tell him the truth about her sexual problems. No need to waste time.

Then she looked around her large cluttered studio. Wigs, gowns, shoes, boots, fake furs, jewelry, and all sort of objects stared back at her. Lita realized she would have to make room for this man. Yes, she'd have to put a lot of this mess away, tend to the things in the large closet, and become more organized. No man would want to live in this confusion. But if she found a real man who loved her, then she would get a larger place, a big bed, and plenty of room for both of them. She dreamed of a kitchen. Yes, she would learn to cook. New furniture, a new television, and all the comforts to go with love.

These ideas excited Lita. A new project for a transsexual who had no other project except putting more and more silicone in her body. Even she knew that everyone needed love and wanted love. Now she would go to the streets and find it! She took another good sniff of her cocaine and looked in the mirror. The drug always boosted her ego. It made her proud and beautiful. Tonight, she would wear her red dress. That dress attracted much attention. Men loved red!

She went to the closet and opened the door. It had to be hanging right near the light switch. When she switched on the light, there was the dress. She snatched it off the hanger. She turned out the light and quickly shut the door. The closet was not her favorite place. My God, how had she forgotten! Quickly she sniffed some more drug and drank the remainder of the brandy. Love! She wanted love. She remembered now why she could never have love. Methodically, she walked back to the closet, opened the door, and stared at the large garment bag containing many of her gowns.

It was a bag she never used or disturbed, because it contained his body, and she remembered about the lesson of love. She laughed softly, closed the door, and ingested more drug. The body of the man she had loved was in her closet. She would always own him. He had claimed to love her, had sworn she was the only one. They had only been together one month, and she discovered he had lied, cheated, and stolen from her. When she protested his behavior, he beat her with a wire coat hanger then locked her in the dark closet. He would only allow her out to go to work. She could have run away, but it was her apartment, and he refused to leave.

Lita was sure he would get tired and leave but he stayed, made fun of her, and called her names that caused her sadness. He'd bragged about his affairs with other women and informed her that he was not planning on leaving her, because she had made his lifestyle easy, and she was stuck with him no matter how unhappy she might become. She became tired of the abuse. It reminded her of the physical abuse she had suffered as a child and later when she went so innocently to have her sex-change operation.

There was a darkness to Lita that this man had no idea existed. He did not realize that he was in danger. Lita never threatened or warned him. She waited for the first opportunity when he would come in late at night, intoxicated and smelling of other women. It had not been long before he arrived in that condition. As he lay sleeping, sprawled on the bed, face down, Lita simply went to him, sat on his back, lifted his head just enough to cut his throat with a sharp razor blade.

She never shook or cringed in the act. She merely dragged his body to the tub, where she made extra razor incisions that allowed the blood to drain quickly before clotting occurred. Then she washed his body and dragged it onto the floor where she had spread a shower curtain covered with plenty of muslin. He had thought that she was making a new dress when she came in one day with all the material. She had laughed at that.

She brought out a large shopping bag filled with boxes of baking soda and began the process of pouring it over the entire body. After it was well covered, she let the body set for an hour. During that hour, Lita sniffed her cocaine that he had denied her and drank her brandy. She had vowed no more lovers. Then she returned to the job of tying the hands together at the wrist and the legs at the ankles so that they would not fly in all directions.

Slowly she rolled the body in the muslin, as in a carpet, until it was securely wrapped. She worked faster now, because the body would become very rigid and difficult to handle. She placed the large garment bag beside the muslin-wrapped body, which she rolled into the bag. There she also put many articles of clothes she would never wear again. The bag was dragged into the closet and put in the corner, and there it stayed and would stay until Lita died.

Now the memory of that incident along with the ingestion of the cocaine made her realize that she could not bring a lover to this place. Not to this small, shit-ass, hole-in-the-wall dump with a body wrapped in muslin, long mummified, and packed away with her drag clothes. Lita snapped on the radio. Get real, bitch!

Spanish music blared out at her. *Good,* she thought, *I am Spanish and I need this music.* Lita danced short sexy moves. She watched herself in the mirror as she swayed her body to the rhythm. Lita knew she could have been a star. A movie star, a Broadway star, if only her life had not been fucked up by the world. Even if she had stayed in Mexico, she would have been a star. More sniffing of the cocaine and sips of brandy convinced her of her beauty.

She began to apply her makeup. Not too much, but she had to remember the slight beard that would begin to show. Tonight she would dress in red. The color seems to excite men, and she always made good money when she dressed in red. Now she was happy, despite the loneliness and the body in the closet reminding her that she could not invite a lover to live with her. Another sniff, and Lita was out of the door, ecstatic and determined to be the best whore on the stroll.

It was almost three in the morning, and Lita had made over eight hundred dollars. She was tired and glad the night was over. When she approached the building on Tenth Avenue, where she lived, there was a young man sitting on the steps. He was the superintendent's son.

"Hey, Alberto, how are you? Why are you sitting here like you have no home?"

Alberto, nineteen, was handsome, with dark-set eyes and square jaw line. He was of medium height and well developed. Lita admired his good looks but was careful to hide her admiring glances. This was where she lived, and she never played those games close to home. She could never leave her small place and did not want any trouble from the super over his son.

"Ah, my dad and I don't get along. He gets on my nerves. Always finding something for me to do."

"Go away. Move out. You're a grown man."

"I ain't got a job, and I ain't got the money."

"You don't want a job, Alberto. You could get a job with no problem."

She pushed by him and started up the stairs.

"I don't see you going out to work in the daytime. Why don't you get a job instead of being a drag-queen whore?"

Lita didn't need an argument. She continued up the steps to her apartment. Lita quickly entered her apartment. She sighed with relief. *That little bastard,* she thought. She knew that he was a piece of shit, and she had to remember that, no matter how good he might look to her. Because he was the super's son, she had to remain courteous but aloof. She had heard him curse his father and refuse to help out in the building. The sooner he left his father's house, the better for all concerned.

Lita's first move when she got home from working the streets was to put her money away. The small box on her dresser always contained at least five hundred dollars in small bills. She had cleverly lifted a floor board and secreted away all the cash she made on the streets. The bills were all hundreds, and Lita knew exactly how much was there. Once a week she counted each pack. She had exactly twenty-five thousand dollars in one-hundred-dollar bills. The other money she kept laying around for her pleasure to look and to buy whatever she wanted. There was no need to hide it. She never allowed any visitors to her small place, and she had no boyfriend or girlfriends, and the thing in the closet was no harm to anyone. Lita was a loner.

Now Lita was tired, and that made her feel dissatisfaction with her drug. She had sniffed enough to be more awake, alert, and energized. She'd have to speak to her supplier. He would have to come up with a better quality. As she lay awake in the bed, awaiting sleep, she already had plans to go to Dr. Edgewater's. His new girlfriend was just what she needed to continue her silicone treatments. Edgewater would be glad to get the money, and he wanted Belinda to learn. Sure, she'd let Belinda pump her up. That would teach Ms. Jolena a lesson.

Alberto continued to sit on the steps. He was in a bad mood and hated everyone tonight. He knew that Lita was a drag queen and a whore. He never had anything against her or whatever she did to make a living. She never bothered anyone in the building. But tonight, he hated everyone, and tonight, he was broke. He should have asked Lita to loan him a few dollars. It was too late now. He wouldn't dare ask after hurling the insults at her. Maybe he should learn to be more kind. Calm his temper. He got up and went into his father's apartment. Maybe tomorrow he'd look for a job.

26

Arnold Brown changed his hospital "drag outfit." He showered, slipped into his designer bathrobe, and strolled through his small apartment, sipping brandy from one of his elegant crystal glasses. It was early evening, and his thoughts were clouded with ideas of how to manipulate his future. The very thought of going out into the streets tonight or any future night began to be a living nightmare. He could hardly believe this good fortune had descended upon him. Surely, one could say that having to care for Louis Frazier was not exactly good fortune, but it was the money that Louis would bring with him that was a saving grace for Arnold.

He had to remember that he was forty years old and had been working the streets nearly twenty years. He was tired! Twenty years of street work was comparable to forty years on an ordinary job. It would be nice to have his own little shop. Antiques, of course! Just the thing for him. He knew antiques. With three quarters of Louis's money, he could start his own business, and until it began to make money, the other money would take care of their expenses. Yes! This would work. He looked around and planned where he would put a bed for Louis. No, not in his antique four-poster.

Arnold thought of the changes he would have to make, but then, he was ready to accept those changes. After a few more sips of brandy, he remembered his one problem. Clarence. Oh, God, how was he going to explain this to Clarence? He looked at the clock. Clarence, who worked the midnight shift, would be stopping by to get some loving. How would he break this news to Clarence that the relationship was over? Arnold laughed. It was Clarence's fault anyway.

First of all, he should never have requested that Arnold suck his dick. Did he think he could sip champagne from this slipper and not want more? Second, he should have gone away, not try to make an honest person out of Arnold. He would explain that to Clarence. After all, Clarence could not dictate his life. Arnold was free to do as he pleased. Clarence was a married man, a father, and with a responsible job. He had voiced his dislike of faggots, so he should have stayed away after the first taste. But he kept coming back again and again. Now he'd have to stay away forever. Arnold knew that he could live without Clarence in his life. But he began to wonder about Clarence. Could he live without Arnold?

The doorbell rang. Reluctantly Arnold answered.

Arnold felt extremely lonely after Clarence left him that evening. He knew that it was not because he missed Clarence. He missed Louis! Louis had become an important part of his life. Maybe even his future. He could trust Louis, and that was only because he could not move. Arnold stopped thinking about if he could ever move. He was only concerned with the fact that he was not moving now. Yes, Louis was his answer. Tonight, he would go out and celebrate by walking the streets, beautiful in drag, and not picking a single pocket.

Yes, he had reformed, born again out of the relationship with Louis. Tonight would be his last stroll. Tonight, he would walk with a purpose. Quickly, he dressed in his most outrageous drag outfit. He added extra touches of makeup. Tonight would be the exit to this life. Once he got Louis moved in, he would explain his secret existence to him. He knew Louis would accept him as Arnold. After all, Lottie and Arnold were one person.

The late spring evening was beginning to get warmer. Lottie Lee sashayed her way to Central Park South. She was more than striking in her outfit tonight. The change in the weather caused an increased traffic of prostitutes and thieves. Lottie greeted everyone she knew and didn't know. One familiar face stopped her and asked if she had scored.

"Sweetie, I am not working tonight. In fact, I will not be working anymore. This is just my final walk."

"What in the fuck did you score? A suitcase full of money?"

"No, I scored love. Love, darling, and a man."

"You got a real man?"

"Yes, a real man. Not a freak like some of these men we meet."

"So you finished thieving."

"Oh, please, don't put it so harshly."

"Well, that's what this was."

Lottie could see this conversation developing into an argument. She walked on.

"See you later, much later."

Lottie decided to walk all the way to Fifth Avenue. As she waited for the traffic light to change at the entrance to the park, some inner voice told her to look back. At the first glance, she saw the girls being herded into the police van. *Oh, shit,* she thought, *I got to get the fuck out of here.* Quickly, she started through the park. She realized she had no knife. *Oh, shit, I ain't got no protection. What if I run into a fuckin' mugger.*

But Lottie knew that she had to keep going until she came out of the park near Seventy-sixth Street. There she could get a cab. As she maneuvered her way through the bushes and rocks, she could hear the sirens coming through the park. She lay down. It was not a good place to lie. It was muddy, and Lottie knew that her best drag outfit was in ruins. After all was quiet, she got up and continued toward the uptown section of the park.

My God, she thought, *I almost got picked up and for nothing. Just having a nightly stroll. Does it really pay to be honest? A girl can't even have a nightly stroll. Well,* she thought again, *I really had no business out here. What if I got picked up and Louis would be waiting tomorrow. Yeah, Oldtimer would have a ball punishing poor Louis.* After a while, Lottie came out of the park and flagged a cab.

"I'm going to the Bronx. I just came from a costume ball and must get home before my wife sees me like this. I'll pay twenty dollars."

"Jump in."

The cab driver knew the deal. He had been cruising his cab around Central Park South and seen the van plucking the girls off the streets. *Well,* he thought, *this one got away. Good for her.* He could use that twenty. It was a slow night.

27

Today would be the happiest day in the life of Louis Frazier. Today, he would leave the hospital. Today, he would go home with his Lottie. Today, his whole life would change.

Every footstep he heard aroused Louis. He kept his head constantly turned toward the door. It was already ten o'clock, and she had not arrived. Oldtimer had been shuffling in and out of the cubicle just to watch Louis's anticipation. He hoped that Lottie would not come and get Louis.

"I doubt if she will show up. It's ten o'clock, man. When is she supposed to be here?"

"I got time. The ambulance won't come until eleven. Don't worry about it. Lottie will be here," Louis reassured him.

"I ain't the one to worry. You worry." He pointed at him with his cane. "You is the one that's got to get out of here. And if she don't show up, they are going to take you straight to that nursing home."

Louis did not want to show his fear to Oldtimer. He prayed that Lottie would show. Oldtimer did not know about the check he would be receiving and the extra money that would come in each month.

Suddenly, Louis heard voices getting closer to his cubicle. Oldtimer quickly made his way toward Louis.

"They coming, man. And ain't no Lottie with them."

"Who's coming?"

"The ambulance people coming to take you away."

"They have to wait for Lottie."

"They ain't waiting for nobody."

"I ain't leaving till she gets here," Louis yelled.

"How you going to stop anybody? You can't move!"

Louis saw the two man dressed in green uniforms looking down at him. The nurse was with them holding what seemed to be important papers pertaining to Louis Frazier.

"Mr. Frazier, you will be going to a nursing home in the Bronx unless someone is here to take you home."

"She's coming. She's coming."

"Who is coming to get you? They should have been here." She made notes on her clipboard.

"Lottie Lee. You know her. She works here. I am going home with her."

"Yes, I know Ms. Lee, but she doesn't work here any longer. She quit yesterday. She has no intention of coming to get you."

Louis was devastated.

"Wait! Wait! She'll be here!"

"I'm sorry, Mr. Frazier, but the ambulance cannot wait. She is not here to give instructions to take you to her home."

"Where they gonna take me?"

"To the nursing home. I already explained that to you."

"Oh, no," Louis cried softly. The tears poured down the sides of his face.

Oldtimer was pleased. He remembered how Louis had bragged about being such a lover and had Ms. Lottie Lee under control. Now the nursing home would be his last ticket.

"Sorry, my man, but you gotta go," Oldtimer added.

Louis wished for death. Not even that would happen. As they moved him out of his cubicle, he looked around to see if maybe Lottie was hiding somewhere and did not want to even say good-bye to him. He could not believe she had lied. How could she do such a thing to him? They had made plans. Slowly the stretcher was wheeled down the hall and to the elevators. Louis had not seen an elevator in a year. It seemed so large. He realized now how small and insignificant Louis Frazier had become. He'd close his eyes, and he never would speak again, nor would he eat again. He'd just die. The men continued wheeling Louis into the main corridor of the hospital toward the waiting ambulance. Louis shut his eyes.

"Stop! Stop! I'm here! I'm here! Louis, Louis open your eyes. It's me, Lottie! I'm here. I'm late, but I'm here. You are going home with me!" Lottie, in all her largeness and drag outfit, leaned down and kissed him.

Louis could not believe he was hearing her voice. His eyes opened. He could almost feel his arms reaching out to hold her. He couldn't move, but it didn't matter. She was here. She kept her word.

"I'm so sorry. I overslept." She directed her attention to the ambulance drivers. "This is the address where we are going. He is my brother, and he will be living with me. Right, Louis?"

"Right!" Louis never hesitated.

Louis was placed in the ambulance, and Lottie Lee rode beside him. He was laughing and crying at the same time.

"I thought it was the end for me."

"No, no. It's the beginning, Louis, it's the beginning for both of us."

Lottie held his hand tightly. It was a new beginning. The only person she'd have to confront would be Clarence.

28

She was tall, blonde and extremely attractive. Her manner of dress was done so as not to attract undue attention to herself. She was confident of her beauty and knew she could attract much attention, but this was not her purpose at this time. She merely wanted to rent a room at the modest hotel until she found an apartment. Here she would stay and become one of the many hundreds of young ladies looking for success in New York. She never doubted her successful future. All she had to do was make it work.

Pamela Thorn had decided a long time ago that she would become one of the top models in the world. There was never a doubt in her mind, and all she had been through made it more essential to obtain her goal. After registering and being shown to her room, she quickly showered, put on a fresh pair of jeans and white shirt. She added a sweater because the weather was getting a little chilly in New York.

She studied her face in the mirror. She was pleased. The makeup she applied was modest. There were no scars or blemishes to hide. When she went to the agency, she knew that they would scrutinize her. But they also knew beauty and potential when it appeared in front of them. Sure they would take a chance on her. Why not? She as the typical American beauty, white, blonde, bluest of eyes, slim, a face perfectly set with jawline and neck almost unbelievably correct.

She studied the mirror and smiled proudly. There were no traces of Honey Babe or Thomas Blake. Those names and lives were behind her, cut out and thrown away somewhere in Canada. She now had a new and permanent name. Pamela Thorn. Simple enough. Born in Canada. Simple enough. Twenty years old. Simple enough. No experience as a model. Simple enough. Everything kept simple enough to prevent her background from being questioned too intensively.

When Pamela entered the office of Model Members she was at first taken aback by the flurry of people and the various wanna-be models sitting and waiting to be seen. She went to the reception desk and was told by a receptionist, who never looked at her, to write her name and have a seat.

While Pamela sat and waited, she used that time to observe the other girls waiting for their interviews. A few of them had pictures, but many, like Pamela, did not have pictures. *Maybe,* she thought to herself, *that was a big mistake. I should have had pictures done.* Well, she'd find all that out during the interview. Pamela noticed that some of the girls did not look so beautiful. She measured herself against many of them and was confident she would lose no points. Her obsession with this project had been long, painful, and enduring. Nobody and nothing would stop her. The sound of her name broke through her thoughts. She quickly moved toward the receptionist's desk.

"You can go in to room Three. Someone will come in to interview you."

She murmured a thank you and disappeared into the room.

It was small with a few successful model pictures on the wall. Pamela was not in awe of the pictures. She only wanted to see her pictures. She was only interested in self. She did not sit but went over to the large picture window that overlooked Manhattan. Pam stared down into the city and smiled. *The beginning,* she thought, *is down there, but now I am up here and it will all be different.* She wanted to be in front of that window when whoever came to interview her entered. Soon, the door opened, she turned, and the tall, graying, but still handsome, man and she met face to face. He stared at her intently. She held out her hand to greet him.

"My name is Pamela Thorn. And I want to be a model. The best model in the world."

"And I am Jonathan Reeves, and I want you to be the best model in the world."

He took her hand. It was cold and moist, and he knew she was nervous and somewhat inexperienced, but he felt another kind of experience that made him realize she had the fortitude to succeed. He was fascinated by the blue eyes, perfect nose, lips, different and sensuous, and the swan neck. Once every three or five years, this kind of beauty would wander into the agency and boost their ratings. She was perfect. The catch of the day and, at least, the next five years. But surely something was wrong. He began his intense questions.

"How old are you?"

"Twenty going on twenty-one. Born March 22, 1957."

"Married?"

"No."

"Have you a boyfriend or lover ruling over you?"

"No, and I am not interested. Career and romance does not mix well."

How is she so knowledgeable? he mused.

"How long have you been in New York?"

"I arrived today from Canada. That's where I was born and raised."

"Have you signed with anyone else, here or in Canada?"

"No, this is the first time I have been in any agency."

"Any pictures?"

"No."

"You need pictures. We have to know how you photograph."

"Tell me where to go. If it's going to cost me, I have a few dollars saved. Not much." She was humble.

"Don't worry about it. You look like a good investment."

Quickly, he went to the phone.

"Maria, come in here. I want you to see someone."

In a matter of minutes, the door opened, and a short, slightly hunched, bespeckled, graying lady entered. She took one look at Pamela and sighed.

"Jonathan, where did you find her?" She laughed and rubbed her hands together as if she was ready to feast.

"She found us! By the way, how did you find us?"

"I looked under 'Model Agencies' in the yellow pages."

"It pays to advertise." The both spoke in unison and laughed.

"Well, Maria, what do you think? Do we have a winner?"

"Does she have any experience?"

"None!"

"She's never been seen or signed?"

"Nothing. She doesn't even have pictures."

"Let's get her downstairs to Burt and have him do some photos on her."

"But I need makeup and clothes—"

"Don't worry, we have everything downstairs. If you come through like we think you will, we will take care of everything. You will belong to us. We will make you famous." Maria stared at her. "That is what you want, isn't it?"

"Yes, that is what I want besides money. I will need money."

Jonathan heard her wish, and he heard in her voice an experience he could not quite put his finger on.

"Maria, take her downstairs. I want to see those photos today. If she works out, the winter collection will be shown soon, and I want her on that runway."

"She has no experience, Jonathan. How can we put her on a runway within two months?"

"You'll find a way, Maria. If things work out, this will be our new million-dollar baby!"

Pamela was ecstatic. She followed Maria out of the room and into an elevator. This would be the ultimate test. She would have to bare herself to the makeup artist and the people who would select her change of wardrobe for the photo shoot. Carefully she would observe if anyone looked at her in a suspicious manner. So far, she had come through with flying colors. It was comforting to know that height was preferred and accepted in models.

29

Alberto was a liar and a thief. The thief had found his way into Lita's apartment. He could have used his father's master key but noticed that Lita had an extra lock on her door. There were other apartments he could have entered without any problems, but he wanted cash, and he knew that cash would be in Lita's apartment. He knew the bitch made money and was too stupid to put it in a bank. Whores never put money in a bank. It was right there in her apartment, and with that thought in mind, Alberto was more determined than ever to get it.

He felt entitled. Why should he get a job washing dishes or cleaning floors when drag queens, like Lita, were walking the streets for a few hours making all that money and he had to work a whole month just to make what they made in a night? No way! He knew a way to get into that apartment and take what he needed. He had a plan. Just get in and take a little each trip. The bitch wouldn't miss it. She couldn't remember everything. He could bet she was high on drugs. All whores got high off of drugs.

The way Lita's apartment was situated enabled Alberto to enter through a bathroom window, just large enough for him to squeeze through. Lita, he was sure, had no idea that the window could be approached from the roof. All it took was a strong young man to lower himself down to the window and come in. Lita always kept the window opened, especially in the spring and late into the fall. And he had noted lately that she had not changed that habit. Tonight, when Lita went out, Alberto would make his way into the apartment to take a look around and see if it was going to be worth the trouble. He was sitting on the stoop when Lita was going out to work the streets.

"Alberto, baby, did you find a job?" She laughed.

"I don't find it funny."

"I only ask, baby, because I know how hard jobs are to find."

"What do you know about a job? You got one?"

"Yeah, I got one." She sneered at him.

"Right! Like selling your body on the streets every night."

"Right! At least I ain't giving it away. Don't have an attitude with me, Alberto. I ain't the cause of your problems. I'll talk to you later."

Lita walked away. There was something about him she did not like. He came across to her as sinister and devious. She shuddered at the thought of him.

Alberto hated her. He felt she saw right through him. But he had no fear of faggot whores. He would get into her apartment and take what he wanted. He waited about one hour, then proceeded to the roof. He just prayed that the window was open. As he inspected the roof and the structure, it looked even easier than he had imagined. His one problem after getting in was to get out. He had to come out the same way. He looked and saw many accessible ledges. This was easy. Ready-made for Alberto, the thief.

Slowly, he eased down towards her window, and it was open! Alberto turned and twisted until he was in the bathroom. He laughed. It was too easy. He was on! He made his way into the large studio room that Lita called home. Already, without remorse, he had invaded her privacy; he had raped her home and would inflict such a stigma on her place of peace and quiet that even Alberto would never be able to compensate for.

He went directly to her dresser, and there was a pile of money. He could snatch it all, but that would be foolish. No, he'd take some and return another day and take some more. It would be like a steady income. Lita would never miss a little. And then he saw the small glasine bag containing the white powder. "Goddam," he whispered, "the bitch sniffs."

Methodically he opened the bag and dipped his fingernail into the powder and lifted it to his nose and sniffed. Damn, cocaine! Alberto laughed. He had hit pay dirt! Not only had he found some money, but drugs. Sure, he had had a few sniffs of cocaine but never this quantity and quality. Maybe he should have been more kind to Lita. She might have invited him in and shared her drugs with him. But then, he would have had to pretend he liked her. He, Alberto Perez, did not like freaks or faggots. He considered himself a man.

Now he felt that what he was doing, this job of thievery, was his duty to society. He would right all the wrongs these faggots did by taking back what they took from others. With all of that in mind, Alberto sniffed a little more than he planned. Quickly, he put the bag back in place. Lita was no fool. He did not want her to suspect anyone had been in her apartment. From the money pile, Alberto was careful to take only a hundred dollars, although he had counted six hundred. He took five twenties. Already, he had calculated how his visits should be planned. If he came each night and took one hundred dollars, he could be way ahead of the work game. Included in those visits was the privilege of free sniffs of cocaine.

And so, Alberto stuffed his pockets with the twenties and went back through the bathroom window, carefully lifting his young, agile body up toward the roof. From there, he descended into the society of acceptance. Alberto felt good about himself. He felt justified. He planned many more visits to Lita's apartment. What he also did was to avoid her when she came out to go to work. She might be missing her shit and ask him a question about it, and then Alberto would get mad and want to hit the faggot.

Within one week, Alberto had made five visits to the apartment. Greed had overwhelmed him, and he was enjoying the cocaine almost more than the money. It had become so easy that Alberto laughed after each visit about the no-risk venture he encountered. It couldn't get much better. He never thought about being caught. So what if she caught him? She wouldn't dare call the cops with all that cocaine in her apartment. The best move she could make for herself would be to open the door and allow him to walk out instead of climbing through the window. But then, Alberto did not plan on being caught.

Lita knew someone had been in her apartment. The first night, she sensed something wrong. She didn't believe in ghosts and immediately checked her closet. Nothing had been touched. In fact, no one had entered the closet. She counted the pile of money she always left on the dresser. Instead of the six hundred, there were only five. And her bag of cocaine was way down. Yes, someone was coming in when she was not there.

As tired as she was tonight, she'd have to solve this mystery. First, she washed her face clear of all makeup. The water was refreshing. Then she went to the bag of cocaine and took a big sniff. A little drink of brandy, and now she'd have to start thinking. Who did she know would dare try to enter her apartment? The super could not come in. She had an extra lock put on the door. She checked the lock. It had not been tampered with. The one window in the studio was a sheer drop. No one could enter there. What other way? She was puzzled.

Who knew the building this well? Who knew her schedule? It had to be someone right in this building. None of the tenants spoke to her. They all pretty well knew what she was and what she did, and they ignored her. The only person she ever had words with was Alberto. Alberto! She took another sniff. That little fuck! It was him. Of course. But how did he get in and out?

She looked again at the window. It had not been touched, and besides, he would have fallen and broken his ass even if he tried from the roof. Her mind raced. *The bathroom! Goddam him,* she thought, as she ran to the bathroom. *I always keep the window open. How could anybody get in and out of that window, and from where?* Lita stood on the toilet seat and leaned out of the window. No, she could not get her siliconed wide-ass hips through there, but a narrow-ass boy like Alberto could squeeze in and out like a snake. She looked and saw where he could hoist himself down from the roof, grab a hold of a convenient ledge and slide right in.

She closed the window and slowly began prancing back and forth. What to do about Alberto? She could double back and catch him, but then, he knew about her cocaine. She didn't want any trouble with the police because of what was hidden in the closet. So the little fuck had her but did not know the whole story. No, he was too busy stealing her money and sniffing her drug to be interested in anything else.

She could kill him, but one body was enough in her studio. And that would bring too many inquiries about the missing Alberto. No, she had to plan something else for him. At this time, she had no choice but to continue to act like nothing had happened. But she'd have to do something soon, because nobody was going to rob Lita Lopez and just get away with it. No, Alberto would have to die. She didn't know how and when, but just as she had planned the other murders, she would plan his.

30

They took Pamela apart. It was like a car being disassembled and put back together. Burt, the photographer, whistled quietly under his breath when he saw her come in with Maria.

Goddamn, where did they find her? he asked himself as he got ready to go into the dark room. His dick got hard when he thought about fucking her. She was young and dumb. He'd have her soon.

Maria led Pamela into the makeup room; there were racks of dresses and outfits used just for photo shoots. Pam's heart raced. At last she would get to see herself as she had dreamed. She had no doubt about her ability to succeed. She would. She would be the most talked about model in years. And how well she had covered her tracks. She thought about Jonathan upstairs, still lusting for her. Pam smiled. Good, let him lust. When the proper time came, he would have his chance.

"Tania, Tania." Maria called loudly. Finally, there appeared a small, elderly woman from a back room.

"Yea, Maria. What is it? What is it?"

"Tania, I have a new girl. Take care of her. Burt is going to do the standard photos of her. You dress her. I've got to talk with Burt. Where is Bruno? I need him to do her makeup."

"I'll get him," Tania replied and disappeared again. Quite soon, she returned with a handsome boy who was apparently the makeup artist. His mannerisms were openly gay.

"Hi. My name is Bruno, and I'll be doing your makeup. God, you are lovely! Where did they find you?"

"I found them," Pam laughed.

She remembered to be kind and not to be difficult with these workers. She needed them. Pam was relieved of her own clothes and re-dressed in a sports outfit. She looked stunning. Then Bruno began his makeup artistry. He was good. He danced around her, dabbing and dotting life into her face. She wondered if he could feel any of her male presence. *Stop,* she thought, *there is no such thing.* No one questioned her. Her body had been exposed, and all Tania could say was that her skin was lovely, her shape perfect, her breasts perfect, her buttocks perfect, her blondness perfect, her face perfect. Bruno was ecstatic.

"Is it that my makeup techniques are getting better, or is it that your face is so lovely, it is accentuating my makeup?"

"Let's say that." Pam joined in with laughter.

"I have to do your hair, because our regular guy is out today, but I can fix it. You have gorgeous hair, So silky and blonde. Are you a real blonde?" He asked as he inspected the roots of her hair closer. "Oh, don't answer. Yes, you are!"

Pam laughed. She was pleased.

"Yes, I'm real all over."

In one hour, Pam had been transformed. She was ready for the camera. Burt could tell she was a novice, but a beautiful one. As he looked through his lens, he could see she would photograph well, but he needed something from her. Sure, she was young and did not understand what she had to do for the camera. The first roll was ordinary. Just showing that she photographed well, but he needed more out of her.

"Pam, come here and sit."

Pam made her way to the chair beside him.

"I know what you are going to tell me. It's just ordinary pictures. I'm not doing anything for your camera."

"Right, right. You know that?"

"I feel that. I'm sorry. I just don't know how."

"Pam, think of a time when things were difficult for you. Maybe when you were most unhappy or needed money or some tragic time in your young life—if you ever hard a tragic time. Then work with that. Give me that look in your eyes and your face. Translate to me."

If that was the answer to Pam's success, then it was solved. She returned to the front of the camera, the music was turned up, and she began remembering the time her parents were killed, the time the uncle molested her, the time she worked Lake Shore's richest men and then when she was Ms. Honey Babe walking the streets of New York. Remembering the rejections and insults she had endured while dreaming of this moment enabled her to project into the camera all of her beauty and talent. This day, she made the camera. It did not make her.

The photo shoot was a success. Burt knew that there was a new rising model. She would add new excitement to the business. He himself took the photos to Jonathan.

"She's a winner! She's a million-dollar property."

"Wow! Damn, look at her! Was she difficult to work with, Burt?"

"She's young and inexperienced. But aren't they all?"

"I want her to walk in the upcoming spring collection."

"Can she walk runway?"

"Probably not, but we will teach her."

"What else are you going to teach her, Jonathan?" Burt asked, his brows knitted together.

"Believe me, I am not going to touch her."

"You say that about all the girls." Burt laughed and got up to leave.

"Keep these photos a secret. Tomorrow we'll do some more. I don't want anybody to see her yet. Not until the show."

Maria barged in.

"Did you see those pictures? She's good!"

"No, I'm good," Burt added.

"But of course, darling."

Pam followed Maria into the room. She sat quietly in a chair. All three were staring at her.

Jonathan walked over and gave her a few photos. Pam inspected them carefully. She smiled. She was pleased.

"I look great. I look great!"

"You are going to be great. But you must listen to me, Pam. You must listen to all of us. Your life will change. Very little of it will belong to you." Jonathan was pacing the floor and talking.

"We do not want these pictures to be seen. Not yet. We do not want you to be seen. I want to put you in the spring show. I know you don't know how to do runway, but we will teach you. When you come out on that runway, everyone will be wondering who you are. You will be the sensation! Now, where are you living?"

"At the Barbizon."

"Good. Stay there. Do not socialize with anybody for the next two months. We will have a schedule mapped out for you. Don't tell anyone where you work. Don't tell anyone anything about you."

Pam could have laughed. Her whole life so far had been a secret, and now it was another secret. She knew how to do that well.

"I will do as you say."

"Do you need money?"

"Yes." Pam was not going to refuse money.

"Maria, make out a check for her. Five hundred dollars. Pam, open up a checking account. In a few days, we'll get a contract together for you to sign. Now, go home and get plenty of rest, and do not gain a pound. It's very important for you to keep your weight exact. No boyfriends and no smoking. Both are bad for the lips."

With those directions thrown at her, Pam left the agency. Once outside, she walked toward Central Park South. There she lingered and looked up and down the street. These streets were very familiar to her. Now she was able to walk them in plain daylight. No more lurking beside buildings, waiting for a trick. All the rejections she had received when she was working the streets will not happen to her again. She would be the one to reject. She would be the one to decide. She would be the one in charge.

31

When Rudy, the young, slim man displaying all the gay movements, asked Pam if she knew how to walk runway, she smiled and replied no. But in her heart, she knew that it would not take long for her to learn. She had walked the streets of New York; this would not be a difficult task.

Rudy led her to a room where a runway was already set up.

"This is our practice room, and I am going to show you how this runway-walking goes. Watch me, and listen to what I say, and you will have it down pat in no time. I can look at you and see the talent in you."

He led her onto the runway.

"You've got to find a style. What I mean is, to walk in a certain way. We've got to find something unique for you. Something that will call for attention; make them wait for you to come out; hypnotize them when you come out; make them silent when you come out; make them gasp as you stroll by their envious eyes."

Pam listened intently. She had practiced in secret the walk of a model but had never been given this particular insight that Rudy was giving her now.

She watched intently as he demonstrated. He began walking and explaining.

"Chin up. Head held straight and forward. Lead from the pelvis, and have your torso lag slightly behind."

She watched in amazement as he started walking. He was good. But after all, he was the teacher.

Again, he called out more explanations of his movements.

"Upper body should be held erect. Arms swinging with opposite leg. Movement must be fluid. Keep it fluid. No jerking. Curve those hands and fingers, gracefully! Now place one foot in front of the other and sway the hips. Hands are used only to compliment the fashion, not to keep your balance. And remember, use short steps. These show the movement of the hips."

And as he strolled and demonstrated, Pam was anxious to try it. She knew she could do it.

"Your turn, sweetheart," he beckoned to her.

As Pam attempted to walk as Rudy had done, she found it very difficult.

"Why is it so hard for me to do?"

He could see she was upset.

"Pam, listen, just learn the basics of the walk, and then you will be able to put the flair into it. Remember, you are advertising. You have to look sexy, but make it a class act."

Pam understood what he meant. She smiled and slowly began the basic steps again. With Rudy guiding her, she began to feel better about the walk.

"You're getting it. Slowly, but surely. And you'll get it better. Just keep practicing until you feel it. You must begin to feel free and acquire a sense of confidence and nothing to hide. You must develop a walk for the runway, turn, walk back, and be gone! All of this in one minute's time."

Pam began to understand. She would concentrate and work on this until it was perfect. After all, everything else was perfect.

"Rudy, can I come here and practice alone? Then I can concentrate until I get it."

"Darling, you can practice until you drop if that's what will do it. You must get this. They want you to do runway, so you have to learn the walk. And I think they want you for the spring show, and that will be in a few months. Enjoy yourself. I should have been born a woman. I would have been the greatest. Oh, well, no need to lament. I must go now. I have other duties in life."

"Thank you for helping me, Rudy. I'll call you in a few days so you can see if I am getting this right."

Rudy, glad to be free, answered her good-bye with a quick hug and left.

Pam was alone now. She was amazed that everything was working almost—better—than she had planned. No one had questioned or suspected her. She had covered her tracks well. There would be no one to surprise her with recognition. Now she looked at the formidable runway. She had to learn this walk. Pam began practicing. Again and again she walked, slowly, then faster. She watched her hands, her arms, her legs, her hips, her neck, and her face in the large mirror that was set at the end of the runway. With each practiced step, she began to look more professional. After an hour, Pam prepared to go to her hotel. Tomorrow, when she had free time, she would come back to this studio and practice until she was perfect.

32

Louis was dumped right onto Lottie's antique four-poster bed. Lottie was truly upset but did not show her concern to Louis. Immediately, she called a medical supply place for a bed to be delivered. Pronto! It would be two days before the bed was available. She also ordered a wheelchair, for she was determined that Louis was not going to lie in bed all day long, as he had in the hospital.

Louis was pleased with Lottie's apartment. He noted that Lottie had surrounded herself with fine furniture and artwork.

"You have a beautiful place, Lottie, and wonderful artwork. I ain't too smart on art, but it looks good."

"I love antiques and art. I'd like to have my own little antique shop, but we did talk about that."

"Yes, and I have a number for you to call and tell the insurance company where to send my check. Also, the man said that I should have a power of attorney drawn up, so you can sign all my papers for me."

"Oh, yes, I know about that. I will get that done today."

Lottie's heart was beating fast. This was really happening. She would get her shop, even though the price was somewhat complicated. However, the one bothersome item, besides Clarence, was how to tell Louis that she was not a woman but a man dressed like a woman; she was tired of all that "dragging" and just wanted to dress in men's clothes and be gay. *Now, how in the hell,* Lottie thought, *was Louis going to handle that revelation?* Then she had to remember that Louis had no choice but to accept whatever she or he was. She would simply sit down and tell him the truth about everything. Better to clear all that out of the way. Both of their futures were at stake, and they both needed each other.

"Also, we will be getting almost five hundred dollars every month," Louis reminded her.

"Five hundred dollars every month?"

"Yes, and for as long as I am in this condition."

"You mean for as long as you cannot move or walk?"

"Yep."

Lottie came over to Louis and started feeling on his arms and legs.

"You ain't got no feeling yet?"

"I don't feel you touching me."

"Well, Louis, they took out that tube, and now there is a urinal there. Do you know when you have to pee?"

"No." He felt embarrassed.

"Don't worry. We'll just keep it there, and I will empty it."

Lottie was becoming extremely aware that maybe Louis had some truth to tell her. She had heard rumors at the hospital that he would never walk but had discounted them after listening to Louis brag about how he would walk. If the rumors were true, Lottie needed to know, because it would become increasingly difficult taking care of him. She'd have to sit down and map out a plan. There would be many supplies she'd have to buy, and a schedule would be important. There would be the problem of keeping him clean and fed. At least he could watch television when she went out. Maybe later, she could hire someone to help her, especially after she got the store. *Oh, well, twiddle-de-dee,* she sighed, *a girl must do what a girl must do.*

Now, what about Clarence? In a few nights, he will be ringing that bell. What a surprise when she opened the door and he saw this big black man lying in her bed. What could he do? He would never risk job and family. Lottie knew that she would be rid of him. He'd quickly find some little transvestite waiting for a ride home. *Good riddance,* she thought. This relationship with Louis was business and an answer to her future. Now Lottie could stop pretending to be what she wasn't and just be Arnold Brown, antiques dealer and lover of Louis. Now she must explain all this madness to Louis. He had no other choice but to accept.

"Louis, I have something to explain to you. First, I want you to understand that I care for you very much."

It was then that Lottie began to remove her stockings and dress. Louis was smiling. His Lottie was going to strip for him. Suddenly, she disappeared into the bathroom. Louis waited patiently. He figured she would come out in some thin sheer gown. However, his smile turned into a frown when Lottie returned with face void of makeup, no clothes, and a man's body appeared in front of Louis.

"Lottie, Lottie!" Louis called frantically. His eyes were wild, his head turning wildly. Where was Lottie?

"Calm down, calm down, Louis. It's me. But my name is not Lottie. It is Arnold, and I am a man. I have always been a man. I just dressed in drag."

"You is a faggot! Oldtimer said something was wrong with you."

"There is nothing wrong with me. Listen to me. Look at me. I am not going to hurt you. I am going to take care of you. We both have disabilities. We will help each other! Without me, where would you have ended? How long would you have lasted? Without you, where would I have ended? How long would I have lasted? I worked the streets, Louis, before I got that mammy-yammie job and met you. Don't you see it's our destiny to meet and be together? We can save each other. I never liked the life I lived, and you, what fuckin' choice do you have? I'm it! I'm going take care of you, and we don't have to be lovers. I'm not asking you to love me or kiss me or touch me. We can be good, true friends, Louis."

Louis was inconsolable. As he lay there and cried, he thought of how he could get out of this situation. Arnold dried Louis's tears, even though Louis had expressed angrily not to touch him. Later, Arnold dressed in his boy clothes and looked quite handsome. Louis was full of questions.

"You ain't going to try and make a faggot out of me?"

"Hell, no!" Arnold laughed.

"How am I going to protect myself from you?"

"Dearest Louis, I am not going to hurt you. Only take care of you."

"I better tell you now that they told me I would never walk or move my arms. Nothing will move but my head. Nothing." Louis began to cry.

"Don't cry, Louis. Can't you see how it is with both of us? We need each other. We can help each other. I'm strong and ambitious. I'm going to open the antiques shop and make a lot of money and get you the best care possible. It will be okay."

Arnold, ex-drag queen and thief, realized what a monumental task was in front of him. But he had managed all these years against insurmountable odds, and he would survive now. He would be a success, and Louis would get the best of care. As far as Clarence was concerned, Arnold knew how to handle that with one phone call. He would call Clarence's house, and if Clarence was not available to talk, he would leave a message with whomever answered that the message was from Arnold and please do not call him again.

Louis had stopped crying. At least he knew the truth, and that was somewhat consoling for a man in his position.

"Arnold, I'm sorry. I've been thinking. We do need each other. I'm glad I'm here, regardless of the truth. But I must admit, you really had me fooled in that hospital."

Arnold smiled.

"I guess that was my last great drag show."
They both laughed.

33

The makeup artist had been called in to do the first makeup on Pam. Afterwards, there would be many photographs taken. It was very important how she photographed because even though they had her set to be a runway model, her worth would be much more if she photographed well.

Lola Davis was one of the best in makeup. She could make an ugly girl beautiful, but when she saw Pam, she sighed.

"Damn, where did you find her?"

"She found us," Maria replied.

Lola could not take her eyes off the beauty that Pam radiated. Few people knew Lola was a lesbian. She knew beauty when she saw it. And this was real, natural beauty. The clear white, perfect skin and the natural blond hair. She wondered if it was like that below. Lola had to walk around a few minutes and compose herself. *Think about the makeup you are going to use, bitch,* she told herself. The pleasure she would have in touching Pam would be more than pleasing.

"Her skin is so perfect that I will want to use almost a porcelain base so close to her skin. I'll do her eyes beyond comparison. They are green and lovely. Her mouth I will accent, and yes, yes, she will be more than beauty. Even the camera cannot ruin this face. She is perfection."

Lola had all her makeup products ready. She held Pam's face and began a transformation. She avoided looking directly into her eyes. However, Pam stared directly at her and met her eye to eye when Lola's gaze lingered. Pam realized that Lola had lesbian tendencies, but she had to meet her head on and act like she had no idea that she had seen the transmissions Lola was sending. Pam remained cold and indifferent. She had no time for romances with makeup artists, photographers, directors, or assistant directors. Pam had come too far to settle. When the right person presented himself, she would know. This was just the beginning. As she became more and more famous, then she would choose the proper suitors, and they would be very very rich. Never would she be vulnerable again.

The makeup transformed Pam into an indescribable beauty. Many of the employees came to watch the photo shoot. Pam who had never taken a picture in life or posed for a picture was stimulated by the music that was played as the session began. She allowed her body to be led by the music. She remembered all the way back to childhood and the many movies she had seen with all the beautiful movie stars. She recalled all of that as she moved to the photographer's direction.

"Pam," he yelled, "I want a somber mood from you. Deep and intense."

She thought back to when her parents had been killed. She gave him what he wanted.

"Perfect, perfect, now I need pleasure, sheer pleasure."

She thought back to when she dressed in her aunt's clothes. She gave him what he wanted.

"Baby, baby, you got it! Give me sadness. Make a tear. I want a real close shot of your face with sadness."

She thought back to when she had to endure her uncle raping her repeatedly with anal sex. The pain and humiliation helped her give him what he wanted.

"Okay, Pam. Great, just great! Now walk and pose, stop and pose. Do it, baby! Do everything that lights up that face. Do all the good and ugly."

Pam thought about the streets. The long walks along Sixth Avenue. The money she made. The dicks she sucked. The plan she made that had worked out perfect. The silicone shots to the body that had helped make her perfect. The operation that had taken her from a man with a dick to a woman with a vagina, waiting to capture the richest man she could find. All of that enabled her to give the photographer what he wanted.

Lola watched in amazement. She thought to herself how different this girl was from all the others. Beautiful and mysterious. She wished she could be part of her life, but then she remembered the icy cold stare Pam had given her, almost like a knife directly into her eyes. No, she couldn't get involved with this one. This one had definite plans for her life. Lola wondered what could have happened to make her so cold and distant. She turned to Maria.

"Looks like you got a million-dollar model! Where in the hell did she come from?"

"Canada. Just walked in a few days ago. And I saw it right away. Yes, she will be the one. In fact, we are going to put her on the runway for our winter presentation."

"God, she will look beautiful in lynx." Lola murmured.

"She'll look beautiful in anything, or nothing."

Later, as Pam was preparing to leave, the director, Jonathan Reeves, approached her.

"Pam, how about some dinner? I'd love to take you. There is a lot we can discuss."

Pam smiled graciously.

"I'd like that very much, but I have a previous commitment."

"You can't cancel?"

"No, I'm so sorry. A rain check, please?"

He couldn't refuse.

"Of course." He was disappointed. His plans had been trampled on with such graciousness. He wanted to be the first to have her. Was she naive or clever? Did she suspect that he planned to seduce her this very evening?

Pam was well aware of how it would go if she went out with anyone in the agency. She was there for business, and no one would have Pam Thorn. Quickly, she left and disappeared into the crowded streets.

34

When Jolena greeted Mark on the day of his appointment, he did not appear to be his usual jubilant self. She sensed something wrong.

"Are you okay today? You appear to be preoccupied. Is there something on your mind? Some deep dark secret you want to tell Jolena?" She laughed.

He managed a smile.

"Just thinking about some business I have to take care of back home. Everything is great. Is he here?"

"Yes, and I want to tell you that a few things have changed. He has an assistant. I no longer go in the room for consultations, examinations, or treatments."

"Oh, we're getting high class now."

Jolena knew it was best to bring that conversation to an end.

"Let me see if he is ready for you."

She spoke over the intercom to the doctor.

"Mark Hunter is here. His chart is on your desk." She switched off the intercom and directed Mark to go in.

Jolena prayed that the doctor would refuse to do the surgery on Mark. It was not a perfected operation and many postop complications occurred. After fifteen minutes, he was out of the meeting with the doctor. Jolena figured that a short meeting was like was a refusal of surgery. She was glad. Mark appeared in her office. He gave her one big hug and was exultant.

"Jolena, Dr. Edgewater said to give me an appointment for the surgery!"

Jolena looked at him in shock.

"You are going to have surgery?"

"Yes. Of course, he explained it was the first stage and could be done in the office. He said to book it for next Tuesday."

Jolena could not believe what she was hearing. *Surgery that complicated in the office! My God,* she thought, *what is Edgewater thinking about?*

"Mark, are you sure you want to do this? What about your wife? Have you spoken with her? Have you explained the whole situation to her?"

"Ms. Taylor!"

The voice, familiar, startled Jolena. She turned and found Belinda behind her.

"What business have you to question the patient about his decision after he and the doctor have already decided on surgery?"

Jolena was shocked and angry. But the anger only surged when she turned and stared with a hatred in her eyes that Belinda would never forget and always fear.

"How dare you speak to me in that manner and in front of a patient who happens to be a personal friend. Furthermore, don't ever question my actions. And never, never spy on me again!"

Belinda, surprised at the rebuttal, quickly turned and disappeared into the doctor's private office.

Mark was bewildered.

"What was that about?"

"That was the doctor's new assistant."

"You mean new pussy," he joked.

"I think this one is serious. She works here in the office, and she lives with him. Enough of that. Mark, let me call you and make the appointment. I am a little upset at this moment."

"I can see that. Calm down. You can handle it."

Jolena smiled wearily and told Mark good-bye. The waiting patients overheard the entire scenario. There were whispers and questions among themselves about this new person the doctor had brought to work in his office.

Jolena put the next patient in the treatment room and announced over the intercom system to the doctor that the patient was ready. She rarely used the intercom system before Belinda's arrival. Now she welcomed the device. It was clear that the road ahead was not going to be smooth. That encounter would be only one of many. Jolena could feel her back getting close to the wall. She refused to be trapped in this job with some young, inexperienced bitch giving her orders. The anger was pent-up within her, and when angry, she cried. But not this time. No crying! She had to think! Things were changing. No need to speak with the doctor about Belinda. He was in love and would never understand Jolena's side. Belinda was here to stay; Jolena knew that the enemy was in the camp.

Belinda shut the door of Dr. Edgewater's office with a bang. He looked up, startled.

"What's the matter, sweetheart?"

Belinda's lovely face was red with fury.

"That nurse out there!" She pointed with her well-manicured hands. "Do you know what I heard her saying to that patient, Mark?"

"What was said, dear?" He spoke with unconcern in his voice.

"She had the nerve to question the patient as to whether he should have the operation you are going to do on him."

"Well, Jolena and Mark are very good friends. They have been for a few years. I'm sure it was only a kind gesture. She tries to make the patients feel that we have their best interest at heart."

"But you don't understand. She was not respecting your decision. You should speak to her. There are probably a lot of things she says and does with patients that you know nothing about."

Belinda looked for a sign of annoyance or anger, but he quietly consoled her.

"I trust her judgment, Belinda. She's been with me for almost five years. Just let it alone. I have plans, and I am the doctor." He smiled and held out his arms to her. "Come here to your daddy, and let me hold you. I hate to see you upset." He wanted to calm her anger.

Belinda moved quickly into his arms. He held her tightly and kissed her. She stayed in his arms for a few minutes, but her encounter with Jolena still rankled. She hated her. She wanted her out! Peter was kissing her, and Belinda knew that soon his dick would be hard.

"She insulted me, Peter. When I confronted her about what she said to that patient, she insulted me."

"Now, pet, don't let it bother you. I'll speak to her."

His penis was hard. He'd say anything to soothe her.

"Feel how hard my penis is for you, especially when you're angry. You are more beautiful."

Belinda quickly understood what she must do. Quickly she unzipped his pants. The small penis was erect and ready. Falling to her knees, she carefully caressed the penis in her hands and then in her hot, wet mouth. Peter threw his head back in ecstacy. He reached his climax in seconds.

"Oh, I am so sorry. I was so excited. I wanted it to last." Belinda looked at him tenderly, but she was not sorry. The faster the better.

"Don't forget to speak to that nurse," she demanded.

However, Peter's mind was savoring his last ejaculation and wondering if he would be able to get his penis hard later that night.

Belinda went to the bathroom and rinsed her mouth. The taste of Peter in her mouth was disgusting. She wondered how long she would have to endure his sexual desires. All he ever wanted in sex was for her to suck on his dick. He never even went down on her. She wanted that. Her thoughts quickly went to the last time she was with the boy in Co-Corp. She was glad she had some place to go and get her satisfaction. Peter was taking up too much of her time. She had to go home more often to see her parents. Belinda would make that clear to him tonight, and tomorrow she'd take the day off. And she vowed to herself that the entire day would be spent in bed with someone who could satisfy her.

35

A murder, to be planned by Lita Lopez, was a real project. Just as a serial killer would plan his murders, carelessness had to be avoided. It was done with much forethought and malice. Guilty as charged. Premeditated to the asshole. She wished in this killing that she could be there to see him die. Whenever anyone did anything terrible to Lita, it was always her joy to see that person suffer and die. But unfortunately, in this case, it was not to be. The joy in this was to get away with the deadly deed. So one quiet afternoon she began her plans.

First, she poured her brandy and began to sniff her cocaine. Yes, she became particularly brilliant when she sniffed in the afternoons. Her mind would entertain all kinds of shit. How to kill. When to kill. Why to kill. What to kill. Who to kill. She sniffed and paced. Paced and sniffed. To the bathroom and back to the bed. From the bed to the bathroom, passing the closet. She stopped, remembering the body that still occupied that space. It would always be there. No doubt about that, and no problem about that.

The problem now was how to make Alberto a corpse. She went to the bathroom with her packet of cocaine and sniffed. Lita looked at the window. This was the way the little motherfucker got in. It was closed now. She opened it. Impossible to lock unless she nailed it down. No, she did not want to do that. She wanted him to come in again, overconfident. She wanted him to become overconfident. That is when he would make a mistake.

Lita looked out of the window and again studied how he had made his descent from the roof. He used the ledge to stand on after lowering himself down. The window was an easy way in. Now she inspected the ledge. Very sturdy; built with old strong wood no longer used in buildings. Suddenly she knew the answer! Dressed in a raincoat, scarf, and dark glasses, she left her apartment. At a nearby hardwear store, Lita purchased a small hacksaw. After returning to her apartment, she again sniffed her white thinking powder and laughed.

"Now I got you, little motherfucker. Fuck with Lita Jose Lopez, and see what happens!"

Returning to the bathroom, Lita opened the window and began sawing the entire ledge away from the window. It was a tedious job. But she didn't want to remove it entirely by sawing. She wanted to break it off so it would look like whoever stepped on it had caused it to break by his weight. When she was able to break it off, Lita took it and soaked it in water for about an hour. That caused the wood to appear warped. Then she soaked it in a dark makeup solution she often used on her body to hide the bruises from the silicone injections. That way, the wood did not appear to be freshly sawed only freshly broken.

Now she handled the ledge with gloves and replaced it carefully at its original site. One step on that ledge, and Lita knew something that Alberto would not expect. It would be a long, deserving fall. She only hoped that he would have time to realize that it was not a mere accident. Lita enjoyed another sip of brandy and a big sniff of cocaine. She was proud of her accomplishment but must save the bigger celebration for when she would hear about the death of Alberto.

Lita reminded herself it was Wednesday and remembered her appointment at Dr. Edgewater's. Belinda was doing her silicone injections, and although she knew the job would never be comparable to Jolena's, she settled for Belinda, because Lita discovered that little Belinda like to sniff cocaine. Now she was her main supplier. How close they had become! Like two girlfriends. Laughing, gossiping, and sniffing there in the treatment room.

The effects of the cocaine made Belinda's mouth spill out many secrets about her relationship with the doctor and, of course, the boyfriend who waited for her every week in the Bronx. When she paid Belinda the money, Belinda would lie to the doctor about how much Lita had given her. Once the doctor asked Lita how much work she had received. Already the answer had been planned between the two friends. Now Lita did not have to confront Jolena because Jolena no longer worked on Wednesdays.

At first, Lita was glad, but later, she felt somewhat lost without that confrontation. And when Belinda would try to talk bad about Jolena, Lita would not join in but rather abruptly changed the subject. Lita found listening to Belinda's devious little activities more interesting than talking about Jolena. After all, there was nothing bad that Lita could say about Jolena. All Jolena ever tried to do was to tell her the truth, and Lita did not want to hear the truth.

One day, Belinda slipped and referred to Jolena as a nigger. Lita cringed but remained quiet. She realized that since she was Spanish, that made her a spick. She was sure Belinda laughed and made jokes about her to the doctor and to her boyfriend. Her imagination was vivid with all the various names they probably used to describe her, such as transvestite, sex change, man-made beast, and spick.

A few hours later, Lita lay on the table and allowed Belinda to fill her buttocks, legs, and ankles with silicone, knowing damn well she did not need any more pumped into her body. But she wanted it, and Belinda did it without question.

As Belinda labored over her buttocks, Lita pulled the pack of cocaine out of her bag.

"Here, little friend, take yourself a one-on-one or a two-on-two if you need it. Peter isn't here yet, is he?"

Belinda immediately stopped her work and began sniffing greedily.

"No. I think he'll be about an hour late. I wouldn't care if he never came."

"Now, you can't say that about Peter. He loves and adores you."

"I am well aware of that. But I want to be married. I want to be a doctor's wife. I am tired of working here. He promised, and so far, I am just living with him. No word on marriage."

"Don't worry. Give him a chance. Soon as he rearranges his office like you said he is doing, he will marry you."

Belinda continued working on Lita, regretting that she had to give up the cocaine for the present.

"Did you bring me a pack like you promised?"

"Oh, yeah." Lita reached into her bag again and brought out a medium-sized glasine bag. "Better put it away before he walks in. If he sees that shit, he will have ten fits."

Belinda quickly retrieved the bag and put it in her bag under the counter.

"When are you going to see your lover in the Bronx?" Lita inquired.

"I can't get to him until the office is covered. That means I have to wait until Jolena is here."

"When Jolena leaves, that will cramp your style, won't it? You won't be able to get away."

"It will never cramp my style! The sooner she gets out of here, the better for me."

She continued to push the silicone into Lita's thigh but began to notice a large lump developing. Quickly, she pulled out the syringe and needle, and the silicone began to leak all over the table.

Lita looked down to see what was happening.

"Damn, Belinda, all my money is leaking out. Do something!"

Quickly Belinda put pressure on the needle hole. After a matter of minutes, the leaking subsided.

"See, I took care of it." Belinda remarked proudly.

Lita knew Belinda was a fool; she had no idea what she was doing. A few more sessions, and Lita knew she would not be coming back. Allowing Belinda to do her body finally convinced her that she had enough. Lita also had enough of sharing her cocaine with Belinda, listening to her fantasies, lies, and racial slurs. Lita hated greedy people, and although she had tolerated Dr. Edgewater's greediness, she did not like the greediness that was Belinda's. At least Jolena never lied, neither had she been greedy.

Belinda, on the other hand, thought that she had complete control over Lita. She never suspected Lita's feelings. However difficult she had found the job of pushing silicone into Lita's rock-hard body, she was glad to be rid of Jolena if that was the price she had to pay. Her over indulgence of cocaine had made her more self-confident. She could handle this office alone. There was just no need for Jolena any longer. She'd have to start reminding Peter of that fact. He would be proud of her now.

And even though he was paying her a salary, she secretly thought that he should give her more now that she was doing the silicone injections. It was not easy work, and most of the time, she was completely confused on where to put the needles and how much to put into the body.

Also, there was the problem of the glass syringes breaking. Peter got very annoyed when the syringes broke. He said that they cost a lot of money to replace. So he reminded her not to sterilize them. Just wash them out with soap and water. That would do the job. Most times, Belinda just used the same syringes over and over. She never intended to wash syringes. After all, she was not a maid, she was a "physician assistant."

36

Bernie had not heard from Jolena for a week. He had called her apartment and left a message on the machine, but still no reply. He began to worry and feel a little depressed. His memories were filled with the last time they were together—that beautiful afternoon filled with love and affection and trust between them. He was aware that he was not the dashing handsome man desired by most women. Especially a woman like Jolena. He was certain she had experienced many love affairs far more passionate than theirs. However, none of that mattered to Dr. Bernie Charles.

He liked Jolena, maybe even loved her. He had known her for years. It was like she had always belonged to him but he had never taken possession of his great prize. He wasn't young, and time moved faster for people of his age. Enough of the unhappiness and memories of a wife who had betrayed him. It was Jolena he wanted now, and he intended to move in haste to capture her. It was at that moment of his thoughts that Chun announced that he had a phone call. He prayed it would be her. That was the line on which she always called.

"Hello, this is Bernie Charles."

Then the soft voice permeated his brain.

"Bernie, forgive me for not calling. A lot of things on my mind. I guess on your mind also."

"Yes, yes, Jolena. Please come see me. I want to see you. I miss you," he pleaded.

This really set Jolena back, for she had not expected that he would express openly such a desire to see her.

"Bernie, I missed you. Yes, I'll be there tonight after work."

"Come right up. The doorman will let you in."

Bernie was elated. He requested that Chun bring him a brandy and that he prepare a light salad for later that evening so Chun could leave early. All Bernie could remember was the voice, the sound of that voice when she said that she missed him. Were these the cards life dealt him? After all these years, he meets someone and falls in love. Someone he already knew for years.

How shocked the few friends he had left would be when he presented her. How shocked the synagogue would be when he took her there. How shocked the hospital administration would be when he withdrew the fund he had set up for the plastic surgery division when he died. How shocked his lawyer and advisor would be when he changed his will. All his millions, which never meant much to him in the past, would now bring him and the woman he loved much happiness. He wanted so much to tell her this, to explain how he felt. He wanted her with him forever. How could he tell her this and not be sure she would reject him? He knew well, from his experience, to wait. Everything that was supposed to happen would happen.

When Jolena entered Bernie's building, she was allowed to go right up to his apartment.

When she saw Bernie, and it was the first time she had seen him since their sexual encounter, Jolena went directly to him and put her arms around him. Bernie had already opened his arms to her. They embraced each other for more then a few minutes. No words were uttered between them until Bernie broke the silence.

"My God, I missed you. I didn't think I could miss a person again."

"I missed you also and didn't know it until now, being here with you. Is this all making sense?" she murmured.

He kissed her on the cheek.

"Let's not try to make sense. We've been making sense all our lives, and we end up unhappy. I am happy now for the first time in a long time."

"You're right, Bernie. I feel good about you. I never expected things to happen this way."

"Come, let's eat. I have some cold salad dishes in the refrigerator that Chun prepared."

She followed him through the magnificent suite of rooms and into the kitchen. She had never seen the kitchen, since it belonged exclusively to the male servant Bernie had in his employ all of these many years. It was large and very well stocked. Pots and pans Jolena had never seen except in magazines. She watched Bernie open the large sub-zero refrigerator, which was fully shelved with many items to cater to Bernie's every dietetic need and whim.

"What a magnificent home you have! A house in the sky!" She laughed.

"I've lived here forty years, Jolena. My wife and I. After she died or, rather, killed herself, I planned on moving, but where could I go and live any cheaper and any more luxuriously than here? Now it has become a great investment."

Jolena joined in and helped lay the meal on the small table in the kitchen.

"This is also a great place to eat."

"Yes, many times I have come in here and ate with Chun."

"Bernie, tell me about your life after your wife's death. I remember that. I was working for you. I felt so sad for you. You fell apart. I wanted to reach out to you, and you did allow me to hold you and comfort you with my words. You probably don't remember, because during tragedies, we tend to forget a lot of things happening around us."

Bernie was able to talk about it now without being sad and feeling sorry for himself.

"Well, Jolena, it was pure and simple. She was going to leave me for another man. Or so she thought. I knew she was going out with him. Even at the various cocktail parties and hospital social events, it was evident that she was crazy about him. He used her to get to me. He was a doctor and wanted to study with me. We had no sex life. She had no desire for me, and although I loved her, I had ridden the top of the crest for many years, but medical ideas and techniques were changing. I knew the glory would soon be over for me. Rumor was floating that they were going to discontinue my teaching program. Anyway, she begged me to allow him into the program, and I did."

Jolena was thinking back to the doctors who passed through Bernie's operating room, studying his techniques.

Bernie continued.

"He learned well, and I could see that with the proper intentions, he would be come a very skilled doctor in gender-change surgery."

Jolena's brain was quick.

"Oh, my God, no. Not Edgewater?"

She stared at Bernie in amazement as he continued.

"Yes. Dr. Peter Edgewater. He seduced my wife and pounced upon her weaknesses. He promised her a new and exciting life. He promised her marriage. He wined and dined her. She already drank too much, and he saw to it that she drank more. Using her weakness, he put himself into a powerful position. I can't tell you how inadequate and low I felt. It was so hard, Jolena. Seeing Gloria come in night after night, drunk, beligerent, and bragging about how he made love to her. I felt sorry for her, and I felt sorry for myself. To come to work the next day and operate and see him was almost more than I could bear. And you were there, and you helped me so much. I remember during surgery, at times you would reach out and touch my hand when I was confused or about to make a mistake. You knew I was troubled but not what I was troubled over."

"I thought you were sick. You had lost so much weight. I had heard rumors you were having problems and that your wife drank a lot but never the gossip about another man and certainly not about Edgewater."

"We hide things well. However, near the end of the program, he began seeing less of her. She called him constantly until he changed his phone number. She drank more and more. I couldn't do anything to stop her. As she wandered through the house in a drunken stupor, she would say things about him. How he had made love to her. How he had begged her to get him into the program, and that was true, because I would have never considered him except for her persistent persuasion."

Bernie was finished eating. Jolena was finished but was mesmerized by the story. He got up and led her out of the kitchen and into the large, comfortable study.

"Sit here with me. I'll pour us a nice drink and finish telling you what happened. We'll both need a drink."

Jolena watched him as he brought the drinks over to the large leather sofa. He was older and time had taken its toll on Bernie, but there was something about him that Jolena admired and cared about. Maybe it was because he cared about her. She began to realize that at both of their ages in life, it was important to be loved by someone and not spend your life alone. He handed her a glass of wine. Tonight it was wine. White wine, and it was delicious and mellow. Bernie settled down into the sofa and began again.

"He did not call her again. A month passed. I discovered she had given him a most expensive emerald ring I had purchased for her during one of my trips to South America. The stone was very valuable. I had too much pride to ask him about it. I'm sure he would have laughed at me if I had asked him to return the ring. She was too drunk and weak to confront him. I couldn't bring charges and have all that publicity. Gloria was now under a doctor's care, and they were trying to get her off the alcohol. One night I came home from a case very late. You remember that case. We worked till almost eleven o'clock."

"Oh, yes, the patient who turned out to be a severe bleeder and the trouble with the anesthesia. Yes, I remember."

When I got home, I looked in her bedroom to see if she was there, and she was sleeping. Or at least, I thought that she was sleeping. I showered and went to my own room. I had a report I wanted to read before morning. I read through it, but there seem to be an intense quietness in the house. For some strange reason, I got up and went back to her room. This time I went into the room. Then I saw the empty pill bottles and the gin bottle. I could feel death. I touched her, and she was lifeless and cold. That was the end of it. The rest you know about. The papers. The gossip at the hospital. I tell you, Jolena, I almost had a nervous breakdown." He shook his head in disbelief at his own words.

She could see the agony on his face.

"Stop. Don't talk about it anymore. I know it was hard on you. I remember the agony you went through. I just wish that I had been closer to you so I could have comforted you more."

"I had to leave. I couldn't stay there any longer. I'm so sorry I put you out of a job. I closed down a whole department. Well, they were going to get rid of me anyway. The board had big plans for all that I had set up. But, of course, those plans did not include me."

"Let's not talk about it anymore." She reached across and enveloped him in her arms. She held him tightly and felt him cling to her. He relaxed in her arms; all his tension seemed to flow out of him. Bernie enjoyed the comfort she had given him. For minutes, there was silence between them.

Jolena broke the silence.

"Bernie, there is something I'm curious about. I know you know the answer." He broke from her embrace and looked at her with interest.

"Why is this female-to-male whom Edgewater did surgery on a few years ago, bleeding from the small orifice at the perineum?"

"Did he do a complete hysterectomy on her?"

"Yes."

"Did they say what color the blood was?"

"Bright red spotting. Off and on for almost a year. The patient wants to have a penile attachment but has become concerned about the bleeding."

"Oh, my God, no. That operation will never work. There are so many complications!"

Bernie got up and reached for his drink.

"I wonder if he ever checked her history before the first surgery to see if the mother ever took diethystilbesterol. That drug did cause cancer of the vagina twenty years later in females born to those women."

"I doubt that he ever checked anything from Mark's past. It was easy money and less complications, especially without the penile attachment."

"What a problem he will have if he goes ahead with this procedure. The end results are never guaranteed, and before it ever heals, there can be complication on complication."

"But he's going to do it. And in a few days or a week. I am glad I am no longer the number-one assistant. I am glad that Ms. Belinda is there and that he has reduced me to a secretary. I am glad I don't have to watch those atrocities any longer. I wish I never had to go back there. I'll leave soon. I am going to go back into the hospital and work."

She had finished her wine. She put her arms around Bernie and held him close to her. He enjoyed the warmth of her body, and she enjoyed comforting him.

"Don't leave me tonight, Jolena," he pleaded.

"Well, all I have waiting for me is an old cat." She smiled at him. "Animals are loyal," she continued. "She'll wait. In the meantime, let's get naked, go in the shower, and go to the bed!"

She jumped up and started down the hallway. Suddenly, she turned, laughing.

"Bernie, I don't know where the bathroom is."

He laughed. He was happy. He was in love, and now he knew it. This would be the woman he would spend the rest of his life with.

"Come, my darling, let me lead you. One day you'll get used to this 'house in the sky.'"

Jolena quietly slipped out of the apartment and caught a cab uptown. It was six in the morning, and it was the first time in a long time that she had spent the night away from her own bed. She and Bernie had fallen asleep together in each other's arms. Jolena could hardly believe how good they seemed to be for each other. He seemed to need her so much, and she was beginning to feel the same toward him. But he was white and very rich. Surely he did not want her for the rest of his life. But then Jolena reminded herself to stop that kind of thinking. Why not her? She was human and as good as any other person. She did not have to be white to be wanted or accepted, and apparently, it has been proven right in this relationship.

Once in her own apartment, she showered, then read the morning paper while she enjoyed two cups of tea. The cat was prancing up and down the apartment, showing her joy because the mistress had returned after an unusual length of absence. Jolena did not have to be at the office until ten o'clock. She would miss the kinds of hours enjoyed for so long. Why did it have to come to an end? Why did Peter Edgewater turn on her so suddenly? But after listening to Bernie's story concerning his wife, she began to understand that there was a very devious side to Peter Edgewater. She was experiencing it; now she wondered when Ms. Belinda would have the opportunity.

37

Jolena was working the day that Dr. Max Snyder came to the office.

"I have an appointment with Dr. Edgewater. If he is not in, then please allow me to wait in his office, because I do not want to be accosted by any of his patients."

Jolena understood what he was referring to.

"He will be in shortly, and he is expecting you. Let me show you into his office."

Jolena guided him into the office. He appeared relieved as he followed her.

Jolena returned to her desk. She wondered why Peter would be consulting him. Then she remembered Mark's approaching surgery and the bleeding problem. Maybe he's going to seek help. Jolena wished she could stop Mark from going through with this surgery, but it was useless to try. He wanted a penis at any cost. Less then ten minutes later, Dr. Edgewater arrived.

"Good afternoon, Jolena, how are you today?"

He appeared annoyed. She was surprised he even asked how she was.

"I am well, doctor. Dr. Snyder is waiting for you in your office."

"Good, good! Don't allow anyone to disturb us."

He rushed to his office, and Jolena knew that the conversation would be most interesting.

Peter greeted Max with enthusiasm.

"My God, Max, it's good to see you!"

Max Snyder managed a smile and returned the greeting. He knew that Peter had a problem. That was the only reason he called on him. He hadn't seen Peter since his last problem nearly four years ago.

"Well, Peter, what's up? What complication are you faced with now?"

"Oh, Max, don't talk like that. We are both doctors and friends. Of course, we don't see each other socially like we should, but then, we are both busy. But you are right! I do have a slight problem. Not a complication yet, but it could turn into a lot of things."

"Who did you rearrange now?"

"Well, he is doing quite well. It's a female-to-male transsexual. He has established a good relationship with a woman. They are married, and their sex life would be perfect if he had a penis. Now he wants me to erect some sort of phallus. To make matters worse, he wants to urinate from it."

"Forget it. You know the complications, and it's almost impossible without such complications."

"But to have this penis is important also to his social life. He wants to be able to stand up and urinate and have sex with a penis."

"Well, what do you plan to do, Peter? I know you. You will try to make one, come hell or high water."

"I have already told him I would do the first stage. I intend to make a skin graft, thigh flap, allow it to grow, and later, make it into some sort of penis."

"What about his clitoris, which I hope is still there?"

"I wouldn't make any attempt to interfere with the blood supply or the nerves to the clitoris. It will remain hidden under the reconstructed penis. I really have everything ready to go, and I know it will be successful. However, my patient is having one small problem, and that is why I called you."

Max knew that it was something that Peter had not yet figured how to get around. Peter always used people until he could find his own way out of the problem.

"I knew there had to be more to this. So, talk."

"He called me the other night and told me that he was bleeding."

"Bleeding? Bleeding from where? I hope not the vagina."

"Yes, in fact, that is exactly where the blood is coming from."

"Cancer of the vagina?"

"No, it could not be that serious."

"Why not? Remember that gynecologists were using diethystilbesterol without any reservations. Twenty to twenty-five years later, here comes the diagnosis of adenocarcinoma of the vagina and or squamous carcinoma of the vagina. Did you ever get a history concerning his mother?"

"Hell, no!" There were a few moments of silence. "Well, it's important to him that he have a penis. So, will it hurt if I just go ahead with the surgery? If he has squamous call carcinoma, he is going to die anyway. He might as well die happy."

Max got up from the comfort of the chair and poured himself a drink. Even Dr. Max Snyder, who had performed his own small unethical procedures, squirmed at the thought of this procedure.

"Why put him through all this misery? You know that an erected penis is going to give nothing but problems. It's difficult to keep the inner skin clean, and the odor can be very foul. Also infection can be devastating. Does this person want to go through all of this just to be able to stand and piss? The penis itself can't even get hard. Tell him the damn truth."

"I don't think I will tell him anything. Sometimes people are better off not knowing. He wants this operation. You want a drink?"

Max looked in astonishment at Peter.

"Yeah, I need one myself. Well, how much money are you getting for this job, Peter? I know that is has to be a healthy sum."

"A little over six thousand." He lied. In fact, he had given Mark a price of ten thousand. Mark had agreed to pay.

"Peter, I advise you to send the man home to his wife and let it go. You are going to make his life miserable before the cancer sets in, if that is the reason for the bleeding. You never questioned him about his past. Your thing is to cut, close, and send them home."

"I didn't call you in here for you to insult me. I asked you to come in for advice and even asked for your assistance with the surgery. There is a nice cut in it for you."

"No, thanks. My advice is to not do it, and I am not going to even charge you for the consultation."

Peter poured another drink.

"Don't you need a little extra money for those horses you feed each evening?"

Max laughed.

"I sleep good at night, Peter. The little devious procedures I do in my office are nothing in comparison to what you do here and in the hospital. How do you stand yourself?" Max gulped down the remainder of the brandy and stormed out of the office. He looked at Jolena and remarked. "How do you stand to work for that man?" Quickly, he made his exit.

Jolena knew that there had been an argument between the two doctors.

Peter appeared at the door. His face was flushed.

"Jolena, has Belinda called? Or is she in the treatment room?"

"Belinda is not here, and she has not called."

"Are any patients here yet?"

"Only one. Your favorite. Lita."

"Forget it. Let her sit until Belinda gets here."

"Whatever you say, doctor."

Jolena was professionally cool as she announced to Lita that she would have to wait until the doctor's assistant arrived.

Lita glared at Jolena. Jolena returned a smile.

"You finally got cut down to size, Ms. Secretary." Lita snorted.

"Not like you got cut down to size. Now be quiet, and leave me alone."

Lita made no more comments.

Jolena herself began to wonder why Belinda had not arrived. These absences were becoming more frequent and lengthy.

The door opened, and Belinda entered. She was in slight disarray. Without acknowledging anyone, she went to the bathroom. When she emerged, the white coat was on and she was in control. She never looked at Jolena and told Lita to go into the treatment room. Then Belinda entered Peter's office.

Jolena strained to hear any loud outburst. Only at the beginning, loud, harsh words were heaped upon Belinda. Then Jolena could hear soft sobbing and pleading. Very soon, sounds were back to normal. Belinda walked out from the office, smiling. Jolena assumed, as always, that Peter had been satisfied. She could see that he was truly taken by Belinda. Everyone had their degree of love. Even Bernie was attempting to show Jolena that he felt love for her as she was developing love for him. Jolena didn't feel left out anymore. Someone cared for her also She realized how important this was for everyone. She flicked on the intercom to Peter's office.

"Goodnight, doctor, I am leaving. Have a good night," she announced in a very soft and soothing voice.

38

Today was busy in Dr. Edgewater's office. He was not in a good mood; Belinda's mother had been sick, and she spent Sunday night in the Bronx with her. What could he do about that? Nothing! He just had to be alone, and now that he had gotten used to her body next to his, he found it very difficult to be alone. Of course, he had called to make sure she was there, but then he could not call all night long; it had kept him awake most of the night—wondering. Suspicion overwhelmed him, and by morning, his mood was sour.

Having to perform surgery that morning caused the entire operating room to catch hell. And everybody was wondering where was little Ms. Belinda, his assistant. Naturally, he made an excuse that she would be late due to the illness of her mother. But when she did not show at all, he was secretly furious. On his first break from surgery, he called her, and she told him very matter-of-factly that her mother was still not feeling well, but she would be at the office at four o'clock. Edgewater was not at all pleased. The next time her mother was sick, he would tell her to hire a health aide to go there and take over.

By the time he reached the office, his mood was still dark. He was rather glad that Jolena was still with him. Maybe he'd better think twice before he got rid of her. He greeted her with a mumble and went to his office and poured a small glass of brandy. Then he returned to converse with Jolena; he had to show a good face. He didn't want her to know that he was upset over Belinda's absence.

"How are you today, Jolena?"

She smiled that beautiful smile and replied in a melodious voice.

"I am well, Dr. Edgewater. And how are you doing? We don't get to talk much these days."

"No, we don't. I'm well, Jolena. Yes, you're right, we don't get to talk much. Oh, by the way, has Belinda called in?"

"No, but I'm sure she will be here soon."

Jolena diverted her eyes elsewhere. She could sense that he was troubled. Now, at this time in her life, she did not want to know about his troubles or problems. He had dismissed her from his private and, almost, his medical life.

"Are we going to be busy today?" Edgewater asked.

"No, not too busy. A few postops, and of course, Mark is due to come in today. Do you remember this is the day for the first step of his surgical procedure?"

"Oh, damn! I almost forgot. Now, where in the fuck is Belinda? I need her to get things started in the treatment room so I can set up for that surgery." Jolena remained quiet. She had no intention of volunteering her services.

At that moment, the door to the office opened, and Belinda entered. She hurried toward Edgewater, hugged him, and before he could begin questioning her, she pulled him into his office.

"Where the hell have you been? Don't you remember that I have a surgical procedure here today? You should have been here hours ago, so get this place in order!"

Belinda began kissing and fondling him. It was only a matter of seconds before he responded.

"I missed you, dammit," he told her.

"Calm down. I have something for you. You know I always have something for you. Do you want it now?" She had his penis out and in her hands. She could feel the wetness wanting to seep out.

"Yes, yes,"

Edgewater quickly locked the door and lay down on the floor. Belinda spread his legs, took his penis, and quickly started licking it up and down. She knew that it would be only a matter of minutes, and she would finish him off and once again be in his good graces. He came almost immediately.

"Oh, God, baby, don't leave me like that again. I couldn't sleep. I almost wanted to come up there and be with you."

Belinda was glad he did not follow through with that idea, because the truth was that her mother was not sick but she and Ricky had spent the entire evening and all night together at her parents' apartment. That way she was able to answer the phone in case Edgewater had called, and, indeed, he had called.

"You can't be mad at me because my mother was sick. You have to understand."

He was like a little boy now that he had come.

"I understand, baby. I understand." He put his arms around her and held her tight. He thought about marrying her as soon as possible so he would have a tighter hold, but held back talking about that.

She broke away from his grip.

"I better go and get things started."

Quickly, she headed towards the treatment room. Belinda was doubly glad to get away from him and not have to face Jolena. She knew that Jolena was not stupid, as she had once thought her to be. Belinda was angry that Jolena sat on her ass interviewing patients, collecting the money, and she, Belinda, had to deal with all the dirty, stinking work in the treatment room. Well, it is what she had wanted. To be in charge of patient treatments. After all she was the physician assistant, and that was her job. She hated it, but it would not be long before Peter married her and she'd get away from this horrible office and that horrible hospital.

Belinda was proud of the plans she had formulated and how well they were working out. She had even managed to keep Ricky on the side, and she needed him and her little drug habit, which she was proud to be able to handle so competently. Ricky had been impressed with the cocaine she had brought to him and had suggested that if she could get him a sizable amount, he would be able to make a lot of money. Belinda now gave thought to Lita. She would be in this week, and she'd see if she could make some kind of deal with her in exchange for extra work she would give to her.

Peter had regained his usual composure. After finishing the regular examinations of the postop patients, he told Belinda to set up for a small skin graft he would be doing on a patient that afternoon.

Jolena was well aware of the friction going on between Belinda and Peter. She suspected that Belinda was clever enough to know how to soothe Peter's sexual appetite and calm him back to normal. It was almost two o'clock when Mark entered the office. Jolena had hoped that he would never come back. Why didn't he just leave this thing alone? He was living a good life.

"My darling Jolena," he greeted her with that handsome smile, "I am so glad to see you again. Well, today is the beginning of my dream."

He came around into her little office and embraced her.

"Please don't say I said this to you, but please reconsider doing this procedure. It is not that perfected. There must be another way, or you can just wait until a better procedure is discovered."

He looked at her and smiled. He seemed so sad at that moment.

"I know you are looking out for my best interest, but, Jolena, you have no idea how incomplete my life is. And even though my wife is happy and life has been good, there is that one missing thing that I need."

Jolena knew it was useless to try any longer to discourage him. She could hear the intensity in his voice and knew that his mind was made up.

"Okay, Mark. Okay. Everything will work out for you. I'm sure that Dr. Edgewater will do his best job on you."

"Thank you, Jolena, for your support. I need your reassurance. I told him about the bleeding, and he's going to check that out also."

"Has it increased, and what color is the blood, bright or dark?"

"Bright red and sometimes dark. There's no pain or discomfort, but it's embarrassing."

Before he could impart anymore information, Belinda appeared at the door.

"You can come in, Mark."

She completely ignored Jolena's presence. In fact, she hadn't spoken to her since she entered the office. The feeling of hatred was mutual. Only now, Jolena wished there was some way she could walk away from this office and this job forever. She felt sorry for her friend and the complications he would probably endure for the rest of his life. Jolena finished recording on the files and put them away. As she sorted the mail, she saw there was a letter from the bank.

She had never spied on his mail before, but suspicion and curiosity had begun to grow in Jolena. She scanned the letter quickly, noting that it was from the bank concerning his safety deposit box with an enclosure of a signature card for Belinda Koski. The safety deposit box where Peter probably hid all his treasures. Jolena quickly put the letter into her pocketbook. And quickly a plan formulated in her brain. It could work, but she'd have to plan it carefully, or she could end up in trouble. She quietly left the office and Mark's fate to Dr. Peter Edgewater.

39

Dr. Peter Edgewater was not in the mood to do surgery on anyone this day, no matter how big or small the procedure. Despite his sexual appetite having been fulfilled, he remained extremely annoyed with Belinda. He was beginning to doubt her story. Where was she all day? Of course, she had said that it was her parent's illness that had kept her away, but he was becoming suspicious of her recent disappearances. *Well,* he thought, *stop thinking like that. It will just destroy your relationship, and you are enjoying her. She has been an advantage and an asset. You are pocketing more money now that she is doing the difficult work on the drag queens.* He had never realized how much money had gone to Jolena. That was all settled now. The only other move he had to make was to slowly cut Jolena's days down to two, and then, he was sure, she would just leave voluntarily. That way, they could part friends. After all, she had not done him any wrong.

"Belinda, do you have everything on this table that I need?" He inquired as he put on his gloves.

"Oh, yes, Peter. It is all set up."

"Mark, how are you doing?"

"I'm as well as can be, now that I am getting this procedure started. Oh, by the way, don't forget to check the bleeding I told you about."

"Oh, yes. I couldn't forget that."

In fact, he had already forgotten about the entire conversation between him and Mark. Now he was further annoyed with having to deal with that problem. Probably something minor. It couldn't be as serious as his friend had suggested. Some doctors, he thought, tend to be overcautious. And he remembered Dr. Bernie Charles. He always preached to take extra caution and time. That's what caused Bernie to lose his wife. Taking all that time with patients and not tending to home.

When Peter met her and realized how weak and alcoholic she was, there was no problem in having her. The rest was history, and now he did not want to think about all of what had happened. But he would never forget Bernie's face when Bernie came up to him after her death and told him that one day the same scene might be played again, but that he, Edgewater, might be the victim. He had laughed at his prediction. Edgewater had no intention of becoming a victim.

Mark was on the table and had been scrubbed down with antiseptic wash. His legs were spread, and if anyone had walked into that room and saw this handsome muscular man lying on a table, legs spread-eagle with what appeared to be a scrotum and no penis, they could become thoroughly confused.

Peter inspected the small hole that had been left open after the complete hysterectomy. When he touched it with his gloved fingers, bright red blood oozed. Peter felt cold deep inside, and a chill ran all the way up his back. Belinda, who saw the bleeding, looked solemnly at Peter to see his reaction. She only noticed that he seemed whiter than usual. She said nothing.

"Well, Mark, there is some bleeding here, but I don't think that it is anything to worry about. We did do a complete hysterectomy on you, so maybe it's a little irritation along the lining of the vagina. Let's not worry about it. We will keep an eye on the bleeding. If it gets worse or, what I mean is, if it becomes heavy bleeding, then you call me immediately."

"Oh, thank God. I was worried, but now that I got the word from you, I can put that aside."

"Okay, now we are going to start. I will be using a local anesthetic. So you will have a little discomfort while I anesthetize the area from where we will take the graft."

Edgewater very meticulously lifted a piece of skin from the left femoral region of Mark's upper thigh. Then a piece of the skin, now a flap, was brought over to the front of Mark's clitoral area. He rolled the skin into a phallus shape. The next procedure was to make a small incision above the clitoris and attached the graft to that area. Hopefully, the graft would take, and later, he would be able to drop it down and over the clitoris, thereby creating a phallus. At least Mark would be able to stand when he urinated.

However, much more work would have to be performed if he were to urinate from the tube. There was the long-standing problem of taking care of the inner skin of the tube. There would be problems in keeping it clean and preventing infections and odors. Peter knew that he'd have to leave both ends open. Mark would not be happy with that, but for now, he'd have to settle. Peter prayed that no hair would grow inside the tube or outside. That was always another problem. As he attached the tube to the other incision, Peter tried not to think of any complications, known or unknown. He just wanted to finish and get out of the office.

"Mark, I've finished first stage, and it looks pretty good from here. We just have to pray that the graft takes. Now what you have to look out for is any foul odor or bleeding from the graft site. Try not to get it wet. I know you might want to shower, but for at least the next two weeks, you have to sort of bird-bath."

Mark was overjoyed.

"Don't worry. I'll do everything you say."

"Belinda will clean you up and put on the dressing. Call me in three days, and we'll talk. Belinda will give you some antibiotics."

Belinda began cleaning and dressing the operative and graft site. Edgewater scribbled something in Mark's chart.

"You can give the check to Belinda. Talk to you in a few days." Dr. Peter Edgewater left the treatment room for the sanctuary of his office and a large brandy.

Mark felt somewhat lost without the guidance of Jolena. He could see that Belinda was inexperienced, even with applying the dressing. He would call the office tomorrow and speak with Jolena. At least this was a start in his hope of having a penis hanging down in the front. Surely, later on, someone would develop a penis that could erect and be used to have sex. He would settle now for one from which he could urinate.

After dressing, he wrote a check for twenty-five hundred dollars and gave it to Belinda. Quickly, he left the office. He would go to the hotel, rest, and return home in the morning.

Belinda sauntered into Edgewater's office and gave him the check.

"That's a lot of money for a quick procedure. And you don't have to share it with the hospital."

"That's what I've been trying to tell you. This is going to be the future. Office surgery. It will be called surgical clinics. That is what I want to open. I'll soon close this office and open a real surgical clinic."

"You're going to need more help."

"Well, sweetheart, that is where you will come in. I am going to make you my office administrator, and you will take care of all the hiring and running of the office."

Belinda glowed. This is what she wanted. To be in charge.

"And what about Jolena?"

"Don't worry about Jolena. She'll be gone by then. Soon, I'm going to reduce her days down to two days. She'll leave on her own. I don't want to make enemies."

"Why? You don't need her."

"Never know when you might need someone."

The brandy had penetrated deeply into his thought processes. If he had still been Bernie's friend, he could have consulted him on the Mark problem. Peter knew that it was still a problem. Something was not right with that vaginal bleeding. Maybe he should have taken a biopsy. Well, he'd wait and see what Mark has to say in a few days.

"Will we still be doing the silicone?"

"God, yes! That's where our cash comes in, and it's one hell of a cash flow!"

"Sometimes I get tired. Maybe I need help."

"No, we can't have anyone helping. You wanted to be rid of Jolena so bad, and I've given you the job. Therefore, you have to do it alone. She did it alone. And now I am not going back and ask her to do it again. If I do that, she will know I need her, and I know she'll ask for more money."

"It's all right, Peter, I'll manage." Belinda knew that she'd find a shortcut without Peter's help.

"Now come here to your daddy and kiss me. I haven't touched you for almost twenty-four hours."

Belinda went to his arms. She did not show her reluctance. She only pretended that he was Ricky. As she stuck her tongue into Peter's mouth and passionately kissed him, she thought that she should have been an actress. She would have made a perfect actress. Now she played her role to the fullest as she slowly unzipped his fly and found his waiting penis.

40

When Jolena left the office, she went straight home, showered, and called Bernie. She had been troubled about Mark but knew it was out of her hands.

"Bernie, I miss you." All of a sudden the words had come out; without forethought, it came out. She stopped and spoke again before he could answer.

"Sorry, I do miss you, but I didn't mean to sound desperate. I guess I did sound rather desperate."

Bernie answered immediately.

"I understand, Jolena. The truth is that I miss you, and I think you do miss me. Anyway, when will I see you again?"

"Bernie, I'd like to see you as soon as possible. Remember, I told you about Mark and his surgery? Well, Edgewater started today on creating a tubular graft. I feel so sorry for Mark. But Mark is desperate."

"Where are you now?"

"I'm home. He doesn't want me there when he does surgery."

"Come down. Do you want to stay the night? I'd enjoy your company."

"Yes. I'll be there within the hour."

She hung up. It was a relief to have Bernie to talk with now. After dressing, she put some extra food down for Ms. Meow. "Here, little cat, is some extra food until I get back and that won't be until tomorrow." Ms. Meow looked rather lonely.

Jolena looked around her small apartment and felt that she had somewhat abandoned her small home for Bernie's. She reminded herself not to get too comfortable at his place. There was no telling when he might get tired of her, despite all he had told her.

When she arrived at his apartment building, the doorman very respectfully directed her to go right up. When the elevator opened to his apartment, he was waiting. As she stepped off, he immediately took her into his arms, and they embraced. Jolena found herself returning his embrace, surprised to discover that she was finding comfort in this man.

"Come into the study, Jolena. I am so glad to see you."

She followed Bernie into the comfortable study. Now she almost knew her way around the large apartment. He handed her a brandy.

She sat on the large leather sofa. Bernie joined her.

"Jolena, don't be distressed about Mark. He is set on his destiny, and you cannot divert destiny."

"I know. But I feel so sorry for him."

"Maybe you should quit the job. Now!"

"I want to, but something holds me there. It isn't loyalty to Edgewater anymore. I think it is that I don't want to be defeated by Belinda. I know she hates me and for no reason, except I do think she is rather prejudiced."

"All the more reason you should get out of there."

"Yes, I will. I'll start looking for another job. This time, it will be in a hospital."

"If you need any help, I'll be glad to give you a reference."

"That is one thing I need Peter to write for me, and in fact, I must ask him to do that this week. That should make him happy. I know he wants me to quit, and he shall get his wish."

"Good! Now that's settled, this evening we shall go out to dinner."

"We are going out to dinner?" Jolena was surprised.

"Well, don't sound so shocked. Why shouldn't I take you out to dinner?"

Jolena quickly surmised that he was right. The only time they had spent together was in his apartment. She would be interested to see how comfortable he was with her in public. Jolena was glad she had wore a well-fitting suit and her cashmere wrap coat.

"Let me check my hair and face." She laughed and ran to the bathroom. The face reflecting back to her was happy. For once in a long time she was happy. *Please God,* she thought, *don't let anything spoil this relationship.* She combed her hair neatly and touched up her makeup. Jolena had to admit to herself that she had never looked better. She was ready to make her debut into Bernie's world.

When she emerged and announced she was ready, Bernie smiled proudly.

"You're a real beauty, Jolena. I always saw it, but I never ever thought I would be able to be a part of your life."

The cab pulled up in front of the Carlyle Hotel. As they walked toward the entrance, Bernie spoke.

"I dine here many evenings. One of my favorite restaurants. All the waiters know me. The food here is excellent, and the service superb."

"I've never been here. Well, I've never been to any of these plush restaurants."

They were immediately led to a choice table. Jolena noticed a few heads turn when they walked into the restaurant. She expected that to happen. The service was all he had described.

"Bernie, please order for me. I trust your selection."

He was pleased and proud. He ordered a bottle of white wine, which was very pleasing to Jolena's taste.

"Do you like that wine, Jolena?"

"Oh, yes. In fact I like anything you order." She smiled tenderly at him.

"Jolena, I am so happy. You have no idea how you have filled the void in my life."

Jolena raised her glass to him.

"Here is to you, Bernie, my friend, my confidant, and my lover. You handle all three jobs very well. You have so much class, Bernie. How could any woman not want you?"

"Thank you, Jolena. But remember it's up to me who I want. And I know who I want." Just then, the waiter arrived with their food. "We'll talk later, after we get back to the apartment."

Later that night as they lay in bed, Bernie took Jolena into his arms.

"I've told you before that I think about you all the time. I really think that I am in love with you, Jolena. And I am not upset about it. I am very happy about it. I know you care for me, because I get that kind of feeling from you. The way you touch me. The way you respond to me, and the way you make love to me. I need you very much. Tell me, Jolena, why you do not have a boyfriend or even a husband. What happened in your life to make you that cold and distant person when we were working together and until our relationship began?"

Jolena took his hand and led it to her stomach.

"You must have seen this small remnant of a scar."

"Yes, and I meant to ask you about it. Me being a doctor, I was curious, but I really forgot. What happened?"

"A long story. But I am going to make it short. It all happened a year and a half before I came to work with you. I had met this man. It was one of those accidental meetings. Something you never expect. That one person you never expect to meet. That one person that when your eyes meet, you know it's forever. He was older but so—how shall I describe him?—suave, so full of life and excitement. His name was Ricco, and it was a magic name in Harlem. His legitimate business was restaurants. His other business was numbers. Oh, yes, he had money. And also had a wife. A very jealous wife.

"But he and I were always together. We traveled. We laughed. We made love and enjoyed life. We were in love with life and each other. I did not expect him or ask him to leave his wife, but four months after we met, I became pregnant. I was happy about it, but he was ecstatic. He told everyone. He was so proud to become a father. Something he had never been. He was with me all the time. Carol, his wife, stalked him day and night. Finally, I urged him to go home and try to comfort her. She knew about my pregnancy. I could understand how devastated she had become."

Now, Jolena sat up in the bed. She leaned her head against the headboard. Bernie listened intently as she continued.

"He had to pick up some receipts from one of his restaurants in the Bronx. He called and asked me to go with him. He explained to me in the car that he had asked Carol for a divorce and further told her that if she did not give it to him that he was leaving anyway. At that point, I did not care about Carol's feelings anymore. I wanted us to be together. We drove to the restaurant. He went in, picked up the receipts and headed back to the car.

"Then it all happened so quickly. I saw her! She had a gun! I blew the horn to try and warn him. I jumped out of the car to run to him, and then she turned the gun on me. She shot me right in the belly. I could feel the life oozing out of me. I fell across his body. I knew he was dead, and I knew that I was dying."

She was crying.

"Oh, my God. Jolena. Ah, stop, you don't have to tell me."

"No, no! I want you to know. Ricco died. I was taken to the hospital, barely alive. I was seven months pregnant. The baby died. They told me it was a boy. The incident rendered me sterile. No children for me, ever. I survived, and a few months later, I came to work at the hospital and in your department. Poor Carol. Her life was in shambles. She was declared insane, and today, she is still out at Creedmore. For a while, I felt guilty about her state of mind, but then, she would have done it anyway. So I became the astute, correct, and cold nurse. I did my job well. Didn't I?"

"You were the best." They were both quiet for a short time. "You did not have to tell me."

"I wanted you to know. I knew all about you and your tragedy. So now you know why I have a cat." She laughed and cried at the same time.

He held her close. She cried and later told him.

"You know, Bernie, I don't think I will cry over that anymore. It's all gone. Time and you have helped it almost disappear from memory. It's so strange. All the time you were in my life, I never figured that you would be the one to make such a wonderful change in me. I've been so unhappy. Even the job was somewhat of a salvation, until Belinda came along. I can't fault Edgewater for falling in love, but I can fault him for the way he just dismissed my ability and loyalty. It's like he had developed a jealousy toward me."

"You hit it right on the head. He did become jealous of your talent. You created the best faces and bodies. You developed an artistic eye and touch. That doesn't happen all the time."

"Do you really think that was the reason?"

"Oh, yes. Also, you are a nurse. What doctor wants his nurse to be more adept than he? And you are black. Prejudice still looms out there."

"I can't believe he'd think like that."

"Believe me. I was in the field almost a lifetime. I heard many remarks concerning all races. Remember also that this little P.A., Belinda, probably had a lot to do with his sudden attitude."

"Yes! That's when his attitude began to change."

"Leave there. Find another job. If that is what you want to do. Let's go to the kitchen and drink some tea."

He got out of bed, put on his robe. He then gave her an unwrapped box.

"Open it. It's yours."

He watched intently as she opened the box. It contained a silk and cashmere robe. Jolena could see and feel the richness of the fabric.

"Oh, my goodness! Oh, Bernie. I love it. You are so clever."

She jumped out of the bed in all her beautiful black nakedness and hugged him. He smiled and returned the embrace. She put on the robe, and it made her all the more beautiful.

"You are beautiful with and without clothes. Come, let's go to the kitchen before we end up back in bed now."

They laughed.

Later, in the kitchen as they drank tea, she watched him, observed his movements and hung on to every word he spoke. She wanted to get to know this man and all his mannerisms and ideas. It seemed to her as if they were being hurled toward each other.

"You don't have to stay at that job, Jolena."

"I know, and now I do have a few dollars saved thanks to one dear patient I will never see again, because she is gone away forever."

"You don't have to work."

"Bernie, I keep hearing references from you about my not having to work. What exactly are you talking about? Be exact."

He looked straight at her and spoke in clear concise tones.

"I can take care of you. I have plenty of money. You know that."

She smiled and shook her head.

"I don't want to be a mistress. I don't want to be your mistress. I'm over forty now. I want to be with someone for the rest of my life. Not living in limbo. And I don't want to be mistress to a—"

"To a white man, right." He had cut into her statement.

"To any man."

"But, Jolena, I never suggested that to you."

By this time in the conversation, they had moved back into the bedroom. Now he was holding her in his arms again.

"What are you suggesting, Bernie. What did I misinterpret?"

"You can marry me. You can be my wife. We can be husband and wife. You can be Mrs. Bernie Charles. You can live here. You can have all I have. You and I can be happy. How much time do we have left? How much time do I have left to be happy? I don't want to die alone. I love you and I want you to be with me."

She turned and kissed him passionately. As she caressed him, she felt she was on another planet or in a dream. She thought about Ricco. It was like she was with him again. Was it like he always said that it was meant to be?

"Bernie, you have made me a offer that is very hard to refuse. Allow me a short time, and I mean a short time, to think about it. But now, tonight, I am going to make love to you like you have never had before."

She could feel his body relax as her kisses left his neck and continued down to his nipples and finally down to his penis. Passionately she stroked his penis in and out of her mouth. She closed her eyes and allowed her mind to communicate with his. She could feel his penis grow larger and hard in her mouth. His moans filled the room, and very soon, he released all his passion to her. He reached down and pulled her to him. She could taste the tears from his eyes as they kissed.

"I loved you so much. I'm not even going to try and wonder why I love you. I don't care why! It has happened and I want it to stay that way," he murmured.

"I love you also, Bernie. Maybe not with the intensity that you love me, but you are becoming my very life."

"I want an answer soon, Jolena. There are so many things I want to do with you. So many places I want to take you."

"I will let you know."

"Jolena, let me make love to you."

"Whatever you want to do, Bernie."

He indeed took her to another sexual plane. In her lifetime, she had experienced various lovers who had performed either the same or different sex acts with her, but Bernie was different. Her body moved to a rhythm he helped create as he suckled each breast to it fullest sexual height. Her nipples remained hard as he manipulated her legs around his head. The moment his tongue touched her clitoris she could feel a difference from all others. His tongue was hot and smooth. The strokes so different. Jolena knew they were strokes of love. And when she came, she knew that they had communicated.

Later, as they lay in each other's arms, he fell asleep first. With so much on her mind to think about, Jolena drifted in and out of sleep. At one point, she got up, put on her robe and strolled through the apartment. The maze of rooms seemed unending. She noticed that he had closed off most of the rooms. It was the living room that was most inviting—large, with a fireplace and overlooking Central Park.

Jolena stood at the window and looked out into the deserted night. Here she was, Jolena Taylor, registered nurse and almost unemployed, standing in the living room of a millionaire doctor who has just asked her to marry him. That marriage would change her whole life. She sighed and looked around the room. Could she handle such a rich life? What would she do in such a rich life? Jolena knew she'd have to make a decision. Now she would talk to Wilma. The one person who had been her friend for twenty years. Bernie could not help her with this problem. His question had created the problem.

41

When Alberto lowered himself onto the ledge of Lita's apartment, he never anticipated his fate.

He landed on the outside window sill without incident. He thought he felt a slight movement of the ledge but quickly discounted it. His main object was to get into her apartment. He had seen her leave and knew she would not be back for several hours. Alberto needed some cocaine. His supply was exhausted, and this time, he vowed to take more cocaine and more money or all the cocaine and all the money. That way, he would never have to make the perilous trip again. What did he care about her finding out that she was slowly being robbed or completely robbed? She was nothing but a stupid drag queen.

This time, Alberto discovered that a large treasure awaited him. *The bitch,* he mused, *had forgot to put away her supply of cocaine. Good,* he thought, *I think I'll just take the whole bag.* Yes, he was more brave at this point. He sniffed a large amount. Alberto looked around the small studio apartment. He noticed the closet. He had never taken time to inspect the closet. No telling what kind of treasure was there.

Another sniff and he strolled toward the closet. When he opened the door and switched on the light, he looked around and saw just a mess of dress, gowns, shoes, and clothes all in disarray. Now he only wanted to sniff more drug and search for extra monies she might have stashed. He closed the closet door. *Nothing in there but junk,* he thought. He did remind himself that he would thoroughly inspect that closet, but at a later time. He returned to the dresser, and as he sniffed more cocaine he looked through the dresser for money.

At intervals, he'd catch a glimpse of himself in the mirror. The reflection shot back to him a very handsome and clever person. While rummaging through Lita's underwear, he found it! A pack of money! *There must be at least a thousand. Take it all,* he thought. He looked at the door to the studio apartment. If there was no double lock on that door, he'd just walk straight through it and be gone. No, he'd have to take just a few of the hundreds and come back. Alberto promised himself that the next time he came back would be the last trip. He'd wait at least a week, and when he returned, he'd take everything he could find that was worth anything. And that would only be cocaine and money.

So, being the smart thief he was, Alberto left a little cocaine and half of the money. He was high now. He felt powerful. He thought at one time that he should just lay up in the bitch's bed and wait for her and demand all she had to give. No, no, Alberto was smart. He'd come back, and when he did, he'd make that freak bitch pay the price. Next time, he'd take it all and wait for her. He'd kick her ass if she did not give him all of her money and drugs. He laughed. Yes, Miss Lita Lopez, you will have a big surprised awaiting you.

Alberto sniffed more and knew he had stayed too long this time. It was time to get out of this place. Quickly, he climbed through the window. He stood on the outside window sill and reached up and grabbed his rope.

Then it happened. Then he knew. Then it was too late. Then he saw the window sill fall away. Then he was without footing. Then he knew. Then as he dangled in the air holding onto the rope, he wondered how long she had known. Then he knew he did not have the strength to manage himself up the rope and make the roof. Then he knew that his arms were getting weak and his hands were burning. Then he knew that she was not as dumb as he had thought. Then he wondered when he fell whether he would survive the fall. Then he wondered whether he could get to the cocaine he had stashed in his pocket and take a sniff. Then he wondered whether he would die before he hit the concrete. Then he wondered how it would feel when his body hit the concrete. Then he took one arm and reached for his cocaine. Then the other arm could not hold him onto life any longer. Then he fell through the air, arms and legs flinging as he screamed and the cocaine disappeared into the wind. Finally, he realized that Lita had been very cruel and extremely clever.

42

Jolena and Wilma Green were best friends for almost twenty years. Although they lived in the same building complex, they might not see each other for a period of three months. However, they were in constant contact by telephone. Wilma had sat through all of Jolena's sadness as Jolena had sat through Wilma's.

Jolena had never told Wilma about her affair with Bernie because she had thought of it, after that first day, as just something that would never occur again. But it had happened again and again; however, the last happening left Jolena confused and in need of discussion with Wilma.

When she arrived at Wilma's apartment, the look on her face let Wilma know that something serious was on her mind.

"You said you wanted to talk to me about something. What has happened, Jolena. Please, no bad news."

Wilma was in her kitchen preparing a ham. She was a large, dark-skinned woman, a good-looking face that in her younger, thinner days had been attractive. The good aromas that came from Wilma's kitchen was one reason Jolena did not visit often. It was hard to resist the offer to eat. It was hard to compete with the way Wilma cooked a ham.

"Wow, it smells good. I know you have potato salad."

"Yep. And I'm fixing you some now. You can use a little meat on those bones."

"Wilma, if I made one trip a week over here and ate your food, I would be big as you."

Wilma dished out some potato salad for her and Jolena. They sat down and began eating.

"Tell me why you're here. You must have something to tell me." She stared intently at Jolena.

"Wilma, you won't believe me, but I think I am in love."

"Please, Jolena, don't take me through this again. I thought you had been cured. Men have always been trouble for you."

"But this is a different kind of love and a different kind of man. He is a white man!" She watched for Wilma's reaction.

"Then I know he's rich." Wilma got up and dished out more potato salad. Jolena indicated that she did not want anymore.

"Yes. He is very rich."

"Then I can understand you being in love. But does he love you, or is he using you?" Wilma's tone was serious.

"Wilma, this might seem weird, but we are in love with each other. Remember the doctor I used to work for when I was working in hospital?"

"Yeah, Dr. Charles."

"That is the man I am seeing."

"How in the hell did you two get involved now? He's much older than you."

"That doesn't matter. But I always kept in touch with him and would go by and see him, and one afternoon, it just happened. Wilma he has been so kind to me and loving."

"What has he given you?" Wilma spoke with a tone of sarcasm.

"I really never looked for anything. But listen to this Wilma. This is my problem. He wants to marry me."

Wilma, startled, stared into Jolena's face. How many years she had watched her beautiful friend go from joy to sorrow back to joy and return to sorrow. She knew that the death of Ricco and her near escape from death plus the death of the baby had devastated her beyond words.

"This is serious. He really wants to marry you? You mean he asked you, or was he just speaking during a passionate interlude?"

"He has asked me, and he is ready anytime I am."

"You mean to tell me that you will be the wife of a rich doctor and be living downtown, doorman and all that kind of stuff?"

"Yes." Jolena smiled that beguiling smile.

"Then marry him!"

"I wanted to hear you say it. But I'm still afraid."

"You weren't afraid when you were with all those wrong men. Just stop all this thinking, and do it, and do it as quickly as you can!"

"I'm going to do it, Wilma. I'm going to do it!"

"Just tell me one thing." Wilma leaned close and looked Jolena in the eye. "How is it making love to a white man?"

They both laughed.

"Wilma, after the first time, I never thought of him as white anymore. Just a man. A very loving and kind man."

"Well, my friend, his friends won't like the idea of him having a black wife, but I know you can handle them."

"We will handle them."

"So when is the wedding?"

Jolena finished eating and was now prancing around Wilma's apartment. She always liked the apartment because it was full of old fashioned chairs with big pillows and an overstuffed couch. Many times she sat in those chairs and fell asleep.

"No wedding. When I tell him that I will marry him, we are going to do it privately. If I am going to be his wife, I want nothing or nobody to interfere."

"Smart, smart, because they, and I don't know who 'they' are, will try to throw in the big monkey wrench."

Jolena looked out of Wilma's window. Children were playing outside now. The weather was getting warmer. It would soon be summer. It suddenly became apparent that there was something else she had to do before she could go to Bernie and say she was ready to become his wife.

"Wilma, got to go. I have a few loose ends to tie up. I'll be in touch and let you know the moment I am Mrs. Bernie Charles."

Wilma laughed and said good-bye. She returned to the preparation of her ham. This was almost unbelievable news. At long last, Jolena had caught the big one. However, Wilma had her doubts about Jolena marrying this man.

43

Clarence Brown drove his car like a madman. He could not get to Arnold's house fast enough. How dare Arnold hang up the phone on him after telling him he did not want to see him anymore and that he had someone else and that the 'someone else' was living with him. *That faggot bastard,* Clarence thought. *After pulling me in with his sex thing, he just thinks he is going to up and quit.* Clarence could still feel Arnold's delicious tongue licking him all over. Now, besides being mad as hell, his dick was hard. He knew that the moment he saw Arnold, he would quiet down. But he also had to see who this motherfucker was that living with him. Yes, Clarence Brown was ready to kick ass.

Arnold knew that the shit had hit the fan! He was only trying to make the breakoff easy for Clarence, trying to be honest with him, but that did not work. Of course he would prefer to have Clarence in his life instead of Louis because of Clarence's sexual ability. But Arnold had principles now. More than he had before. He refused to allow Louis to be hurt in any way. Louis was his benefactor. He saved him from the streets, from pickpocketing, and going to jail for the rest of his life. Now he would never have to perform jailhouse fellatio the rest of his life. Already he had signed the lease to enable him to open his small antiques shop.

Louis noticed that Arnold looked worried this morning and did not have too much to say except good morning.

"What's the matter, baby? You look worried."

Arnold had quickly decided that he would tell Louis the whole story so if Clarence appeared at the door as he had threatened, at least Louis would not feel deceived.

"Louis, I have to tell you something. All of this happened before I met you. I want you to know that I care for you very much, and I am not going to let anything happen to you. We will always be together."

Arnold sat on the side of the bed and took Louis's hand in his and then he began to tell him about his past life and Clarence.

44

When Lita approached her apartment building, she saw the police cars and the ambulance with all the lights glittering. There was a crowd of people, all stretching their necks to see the body that had been pulled out of the alley. Lita walked amongst the crowd, listening to the various rumors.

"Some guy either jumped or was pushed."

"Probably pushed. That was Alberto. He was a nothing."

"He was probably trying to get in someone's window. He was a thief."

"His father won't miss him. He was lazy and useless."

Upon hearing all these accounts concerning Alberto, Lita felt more justified than before. She had made the right decision. She wondered how he felt flying through the air, knowing damn well that he had fallen into her trap. Lita decided to go back to the bar or work the streets for the rest of the night. She did not want police knocking on her door, so she'd just go get high and stay away for another day. Besides, it was time for her to go to Edgewater's and let little Miss Smartie Belinda pump her body again. She had promised Belinda a larger amount of drugs for that boyfriend she had hidden away in the Bronx. *Imagine*, she thought, *if Edgewater ever found out about that little episode. That secret might be worth saving for the future.* So Lita strolled the streets toward her nightly haunts, feeling satisfied that she had killed again.

Arnold jumped when he heard the pounding on his door. Louis, unable to move his body, quickly turned his head towards the door as Arnold went to open it.

Clarence Brown burst into the apartment and immediately grabbed Arnold.

"Let go of me you dumb motherfucker. You are about to ruin your whole life and career."

Clarence had his hand raised to hit Arnold, when he saw Louis in the bed.

"So are you the motherfucker living here now. Getting your dick sucked, or are you sucking his dick?"

Clarence screamed at Louis and started towards the bed to attack him. Arnold quickly jumped in front of Clarence.

"If you touch him, motherfucker, I'll kill you. He has nothing to do with this. Look at him!" Arnold screamed. "Look at him! He's paralyzed. Completely. He can't move anything. I met him in the hospital, where you insisted I get a job. I care for him, and he cares for me. I don't have to work streets anymore. What could you do for me? Nothing! I just satisfied your sexual needs. Go home and teach your wife to suck your dick. Leave us in peace. I'm just not the same person you brought home that morning from the jail."

Clarence was stopped in his tracks. He stared at Louis lying in the bed. Louis had not moved a muscle. Arnold was right. This man was paralyzed. He looked at his face and saw that his eyes were forming tears, which he couldn't even wipe away. Clarence hung his head. He felt ashamed.

"Man, I'm sorry," he directed his words to Louis, "I had no idea. Forgive me. I really lost it. Look, Arnold is a hell of a person. He's a good person. You are really lucky. He'll take good care of you."

Clarence turned and slowly walked out of the apartment.

"Well, that takes care of Mr. Clarence Brown." Arnold remarked proudly.

Louis was sobbing uncontrollably.

"Why are you crying? Don't cry, Louis. Everything is okay."

"What kind of man can I be for you? I can't even protect you."

Arnold got tissues and was drying his eyes.

"Don't you worry about all that man stuff. You are a person, and you care for me, and together we will be okay. I am man enough to take care of both of us and can be a woman if and when it is necessary."

They looked at each other and laughed.

45

Jolena knew that if she was going to go through with the idea that had suddenly occurred to her, she had to move fast. It was apparent that her working days in the office were numbered. Now Jolena planned to get into Dr. Peter Edgewater's safety deposit box. She had thought about it all that night as she drifted in and out of sleep. It had to be done quickly and without a mistake. She knew that Mark would return on Friday to have his dressings removed and the doctor would have to spend time looking over the incision and graft to see if everything was going well. It was during that time while he and Belinda were busy in the treatment room that Jolena would do what she had to do.

On Friday morning Jolena called Mark at the hotel to make sure that he would keep his one o'clock appointment.

"Don't forget your appointment today, Mark. By the way how is everything?"

"I'm not too happy with the smell, but I guess it's going to be all right."

"Of course, when he changes those dressings, it will be better."

After Jolena hung up the phone, she sadly shook her head. The smell was a bad omen. The graft was probably infected or on its way to becoming infected, and that meant only one other thing. The graft had not taken and was probably infected. Jolena wanted to get up and leave forever. She didn't want to see the look on Mark's face.

A few days earlier, she had gone to the bank to become familiar with the area where the safety deposit boxes were located. It was a small bank, and the boxes were located in the basement. She didn't bother to go in. One trip would be enough. Again and again she had read the directions. She would need to bring the signature card, signed, and some identification; however, the request was not for picture identification. This was the only reason Jolena was confident she could get away with this small crime.

Since it was obvious that he had not provided this for the bank, Jolena was going to provide it all. She would be Belinda Koski that short time while the two geniuses were busy fucking up Mark's life. She would simply go to the closet, take his keys, remove the safety deposit key, and take Belinda's identification. She had practiced the signature all morning and it was good enough to pass.

A little after twelve noon, the duo came into the office. There was only one person to see besides Mark.

"Has Mark called?"

"No, but he is on his way."

"Oh, good, when he arrives, let me know so I can get started on that dressing. Belinda and I will be inside if you need us."

"Fine, doctor."

Jolena had less and less to say to Dr. Peter Edgewater. She watched them hang their coats in the closet. *Good*, she thought. *Just the place they are supposed to be. So when I am ready to go after what I want, it will be waiting.*

Mark appeared at the door, and when he moved toward Jolena's desk, she could smell the foul odor. *Oh, my God*, she thought, *don't let it be infected*, but Jolena was experienced in smelling the foul odor of infection.

"Hi, Jolena. I am not too good today. I feel sick. I'll be glad to get this dirty dressing off."

"Come, Mark, let me take you into the treatment room."

She took him there and told him to lie on the table. She would get the doctor.

Jolena rang the intercom to the doctor's office.

"I put Mark in the treatment room, and he is waiting, and the smell is overwhelming."

Her voice was firm and without hesitation. Edgewater knew her long enough to know what she was insinuating. In a matter of minutes, he and Belinda were in the treatment room. Jolena knew this was the time to move fast. She put the phone on mute so there would be no calls. Quickly, she moved to the closet. She prayed no one came out of the treatment room, but then why should they? Quickly, she dug into his coat pocket and found the keys. Then she went to the bathroom, where she removed a safety deposit key. There were two identical keys. She returned the keys to his pocket and searched through Belinda's coat for a wallet. Nothing! Damn! Then she looked on top of the shelf and saw the pocketbook. Quickly, she searched and found a wallet. She'd take the whole wallet. That way she'd look more effective. Now Jolena threw on her jacket, gathered up her bag, and left the office. Just to be on the safe side, she left a large note on desk: "Be back in five."

The walk to the bank took but a few minutes. Once inside, she entered the elevator and rode one flight down to where the safety deposit boxes were kept. There was one person on duty, an elderly gentleman, neatly dressed and bespeckled and reading a newspaper. Jolena smiled and greeted him warmly.

"Good afternoon. I have a signature card that Dr. Edgewater wants me to sign so I will have access to his box, or rather our box."

"Very well. Do you have identification?"

"Yes, I do and the card and key. The vault number is 963."

The gentleman searched through a small file box and came up with a card.

"Yep. That's the right number. Okay, Ms. Koski, Belinda, right?"

"Right!" She smiled.

"You sign right here." He pointed to a line on his card. Jolena signed as if it had been her name forever. "Very good. Now, let me have your card we sent you, and everything is set. Did you want to go in the box?"

"Oh, yes, I have some papers to put in there."

"Follow me."

Jolena could not believe it was this easy. Surely someone was waiting to arrest her. She followed him into the large vault.

"You give me your key, and then you can take the box in one of the private rooms and take care of your business."

He handed her the box, which was heavy, and returned her key.

Jolena hurried to the small room, shut the door, and almost collapsed into the chair. Her heart was beating faster and faster. Surely this was not going to work. But it was working, and she had the box. Slowly, she opened it. There were many envelopes labeled as stocks and bonds. One envelope was thick with hundred-dollar bills. She saw the familiar name of "Treasury Bond" on several documents. Many of these things she had read about but hardly understood the value. However, it was apparent to even Jolena that he had managed to accumulate a small fortune. But she had no time to look through papers; she had come here for one purpose. She was looking for one item, the emerald ring.

Then she spied a small velvet envelope and opened it. There was the ring. She was hypnotized by the beauty and size of the green gem. Never had she seen such a magnificent piece. She had no more time to waste. Quickly, she placed the ring in her pocket but left the velvet pouch there. It might be a while before he missed it. Quickly, she returned the box to the gentleman who locked it away and returned her key.

"Thank you, sir. Have a very good day."

"And you, too, Miss Koski."

When Jolena returned to the office, she was relieved to note that she had never been missed. Jolena returned everything she had borrowed to its place. Now she knew that by next week, she would no longer be working in this office. The ring, the ring. What a surprise she would have for Bernie. This weekend would be their weekend. She smiled and was quite pleased with herself for being the thief. But then, she had taken nothing that belonged to Edgewater. The ring had been Bernie's wife's. Edgewater never deserved it. She thought about the cash she had seen in his box. If she was a real thief, she could have helped herself. But that was his money. That was not what she was after. She'd only wanted the ring to return to Bernie, and if it had not been there, she would not have taken anything.

When Mark emerged from the treatment room, he looked pale and aged.

"Jolena, please call me a taxi. I am a little too weak to hail a cab right now."

"Come with me, and I will get you one right now." She helped him to the door. She was angry that Edgewater had made no effort to help the patient.

"Mark, go away. Don't come back here. This is not going to work. You are going to end up infected and possibly dead. Please go home and find a doctor who will work with you. There are other gender-change doctors in this world. Please listen to me."

"I'm listening, Jolena. I know you are right, but he swears he can do it."

"Don't listen to him. Trust me. I'll find the name of one and leave a message at the hotel for you. Promise to go away. Write me when it is better, or call."

She scribbled down her phone number and shoved it in his pocket as she helped him into the cab.

Jolena returned to the office. Edgewater was waiting.

"I got him a cab. He didn't look too good."

"Oh, he'll be okay. I just hope that graft is going to take. It's so hard to make patients follow directions."

Jolena did not answer. He had known her long enough to know that she had always been fond of Mark. He also knew that she had sensed a problem.

"I'll be leaving early today. Is that all right with you?"

"Of course, Jolena." He was glad to see her go early, because her presence and knowledge bothered him. He would be glad when she was gone forever.

Jolena then smiled that beautiful smile, reached out and took his hand. *Amazing how smooth and soft surgeons' hands are*, she thought.

"Peter, next week will be my last week. Please have my small check ready, because I will need it. Thank you for the good years. I had once enjoyed working for you, but all good things come to an end."

He was surprised. He had not expected her to quit this soon. Was he going to be able to manage without her? Of course. He had Belinda. Yes, he and Belinda would take care of it all. How convenient she had made her departure for him.

"Jolena, I never expected—"

"Yes, you did. This is what you planned, and it worked for you. There is no more for us to discuss."

Jolena turned and left the office. She was sorry she would have to return next week, but it would be for only two days.

At the corner, she stopped and decided to call Bernie. She'd tell him that she had quit. No, she would wait. She would have to see him in person. There were a lot of things she had to tell him, especially about having secured his ring. Jolena was not quite sure how Bernie would accept her being clever enough to get into Edgewater's safety deposit box. Maybe it was not good to allow him to know how exactly how she had manipulated to secure the ring. No, she would not say anything yet. The time would present itself.

Jolena decided to walk a few blocks before catching the bus home. She felt good being free. Free from that horrible office and various problems that would never be solved. She wanted a different life, and for the first time, she was sure that if Bernie was serious about marriage, then she was ready. Ready for a new and very rich life.

46

Jolena could not believe she had actually quit her job. *My God,* she thought, *where did the nerve come from to walk away? Was it because of Bernie and the promise of marriage?* which she still refused to take seriously. *Tell me that, Bernie,* she thought, *in front of the world.* At home, she emptied her pocketbook and closely examined the ring. This was the first time she had ever seen a green stone that was almost hypnotic. It was perfect. Large, but perfect, and truly a beautiful piece of jewelry. She knew it had to be worth a fortune. She had read that fine emeralds were rare and very expensive. Bernie had no idea she had this ring. No one had any knowledge of her having this ring. This ring actually never existed.

The only person who could be blamed would be Belinda. After all, it was her signature on the bank safe deposit slip as the last person to visit the box. Maybe she should have taken a few other valuables out of the box, but it was difficult for her to be a thief. She did not hate Peter. After all, they were his possessions, except the ring. So this act was not an act of thievery but an act of recovery. She never had to tell Bernie, she could just keep it until years passed and then sell it. But that was not the reason she had taken the ring. It was done for Bernie, who had been hurt by Edgewater. She'd call Bernie and ask to come and see him. Then she would explain to him why she had done it. Her thoughts were disturbed by the ringing phone.

"Hello."

"Jolena, it's Bernie. I've missed you."

"I was just getting ready to call you. I quit the job. I did it. I quit!"

There was a short silence on the other end.

"I'm glad, Jolena. I am so glad. Please come and see me tonight. We have so much to talk about."

"Yes, Bernie. I must see you soon." She hesitated. "I need a couple of days, Bernie."

"Take the time you need, Jolena, but please come with an answer."

"An answer?"

"Yes, an answer to what I asked you." His tone was firm.

She paused. He was really serious.

"Yes, Bernie. I will come with an answer."

"Time is short for me, Jolena. I want happiness, and with you I am happy. Please understand."

"Yes, Bernie, I understand. I will see you soon."

She hung up the phone and slowly paced the floor. Ms. Meow followed her every move. He was really serious. She had to give him an answer. If she said yes, then it would mean that she had to give up her freedom; give up her small apartment; give up living in Harlem; give up worrying about bills; give up not having charge accounts; give up not having a doorman; give up not having to worry where the next dollar would come from; give up being alone; and give up being poor! But she would have a man who loved and adored her. Someone she could trust and return love and care for. Someone who needed her. Jolena knew they needed each other.

She immediately called Wilma.

"Wilma, what am I going to do. He has asked me again, and now he wants an answer."

"Marry him, fool, or, excuse me, you will be a fool if you don't."

"But, Wilma, my freedom and my life. Everything will be different. Can I get used to the changes?"

"You like him don't you?"

"Yes."

"He's not obnoxious. He's refined. He cares for you. It can work. If you don't marry that man, you will learn that the freedom you think you have now is not so free. Money is freedom. Believe me. Look at me. How free am I? I have nothing but welfare. He cares for you. You are in control. And always stay in control. Marry him, Jolena! Make him happy and make yourself happy. Stop waiting for the next Ricco. There are no more Riccos. Live your life. And whenever you miss Harlem, come and visit me."

Wilma had said it all.

"Okay, Wilma, that's it! And if it doesn't work out, then you and I will be living together."

"If it doesn't work out, then I will be your maid. Have you heard of alimony?"

Wilma laughed.

Jolena sighed.

"Talk to you later, Wilma. I have a lot of things to do."

47

Peter Edgewater was not going to reveal to Belinda that Jolena had decided to leave. He would wait a few days until after Jolena left, then he would tell her. It would be a large and important responsibility for Belinda. However, so many times she had bragged about how effectively she could run the office.

Peter heard what she was saying but could not believe she had the nerve to say it out loud. Slowly, she was beginning to sound stupid. The only thing that Belinda could do in the office that amounted to anything was to suck his dick. She was pumping Lita with the silicone, but Lita was about the only person he could trust her with, because Lita was so greedy and did not care who put it in or where.

Now he would have to get the other patients used to Belinda, and that might be a problem. But if they wanted the injections, they would have to accept what he offered. Belinda's lengthy absences were beginning to bother him. Also, he had decided to leave her just a certain amount to inject into Lita. He knew Lita was clever and might try to bribe Belinda into giving her more silicone and even suggest to Belinda that she did not have to tell him. Once Belinda started getting clever enough to think she could do things in the office without his knowledge, it would spell trouble.

Now the fact that Jolena would be leaving began to trouble him. But that had been his plan. He had orchestrated the situation, and it had worked out perfectly. She had quit, and that also meant he would be relieved of the burden to pay compensation. However, he felt uneasy about her leaving. Something just kept gnawing at him about Jolena, and he could not put his finger on it. Why had she not made more of confrontation about how he had actually disrepected her position the last few months? Why had she gone along with his plan without any protest? Maybe he should have asked her to reconsider. After all the years she had devoted to his office, that would have been the correct thing to do.

However, he felt that that would have never worked. He had already done damage to their professional relationship. *Well,* he thought, *forget about it. Changes are always good.* This would now give him a chance to see just how well Belinda would be able to handle the office and the patient load. One thing for sure, she would not have time to be disappearing to her mother's house.

"Belinda don't forget to clean up the treatment room. And your favorite patient is coming today."

"Oh, God! I forgot. Lita! Wow, I really am tired. But I guess I must."

"Yes, you must! By the way, I am giving you only enough to do her usual thousand dollars' worth. No more than that," he commanded.

Belinda was not happy about having to do any work, especially on Lita, but today Lita was bringing the package she had requested. This would help her boyfriend make money. She would be sure to remove a little of the drug for herself. It was difficult for her to obtain any except through her boyfriend and Lita. Now Peter had thrown a wrench in her plans. She had promised to give Lita extra, and now he was not going to leave enough. How was she going to handle that?

He had really messed up her plans. She could not do it for an even exchange, as Lita had once suggested, because she had to show Peter the money from pumping Lita. He always checked on the money, and he never gave her back much for herself. She noted that maybe he would give her two or three hundred a week, despite all the work she did. Even though it did not cost her rent and food, she wanted other things in life. A car would be nice, but she could not drive, and Peter told her it wasn't necessary because she would always be with him, and they only needed one car. He explained that it was too much expense with insurance and garage.

Belinda was beginning to get an uneasy feeling living with Peter. He was actually running her whole life. Telling her what to wear, when to get up, when to go, where to go, where not to go, to be at his beck and call at all times. It was getting very annoying. She had expected a better life than this. First of all, she expected to be married, not to be working in the office. She hated the place. At first, she thought she would like being in charge but now realized that it was just because Jolena was in charge. Her intense hatred for Jolena she now found was false. She just did not like black people, especially when they act as if they knew more than she.

Now, after giving it more thought, she realized that Jolena should have been doing all the work, as she had before Belinda arrived. Maybe she had better talk to Peter and see if he could keep Jolena and give her back all those duties. If Jolena left, then she, Belinda, was stuck with the whole, big, stinking mess. Belinda had never smelled stink as the ones that passed through the office. A person needed drugs to be able to maintain a straight face once the smell permeated the room.

She wondered if all Peter had promised her, marriage and comfort, was going to be worth the sacrifice she had to make. Sometimes she found herself hating him. Especially when he insisted that she suck his dick again after she had already made him come. Who did he think he was? Superman? Often her neck ached from having to spend twenty to thirty minutes over the limp dick still without success.

"Belinda, pet, I am going to the apartment. You come as soon as you are finished with Lita."

Dr. Edgewater left the office. He was tired and glad to get away and comfortable now that he had Belinda to do the one procedure in the office that made him cash money.

Belinda had kissed him good-bye and tried to act civil, but she was mad as hell. After he left, she kicked the furniture, overturned a chair, and screamed out loud. Of course, no one could hear her.

"Hurry up, Lita, hurry up. I need some cocaine!" she moaned.

Suddenly she remembered that he had not left her enough silicone to satisfy Lita. Belinda started searching through the cabinets to see if she could find the large bottle he kept.

"That bastard! He took it with him."

But she had an idea. She grabbed her pocketbook and keys and went to the drugstore. There she bought a large bottle of baby oil. She was clever enough to buy the unscented kind. That way Ms. Lita Lopez would never know the difference. It all looked alike. She returned quickly to the office and poured the bottle of oil in with the silicone. No one could tell the difference. Belinda was pleased with her cleverness.

A few minutes later, Lita was at the door. When the bell rang, Belinda was almost at the door.

"Damn, you sure can get to a door fast."

"I've been waiting."

She beckoned her to the treatment room. Lita followed, smiling. She knew what Belinda needed.

"Don't worry, I have your package. I told you I would bring it."

Belinda was relieved as Lita pulled out the small, neatly packed drug.

"I want to try some of it," Belinda demanded.

Lita laughed. She could try all of it. Lita didn't give a shit. She gave Belinda the pack. Quickly, she made a slit and sprinkled some on the counter. Lita watched her as she sniffed the drug.

"Better save some."

"Oh, I'm just testing it."

"It's good stuff."

"Yes, yes, it is. He'll be pleased."

"Now, how much discount am I going to get off of my body work?"

"Lita, I have to work it in a way Peter won't suspect. You always get a thousand dollars worth, so you give me seven hundred, and I'll give you like three hundred extra for the cocaine."

"But the cocaine is worth more than that."

"Okay, okay, I'll pump you more. Wherever you want it. That way we will be even."

That sounded okay to Lita. She wanted more in her breasts. Lately she had become obsessed with larger breasts. Of course, her breasts were large, but hard and discolored, and not even Snyder would touch them. Lita knew she had what Belinda needed and would do anything to get it.

48

Jolena felt rather sad that this was her last day to work for Edgewater. The years had been good, and he had been fair, and he had been a fine, brilliant doctor in the beginning. She felt, however, that greed had set in somewhere along the way, and Peter had changed. Not to mention love! Love changed many people. Its mysterious, magical feeling made many changes in a person. Jolena had been there. She knew! She had learned.

The office was empty when she arrived. She methodically began to gather her few personal belongings, but as she passed the file cabinet, Jolena decided that for her own future safety she would remove some files. Very important files on patients who might later come back to haunt Dr. Edgewater. She went through patients' files that might contain her name or a note she might have written. They were all removed. Jolena wanted it to be as if she had been only the secretary. She took the entire files on Mark and Lita. He had never made notes on them anyway, and Belinda never bothered to ever look at the files. These files would be her insurance against Edgewater's wrath when he finally figured out who had gotten into his box. She smiled and wondered how long it would be before he discovered the ring was missing. The ringing phone interrupted her thoughts. Jolena answered and listened to the troubled message.

"Tell him I'll be right there," she replied to the party who had called.

Slowly, Jolena hung up the phone. She was shocked. The voice had told her that a patient of Dr. Edgewater's, Mark Nelson, had been admitted and was in serious condition.

Jolena methodically gathered her belongings and left the office. She had to go to Mark. She'd call Edgewater later. If there had been any lingering regrets about quitting that job, they were now dissolved.

Mark lay in the hospital bed attached to monitors and two intravenous fluid setups. The doctor had explained that his previous operation, the skin graft, had become seriously infected. A staphylococcus infection had already set in. They were giving him antibiotics and hoping that the infection would not spread any further.

The skin graft was definitely destroyed. His body was toxic from the overwhelming infection. They would do all possible to save his life, but this type of infection was very difficult to treat. Also, investigation of his previous situation and the bleeding from the perineum suggested that he might have a possible vaginal carcinoma. Did his mother ever take diethystilbesterol? Mark had no idea what his mother ever did. The doctor explained the situation to him, and Mark could see and sense the despair and disgust on their faces. Finally, he asked them to please call the doctor's office and ask Jolena to come to the hospital. He did not want to see Edgewater.

When she walked into the room, Jolena knew that Mark was in serious condition. She eyed the monitors and IVs. She could smell the faint odor of rot and infection.

"Oh, Mark, my God, what happened?"

"It's not working, Jolena. It's infected. It's not even going to work."

"Oh, Mark, don't worry about that. You're alive, and you're going to be okay. Did you call your wife?"

"No, no, I don't want her to see me like this!"

"Give me the number. I am calling her. If she is as wonderful as you described, then she will support you."

He beckoned toward the nightstand. Jolena searched and found his wallet.

"The number is there. Her name is Cindy."

"I'm calling her now. I'll be right back."

Jolena went to find a telephone. She knew he was depressed. It was important to get his wife here as soon as possible. The telephone was picked up on the first ring. It was Cindy. She had been frantic with worry. Mark had not called her in two days. Jolena explained the situation and advised Cindy to get to New York as soon as possible. Cindy said she would leave immediately. After the phone call, Jolena sought out the doctor who was in charge of Mark's case.

"I'm his friend and the nurse who works with Dr. Edgewater."

He surveyed her with a serious expression.

"What kind of operation or procedure was he planning to do to this person?"

"I have no idea. I have been barred from his little operating room. Did Mark tell you his history?"

"Yes, that he was once a woman and underwent the necessary changes to live his life as a man."

"He has lived a well-rounded respectable life and has a wife. He was happy except for one problem. I tried to discourage him from seeking that operation. I told him to go back and be happy."

"Then you knew that this was not an acceptable surgery. It does not work. At the present time, it is impossible to make a phallus that can function one hundred percent."

"I agree."

"Does that doctor you work for know that?"

"He should. He's a doctor."

"I would like to speak with him. In fact, it is very important that I speak with him."

"You have the number. Please do call him and ask him to stop doing this kind of surgery."

"Mark is also bleeding from the vagina. It could be serious. Also the infection is so overwhelming, he will be lucky if he survives. Staph spreads rapidly. It has already spread to the legs."

"Oh, my God," Jolena moaned. "I have to go to him. He has no one until Cindy gets here."

Quickly Jolena returned to Mark.

"I called her. She is on her way."

"Jolena, I am so sick. What is going to happen to me? I can't live like this."

"Just hold on. Everything will be okay. I'm going to stay with you until your wife gets here."

Jolena stroked his hair. His handsome face appeared tired. He held her hand. Jolena held back the tears.

"Don't worry. I'm here with you. Think about the times we laughed about so much in that office. And guess what? I might have a big surprise for you, but I'll tell you when you are feeling better." He managed a faint smile. "Don't try to be clever with that smile, Mark, and stop begging with those eyes for me to tell you anything now. Just wait! Go to sleep and rest. Everything will be okay for you."

Jolena hated Edgewater at this moment. Maybe she should have emptied his whole box. Well, enough of that thinking. She had to call Bernie and tell him she would not be there tonight. But she would not call Peter Edgewater. That was not her job. Let the doctors notify him. Then they could all have a conference together. Whatever happened in that office, Jolena Taylor had removed herself from all responsibility.

49

Lita returned to her building about six in the morning. All the police and onlookers had disappeared. Once in her apartment, she closed the bathroom window and nailed it shut. That took care of him and anybody else who might decide to attempt to climb into her window, she surmised. Quickly, she showered and would try to get a few hours rest before going to the office and get herself worked on by Belinda. The two had made a deal. Belinda would give her five hundred dollars' worth of work in exchange for a medium-sized bag of cocaine. Of course, Lita would pay only five hundred in cash and that way, Edgewater would not know anything about the whole deal. She was pleased with this little setup. There was no way she could have worked such a deal with that Jolena. And Belinda was so stupid that she had no idea the drugs she was getting were cut down to the minimum and not worth two hundred dollars. *Well, that's life,* she thought, *little Ms. Smartie would just have to learn.*

Belinda was at the office early today because Peter had informed her that Jolena would not be in for a couple of days. That meant Belinda had many things to do on her own. She always had to clean up after Peter. He was sure a pig in the office. Never picked up after himself. She had no idea if the syringes were dirty or clean. She had no idea if the needles had been used. She had no idea of what to do with anything, so she just rinsed off the syringes and needles and put them all back together in the same container with the supposedly clean equipment.

Belinda had done her duty, and she was beginning to realize that this job was no picnic. The last time she had been with Ricky, her decision was that she should try to make friends with Jolena. She would speak and be more cordial. In fact, she would even suggest to Peter that he should not get rid of Jolena. She would start to praise her services as most essential. Belinda knew now that if she was in that office by herself, she would never have time to see Ricky. Never have time to relax and sniff her drugs. Never have time to shop. Never have time to have her nails and hair done. All her time would be with Peter and in that damn office with all those freaks. She hated all of them and hated that Lita most of all, but Lita had something she wanted—no, needed. Now she needed the cocaine, even though she was sure that whenever she was tired of it, quitting would be very simple.

Peter arrived at the office almost immediately after Belinda.

"Hi, my love." He embraced her and could feel his penis getting hard.

"Not yet, Peter. Lita is coming early today. We have plenty of time tonight. Lita is a very trying situation for me."

"She's coming again so soon? She must be pleased with your work. Well, after you're finished, we will go out and have an early dinner. Maybe even take in a show."

She would enjoy that. It was about time he started taking her out to the theater.

"Peter, I've been thinking that maybe you'd better not get rid of Jolena. I've noticed that she runs this office very efficiently. I am so sorry I never realized that before, and I am sorry that I have been so short with her. Tomorrow, when she comes in, even though it is her last day, I am going to apologize to her and try to form some kind of relationship. This is not an easy office to run, and doing these injections are not easy. I know you'll agree with me. You never really wanted to get rid of her. You had always praised her loyalty and the manner in which she was able to keep the office going."

Belinda had spoken with a most sincere tone. Peter was proud of her but realized that Belinda was too late in her assumption.

"My darling, I am so proud to hear that you have thought about the work that has to be done here and have given it so much thought. However, I don't think Jolena will reconsider."

"Well, call her up and ask her to come back. In fact, beg her to come back," Belinda demanded.

"She won't come back."

"I'll call her."

"I don't think she would want to talk to you. No, it would be up to me."

"Well, do it, Peter, I can't run this mess by myself!"

Peter could see that Belinda was frantic. He didn't want to upset her any more.

"Don't worry, pet, I'll talk to her and see if she is really sincere about quitting. I'll even tell her that you want her to stay."

"Tell her anything!"

Belinda excused herself and went to the bathroom. There she sniffed the last of her own cocaine. Carefully, she cleaned her nose and returned to the treatment room. She was much calmer now. Yes, it would be necessary to get Jolena back. Peter was in his office now. Belinda heard the bell and knew it could only be Lita.

Lita could see that Belinda was on her way to getting high.

"You look mellow, pretty girl."

"I just had to go and sneak the last of what I had, so I do hope you brought that with you. You do remember our deal?"

"How could I forget? I got just what you want."

In the treatment room, Lita began to strip off her clothes. Belinda could hardly stand to look at the hideous, uneven, discolored body. It looked bigger than before. Lita reached in her bag and gave her the package.

"Better put that away before he comes in here."

Belinda quickly put the bag in the bottom of a cabinet.

"Okay, here is the five hundred. Go and tell him that's all I'm getting today, so he won't think you are cheating him." Belinda took the money but did not move. "Go! I know that doctor. Tell him I sent you in to tell him that this is all I'm getting!"

Belinda turned quickly and went to Peter's office.

"Lita said to tell you that she is only getting five hundred today." She handed him the money.

"That's good! That will take less time. Oh, sweetheart, I am going to have to leave you alone. I have to make a run to the hospital. When I come back, we will go out. Here is the silicone for Lita today." He reached under his desk and gave her the half-filled bottle.

Belinda knew it was not enough for what she was swapping with Lita, but now it was of no concern because she had found a way to supplement the bottle with oil. She kissed him on his lips.

"See you later, Peter. I love you."

"And I love you, pet."

Peter felt pleased. Maybe everything will work out with Belinda if she would just be patient. He had no intention to ask Jolena to stay. However, Belinda would never know.

Belinda felt proud. She stopped in the bathroom, and there she added more of the baby oil. It worked well and was easier to push into the body than the silicone alone. She returned to the treatment room. Lita already lay face-up on the table.

"Okay, Lita, turn over, and we will start."

"No, I want to make my breasts bigger today."

Belinda stared at the large, discolored breasts. She touched them, and they felt hard.

"I never did breasts before. Are they supposed to be so hard?" She was puzzled.

"Oh, just do them. If you are going to learn this business, you have to do everything. Jolena knew how to do everything."

Lita knew that would prompt her.

"I'd better get Peter in here to put the needles in."

"Just do it, Belinda. Stop being a pussy."

Reluctantly, Belinda filled the syringe with the anesthetic.

"Where does Peter usually put the needle?"

"Right here under the breast." Lita pointed to the spot with her long fingernails.

Belinda plunged the needle under the breast. Suddenly, bright red blood returned, so she twisted the needle into a different position. The blood slowed but continued to flow. Belinda packed gauze around the needle to keep the blood from flowing all over the table.

"Now put a needle in the other side, so it will be numb when you get to that side," Lita ordered.

Belinda looked cautiously at the bloody gauze she had placed around the needle already inserted. She walked to the other side of Lita and again plunged a needle in an upward direction into the breast. This time, no blood appeared. She was relieved. Reassured that the needles were in place, she returned to the first injected needle and began filling the breast with the silicone. Her main problem was that the blood kept trying to come out of the needle. She again twisted it until she was able to pump the silicone without a blood flow coming back. The size of the breast rose gradually. Belinda was amazed at how big it got.

"Wow, just look at that breast, Lita."

Lita looked down and was delighted.

"Oh, you are getting to be a pro. Better than Jolena. Wait till I strut these breasts in front of her."

"You won't be able to. She quit."

"What? She quit! Goddam her! So you finally ran her out. Are you happy now?"

"Hell, no! Now I have to do all this fuckin' work. When am I going to get a chance to see Ricky? I told Peter to call her up and ask her to come back to work."

"She ain't coming back."

"She might if he asked her."

"No. No. Jolena is not stupid. She quit for a reason and a good one. She probably has another job already." Lita was disappointed. She would not be able to taunt Jolena anymore. Now she had to deal with this little dummy. "Well, hurry and finish because I have to go." Lita's voice was curt.

Belinda had finished the one breast and was now holding the needle hole with gauze to try and stop the bright red blood from flowing.

"Give me a few minutes, and I'll be finished."

After five more minutes the blood stopped and Belinda dressed the area where the needle puncture was and proceeded to work on the other breast. When she had finished, she noticed that the first breast she had worked on was bigger than the other. She said nothing and quickly put dressing on and helped Lita into her brassiere.

"This one breast hurts, and it looks bigger," Lita remarked.

"Oh, that will reduce itself later. Breasts are very different than the rest of the body."

"Well, I hope so, or I'll be back."

Lita got dressed and left. She was still disappointed about Jolena. *The nerve of her to sneak out on me,* Lita thought.

Belinda cleaned up the bloody mess. She was glad Peter had left. What explanation could she give to him if he had seen all this blood? She didn't have one. She went to the cabinet and got the precious bag. In the bathroom, she took a few good sniffs of the drug. It reinforced her confidence. Now she could deal with Peter and make up an excuse for tomorrow so she would not have to help him in the operating room. No, tomorrow she would be with Ricky.

50

Lita returned to her apartment after being pumped by Belinda. She had wanted to go elsewhere and maybe even try to turn a trick or two before going home, but she felt tired. Once in her apartment, she undressed and looked at her breasts. One was bigger than the other. *That bitch, Belinda, knew that,* she thought. Lita was aware that Belinda did not know what she was doing with those needles and that silicone. And all that blood that had been coming out. She saw it herself. In fact, it flowed all over the table and floor. Needless to have asked Belinda the reason for so much blood. What did she know? Lita pulled out her cocaine and took a big sniff. She would lie down and rest for a few hours before going out into the streets.

Suddenly she felt dizzy! *Damn,* she thought, *what's the matter with me? This never happened before.* And she knew it was not the drug. She never had problems with the drug. The first spell of dizziness passed quickly; Lita was relieved, although she was still troubled. She slept for nearly an hour but was awakened by what she thought was a bad dream concerning her breathing. It had become increasing difficult to breathe. Once awake, she realized it was not a dream. She could only manage to breathe short painful breaths. Lita knew that something was wrong. In all her days, she had never had this kind of feeling. Not with all the cocaine she had ever sniffed did she ever feel this bad.

Now it was becoming apparent to Lita that whatever was wrong with her had to do with the injections she had received from Belinda. *Was that bitch trying to kill me?* she thought. "Oh, no, I'm not going out like this," she said out loud. Lita struggled to get out of the bed. Her breathing was worse, and she felt dizzy. She had to call the office. The only answer was the service operator. Lita did not even leave a message. She knew that it would be useless. What should she do? Who could she call to help her? Jolena? Oh, no, not her! She still had her home phone number that Jolena had given her years ago when they were on a more friendly basis. She remembered quite clearly what Jolena had said: "If you ever have a problem, call me."

Quickly, Lita scrambled through her worn telephone book and found Jolena's number. She prayed that it was not changed. Her breathing had become more difficult. Jolena's phone was answered by a machine. Lita had to leave a message.

"Jolena, this is Lita! Don't hang up. I am sick. I need help. I am going to call for an ambulance. I can hardly breathe, Jolena. I think Belinda did something wrong today with the injections. Please try to find me. I am scared. I don't want to die."

After finishing the message, Lita called for an ambulance. She had painfully dressed and struggled down the stairs. When the ambulance arrived, Lita hardly knew who or where she was. The ambulance drivers managed to get her into the ambulance. They immediately gave her oxygen. They couldn't help but take notice of the swollen discolored legs and the large buttocks and breasts. The illness that had overtaken Lita made her look more monstrous than ever.

Jolena did not get home until almost ten o'clock that night. It was always her routine to check her messages first, and now that Mark was in the hospital, she went directly to the machine. The sole message was from Lita. Jolena was shocked. At first, she thought that Lita was playing a joke or trying to annoy her. But when she heard the part about Belinda's injections, it was clear that Lita did have a problem. Now she would have to check the city hospitals for a Lita Lopez admission.

She could bet that they had taken her to Bellevue, and the call there proved her right. The clerk called her condition serious. Jolena was puzzled. What in the hell happened? Since she was still dressed, Jolena left her apartment and caught a cab to the hospital. Regardless of all the nasty remarks she had made to Jolena, if Lita Lopez called her for help, then it had to be serious.

Almost everyone in the emergency room came to view Lita Lopez. Word spread fast that a drag queen was being brought in for treatment. However, when they saw the difficulty she was having in breathing, the spectacle of viewing ended. Immediately, the doctors started drawing blood and administering intravenous fluids.

"What happened?" the doctors inquired.

"I don't know what happened, but it damn sure wasn't supposed to happen. I know it was that stupid bitch, Belinda, injecting me with that fucking silicone."

"Silicone?" Injections? Are you sure?"

"Am I sure? Look at me, doctor, I have at least fifty gallons of the shit in me. All injected to make me lovely."

Eyes and expressions were immediately concentrated on her by the staff.

"Lita, you are in serious condition. Apparently, you have received an injection almost directly into your artery or vein, and you are in pulmonary edema. This is the reason for the pain in your chest and your breathing problems."

"That figures." She was struggling to speak. "I just got them pumped today and also a few days ago. Beautiful, aren't they?"

All eyes riveted to her chest. The breasts were large and hard on touch. One breast was severely bruised.

"Where did you have this done?"

"Dr. Peter Edgewater's office, and his physician assistant, her name is Belinda, did the injections."

"He can be sued for this."

"I don't want to sue. I want to live. I see all those funny-looking stares you are giving each other. Am I dying? I want to know if I am dying," she screamed, hardly able to summon any more energy.

"Lita, you're in bad shape. You've had a lot of this injected into your body. This is probably not the first time you've had a dose to the arteries or veins, but this is almost a direct hit to the lungs." The doctor spoke with much kindness in his voice.

"I'm tired. I can't talk anymore. I feel bad. The last time I felt this bad I had just had a sex change. And that didn't work."

"Is there anyone we can call for you?" He could see she was more than tired. The blood reports has been returned, and Lita's oxygenation level was low. She was going into pulmonary edema, Lita Lopez had a better chance of dying that living.

"My friend will come. She will come. Her name is Jolena." Lita closed her eyes, and the doctor knew she was entering a semicomatose state.

"Okay, let's get her up to intensive care. Let's try to save her life for whatever it's worth. She is a human being, despite all we have seen."

Jolena sat in the intensive care unit, waiting for some kind of response from Lita and to talk with the doctor who was in charge of her case. When he appeared and introduced himself, Jolena was not impressed. Very few doctors could impress her at this stage of the medicine game.

"I'm Dr. Cohen. I am in charge of your friend's case."

"Lita Lopez, my friend?"

"She said you were her friend. Didn't you realize she was sick?"

"Not until I got the message on my phone. I'm surprised she called me. We are not on the best of terms. I never approved of all the silicone she had pumped into her."

"She stated that she had received some injections from a Dr. Peter Edgewater's office by his P.A. named Belinda."

She watched him as he scrutinized his notes. Jolena offered no information.

"Have you any idea where this office is or who this Dr. Edgewater might be?"

"No, I have no idea. Lita was always very secretive."

Jolena knew then that to know nothing was the best move in this case. Lita had given all that information to these doctors. It was not her job to protect Edgewater and certainly not Belinda. Lita had just charted their future.

"It seems she was injected with liquid silicone. Many times before this last treatment, which happened to be injected directly into an artery or vein, and Lita has pulmonary edema. She will be lucky to live. If there is an emboli on the move, she will die."

"Oh, God! This is terrible." Jolena was truly moved with grief. "Is she conscious or what?"

"She is somewhat coherent. Very tired, and her breathing is very labored. If you stick around, she will be able to talk to you."

Jolena began to wonder why Lita had revealed any names to the doctor. Why had she given them all this information? And why had she called her to come to the hospital? She went to Lita's bedside and stared down at the massive figure. Lita's face appeared larger than before. Maybe, Jolena thought, it was because she had not looked so directly as it as she did now. She pulled back the sheet and saw the massive breasts. Both were bruised and swollen.

So, thought Jolena, *that is where little Ms. Belinda stuck the needle and dealt Lita her most fatal injection.* She wished Lita would awake and tell her why she asked her to be there. Jolena touched her shoulders and spoke to her.

"Lita, Lita, it's Jolena. You called me. Why? Can you hear me. Talk to me, Lita." Lita only mumbled something incoherent and continued sleeping.

Jolena sat in the chair, tired and disgusted. Why has she dragged me into this mess? She wondered if Edgewater knew about all these events that stemmed from his office. Mark was sick in one hospital, and now, Lita in this one. Lita's accusations were most serious. Jolena wanted away from all this. It was too late into the morning to call

Bernie. She certainly did not want to annoy him with all these happenings. After all, he had nothing to do with any of this. Jolena had not talked to him since she retrieved the ring, and she had no intention of ever being involved with medicine again after she returned it to him. She would accept his proposal of marriage. This would change her whole life. She was ready now without a doubt. Suddenly a voice broke through her thoughts.

"Jolena."

She looked up into a nurses's face.

"Yes."

"That patient, Lita, is asking for you."

Jolena hurried to Lita's bed. Lita's breathing was labored as before. She struggled to talk.

"Jolena, Jolena, forgive me for dragging you here, but I need your help. I don't think I am going to make this trip. Belinda has killed me. That bitch doesn't know what she is doing. Oh, I only hope I make it out of here so I can take care of her like I did all those who did me wrong."

"Oh, Lita, I am so sorry this has happened to you."

"It's my own fault. I knew everything. I defied everyone, especially you. But, Jolena, you got to go to my apartment. Get the key out of my pocketbook. It's here somewhere. Go to my apartment. Look by the dresser. There is a loose board in the floor. Under it is almost twenty-five thousand dollars. Please send that money to my mother in Mexico. She doesn't even know I am alive, but I know she is there, and I have sisters. Send the money there for me. I know I can trust you. All the information you need is there. Do it any way you have to, but please see that they get it."

Jolena did not want this burden. She sighed deeply. Lita could see the dismay on her face.

"You gotta do it for me, Jolena. I can trust you. I've known you long enough to know I can trust you. Forget our differences. You were right, I was wrong. That's why I'm here. I see the look on the doctor's face. I hear what they say even though they think I am sleeping or out of it."

"I'm sorry this happened to you, Lita. I pray you will be all right."

"Edgewater and Belinda better hope I am not okay, because when and if I get out of here, I will kill both of them." Jolena could hear the sincerity in her voice. "It won't be the first time I've gotten even," she continued.

Jolena did not want to hear any more.

"I'll go in the morning and get the money. I'll bring you a receipt after I get it sent. I don't exactly know how to send that amount of money to Mexico, but I will get help. Don't worry, your mother will get it."

"Be sure to put a note with the money to let her know it was from her son Jose. It's a long story, and I'm tired. Just take care of it, and, oh, yeah, Jolena, don't go nosing around that place. Take the money, lock the door, and make sure you don't leave any fingerprints there. Do like I say."

"I understand." Jolena spoke quietly. She knew that Lita was into devious operations; however, she had no idea of what she was referring to, but she would do exactly as she had been directed.

51

Jolena finally found her way to the Ninth Avenue apartment building where Lita lived. She looked around at the neighborhood and thought about how well she lived in comparison. Slowly, she climbed the stairs to the top floor. After fumbling a few minutes with both keys, she entered Lita's small apartment.

Jolena stood still for a few minutes surveying the large one room where Lita lived her life. The bed was still unmade. It appeared that it had never been made. The pillowcases were stained with makeup. Jolena assumed Lita probably just went to bed without washing her face. The dresser was littered with various lipsticks, rouges, powders, eyeliner, eyelashes, artificial fingernails, and various other artifacts Jolena could not identify. She did, however, note a small transparent bag filled with a white powder. Probably Lita's cocaine. Even she knew about Lita's habit. Clothes were thrown over chairs and whatever could accommodate them. Even the radiator had become a clothes rack.

"What a mess!" Jolena whispered to herself. "But she told me not to snoop around. Just take the money and leave. And that's what I'd better do. I don't feel comfortable in this place."

She placed her foot on several of the floor boards to see if one was less stable than the others. She touched one that seemed to be loose. On her knees, Jolena pulled at the board, and it moved. She spied a black plastic bag and removed it. In the bag was a pack of one-hundred-dollar bills. Jolena was shocked.

Lita saved all this money, she thought. *What was she going to do with it? Maybe she was going back home. And now she wants it sent to Mexico? How am I going to send all of this money to Mexico? All she has is a name and address. How does she know that this woman is still alive or lives there? Apparently Lita knows. If she's smart enough to save this much money, then she's smart enough to know where it should sent. Twenty-five thousand dollars is a lot of money. I never had that much money, at least not in one pile.* Quickly, she replaced the floor board, put the money in her pocketbook, and left the apartment.

Outside, she hailed a cab and went home. She was still puzzled about how to get this money to Mexico. Jolena had no idea about how to do this. She could easily just keep the money, but why take Lita's money? She didn't take Edgewater's when she raided his box. Lita had trusted her. Lita, who had taunted, ridiculed, snubbed, and snickered at her, had only been calling out for help from Jolena, who had profoundly ignored her. Now Jolena realized that Lita, prostitute and cocaine-sniffing and silicone addict, needed and trusted Jolena.

After Jolena left Lita's apartment and returned home she found it necessary to take a shower. There was just something strange about Lita's apartment that made her want to shower completely.

She had not even called Edgewater to tell him about Mark or even Lita. It was all out of her hands. She had taken from the office all that belonged to her and a few files and documents for her "insurance." The way things were going, it appeared to Jolena she had exited at the correct moment. Mark was infected, and Lita did not look like she was going to make it out of the hospital alive.

She carefully began to think of who could help her with this situation. Almost immediately, Bernie came to mind. He would know about things like this that concerned money. Bernie was money. Old money. She picked up the phone to call him. It was time now. She missed him, especially with all these problems that had occurred. When he answered, she spoke softly and with much sincerity.

"Bernie, it's Jolena. God, have I missed you! Forgive me for not calling, but so much has happened these last few days. I must see you. I have many things to tell you, and I need your advice and help with one particular matter."

"Jolena, come now if you wish. I have missed you. I called, but you have been impossible to catch," he replied.

"I'll be there within the hour."

Jolena hung up the phone. She dressed carefully. For some unknown reason, she felt like looking her best today. The beige linen suit accentuated her dark hair and olive skin. The image in the mirror pleased her. Before leaving the apartment, she thought about calling Peter and leaving him a message concerning his up and coming problems, but then, why? Soon enough he would hear all about it, and besides, today had been her last day and he had not even left her check.

When she arrived at Bernie's, he met her with open arms. Tenderly they embraced one another. *Strange,* she thought, *how I really care for this white man.* But she had to stop thinking about him being white, but just a wonderful loving man who sincerely cared and loved her. Jolena realized now that there was no gap left between them. If he put the marriage question to her one more time, she would accept without hesitation.

"Jolena, darling, what has happened?"

"Mark is in the hospital with the worst staph infection you could imagine. I think they have it under control. He is very depressed. I called his wife, and she is with him. The doctors say he has a good chance to survive. But he would have to forget about the quest for the penis."

Bernie was quiet. Slowly he walked to the window and stared down onto the street. *Peter Edgewater,* he thought, *I trained him to do this to patients.* Bernie felt somewhat guilty.

"And to think I trained him! I thought he would be a good doctor."

"He started out as a good doctor, Bernie, but he lost it as he became more and more greedy. I was there. I watched him become less attentive and more careless towards his patients. He acquired dirty habits, and often, I'd have to remind him to wash his hands. The office became a nightmare!"

"I'm so sorry you had to work there."

"The next horror story is Lita. She is in the hospital with pulmonary edema. You should see her, Bernie. Her body is all swollen. Her skin color is black and blue and hard on touch. The silicone has traveled from her hips down to her toes."

"My God, is she still alive?"

"Alive enough to tell the doctors who did that to her. She named the physician's assistant and Dr. Peter Edgewater. Told the doctors that Ms. Belinda with the assistance of the doctor pumped her full of silicone the past weekend."

"How did you happen to see her?"

"She called me from her apartment because she felt sick after Belinda had worked on her. I got the message when I returned home. She begged me to find whatever hospital she was in and come to see her because there was something she wanted me to do for her."

"She called you? I thought she hated you?"

"Lita was sick, Bernie. I had to go to her. She asked me to go to her apartment and get some money she had saved there for her mother in Mexico. All these years, her dream was to go back to Mexico and give her mother this money. Now, this is a problem for me. I went there and found the money, but Bernie, the money amounts to twenty-five thousand dollars and—"

"Twenty-five thousand dollars—" he interrupted.

"Yes," she continued, "and I have no idea how to send twenty-five thousand dollars to Mexico. You have to help me."

"She gave you an address?"

"Yes, here it is, and here is the money."

Jolena reached into her bag and put the money, which she had placed into an envelope, and the address on the table.

Bernie sat down and shook his head.

"This is unbelievable. You could have kept this, and no one would be the wiser." He stared at her with intensity.

"I couldn't do that, Bernie, Lita has no one. She didn't hate me or even resent me. I think I was all she really had in case anything went wrong with her life. Always in her mind, she held me in reserve for that moment. When she got sick, she called me. There was no one else. Do you think she will make it?"

"Not if that shit has seeped into her lungs."

"Can you help me get this money to her mother?"

"Yes, yes, no problem. I'll call my accountant, and he will see that a wire transfer is sent to the bank and create an account in the mother's name. They will contact her."

Bernie went to the bar and poured himself a brandy.

"Well, it might be a little early for this, but at this time, it is necessary."

"I'd like one also, Bernie, because I have one last story for you."

He poured her a drink. Slowly she began to walk the floor of the large room. Many thoughts went through her mind; she had to tell him now.

"I love this room, Bernie. I love this place. I love the way you live. I love the nights we spend together, the small dinners, the drinks the conversation, the bed, the lovemaking. I love how you hold me in your arms. I feel so protected. I hate going back to my apartment or to that job or just out into the world because you are not there. I sometimes wish that all this happening between us now had happened many years ago. But then we understand about destiny." She stopped and made direct eye contact with him. "Loving you as I do now, I hate to see you hurt for anything. I hate knowing how unhappy you were those years when your wife was sick and when Edgewater took advantage of her. When I began to care for you more and love you, I had to find a way to heal that wound of yours, and I found it, Bernie."

Slowly, she walked toward him, reached into her pocket and gave Dr. Bernie Charles the brilliant emerald ring. He stared at the object in complete disbelief.

"Jolena! How in the hell did you get this ring? This is the ring my wife gave to Edgewater. How did you—"

"Well, Peter wanted the girlfriend to have a key to his safe deposit box, and she had to sign a signature card. I received the notice at the office for her to come to the bank and sign the card. So while they were mutilating Mark, I simply took her wallet and walked to the bank and announced I was there to sign the card and wanted to open the box."

Bernie laughed loudly.

"You got away with it?"

"No one asked for picture identification. So I was Ms. Belinda Koski, without a doubt. Bernie, I was scared as hell, but I was determined. If he had that ring, it had to be in there."

"Was the box full of other objects, Jolena?" Bernie was extremely interested.

"Oh, yes! Papers, bonds, and money. A few piles of real cash."

"But you found the ring."

"Bernie, I had to do it. I'm not a thief, but I felt justified in getting this returned to you."

"I have no qualms about what you did. You've made me very happy. It seems like things are back in place. Maybe she can rest in peace now. It was never her fault." Jolena leaned down and kissed Bernie as he sat still looking at the precious object. He kissed her back. "Jolena, all you have said to me means so much. I love you very much. I want you with me. Marry me, Jolena. Marry me now!"

She knew he was serious.

"Now?" She laughed. "This very moment?"

"Yes, we can do it."

"It takes time. Paper work, blood test."

"Are you ready? Now! I will call my driver, and in two hours we will be in Maryland. A little place called Elkton. We will come back man and wife."

Jolena stopped breathing for a moment. She heard Wilma's words. But she was afraid. Ricco! There are no more Riccos. Do it! Do it now.

"Okay! Okay! Let's do it!"

They embraced one another, laughed, cried, and forgot about the rest of the world. Jolena Taylor and Dr. Bernie Charles were going to be married that very day.

When the limousine picked them up at Bernie's, Jolena made one request.

"Bernie, have him stop at the hospital so I can tell Lita that I have done what she wanted, and I must return these keys."

Bernie agreed that it would be the right thing to do.

Jolena was informed that Lita Lopez had been moved to the intensive care unit. When she arrived there, Lita had been intubated, a tube into her trachea, and was on a respirator. She was unconscious. A nurse was in the process of changing the intravenous fluids.

"She doesn't look so good. Is she going to make it?" Jolena asked as she stared intently at Lita.

"It would be a miracle. She's in a deep coma. There is not much hope for this patient. Are you family?"

"No, just a friend. Her only friend, and she knew it."

Jolena leaned over and whispered to Lita.

"Lita, I don't know if you can hear me. But I took care of that for you. Your mother will get the money. All of it. I hope you get well, Lita. Don't die. I feel so sorry for you, but you were so determined to have more and more silicone. I am going away, Lita. I can't help you anymore. I have a new life to live. I'm glad we had a chance to talk. I'll always remember you. The girls will talk about you for years. You will be a legend amongst the queens. You had a lot of guts, Lita, and you even had a plan, but it just didn't work out."

She put the keys into Lita's hand, closed it, and left.

Now in the limousine, she leaned back and sighed. Bernie took her in his arms, and she held on tightly to him as the car sped down the highway to Maryland.

A few hours later at a justice of the peace, Jolena Taylor became Mrs. Bernie Charles. Because there was not time to buy a wedding band, Bernie had slipped the emerald onto her finger. Now a better life was beginning.

In a New York hospital, Lita Lopez's life had just ended.

When Lita Lopez's rent was not paid for two months and the landlord could not find her, he figured that she had run out, skipping the rent, like all street prostitutes eventually do.

Now it was important for him to get into the apartment, because he wanted to rent it. One morning, he firmly decided to go up there and open the door. However, he discovered there was an extra lock on the door. After breaking through it, the door was opened. Enrique, the old landlord and superintendent, was surprised to find that nothing had been removed from the place. It was as if she still lived there. He walked into the apartment, but suddenly a strange feeling came over him. Enrique decided that it was best that he go downstairs and call the police. He did not want to be accused of breaking and entering. What if she came back at that moment?

The police arrived, and Enrique explained the situation. Together they returned to the apartment. The police, in their most efficient manner, walked through, noting that there was nothing but a lot of clothes and nothing of real value. Enrique went to the closet. He was dismayed by the pile of materials and gowns that filled one side. This would cost him a lot of money to have someone clean this trash out.

"Look at the pile of clothes and the mess she left here," he complained to the officers.

They came to the closet and glanced at the scene.

"You said she was a man?"

"Yeah, he dressed like a woman. But I know she was a man. My son told me. He's dead now. Fell from the roof."

One officer proceeded into the closet.

"A lot of junk," he mumbled as he kicked the pile. But his foot hit a more solid mass under the assortment of clothes. "What the hell is under here? Hey, Tim," he called out to his partner, "let's see what's under this pile of clothes."

Diligently, they searched, and it did not take long to unravel the mystery of Lita's closet. The body was still there, almost intact, but began to fall away from its bones from exposure to the air. Perfectly mummified. Perfectly murdered.

There were pictures and newspaper articles and many inquiries about Lita Lopez. No one seemed to know who she was or where she was. One thing for sure was that Lita Lopez was wanted for murder.

52

Pamela Thorn had just returned from Paris. The agency had sent her there to be groomed for the spring collection show that would take place in a few months. They wanted to keep her a secret, but they did, however, cleverly reveal throughout the fashion gossip group that there was a new, stunning model that Jonathan Reeves had discovered and was keeping a big secret. He would not even show pictures of her. Of course, this kind of gossip made every other agency curious. But Jonathan had whisked her away to Paris, and there, she was studied, groomed, and taught all that was needed for her to become a new supermodel.

Jonathan was amazed at how fast Pam learned and at how intent she was to be the best. This was something he had searched for so long in a model. She would bring much fame and fortune to the agency, but he had to keep a hold on her. Sometimes he would notice her just sitting quietly by herself. He'd ask her if there were any problems, and she would smile and reassure him that everything was well with her.

A month later, Pam returned to New York. Her first priority was to look for an apartment. An agency was assigned to find her one, but she stressed that she did not want anything on the East Side and certainly not around Central Park South. Pam referred to that area as a smelly bathroom. But of course, Pam had her own private reasons for not wanting to live anywhere near those areas. She finally took an apartment near Lincoln Center. It was on the twenty-second floor of a very exclusive and expensive building. The agency paid for everything, because at that point, Pam had not earned one dime. This sort of bothered her, moving into such luxury, ordering furniture and all the other amenities, but no money of her own to pay for these. But the agency reassured her that it would all come out of her salary that would grow into hundreds of thousands of dollars.

It was almost three weeks until the big show. Pam was forbidden to go out, and most of her time was spent in the movies or reading. She liked Paris and longed to return but knew that her main objective was to be successful, rich, and famous. This is what she wanted, so she followed the rules and regulations handed down to her. At night, she would stand by the large picture window that overlooked the city. She observed the people coming in and out of the various theaters at Lincoln Center. One day soon, she would be escorted in and out of the finest restaurants.

Romance had not entered her life, and she did not intend for it to enter. First, she must be famous and rich. Pam knew that she would meet many rich men and the opportunities would be vast. She would wait for the right man. The richest man would be the one to win her. The question of sex would be no problem. Each night she would insert the large artificial penis into her new vagina and work it back and forth so her vagina would not close up. The doctor had told her this was a necessary procedure until she began to have sex. Pam never felt any sexual sensation from this maneuver. Maybe when she had a real dick in her pussy she would feel differently.

She had no friends to confide in and had always remembered what Jolena had told her. Trust no one. Her thoughts were often of Jolena. Was she still working at that horrible office? Then Pam remembered that she had her home phone number. She searched though her papers and found it. She wanted Jolena to know how her life was going.

Excitedly, she dialed the number.

"Jolena, Jolena, it's me, Pam. Well, you know my other name. Remember me?"

Jolena had been to her apartment to pack a few clothes to take to Bernie's. She was surprised to hear the familiar voice.

"Oh, my God! Pam? So it's Pam! I am so glad to hear from you. How are you doing? What are you doing?"

"I made it, Jolena! I made it! I did everything like I told you. I returned a few months ago, and I am with an agency that is keeping me under wraps until the showing of the spring collection." Jolena could hear the excitement in her voice. "And Jolena, please come. Please! I want you to see me. I am going to be the next super model just as I promised you I would be. And I hope you are not working at that horrible place."

"Now a surprise for you, Pam. I just got married to a very very wealthy doctor whom I love and care about with all my heart. He has made me very happy. I am happy, Pam."

"How wonderful! Then I will see that both of you get an invitation to the show."

"Pam, make sure you send the invitation personally. We will come, but promise me not to acknowledge knowing me. Make no attempt to speak to me. We never know who knows who. You are on your way to fame and fortune, and there is always someone looking to destroy you. Promise me."

Pam listened intently to Jolena's warning and knew she was right. Another sacrifice for the fame and fortune she sought.

"I promise, Jolena. You are right! But please come."

"We will be there. Send the invitation to Dr. and Mrs. Bernard Charles."

Jolena finished giving her the address, and they said good-bye to each other. Both knew that would be their last conversation in life to each other.

Pam felt sad for herself but happy for Jolena. But this was the price she must pay. Alone and lonely, but one day things would be different. And one day after she had earned her first million, Pam would return to Europe. There she would find and live an even better life and make new friends.

Mark's wife, Cindy, was quite upset with him when he told her that he would not sue Dr. Peter Edgewater, neither would he speak to him again.

"How much money did you give him?"

"Just a deposit. It won't break us. I don't want to talk about this whole scenario, Cindy. It's over and done. I am lucky to be alive. Lucky the infection didn't spread all over my body."

Cindy nodded her head in approval.

"I still love you, Mark. Just the way you are. I never wanted you to do this or go through this misery."

"I know. I know. But it's something I had to try. I thought it would work. Even Jolena told me it would not work. But not the doctor. Why would he do that to a person? I will never understand, which is the very reason we will drop the subject." He held her hand and squeezed it firmly. "I love you. I am so lucky to have you. We were always good together. Now we'll be even better."

Cindy smiled. She was happy all this was over.

"By the way, I have some good news. Good gossip news. I was scanning the newspaper today, and I think you know this person."

She put the newspaper in front of him.

Mark looked at the picture facing him, and then he looked closer.

"My God! That's Jolena. She got married and to a doctor. This is the doctor she used to work for five or six years ago. He's a goddam millionaire. Good for her! Good for her! I remember she told me that she had something to tell me. I was real sick, and she whispered in my ear that I should not die, that I should get well, because she had a surprise for me."

"He's real rich?" Cindy asked.

"Yes, he is!" Mark laughed. "Wait till Peter Edgewater sees this paper and reads all about it." Mark continued to read it aloud: " 'They eloped to Baltimore. She was his former nurse before he retired. They will live in his Fifth Avenue apartment. Her wedding ring was the famous South American emerald, which has not been seen for years. They will honeymoon in Bermuda.' Oh, just this alone will make me well and happy."

He hugged Cindy.

"Find a doctor, Cindy. I think I am ready to go home."

Cindy quickly departed.

Mark settled back in the bed and smiled. The Jolena he had always adored; the Jolena who, from the beginning, had advised and helped him; the Jolena who had rejected his advances but allowed him to hold her close; the Jolena he had always had a passion for had made the correct move in her life. He felt a little sad, because he would always remember her and miss her.

53

Dr. Peter Edgewater, very upset with his personal life, had no idea what was happening in his office. He had not seen Belinda in two days. Those two days included the weekend, so now it was almost three days. He had called her mother's house but no answer, even late at night. Now he had to get to the office because no one was there to meet the patients or to take care of anything. Jolena had quit. He had called the office several times, but no one answered the phone. The phone service had many messages, but he refused to take them from home. He would go to the office and get things straightened out.

Now he began to worry about Belinda. She had never disappeared before. Maybe something has happened to her. He was very angry at her but then felt it was better to wait until she reappeared before he incorrectly judged her. However, Peter was beginning to feel that his world was not quite right. He wanted to tell himself that he had made a mistake loving Belinda and should have never brought her to the office. How well things had been going before he made that move. But Peter didn't want to think about that.

Belinda and Ricky had laid up for two days, sniffing cocaine and solving all of the world's problems. They had also counted the profits that Ricky would make once he began selling the drug. It added up to enormous profits. However, when they had finished with all the planning and plotting, which took two days and nights, it amounted to rhetoric; they sadly discovered that they had used the cocaine. Ricky blamed Belinda for being greedy, and Belinda informed him that he sniffed more than she because he was a man and had a bigger nose. She further accused him of being impotent, because his dick would not get hard and she wanted to fuck. He explained to her that his dick could not work with all the cocaine he had sniffed.

"I'm going back to the city. I know that Peter is worried about me." Belinda got up and began to dress. She looked in the mirror and did not like the reflection.

"When are you going to get enough of that shit so I can start selling it?" Ricky complained.

"You were supposed to start on this bag. It ain't easy getting this shit. And pretty soon the bitch is going to want money or free work. I can't give her either one!"

"Why not? You were going to be Miss Rich Bitch, living with that doctor and taking over the office. You were supposed to be in charge of everything, including the money."

"He ain't stupid. He only gives me a little of the silicone to work with. He promises me more money, but I have to wait until Jolena leaves for good."

"When is this going to be?"

"It's now, I hope," she shot back at him as she finished dressing, "but I'm in big trouble now because I disappeared. I got to make up a story."

"You're good at that. No problem there." His voice was full of disgust.

"I got to go. I'll talk to you later."

Belinda left Ricky's apartment and went to her parents' apartment. They were away for a week, so no phone call had been answered. She quickly got out of her clothes and took a shower. She had to have a clear head when she went to the office. The phone rang, but Belinda did not answer. She knew it was Peter. It would be enough to deal with him in person.

Peter, sensing, as never before, the urgency to get to his office, got there as fast as he could.

The first thing he did was to retrieve his messages from the answering service. There were several calls from patients, the hospital, and some doctor he'd never heard of, but nothing from Belinda. Maybe, he thought, he should call the police and report her missing. No, don't panic. He began to wonder who was this doctor, from a hospital he was not affiliated with, calling him. He put a circle around the number and would call later. Then he remembered Mark. He had not heard from him, so all must be well.

Peter secretly missed Jolena. How he wished now that he had never turned against her. She never did anything wrong to him. She had been his right hand, and even his left at times. How had he allowed love to interfere with his business? Had Belinda left him? Why hadn't she called? He began to feel very depressed. He would take her back if she would just contact him. He had to admit he'd been selfish with her. Just then, he heard the office door open. Quickly, he got up to see if it might be Belinda.

Belinda closed the door and stood against it for a few minutes. She had to get this story together. Suddenly, she was startled by the appearance of Peter.

"Belinda! My God, I've been worried sick. Where have you been? Why did you not call me?"

Belinda quickly composed herself and her thoughts. She went to him immediately, put her arms around him, and waited for him to respond. At first he did not, but soon, he hugged her. They kissed, then she began to explain.

"Oh, Peter, what a weekend. My mother and father insisted I go to the country to see an aunt I hardly know. We drove somewhere in the boondocks. There was no phone service, no place for me to call out. There wasn't even a shower. We just got back this morning. I missed you so. I knew you were worried, but you knew I would be back."

Peter listened to the story. How could he disprove it? Why even bother. At least she was here.

"Why are you here so early?" she inquired.

"There is no one to run the office, sweetheart. Remember, Jolena is gone?"

"You couldn't urge her to come back?" Belinda was truly disappointed. She knew it would be impossible to handle this office alone. The ringing phone interrupted the conversation. Dr. Edgewater answered.

"Yes, this is Dr. Edgewater."

"We have a patient of yours here, or, I'm sorry, we *had* a patient of yours here, but she died over the weekend."

Chills ran down his back. He could feel himself draining. Who in the hell is he talking about?

"A patient of mine? I have no idea who you are talking about. Can you give me a name?" He tried to keep his voice calm. Belinda was listening with intensity.

The voice responded.

"Lita Lopez. It seems she was injected with some kind of oil in your office. The injection was directly into the chest cavity. She died of pulmonary edema."

"Lita Lopez!"

Belinda was startled at the sound of the name.

"Yes, that is the name, and the case is now under investigation by the district attorney's office. It is considered a criminal case."

"I don't know why you are calling me. Yes, I know the patient, but she was never here for any injections," Peter lied. He knew he could never admit to that.

Belinda was nervous. She began to pace back and forth while listening to the conversation. *Now,* she thought, *is the time I need that cocaine to settle my nerves. Lita Lopez, what is that bitch up to now?*

"Well, doctor, it seems she lived long enough to tell the whole story and sign papers stating that this took place in your office, several times, and by your physician assistant and you. It also states that she paid in cash and cocaine in exchange for the silicone or oil injected into her body."

Peter jumped up from his chair. He was aghast.

"Cocaine? I don't know anything about cocaine. In fact, I don't know what you are talking about. I will wait until I am notified by the authorities. I have no more to say to you."

He slammed down the phone and stood quietly over his desk as he gave further thought to what he had heard. Belinda slumped down into a chair. She could feel his eyes riveted onto her.

"What was that all about?" she asked meekly.

"I don't know, Belinda. What *was* it all about? I know that some doctor just told me that Lita Lopez is dead! And that she got herself pumped full of oil and silicone here in this office in exchange for money and drugs." By the end of the sentence, his voice was loud and out of control.

"Why are you screaming at me? I didn't do anything wrong. I only did what you told me to do."

"What did you pump into her? I only left you a certain amount, so you and her could not get slick together, but it looks like you were slicker than Lita!" He came around from the desk and grabbed her out of the chair. "What the fuck happened after I was gone?"

"I don't know. Maybe she pumped herself when I went to the bathroom."

"To the bathroom to do what? Sniff cocaine? So Lita just picked up the needle and pumped herself? What a fuckin' stupid little liar you are."

He slapped her hard enough that she hit the floor. Belinda began crying. Peter walked toward his desk.

"If you hit me again. I'm going to call the police."

He looked at her and laughed.

"You won't have to call the police. From what that doctor told me on the phone, we will be seeing the police soon enough."

"What do you mean?"

"Lita Lopez signed a paper before she died, naming this office and you as the one who put that shit in her. I thought you knew what you were doing. Why didn't you ask me when you did not understand?"

"Why can't we say that Jolena did it? I'll say it! I'll say that Jolena did it."

Peter looked at her and realized that he didn't love her as much as he did last night or that morning.

"Jolena quit last week. She was not here, and since I am going to be blamed anyway, I will not allow you to say anything about Jolena. You are going to take the blame along with me. Besides, you have nothing to lose."

"What about my physician assistant status? I don't want to lose that."

"You were never one. I had the paper made up. Didn't you realize that? Were you so stupid that you did not realize how much time has to be put into becoming a real P.A.?"

"You told me I was one," she screamed back at him.

"Don't raise your voice to me. Sit down and shut up. This is going to cost me a lot of money."

Peter Edgewater slowly lifted the phone to call his attorney. He looked at Belinda and realized that he was stuck for the meantime with a common trashy slut. No wonder she could suck dick so well. He shuddered to think of the ones she must have done before he got her.

"I want to go home," she said quietly.

"You just keep your ass there until I see what kinds of legal maneuvers I have to go through. I'm not taking this by myself. Now, you wanted to run the office by yourself. Well, you finally got the chance. Go out there, answer the phone, and start cleaning up."

Peter practically pushed her through the door. Slowly, he sat down and sighed. He knew that it was only a matter of time and she would be gone. What a mistake he made. He shuddered, thinking that he had even harbored plans to marry her and put her name on his safety deposit box. He felt relieved that he had not gone that far. The ringing phone shook his thoughts. He answered, and it was Dr. Snyder.

"Read about a problem in the paper this morning. Was that yours?" Snyder asked.

"I don't understand what you are talking about." Peter was not answering questions.

"Oh, come now, it was known that the late Lita Lopez was your star patient."

"She was yours also, Snyder."

"Not mine. She never mentioned my name. According to the newspapers, you and your physician assistant were named."

Peter could hear the small sound of joy in Snyder's voice.

"I don't want to talk about it."

"But that is not the real reason I called. I just heard from the grapevine that someone you know well was just married. In fact you know both of them."

"I am not interested in hearing about marriage now."

"But this one you will be interested in."

"So who was it, Snyder. Tell me and let me hang up."

"Your good and faithful nurse, Jolena, and Dr. Bernie Charles. They were married Saturday." Snyder waited as the silence grew louder.

"Jolena and Bernie? I don't believe it! Why would they marry? She hasn't seen him in years. He is almost a recluse."

He could hear Snyder laughing—loud and long.

"She is now Mrs. Bernie Charles, and it seems like this relationship had been going on for a few years. By the way, he gave her a beautiful emerald ring. Almost exactly like the one his late wife gave to you. Now, that could not be the same ring? Or it could be an imitation?"

Peter Edgewater felt sick to his stomach as he listened to Dr. Snyder's gossip.

"Sorry, Snyder, I've got to go." Peter hung up the phone.

Impossible, he thought, *for Bernie to have that ring.* It was in his safety deposit box. No one could get in there. Jolena married to Bernie? How long had she been seeing him? Right under his nose, she had kept Bernie Charles abreast of everything happening in his office. But the ring. It must be a fake, or maybe there were two. But no, this ring was unique. There were not two stones like it. Peter suddenly decided he had better visit his safety deposit box. As he hurried out of the office, Belinda was still in a daze.

She had no idea where to start in the office, but she did have an idea that she was not going to be there much longer. After he left, without every saying when he would be returning, Belinda waited a few minutes and left. Some way or another she would find her way home, and she would never come back to see Dr. Peter Edgewater again. She was not going to be responsible for Lita Lopez's death. After all, he was the doctor. She had no credentials.

At the bank, Peter hurriedly signed his name on the signature card.

"Has anyone else had access to my box?"

"Yes, sir. A young lady named Belinda Koski. Her name is right here. You had requested a signature card for her, and she came and completed the card and had the key."

The clerk gave Peter the card. It was Belinda's signature. But he had never shown Belinda the card or given her a key. The only person who could have known about the card was Jolena because she received all the mail. Not Jolena! She was not that clever. Hurriedly, Peter retrieved his box and sat down in the private room to search through the contents. Everything was there. Nothing appeared to be missing. He searched for the velvet envelope that held the ring. It was there. And then he picked it up. Empty!

How had she managed to do this to him? How long had she planned this? But he had to remember that he had been so involved with Belinda, he forgot that he had created an enemy. She had not always been one, and to prove it, she had taken nothing else but the ring. All these years, she had been a good and loyal nurse to him, but her real loyalty had been to Bernie. How long had they been lovers? Oh, the questions he wanted to ask her. And he smiled at the way she had done it. Such class. She only took what did not belong to him. Slowly, Peter closed the box, and a large part of his life closed with it.

When he returned to the office, it was empty. Belinda had fled. He expected that much. It would be a lonely and costly fight, but he would survive. How he wished he could talk to Jolena. How clever she had been. He would like to congratulate her on her marriage. Peter knew that, financially, Jolena Taylor was set for life. She had grabbed the prize.

54

Arnold awakened suddenly. He jumped out of his delicious bed and looked around. *Bad dream,* he thought. His dream was that Louis was still in his bed. However, Arnold smiled as he remember that a proper hospital bed had been purchased for Louis. He had pushed aside some of his antiques to provide room for his man forever. Yes, he knew that life with Louis was forever, and it turned out to be a good life. The money that Louis had received enabled Arnold to open up a small antiques shop on the main floor of the very building he lived in. The rent was reasonable, and already, Arnold had filled the shop with many antiques and old fakes.

The Bronx was not the most lucrative place to open this type of shop, but since it was the only one, far or near, Arnold's business was booming. People brought in things to be sold, and thieves were always unloading their stolen goods on Arnold. He hated them for being such petty thieves, but then, what could a former pickpocket say? He could, however, say that he had never been a petty pickpocket. He could say that he always picked the best and the biggest. Yes, he could say all that and more, but Arnold had learned to be quiet when it was most important.

It was his sister who talked more and attracted men to the shop. Of course, his sister was named Lottie Lee, and Arnold just loved her. What a life! Occasionally, he would go to the shop dressed as Arnold, and other days, he would go in dressed as Ms. Lottie Lee, fancy name tag and all. In this disguise, he was able to hear all about what was wrong with his shop and with Arnold. If what he heard was constructive for business, he would correct it. If it was not, he merely shrugged it off. Louis's voice broke the silence in the room.

"Hey, baby, you okay? I saw you jump out of that bed like something bit you."

"I'm fine, Louis. I got to get downstairs to business. Your caretaker will be here in an hour. Can you wait breakfast till then?"

"Oh, sure. Well, who are you going to send to work the shop today?"

Louis enjoyed the small show that Arnold put on for him. He still had not made up his mind who he liked better, Arnold or Lottie Lee.

However, when it came to kissing, he preferred Lottie Lee. When he was made love to, it always came from Lottie Lee. Even Arnold enjoyed making love to Louis when he was dressed as Lottie. However, he wished that Louis's penis could get hard. What a waste? So big but so flaccid. Often he thought about putting his own dick into Louis's mouth. After all that was the only part of his body that could function, but he knew that that would destroy Louis's image of Lottie. However, after careful consideration and thought, Arnold knew of an even better way to satisfy his sexual urge.

"I will send Arnold today." He spoke in a deep masculine voice. "Later in the afternoon, I will send Lottie."

They both laughed.

"I have a surprise for you tonight," Arnold said softly to Louis.

"Oh, wow, I can't wait."

"It's very sexy."

"Now I really can't wait."

"Well, you have to wait until Lottie comes in tonight. Now, no more conversation. I have to go."

After Arnold left, Louis thought about his life. Being paralyzed had been a devastating problem, but he accepted and dealt with it. God had sent him Lottie Lee. And Arnold had also been a Godsend. Louis always thought about them as being two separate persons. He and Arnold always related man-to-man. Even though he understood that Arnold was gay, he had no problem with that. It was Lottie he waited for. Two or three nights a week, Lottie would visit him. Her kisses aroused his brain so much, he just knew that his dick was hard. He never asked or looked to see. Lottie just made him happy with her kisses and caresses. He could hardly wait until tonight for his surprise. Today he would ask the attendant, after his bath, to rub his body with the new cologne Lottie had brought him. *Yes,* Louis sighed, *life could have been worse.*

Consuela Lopez had spent almost fifteen years in jail for the murder of her husband. In Mexico, prison life was hard for a woman. All her children had been placed in orphanages, and she never saw them again. She had often wondered about the baby boy she had given birth to. It was directly after that that she had killed her drunk and abusive husband. However, the authorities were not impressed with the facts of abuse from a husband. She was sentenced to jail for twenty-five years but, somehow, had been released after fifteen years. The short, wrinkled faced lawyer informed her that due to some mitigating factors, which of course, concerned money, she had been set free. Consuela could not understand who would ever pay money to free her. The lawyer had mentioned that it was a relative from the United States.

Now she was working in a factory and had found a small room in which to live. She longed to see her children. But she had no idea where they would be after all these years. Her not having any money prevented her from even searching for them. Life was as hard out of prison as it had been inside. Not having any money, just the few pesos she earned, still made her life difficult. However, one day at her job, she was called to the manager's office. Consuela was scared. Her job was important to her. She did not want to be fired.

"Consuela, come in. I have an important message for you."

She could sense that it was not about being fired. The manager, short and rather handsome, smiled and gave her a paper to read. Slowly, she read the paper again and again.

"I don't understand. Why would there be money for me at the bank?"

"I don't understand either," he said with much authority, "but I suggest that you go now and find out how much."

"It must be a mistake."

"How can it be a mistake? You are Consuela Lopez! Go now, and let me know what happened."

Quickly, he rushed her out of the office.

Consuela walked toward the bank. Today, when she should be jubilant; she felt sad. Her spirit had long ago been broken. The aging process had taken over her body and face quickly. She thought that if it was truly money for her, then what a blessing. But if not, there could be no disappointment. She had suffered all the disappointments in life.

The bank manager escorted Consuela to his private office. He appeared very serious but jubilant.

"Consuela Lopez, I have good news for you." Consuela was not impressed. She waited. "We have received a large amount of money, wire-transferred from the United States to you." He waited for Consuela to perk up, smile, scream, faint, or anything. But her reaction was stoic. "Consuela, it is in the amount of twenty-five thousand dollars!"

Consuela could not believe the amount.

"It must be a mistake. Who would send me that amount of money?"

"There is a message saying that a letter would arrive explaining the circumstances. This is your money. Now, I know that it is difficult to handle this amount of money, and I suggest that you open an account here in our little bank."

He certainly wanted her account at this bank. It would mean much prestige for him to have acquired her as a customer.

"Yes, yes, by all means."

Consuela was beginning to respond to what she had heard. Twenty-five thousand dollars in Mexico was a fortune. Now she could even pay to find her children. But she remained bewildered about who would send her this kind of money.

"Excuse me, senora, I will get the necessary papers for your signature."

When he returned, he handed Consuela a sealed letter. She opened it but was unable to read it because it was in English.

"You must read it for me. It is in English."

The manager, Senor Gonzalez, read the letter in silence and then explained to Consuela the contents.

"This person writes that she was a good friend to your son. His name was Jose Lopez. She said that he always talked about you and was sorry that he never got back to Mexico but always wanted to come home. I am sorry to tell you, Consuela, but your son is dead."

Consuela gasped. The boy she had over twenty years ago. Her first boy and last child. She hung her head and cried. The money was no longer a joy.

Senor Gonzalez continued.

"She further writes that she gave him a proper burial in the United States because to send a body back to Mexico would be too expensive. She also writes that he wanted you to have this money, and so, she sent it to you. It seems he knew where you were and that you were in prison, and he was the one who paid to get you out. Also, he was working so hard that he never had the time to come back to see you, but he wanted you to know that he always thought about you, and even though he never saw you, he knew you were a beautiful mother."

Even Senor Gonzalez was moved to tears. Consuela had stopped crying.

"May I please have the letter? It is all I have left of my only son."

"Of course, of course!" He quickly handed her the letter.

"Maybe tomorrow will be a better day to put your account in order?"

"No, senor. We will take care of this today. I have much to do. I have children to find, and with the help of my son and his spirit, I know I will find my children, and we will be a family again."

Consuela Lopez prepared herself for a new and different life. She would always remember her son, Jose Lopez.

55

Today, this afternoon, would be Pam's debut. This is the first time she would be seen in America. She was the new secret weapon the agency had been bragging about. She was the beauty from nowhere. She was the next super model, and she, Pam, was loving it all. Pam had learned a long time ago to keep to herself, don't gossip, smile, be courteous, go home alone, and put the phone on an answering machine in order to screen her calls. The only important call was from the agency.

When she arrived at the grand ballroom, there were about fifteen models. Pam was amazed by their beauty. This was the first time in America that she had met any of the other models; they were from other agencies. Later, in the dressing room, Pam saw all the people from the agency—the guys and gals who dressed, applied the makeup and fixed the models' hair.

Immediately, they started their magic on her. She could see the other models eyeing her with envy. Her hair was healthy, strong, and real blond. It was then curled and twisted into an exciting new hairdo. Her first outfit was a new shade of blue that seemed to match her eyes. Hers was a long chiffon gown, flowing with beauty. Pam was confused.

"Why a gown on my first walk?"

"It will be different, and you will electrify the audience. They know we have a new girl. This gown will show all of the beauty of your shoulders, neck, and face. Who will be looking at the gown on your first entrance?"

Pam became more excited. She was told that she will be the last one out in this segment.

"After that, they will be searching for your return."

Pam hoped that would be true. As the makeup was being finished, she hoped that Jolena would be in the audience. She had remembered Jolena's warning and now began to realize that if she went to the top today, good friends would be very scarce. She could never trust anyone. The show had started, and backstage was in a fury of changes, complaints, tears, and protests. Maria and Rudy were protective of Pam.

"Don't watch those crazy bitches. Keep yourself calm. All you have to do is this one walk and you got it. This is the one to make you, and they know it," Rudy reminded her.

The other models were sneaking side glances at the new girl in town. Many of them knew she was unbelievably beautiful.

Suddenly, Rudy called her.

"Pam, it's time. Let's go."

He led her to the entrance.

"Remember, float, and remember, you are beautiful," he whispered.

And then Pam realized it was her turn. She looked down the runway and all the people surrounding it. She smiled slowly and methodically. It was like the stroll that she used to walk, but this time she would show her femininity without vulgarity.

She began her walk. Although the music was playing, the entire ballroom seemed to be silent. If there was any noise, Pam did not hear it. She thrust her hips forward and held her head high. Her eyes scanned the audience. She was not afraid to look into the eyes of her critics. She saw Jonathan smiling with approval. He blew her a kiss. She ignored him and continued her floating walk to the end of the runway, where she did the little half-turn and step and pause for all to see. Her beauty was mesmerizing. Her lips full and inviting. The tantalizing smile revealed a beautiful set of teeth. She began to walk back. It was important, for this was her last chance to show her beauty. *Is anyone looking at the gown?* she wondered. Then her eyes met a familiar face. She smiled and kept moving. *It's Jolena,* she thought. *She came! She saw me! I kept my promise to her, made so long ago.* Then she heard the applause. It was earth-shattering to Pam. She continued her walk and disappeared into the dressing room. Maria and Rudy grabbed her.

"You did it! Before you even got off the runway we were getting calls. Who is she? Is she signed? We want her for this show and this magazine. I think we already have you for a cover. Do you realize what this means?" Rudy was jumping up and down. The other models were staring in envy.

Pam sat down in front of her mirror and stared at herself. *I did it,* she thought. *I did it! Oh, God, I don't even want to think back to yesterday. My life has just started. I have just been born.*

"Okay, Rudy, Maria, let's get ready for the next outfit. Let's keep this magic going," Pam announced with gusto and confidence.

She stood up, and they began to undress her. She was in control now. She was headed for the top, to fame and riches, to be the most envied woman in the fashion world. Now she was a woman, a real woman.

That night, after Arnold closed his shop, he returned to his apartment. The attendant had left, and Louis was in bed as usual and waiting for Arnold's return.
"Don't forget your surprise you have for me."
Arnold smiled.
"Oh, I have not forgotten. I'll take a shower now and put on my new outfit."
Louis smiled. He was happy! He always liked it when he knew that Lottie would be there soon to visit him and make love to him. His mind was active sexually, but he knew that nothing was happening in the rest of his body. How he would have loved to stick his big dick into her. His thoughts were interrupted by the appearance of Lottie Lee.
"Oh, my, my, what a outfit!"
Lottie smiled. She had a new blond wig on and sheer red, short lingerie. Cleverly, she had tucked her penis between her cheeks so Louis didn't have to view it. Lottie went to the bar and fixed him a drink of brandy.
"First, I am going to give you a little brandy."
"Wow, you never gave me brandy before."
"Well, we will both have some."
Lottie slowly helped him sip the brandy, and then she quickly gulped down a couple of shots.
"That brandy sure goes to the brain fast. I almost feel like I can walk. I feel good! Are you ready to make love to me?"
Lottie knew that in Louis's mind, he was ready, and Lottie was ready tonight to have sex and not have to masturbate. No, tonight she was going to give Louis the sex that she had dreamed of.
Slowly, she slipped into the bed with him. His body smelled good, and she began to kiss him on the mouth. He responded as usual. Lottie wished she could feel his arms around her, but she knew that was impossible. After caressing the top of his body and his flaccid penis, she started to turn him slightly.
"I'm going to turn you over a little. But first, here, take a little more brandy."
She fed him more brandy. He was feeling real mellow.
"Damn, baby, do with me what you want."
Slowly, she turned him over and positioned his head to the side, so he would not smother. Lottie reached down and took off her G-string panties and allowed her penis to fall free. The penis was hard, lubricated, and ready. She lay on top of Louis and whispered.

"From the first time I saw you, I loved you."

Slowly, she started pushing her penis into Louis's rectum.

"I loved you, too, Lottie Lee. Was that my surprise because you never told me you loved me?"

Lottie pushed her penis in more. There was no reaction from Louis. *God,* she thought, *why didn't I do this before?* She pushed deeper and deeper, in and out. *Damn, this is good!*

"So what are you doing on top of me?"

Lottie almost forgot that she had to give him an answer.

"I'm loving you, baby. I'm loving you. I'm licking your back and I'm gonna bite you on your ass and lick it. Won't you just love that?"

"Oh, yeah, oh, yeah. Is it gonna make you come?"

"You're right, baby, it's gonna make me come."

Now Lottie was pushing more and more. She knew that soon it would be over. It couldn't last much longer.

"When I come, I'm gonna give you a big scream. Okay? Okay?"

"Yes, baby, holler all you want!"

And then Lottie came and she collapsed onto him. Lottie bit his ear and screamed and moaned like Louis had never heard in his life. He felt happy and satisfied that at last he made his Lottie happy. Slowly, she moved off of Louis and turned him over. They both fell asleep. Lottie and Louis in love forever and ever.

56

The full moon had settled over the island of Bermuda. The night was beautiful and warm. Dr. and Mrs. Bernie Charles had just settled down into their luxurious suite after a day of shopping and lying in the sun.

Jolena had just showered and slipped into a new, beautiful, and very expensive negligee Bernie had chosen.

"Why black?" she had complained.

"Because it will look gorgeous on you."

Jolena did no further complaining. After slipping into it, she had to admit that she looked gorgeous. Her face was radiant. She combed her silky black hair and twisted it into a bun. She stood on the balcony waiting for Bernie who was still in the shower. A bottle of champagne was chilling, and Jolena wondered how much better could it get. Life at last was much easier. All her life, work, trials, and tribulations; trying to be loyal to employers and always ending up with the short end of the stick. She turned and looked at the luxurious suite.

Bernie had come out of the shower, and he was putting on his elegant robe. *No*, she thought, *he isn't handsome, tall, and dashing, but he is considerate, respectful towards me, affectionate, and he loves me, and I am his wife.* For once in her life she was a wife and to a very rich man. She adored him and would always take good care of him. There would be only him and her. They did not need too many people in their lives. He came out onto the balcony.

"God, what a moon! What a night! And I have you."

He sighed and put his arms around her. She embraced him.

"I am so lucky, Bernie. I am so lucky." Then she stepped back and asked him, "Why did you want me to wear black tonight?"

He reached into his pocket, then handed her a box. She opened it, and there were a pair of black pearls.

"Oh, my God! How did you know?"

"You mentioned it once, many months ago. I always remembered. See how well they go with your outfit tonight?"

He helped her put on the pearls. Jolena looked magnificent.

"These had to cost a fortune," she murmured.

"So what? I have a fortune. Two fortunes, my money and you." They laughed and he opened the champagne. "This toast is to you, my darling. I love you very much, and I am very happy."

"And I love you, Bernie. I am very happy."

Jolena Taylor Charles meant every word.

Later that evening as they lay in bed, they talked.

"Bernie, have you gotten over how beautiful Pam Thorn is?"

"Incredible. She is a very clever girl. She is one of the girls to make it to the top. Not many do, you know that."

"Right you are, Bernie. Not many. Look at poor Lita Lopez. I am so glad that I sent the letter to her mother. It wasn't necessary for her to know the truth. At least not in this case. It's amazing that Lita had had all that information about her mother."

"That's not as amazing as the mummified body they found her closet."

"And to think I was in there. She told me not to be nosy. Just get the money and get out."

"But then she confessed to the doctor to all those other murders she committed. My God, she was a serial killer."

"Wow! Bernie, stop, let's go to sleep." They both laughed.

There was silence for a while and then Jolena whispered to herself:

"As I lay me down to sleep,
I pray the Lord my soul He'll keep.
If I should die before I wake,
I pray the Lord my soul He'll take."

978-0-595-36780-1
0-595-36780-1

Printed in Great Britain
by Amazon